Cutthroat

The grandfather clock chimed eight as she struggled from the chair. Every joint ached when she moved. How she dreaded opening the door to let the dogs in, giving the hoary demon of winter a chance to chew on her bones. Spring was late this year. So was Tom.

At first she thought she saw a ghost outside the open door, a trick cataracts played on her eyes. Then the knife cut her cheek and she knew the specter was real. Drops of blood spattered the snow-white mask.

The next two cuts slashed her palms, raised in terror to protect her face. The honed blade sliced to the bone.

The old woman staggered back against the butter urn. Her wedding ring clanged the copper boiler as she stumbled. Cutthroat sliced the back of her neck while she struggled to stand.

From stove to china hutch, to pioneer water pump, beneath her copper pots and coronation mugs, past Irish crochet and Nottingham lace and rustic sepia prints, the killer stalked her ruthlessly.

"Out with the old."

He cut her.

"In with the new."

Also by Michael Slade and available from NEL:

HEADHUNTER
GHOUL

ABOUT THE AUTHOR

Michael Slade is the pseudonym of a firm of Canadian criminal lawyers specializing in the field of criminal insanity. With a combined experience of forty years in the trial courts, the partners have defended and prosecuted some very dangerous individuals in more than a hundred murder cases. Several major precedents in the Supreme Court of Canada have resulted from their work.

Cutthroat

MICHAEL SLADE

NEW ENGLISH LIBRARY
Hodder and Stoughton

First published in USA in 1992 by New American Library

NEL edition 1993

The characters and situations in this book are entirely imaginary and bear no relation to any real person or actual happenings.

Printed and bound in Great Britain for Hodder and Stoughton Paperbacks, a division of Hodder and Stoughton Ltd., Mill Road, Dunton Green, Sevenoaks, Kent TN13 2YA (Editorial Office: 47 Bedford Square, London WC1B 3DP) by Clays Ltd., St Ives plc.

British Library C.I.P.

A CIP catalogue record for this title is available from the British Library.

ISBN 0 450 58428 3

for
Rebecca
Jeremy and Jarrett

Part One

SKULL

There is no doubt that the inductive and predictive powers of the brain have become exceptionally enlarged in the course of the evolution of man. They have led him to his greatest discoveries about the regularities in the operations of nature and of men themselves. These habits of enquiry are the fruit of the anxious need for the security of knowledge, which is a characteristic and sometimes painful human trait. . . . It has led man to perhaps the two greatest discoveries of all, on the one hand that each individual will die and on the other hand that there was a time when no human beings existed. Such knowledge still dazzles us and leaves many people unsatisfied and unsure, so that they seek for security in the inventions of myth, as Mankind has probably done ever since he began to talk and reason.

—J. Z. Young,
An Introduction to the Study of Man

FIRST ACCOUNT OF THE CUSTER MASSACRE.

TRIBUNE EXTRA.

Price 25 Cents. BISMARCK, D. T., JULY 6, 1876.

MASSACRED

GEN. CUSTER AND 261 MEN THE VICTIMS.

NO OFFICER OR MAN OF 5 COMPANIES LEFT TO TELL THE TALE.

3 Days Desperate Fighting by Maj. Reno and the Remainder of the Seventh.

Full Details of the Battle.

Sioux, emptying several chambers of his revolver, each time bringing a red-skin before he was brought down—shot through the heart. It was here Bloody Knife surrendered his spirit to the one who gave it fighting the natural and hereditary foes of his tribe, as well as the foes of the whites.

The Sioux dashed up beside the soldiers in some instances knocking them from their horses and killing them at their pleasure. This was the case with Lt. McIntosh, who was unarmed except with a saber. He was pulled from his horse, tortured and finally murdered at the pleasure of the red devils. It was here that Fred Girard was separated from the command and lay all night with the screeching fiends dealing death and destruction to his comrades within a few feet of him, and, but time will not permit us to relate the story, through some means succeeded in saving his fine black stallion in which he took so much pride. The ford was crossed and the summit of the bluffs, having, Col. Smith says, the steepest sides that he ever saw ascended by a horse or mule, reached, though the ascent was made under a galling fire.

The companies engaged in this affair were those of Captain Boylan, French and McIntosh. Col. Reno had gone ahead with these companies in obedience to the order of Gen. Custer, fighting most gallantly, driving back repeatedly the Indians who charged in their front, but the fire from the

ies terribly mutilated. The squaws seem to have passed over the field and crushed the skulls of the wounded and dying with stones and clubs. The heads of some were severed from the body, the privates of some were cut off, while others bore traces of torture, arrows having been shot into their private parts while yet living, or other means of torture adopted. The officers who fell were as follows: Gen. G. A. Custer, Cols. Geo. Yates, Miles Keogh, James Calhoun W. W. Cook, Capts. McIntosh, A. E. Smith, Lieutenants Riley, Critenden, Sturgis, Harrington, Hodgson and Porter, Asst. Surgeon D. Wolf. The only citizens killed were Boston Custer, Mr. Reed, Charles Reynolds, Isiah, the interpreter from Ft Rice and Mark Kellogg the latter the Tribune correspondent. The body of Kellogg alone remained unstriped of its clothing, and was not mutilated. Perhaps as they had learned to respect the Great Chief, Custer, and for that reason did not mutilate his remains they had in like manner learned to respect this humble shower of the lead pencil and to that fact may be attributed this result. The wounded were sent to the rear some fourteen miles on horse litters striking the Far West sixty odd miles up the Big Horn which point they left on Monday at noon reaching Bismark nine hundred miles distant at 10 p. m

The burial of the dead was sad work but they were all decently interred Many could not be recognized; among

Gen. Custer, Cols. Calhoun, Yates, Capt. Smith, and Lt. Porter. The unhappy Mrs. Calhoun, loses a husband, three brothers and a nephew. Lt. Harrington also had a family, but no trace of his remains was found. We are indebted to Col. Smith for the following full list of the dead; to Dr. Porter for the list of wounded, which is also ful:

KILLED.

Field and staff. George A. Custer, Brevt. Major General.

W. W. Cook, Brevt. Lt-Colonel.

Lord, Asst. Surgeon, J. M. DeWolf, Acting Asst. Surgeon.

N. C. Staff, W. W. Sharrow, Surg Major.

Henry Voss, Chief Insptr.

A Henry Dallans,.. .. ..Corp.
" G. K. King. .. .. "
" J. K. Armstrong, ...Privt
" James Drinaw,.. .. .. "
" Wm. Moody, ... "
" R. Rowlins, ... "
" James McDonald, ... "
" John Sullivan, ... "
" Thos. P. Switser, ... "
B Benj. Hodgson, ...2d Lieut
" Richard Doran, ...Privt
" George Mask, ... "
C T. W. Custer,.. .. ..Brevt Lt-Col
" H. M. Harrington, ...2d Lt

The body of Lt. Harrington was not found, but it is reasonably certain that he was killed.

" Edwin Baba .. ..1st Sergt
" F[illegible]ley, ...Sergt
" Finkle, ... "

" H. A. Bailey .. ..Blacksmith
" J. E. Broadhurst.. .. ..Privt
" J. Barry.. .. .. "
" J. Conners.. .. .. "
" T. P. Downing.. .. .. "
" Mason.. .. .. "
Blorm.. .. .. "
" Meyer .. .. "
" McElroy.. .. ..Trptr
" Mooney .. .. "
" Baker.. .. ..Privt
" Foyle.. .. .. "
" Bauth.. .. .. "
" Cohner.. .. .. "
" Daring.. .. .. "
" Davis.. .. .. "
" Farrell.. .. .. "
" Hiley.. .. .. "
" Huber.. .. .. "
" Hime.. .. .. "
" Henderson .. .. "
" Henderson .. .. "
" Leddisson.. .. .. "
" O'Conner.. .. .. "
" Rood.. .. .. "
" Reese.. .. .. "
" Smith 1st .. .. "
" Smith 2nd.. .. .. "
" Smith 3rd.. .. .. "
" Stella.. .. .. "
" Stafford.. .. .. "
" Schoole.. .. .. "
" Smallwood.. .. .. "
" Tarr .. .. "
" Vaugant.. .. .. "
" Walker .. .. "
" Bragew.. .. .. "
" Knight.. .. .. "
F G. W. Yates.. .. ..Capt
" W. Van Rieley.. .. ..2d Lt

GREASY GRASS

Valley of the Little Bighorn River,
Montana Territory
Sunday, June 25, 1876, 1:00 P.M.

The arrow struck him in the left eye, the feathered shaft sinking deep into his head as with a jerk his spine arched back, his arms flew wide, and his horse reared up on its hind legs, throwing the soldier from the saddle down to land in a crack of bones at the feet of Lieutenant Colonel George Armstrong Custer.

"Where in hell is Reno?" Custer shouted amid the overpowering din of the battle as he whirled and fired his Webley at a fast-approaching Cheyenne. The pistol shot was good.

The colonel stood near the crest of a hill north of Medicine Tail Coulee, his yellow locks cropped close, his stubbled jaw caked with alkali dust from three long days' ride over rough country. Dirt begrimed his buckskins, the breeches of which were tucked into square-topped cavalry boots, and sweat stained the red kerchief knotted at his throat. His once white broad-brimmed slouch hat—swept off in the heat of battle—now lay crushed in the sage at his feet.

Gone today was the natty, well-groomed cavalier who had led the Seventh Regiment to glory in 1868, when thundering out of a raging storm they had destroyed Black Kettle's camp sleeping by the Washita River. Left in place of the man once reputed to be the greatest Indian fighter in the U.S. Army was a weary, unkempt soldier who—battling desperately for his life—snapped orders at the young bugler by his side.

"Tight, God damn you, tight!"

"For Chrissake, boys, don't run! What is this? A rout?"

"Get Calhoun's men dismounted and deployed as skirmishers!"

Sergeant Robert Hughes of Troop K held Custer's battle flag. A swallow-tailed pennant of red and blue bars with two crossed sabers, its presence indicated the colonel was on the field. As Custer broke open his Webley and fed it .450 brass casings from his cartridge belt, Hughes cried out, "Oh, my Jesus! Tom just got it!" Captain Tom Custer, the colonel's brother, had taken a slug between the eyes, spattering blood and brains all over the horrified flagman.

"Here they come!" the bugler shouted. "Black as hell and thick as grass! Oh God, we're going to die!"

High on the bluff later known as Battle Ridge, Custer's view of the Indian village stretched along the river was restricted by a thicket of giant cottonwoods. Gazing down in disbelief on the carnage unfolding below, it was obvious there were more hostiles here than he had expected. Unknown to the colonel, the Sioux and Cheyenne were camped in seven circles four miles long, formed when three converging bands—each leaving a separate lodgepole trail as evidence of its size—joined together shortly before the cavalry attack.

Custer was a mercurial man of overwhelming ambition. A commander for whom attack and victory were synonymous terms, to ride away from a battle was simply not in his disposition. Three days back, his scouts had discovered a recent lodgepole trail, so he'd ordered the Seventh to follow it across the parched Wolf Mountains to where the Indians were camped. His strategy being to trap them in a surprise pincer attack, he'd split his 615 troops into three battalions. Leading the spearhead charge himself while Reno's column flanked, the colonel had galloped his battalion into a camp of not only those Indians they had followed, but also warriors with the other converging bands. His men outnumbered ten to one, "Custer's luck" had run out.

Like bees swarming from a hive, the Sioux and Cheyenne were responding with a ferocious counterattack. Uncpapa Sioux like Black Moon, Crow King, and Gall had dashed half-dressed from their tepees to blunt the longknives' charge, some wearing the quilled war bonnets of the Plains tribes, others with feathers in their hair notched to mean "cut throat and scalped" or split to indicate "suffered many wounds." Cheyenne braves like

Dull Knife, Flat Hip, and Ice Bear had engaged the *Wasichus* to force their retreat, some firing Winchesters or older muzzle-loaders, others armed with bows and arrows or long feathered lances, others still wielding double-headed tomahawks. Crazy Horse and the Ogallala Sioux—their mounts painted with palm prints to boast the foes they'd slain—had galloped after Custer and his rebuffed men, scattering the whites across the bluff. Through wreaths of smoke, dust, and the cacophony of battle, Rain-in-the-Face and Pemmican and Hump and Weasel Bear shouted the war cry "*Hoka hey!*" as others made the tremolo or shrilled the air with whistles. A Teton Sioux named The Lung galloped by in a beaded jacket fringed with human hair. The Sans Arcs—the No Bows—fought the "sick-looking men" hand-to-hand, their bodies draped with talismans bestowing spirit powers: an owl's beak on a thong or a coyote's skin. Plunging into this confusion of shots and whinnying horses, charging across the battlefield where panicked mounts with empty saddles stampeded wild, came Bad Soup and Comes Again, Low Dog and Spotted Eagle; came Feathered Earring, Bare Ribs, Flying Hawk, and Iron Thunder; came Blue Cloud and Belly Fat and Man-Who-Walks-His-Dogs . . . an endless horde of outraged horsemen riding to the slaughter, cutting the *Mini-hanskapi* down as stragglers, wounded and dying, pleaded for their lives. The fight was now a running fight away from the river and up the ravines . . . up toward the crest of the ridge where Custer stood . . . fighting and falling, turning and shooting, troopers on the run . . . as back, back, pushing them back, the Sioux encircled them.

"Sound the call to stand formation!" Custer shouted.

When the bugler didn't respond, he slapped the man. The trumpeter crumpled to his knees, blubbering hysterically.

"What damn fool move is this, sir? *I* am in command!"

Custer slapped him again.

"Now blow that horn!"

The call of the bugle summoned survivors to the crest of the hill. Hacked-up soldiers dragged themselves across the blood-soaked scrub as Indian horses streaked past, followed immediately by descending tomahawks. Troopers still in the saddle were shooting their mounts to take up positions behind the carcasses. One cavalry man grimaced as a spear ripped through his chest; then halter, lariat, saddle, and blanket broke away from his horse, toppling him to land beneath pummeling Cheyenne hooves.

Bullets zipped into the sage, throwing up puffs of dust. The air turned black from gunsmoke haloing rifle barrels. Seventy-five doomed men formed a defensive circle, the ones in front kneeling so those behind could fire. Mathey, Slaper, Frett, Girard, and Edgerly went down. Luther Hare shouted, "My fuckin' gun is jammed!" "So's mine," Edward Godfrey cried, then a Teton bullet blew away his face.

One by one the Seventh's .45/70 Springfield carbines seized up. Overheated extractor hooks cut shell rims like putty, leaving expended cartridges in the firing chambers. "Stick to sidearms!" Custer yelled as the circle collapsed. Those who heard him drew their Colt Peacemaker .45s.

The battlefield was now so dark that Indian and white alike shot at their own men, friend and foe but shadows in a veil of smoke. The Seventh was down to twenty soldiers still on their feet when a few tried to break away from the ridge. Those remaining promptly turned their guns on the deserters.

One of those attempting flight was a civilian named Francis Parker. A gangly Ichabod Crane of a man, he'd crossed paths with the army column shortly before the charge. During Custer's foolishness he'd remained behind, only to be embroiled in the battle when the troops were driven back.

Another, Lieutenant Harrington, commandeered a horse from a wounded man. Breaking through the Sioux, he galloped down the Valley of the Little Bighorn River. The Indians pursued him with Old Bear in the lead, but Harrington's mount was swift with fright and it seemed he'd get away, when suddenly the lieutenant drew his revolver and shot himself in the head. He died by the unwritten code of frontiersmen: "When in a fight with Indians, save the last shell for yourself."

High on the bluff, Custer and Hughes were the only two left. Gauntlet on one hand, gun in the other, the colonel stood above the bugler thrashing in the grass, a Cheyenne arrow imbedded in the trumpeter's throat. On one knee, Hughes clung tenaciously to the flag, triggering his empty pistol at the Sioux. When a tomahawk split his head open, he dropped with a whimper.

Enraged by the sight of his tattered flag trampled in the dust, the colonel shouted, "Damned if I'll be killed by heathen redskins!"

Muzzle so close its powder blackened Custer's skin, Rain-in-the-Face rode up and shot him in the temple.

With Custer dead, the Indians' fight with the Seventh was over, but half an hour later they still circled the field, whooping while thudding the bodies with arrows or shooting them again, swirling around the Last Stand like rapids around a stone.

The sun had moved but a few lodgepole widths from the start of the fight to the finish.

The aftermath took longer.

Broad shouldered and sinewy, The Lung was medicine chief of the Teton Sioux. He'd shed his beaded jacket for the climb uphill, and now stood bare-chested under the scorching sun. Surveying the battlefield, he thought, *My people's blood boiled hot today, but their hearts are cold.*

Chattering squaws stripped the bodies of the whites. Around them piles of war spoils stood ready to cart away: tobacco, watches, wallets, whiskey, weapons, saddles, flags, and photographs. The stronger women mutilated the dead, cutting limbs and heads from those the braves had scalped. A trio of men rode by with trophies on their spears, one holding aloft the slashed-off whiskered cheek of an army major. The last survivor of the Seventh limped about the field: Captain Myles Keogh's black-maned sorrel named Comanche. Wounded, the horse was half-dead from loss of blood.

Of all those on the killing ground, Captain Tom Custer's corpse was in the worst shape. The colonel's brother lay facedown near the crest of the hill, his skull crushed by repeated tomahawk blows. Every strand of hair had been scalped from his head except for a tuft at the nape of his neck. Rain-in-the-Face had cut out and eaten the captain's heart, an act thought to impart an enemy's courage to the consumer.

The colonel's corpse was the only one that wouldn't

be scalped. Instead someone had stuck awls in his ears to help "Yellow Hair's" spirit hear Indian protests better. There were two wounds in the colonel's body, the shot to the temple and a hole in his chest. As The Lung squatted to address the corpse, Custer's opaque eyes stared vacantly up at him.

"Sometimes, *Pahuska,* dreams are wiser than the waking. That which has occurred today is that which was foretold."

The Lung brushed away a swarm of flies.

"The Black Hills are not melting snow in our hands. They are home to Wakan-Tanka, greatest of all gods. The waters of the hills are tears from his eyes, the earth and what it contains his sole domain.

"In the Moon of Making Fat, you told Red Cloud the hills are ours as long as the grass grows and the river waters flow. The Treaty of Laramie promises you will not enter our land, yet you come anyway as if the hills are yours. This yellow metal you worship, this earth that makes you crazy, is it worth the price all of us must pay? You talk and talk, you *Wasichus,* but in the end your words are like the winds blowing."

Overhead, the first vulture circled the field.

"Wakan-Tanka told Sitting Bull you would come in a dream. Now he's sent Bull a vision of many longknives riding to avenge your slaughter. Bull says we must flee across the Medicine Line, past the stone heaps where the *Shaglashapi* redcoats guard the Land of the Great White Mother.

"*Pahuska,* a people's dream died in your blood today. You have driven us from our land. But moons from now we Lakota will return. In the end the earth is all that lasts."

The Lung was distracted by a frightful scream. Months before this day's battle on the Greasy Grass, Sitting Bull had asked the tribes north of the Medicine Line to join him against the whites. The Blackfoot declined but the Plains Cree agreed, and one of them, White Owl, was taking scalps.

Among the soldiers lay a man dressed in civilian clothes. As the Cree gripped his head and cut away his hair, the white let out a horrid shriek of pain. The cry attracted several squaws nearby, for one of their jobs was to drag survivors away for torture in the camp. Across the river gibbering howls could be heard, and here was another voice to join the chorus.

As the civilian pleaded, the Cree stripped him of clothes. Unnoticed, a notebook fell from one pocket and landed in the scrub. When the man was down to his underwear, the squaws took him away, but not before White Owl claimed his scalp. The Cree, spotting a shoulder bag on the ground, emptied its contents hoping for trophies. Out fell a book and a large yellow skull. *Parker's Journal* was tooled into the book's leather cover.

The skull was two to three times as large as a man's. A sagittal crest crowned it like an Iroquois scalp lock. The fossil was wrapped in fishnet to hold the jaw in place. Its canine teeth projected like fangs.

With a whoop of satisfaction White Owl stuffed the journal and Parker's clothes into the bag. Slinging the satchel over his shoulder, he mounted his pinto. The skull hoisted on his lance, he turned his horse toward the river and left the battlefield.

SNIPER

San Francisco
Saturday, March 14, 1987, 8:12 P.M.

The Walther WA2000 using a .300 Winchester Magnum 180-grain hardball cartridge has a muzzle velocity of 3,000 feet per second and a muzzle energy of 3,600 foot-pounds. In other words, the Walther will drop a grizzly bear. The barrel is the most important part of any rifle, so the barrel of the Walther in the sniper's grasp was hand-finished and rifled to his exact specifications. Its length was longitudinally grooved to dissipate heat and resist harmonic effect. The action was a bull-pup, the bolt and six-round magazine nuzzled up under the killer's masked jaw. The pistol grip had a thumb hole for greater accuracy, while the barrel was set in a rigid frame so the shoulder stock was but a prolongation of the receiver. The recoil force from the shot would be delivered in a straight line to the sniper's shoulder, ensuring the sights wouldn't stray from his target. The telescopic lens mounted in front of his eye was a 2.5 ten-power zoom angled sharply down from the hotel roof. Its sights were focused through the glass ceiling of The Conservatory fifteen stories below, the cross-hairs centered on the forehead of the speaker now at the podium. The killer's gloved finger closed on the trigger.

Within The Conservatory of the Carlton Palace Hotel, the American Bar Association was having its convention. The buzz of a thousand voices echoed in the cavernous room as judges and lawyers sipped liqueurs, chatting while the dinner dishes were cleared. The Conservatory dated from 1909, when it replaced a dance hall that fell victim to the Earthquake of 1906. An opulent salon of gilt walls, velvet drapes, and crystal chandeliers, its ceiling had ten thousand panes of glass. This evening the room basked under a canopy of stars, dimly lit except for a spotlight on the podium. The president of the ABA addressed the crowd.

"Ladies and gentlemen, honored judges, members and guests. It gives me pleasure to introduce this evening's speaker. Arguably the most innovative jurist since Lord Denning, would you please welcome Mr. Justice Hutton Murdoch of the British Columbia Court of Appeal."

To applause, he relinquished the podium to a man in his mid-sixties wearing a tuxedo. As the judge's craggy, handsome face appeared in the spotlight's glare, the din among the conventioneers died to a whisper. His was a presence as commanding as F. Lee Bailey or Edward Marshall Hall.

"Mr. President, fellow judges, members of the bar. Canada is indeed fortunate to have the United States as its neighbor, for your Constitution is centuries more advanced. We therefore have had the benefit of learning from your mistakes.

"When I say 'your mistakes,' I don't mean this in a disparaging way, for every nation is shaped on the anvil of its history. We've had the benefit of assessing your experiments before drafting laws of our own, an advantage not available to the leader in the field. The similarities between our countries result from the constitutional concepts we adopted from you; while the differences reflect those aspects we rejected.

"First the differences.

"America is a republic born from a revolution. For that reason your Constitution guarantees you the right to bear arms. Today we see the results of this clause, for though Canada's population is one-tenth that of the States', in 1985 we had five handgun deaths compared to your 8,092. In the last five months alone 135 handguns were seized from American tourists crossing the border from Washington state, so our Constitution—learning from you—does not, and never will, guarantee this right.

"When America split political power between Congress and the states in the eighteenth century, your Constitution gave the states control over criminal law. Today the resulting mishmash means a killer who crosses state lines must be extradited, while depending on *where* he murders his victim he'll either forfeit his life or may one day go free.

"Imagine how much safer America would be if like our Mounties, your police could automatically hunt felons coast to coast? From sea to sea our criminal law is uniform, for we—again learning from you—gave that power to the central government."

A drunk in the audience yelled out, "Your laws would put most of us out of work. Who wants safety if lawyers are gonna starve?"

Murdoch ignored him.

"America settled its Wild West by opening the floodgates to free spirits in a free-for-all. Consequently, you had to struggle to bring the resulting chaos under control. Your mythic heroes of the West—Wyatt Earp, George Custer, Bat Masterson—were all renegades themselves, for *how* you settled your territory fostered a situation where you were later forced to fight fire with fire. The level of crime in the U.S. today indicates a diminished respect for the rule of law, because your expansion conditioned the ethic of flouting authority."

The drunk cried out, "What's this holier-than-thou shit?"

Murdoch paused a moment to glare at the man. The crowd turned to get a glimpse of the heckler slouched in his chair, finger tapping the ash of a stogy onto the floor, a glass of red wine spilled down the front of his shirt. Embracing the fifteen minutes of fame promised by Andy Warhol, the drunk gave the crowd a little wave.

The judge returned to his notes.

"In the early 1870s there were no white settlers on our prairies west of Manitoba. Canada as a nation had only been in existence since 1867, and already the government feared our demise should you sweep up in the West to seize our unsettled land. American whiskey traders were already entrenched at Fort Whoop-Up in what is now Alberta.

"After the Riel Rebellion of 1870, the army sent two British officers—William Butler and Wilfred Blake—across the prairies in the dead of winter to report on conditions there. When both men recommended forming the North-West Mounted Police, the Force was recruited in 1873. That same year it departed on the Great March West to wipe out Fort Whoop-Up.

"Because the Mounties had to pass through Indian territory, the men were issued scarlet tunics to wear. Historically both the Cree and Blackfoot had respect for Queen Victoria's Redcoats. During their trek to the Rockies, the Mounted Police established detachments along the way, so when the first settlers later arrived to farm the West they found the rule of law firmly in place. From you we learned not to let things get out of control.

"Canada is an obsessively law-abiding country. What other nation is known first and foremost for its police? All our mythic Western heroes—James Walsh, Sam Steele, Wilfred Blake—were officers in the North-West Mounted—"

"You forgot one."

The drunk was back in business.

"What about Preston's dog King? He your hero too?"

Murdoch paused, debating whether to take the heckler on.

The crowd stirred in anticipation, for lawyers enjoy nothing more than an all-out verbal mudsling.

Fifteen stories above the judge, the sniper pulled the trigger.

Because the Walther was equipped with a sound suppressor, the only noise that shattered the night other than breaking glass was the supersonic whip-crack of the high-velocity slug.

The bullet smashed through the roof of The Conservatory below, fragmenting the judge's forehead and atomizing his brain.

Blood and bone were blown all over the startled ABA execs at the head table.

For a moment the judge's headless body was held in the spotlight's glare; then what remained of the Canadian crumpled from sight.

An hour before the shot was fired, Chuck Fraser had been surprised to run into Martin Kwan. Their paths crossed in the corridor outside the doors to The Conservatory.

"Hey, Martin."

"Hello, Chuck."

"What are you doing here?"

"Same thing as you. Cheating the tax department."

Fraser grinned. "Not me. I live here. Don't get a free holiday till next year."

Martin cocked his head, arching an eyebrow. "Chuck, you seem . . . younger. I hardly recognize you."

"Miracle of modern science, pal. You're only as old as you look. If you'd let me know you were coming, I'd have laid something on."

"The trip was spur of the moment. Didn't know I was flying down till late last week."

"Here alone?"

"With my sister. She just emigrated from Hong Kong and wanted to see San Francisco."

"You'll have to introduce me. What's her name?"

"Lotus."

"Pretty handle. A lawyer too?"

"Uh-uh. Business."

"What's her line of work?"

"Pharmaceuticals. She runs Fankuang Tzu."

Chuck Fraser was an attorney who specialized in transpacific finance and Asian immigration. His San Francisco office—he also had one in Japan—was a full-floor penthouse suite high above Montgomery Street. A vitamin-popping fitness freak who played squash every day, Fraser employed his own sushi chef and kept a pair of geishas. Espousing the philosophy "If you can't beat 'em, join 'em," he was at the convention tonight to show off his recent face-lift and implanted hair. Chuck had sipped from what passed these days as the Fountain of Youth.

Martin Kwan—from Chuck's point of view—was a Young Turk in the boardroom, Asian style. In his mid-twenties, the foreigner's oval face surrounded cold, rapacious eyes. His black hair, perfectly cut, was parted to one side, his Cupid's-bow lips and dimples curled up in a supercilious smile. Kwan was wearing a charcoal Chester Barrie suit worth at least two thousand bucks, coordinated with a pale pink shirt and matching silk tie. Fraser imagined him up at dawn, backed by a salmon sky, fluidly running through the 108-move sequence of the Taoist tai chi, preparing for another day of ripping the guts out of North American industry. He was the sort of merciless shark good for Chuck's business.

"How'd your grandfather take the news? Wish I could have helped him."

"He accepted your advice. We have other options."

"I hope he understood it's not our quota system. The U.S. may only take a handful of Hong Kong immigrants a year, and yes, the waiting list is thirteen years long, but with the right connections there are ways around the queue. If not for the company's trade with Hanoi, I could have got him in."

"No need for a rehash, Chuck. He understands."

"That's the problem with a one-shareholder company. The owner is tainted by what the company does."

"We know you did the best you could. There's room at another inn."

Fraser shrugged apologetically. "Fankuang did sell the North Viets thirty percent of their drugs, including the thiopental used to interrogate our POWs. That sort of commerce America's just not ready to forgive."

Kwan glanced at his Rolex, the platinum kind. Fraser took this as an indication to change the subject.

"I hear Fankuang's doing wondrous things with organ transplants. The donor shortage here's created a desperate market. Any chance of a finder's fee if I steer business your way?"

"How much?"

"Say twenty percent of the cost."

"Make it ten."

"Fifteen."

"It's a deal."

Again Kwan glanced at his Rolex. Then at the hotel's clock. He was about to excuse himself when Fraser said, "I have a Japanese client who—like your grandfather—isn't welcome in the States. Think you could slip him into Canada instead?"

"Does he have money?"

"Of course. Or he'd be no client of mine."

"A criminal record in Japan?"

"Laundering problems with the States, but he was never charged."

"I assume he's not been deported from Canada in the past?"

"Hasn't set foot outside of Japan."

"Then there should be no problem bringing him in.

Our Immigration Act encourages offshore investors. If he'll put $250,000 into a foreign-financed Canadian venture fund, or if he'll sink the same amount into creating a domestic business, immigration visas are virtually guaranteed for him and his family. After three years of landed status they'll get full citizenship."

"That's it? No quotas?"

"Not if your client has money. Quotas apply to Sweatshop Suzie, not the financial elite. Ottawa bends over for anyone with cash."

Fraser winked. "I heard you were easy. But that's a lawyer's dream."

"Twelve thousand Canadian passports will be sold in Hong Kong this year. Offshore money's flowing in at the rate of billions every fiscal quarter. Lotus came in last week from Hong Kong under that provision. Of course, she also had me to sponsor her under the family reunification plan."

It occurred to Fraser that something was amiss here. If Martin, a Canadian citizen, could be his family's sponsor, and if his grandfather could easily buy his way into Canada, why had the Kwans approached him the year before to get them into the States?

Yet a third time, Martin glanced at his watch. "Gotta go, Chuck. Lotus has disappeared. I've been trying to find her for half an hour."

"I've got the same problem. Your countryman Smolensky is nowhere around. He should be at the head table when Murdoch speaks."

They parted company forty-five minutes before the shot.

8:21 P.M.

Arnie Smolensky was a very happy man. Yessiree.

Arnie was a specialist in P.I. fender benders from Whalley, B.C., a rotund lawyer of forty-six with a bulbous nose, protruding ears, and a shiny pate surrounded by a fringe of thinning hair. Back home he had a fat wife who ran a dog-grooming salon, three snotty kids who thought their father was a dork, and a thriving, though boring, law practice restricted to personal-injury suits.

As Canada's liaison to the exec of the ABA, once or twice a year he'd attend U.S. bar conventions, where it was his habit "to really cut loose." Cutting loose for Smolensky meant getting tanked in the hotel bar, where often he'd hook up with other attorneys "hunting pussy on the hoof," forging a group of three or four "horny musketeers" who'd whiz around the convention city in an endless succession of cabs, overtipping each driver to find them "the hottest spot in town," before invariably "striking out with the babes" to wind up at five A.M. in some all-night Chinese joint for a feast of chicken chow mein.

But not tonight.

Yesterday after the panel on how to jack up soft-tissue whiplash awards at trial, Arnie had behaved true to form and consequently had slept through till late this afternoon. On awaking he'd quickly dressed for the ABA dinner in The Conservatory—black suit, white shirt, red polka-dot bow tie—before sauntering into the hotel bar for a little hair of the dog. It took a moment for Arnie's eyes to adjust to the smoky lounge, then he caught sight of the "China doll" and "almost shot in his pants."

What a fox! he thought.

From his point of view the China doll was "the most gorgeous gash" he'd ever "felt up with his eyes," sitting alone near the end of the bar sipping a Singapore sling, dressed in red Oriental silk slit high on the thigh, long legs brazenly crossed as one scarlet pump jiggled up and down. Dark eyes set wide apart in a face the color of gold, teeth like Asian pearls peeking through pouty red lips, a white gardenia adorning upswept jet black hair—Arnie thought this babe "a wet dream come true."

With the "big boy" stirring in his shorts, he strolled toward the bar.

It was now two hours later in Arnie's top-floor hotel suite. The ecstatic lawyer was stretched out on the king-size bed, the big boy limp as a noodle from "getting his oil changed." Listening with erotic anticipation to the spray of the shower behind the closed bathroom door, Smolensky thought, *Yessiree, yellow pussy's the best.* He was still amazed he'd talked Lotus Kwan into climbing between the sheets.

Tonight marked the first time Arnie had "porked Oriental skank." Except for a black hooker named Midnight who'd blown him at last April's convention in the Cayman Islands, Smolensky's sex experience was confined to his wife's "nooky-ass." And his books and tapes.

For back home in the bottom drawer of his office desk, locked away from Bunny, his legal secretary, Arnie kept the "wank-aids" he purchased every month. Not *Playboy* and *Penthouse*, that wimpy junk, but high-class rags like *Hustler, Club,* and *Gent,* mags where you got to know the girls—really carnally know them—without being distracted by anything except what nestled between their legs. Arn was a mainstay of the billion-dollar-a-year pornography industry. He considered himself "a connoisseur of cunt."

Sometimes when his wife was out of town and the kids were safely at school, he liked to dress up in Wendy's "undies" to see how he looked. His wife wore chain-store cotton panties ballooning from the waist, and sensible bras designed for support, not display. In Arnie's mind he saw himself in a flimsy G-string or cutaway coquette briefs, jiggling a lacy French bra that showed off his tits, hips caressed by a passionate red or sinful black garter belt. Welted fishnet stockings encased his quivering thighs—for Arnie escaped to a down and dirty fantasy world.

Lotus Kwan was that fantasy come to life.

It was almost as if the Asian had waited for him in that bar, intent on a seduction planned in advance. Could it be their meeting was preordained, a match by Eros, a "wanker's dream"? Everything Arnie asked Lotus to do, the China doll obliged. It was as if Kwan liked "to flaunt her quim" as much as he liked to look.

When the bathroom door opened, Smolensky turned. The sight of Lotus naked parched his throat. Kwan had been showering so long he'd begun to fear this was a figment of his mind, a sexy interlude while he napped. Struggling to keep his voice from breaking like an adolescent's, he managed to croak, "Wanna do it again?"

"Do what?"

"You know. Like before."

"Tell me, Arnie. I love to hear the words."

"Feed me," he said, wiggling his tongue.

Lotus slinked over to kneel, legs straddled above his

face. "Hot damn," Arnie whispered as "Miss Puss" zoomed in. Back in the late forties when Arnie was starting school, one of the big kids had told him Chinese girls were different in that "their slits ran east to west instead of north to south." Arnie was in the process of laying that bogus theory to rest (actually, he'd done so earlier, but who was counting, huh?), wishing deep down in the depths of his mind that he "had a cooze like hers," longing to chuck the practice of law for the job he'd always wanted, photographing "muff" for his favorite magazines, when the fire door connecting his suite to one adjacent—the same fire door he'd forgot to lock after boozing the night before—burst open, and Max Cavandish, the ABA exec from Kansas City, poked his head in to announce, "Arnie, Murdoch's been shot!"

BULL'S-EYE

8:41 P.M.

There was a time once when all homicide bulls were big tough men, when you couldn't become a homicide cop unless you looked like the meanest SOB in the valley. Punk would be sitting in a room down at the Hall of Justice, cool as ice on a winter's day, knowing his people were movin' and shakin' to get him sprung, out of here in a jiffy as long as he kept his trap shut, hip to the fact that ninety percent of the cons in the slam had verbally hung themselves, when suddenly the light beyond the door would disappear. The perp would glance at the hall outside and all he'd see was black. Then slowly it would dawn on him that was because the dude at the door filled all the available space. Homicide bull would say nice and soft, "I wanna talk to you," and seconds later the perp would be spilling his guts to The Man, stringing himself up by his own wagging tongue.

When later the case got to court, the punk's mouthpiece would ask, "Inspector, do you consider yourself a physically threatening man?" Amused, the homicide bull would reply, "Counselor, there's nothing I can do about my size. But I can assure you I didn't touch your client." Truth was, in those days—contrary to legend—there was no need for the bulls to pull out a rubber hose. Truth was, the *look* of The Man, the *size* of the motherfucker—combined, they were rubber hose enough.

Then came the sixties and all that changed. Career enlightenment hit the U.S.A. Soon everyone got an equal shot at every job, so these days your homicide bull could be four feet tall, eat tofu for dinner as a substitute for meat, and drink California Cooler instead of straight scotch. Hell, these days Pee-wee Herman could be a homicide cop.

The two men in the unmarked sedan were throwbacks

to the good old days. Inspectors with the Homicide Detail of the SFPD, they'd caught the squeal on the fourth floor of the Hall of Justice on Bryant, and now were less than a block away from the Carlton Palace Hotel. Ahead, a dozen patrol cars had cordoned off Hyde, while choppers with searchlights buzzed the roof. The sedan's radio squawked with busy air.

"Christ, I hope this ain't a round-the-clock," McGuire said.

"Has the makings," McIlroy confirmed.

"Remember last year? The hooker on the Wharf? Almost didn't get to celebrate Saint Pat's."

"What a party. One of your best."

"Only green *you* wore was the puke down your shirt."

"Pull in here. We'll walk the rest."

Nosing the Ford to the curb, McGuire locked the wheels and set the hand brake. With luck the car would still be here when they returned, not a mile downhill submerged in the Bay. As both giants lumbered out, the balmy night kissed their cheeks.

Six-foot-four and 260 pounds, McGuire was Irish-American by way of New York. Hair blond and eyes blue, he'd come to California when the Beach Boys promised sun, surf, and fun, fun, fun. With Saint Patrick's Day looming fast, McGuire's mind was preoccupied with his annual bash. The Homicide Detail liked to say only the brain-dead whacked someone the day after Mac's party. The bulls roaming the streets were all hungover.

"Tried Kwellada?"

"Huh?"

"You're scratching your crotch."

"I think Silicone Judy gave me crabs."

"You and your strippers," McIlroy said.

"Buddy of mine got crabs once. A field geologist. Discovered 'em the day he was dropped in the bush. Plane wouldn't pick him up for a month. Had to shave his sac with a knife and pour kerosene on his balls."

Six-foot-three and 240 pounds, McIlroy, between the pair, was known as "The Shrimp." Back in '64 when he blocked for Stanford, he was known as "The Thing" on the grid. McIlroy's name in Scots Gaelic meant "son of the red-haired lad," a fitting moniker since he was a freckled carrot-top. As the bulls approached the hotel, he winced at the thought of Mac shaving his sac after one of his parties.

Red-blue-red-blue— The wig-wag lights on the car roofs stained their faces.

"GOLD IN PEACE, IRON IN WAR" read the Spanish motto on the shields they pinned to their jackets.

As the cop guarding the hotel door stepped back to let them in, a news photographer rushed up and snapped their picture.

The flash went off while McGuire was scratching his groin.

Inside, the lobby was a gilt extravaganza of high frescoed ceilings and marble staircases. In the fountain near the check-in desk, cherubs peed recycled water into a basin. Off the lobby was a foyer with coat check racks, and beyond that a ballroom named Champagne Bubbles. A herd of antsy lawyers milled about the dance floor while harried blues tried to determine who was who, who'd seen what, and who was where when.

An assistant D.A. met the bulls at the door to the murder scene. His clothes and tanned face were spattered with blood. The room beyond was empty except for Murdoch and those investigating his death. An M.E. from the coroner's office was bent over the stiff. "Mac. Mac," the D.A. said, acknowledging both cops.

"'Evening, Stan," McGuire said, unwrapping a stick of Wrigley's Juicy Fruit gum.

McIlroy nodded. "What's the rundown?"

The shaken lawyer loosened his tie. "The victim's a Canadian judge, down to speak tonight. He was addressing us when he was shot. Bullet came through the ceiling, probably from the roof. I was at the head table beside the podium. When the crowd panicked and ran for the door, I used the maître d's phone to call Security. The hotel was sealed before anyone got out."

McGuire blew a bubble.

McIlroy said, "Good work. Crowd in the streets would be like shooting fish in a barrel."

"I don't envy you guys," the D.A. said. "Convention's theme is *How to Make the Streets of America Safe*. Keynote speaker last night was the A.G. himself."

The three men crossed The Conservatory to Murdoch's

corpse. Behind them came the lab team, a dozen strong. "What a mess," McGuire said. "Where's the top of his head?"

"You're standing in it," the M.E. said. "Watch you don't slip on the gore."

McIlroy crouched over the wound.

"Bull's-eye," McGuire said, pulling down his eyelid and pointing to his eye.

The M.E. took this as gallow's humor, a common trait among cops. Some sort of Homicide Detail double entendre. Actually, McGuire was saying, *Let's not miss a thing*. Mac and Mac had been teamed so long they had their own language.

McIlroy indicated a hole in the floor. Ident snapped the find from every possible angle, then one of the ballistics techs dug out the slug. "Hardball," the tech said. "Not a hollow point. Have to be to punch through the glass."

The coroner's stewards set to work with their stretcher and body bag. After Murdoch's remains were on their way to the morgue, the same tech used a laser gun to line the hole in the floor up with the one through the ceiling. Mac and Mac followed most of the team up to the hotel's roof, stepping out into a dust storm when the elevator opened.

"God damn!" one of the Hairs and Fibers techs exclaimed, cursing the chopper that whupped overhead. Any traces the killer had left behind were scattered to the wind.

The laser beam from below grazed the edge of the roof, tracing the bullet's trajectory back to where the sniper had fired. In a set pecking order, the techs approached the beam. Portable arcs were turned on to light the ledge, then Hairs and Fibers vacuumed the roof with a MiscO. Hundred-to-one the bag wouldn't cough up in the lab.

Next, Prints dusted the ledge where the killer had stood. They had to wait till the MiscO was done so fingerprint powder wouldn't contaminate any traces. Finally, Ballistics combed the site of the shot.

".300 Winchester Magnum," a firearms tech said.

Mac and Mac turned. Both were staring over the ledge

at The Conservatory below. Through the glass they could see the podium where Murdoch had given his speech.

"Heavy load," the tech said, holding out a cartridge casing in a plastic bag. "Only one shot. The hitter's a pro."

The homicide bulls left the roof team to carry on. As they waited for the elevator, McGuire said, "Take a look around. Mac. Where'd the shooter go? Nothing on all four sides except a plunge to the street."

"Must have fled into the hotel or down the fire escape."

"If it's the hotel, he's cornered inside."

"If it's the fire escape, he's long gone."

"What say we check the alley?" McGuire said.

At the door to the alley, they bumped into Joan Passaglia, the chief gunpowder tech. She was a matronly woman, glasses on a chain, who reminded McGuire of his Aunt Bee in Poughkeepsie. Passaglia carried rifle components sealed in evidence bags.

"Hi, Joan. Whatcha got?"

McIlroy fanned his face. "Phew. Smells like someone cut the cheese."

"Walther WA2000," Passaglia said. "State-of-the-art piece and the gunman leaves it behind? I found it in the alley, broken up. The sniper dropped it from the roof after the shot. Stock and action landed in the garbage bin out back. The restaurant special is Seafood Delight."

Through the door another team of techs was at work. "Ladies and germs," McGuire said, greeting them. Both ends of the alley were sealed by police. The bottom of the fire escape was to their right.

Once they were out of earshot, McIlroy said, "I don't like the feel of this one, Mac. Professional hitter whacks a foreign judge in front of the Bar. The night before the A.G. says, "Let's clean up the streets." Something tells me this one's gonna draw heat."

"There goes the party," McGuire sighed.

"Must be a thousand lawyers inside to interview."

"If that ain't a cop's nightmare, I don't know what is."

"Let's golf it," McIlroy said, nearing the fire escape. "Guy'd have to be brain-dead to want to keep this case to himself."

McGuire spit his gum toward the nearest dumpster,

and that was when he saw the winos slumped on the stairs. Oblivious to what was going on, the bums passed a jug of screech back and forth.

"Time to call in the Suits," McIlroy said. "If the motive's in Canada, does that cross state lines?"

McGuire's eyes followed the fire escape from the bums up to the roof.

"And while we're at it," McIlroy said, "let's bring the Horsemen in. That unit they got up there. X-Men, I think they're called."

THE TRUNK

West Vancouver, British Columbia
Saturday, March 14, 1987, 10:50 P.M.

Ten days ago DeClercq had received an unexpected call. It was eight at night and he was sitting feet-up in the greenhouse of his West Vancouver home, Beethoven's *Moonlight Sonata* backed by the soft patter of rain on the sloping glass roof, his mind deep in the fifth chapter of Caesar's *The Conquest of Gaul,* when his thoughts were interrupted by the phone.

"DeClercq," he said, answering the cellular by his chair.

"Robert. Jack MacDougall."

"Jack, long time no see."

"Yeah, four years, give or take. Am I interrupting anything?"

"Just reading a book."

"Spare me a moment? It's important."

"Shoot."

"I'm in Dundarave. Ten minutes and I could be there."

"Coffee or tea?"

"Coffee please."

Jack MacDougall, DeClercq recalled, was a country & western man. There was only one album in the house that suited his taste, a cassette Genny's brother had sent her six years ago. After making the coffee, DeClercq put Merle Haggard's *Going Where the Lonely Go* on the stereo.

The Jack MacDougall who rapped on the door had slipped a notch or two. Habitually well tailored in GQ style, tonight his blue blazer and gray flannels were rumpled like pajamas. The RCMP crest stitched to the blazer pocket—buffalo head beneath a crown surrounded by maple leaves—was stained yellow by spilled scotch. Insomnia had puffed, flushed, and sagged MacDougall's face.

"I know I look like shit," he said, following Robert and the coffee tray down the hall to the living room and out into the greenhouse.

Except for the La-Z-Boy beside DeClercq's reading lamp, the chairs among the greenery were wicker head-fans. MacDougall took a seat near the German shepherd asleep on the Persian rug while DeClercq filled two mugs on the serving tray. "So tell me," Robert said, passing Jack a cup.

"The DC wants to drum me out of the Force."

"Why?"

MacDougall hesitated. "Because I'm gay."

A shadow of discomfort crossed DeClercq's face, which Jack mistakenly linked to his revelation. In the background Merle was singing "Shopping for Dresses," soon to be followed by Willie Nelson's "Half a Man." *Poor choice,* DeClercq thought.

"How'd the DC find out?"

"Peter told him. Peter Brent. My lover till recently."

"Motive?"

"Spite and cocaine. It's a long, sad story."

There was no need for Jack to explain the DC's reaction. The RCMP are civil cops with military ways, their tradition dating back to the British Imperial Army, from which the first recruits were drawn. Homosexuals are not permitted to join the Force, and the deputy commissioner was a strong traditionalist.

"Peter's a gymnast who didn't make the Olympics in '84. He started using steroids preparing for '88. He got caught and they bounced him from the gymnastic team, so that's when he took to snorting cocaine. When I found out, we had a fight that went from bad to worse. He blamed me for all his problems, for shattering his dream, because of the pressure I imposed to keep our love a secret. Before he stomped out he said he was going to force me out of the closet. He called the DC, and now I'm being forced out of the Force."

MacDougall reached down to scratch Napoleon's ear. Out on the water a foghorn growled. The beam of the Point Atkinson lighthouse played across his face, whitening, then blackening his clipped mustache. A seagull landed on the roof to walk back and forth.

"It's a bad rule," DeClercq said, "that ought to change."

"What do I do, Robert? I need your advice. If I want to save my pension, the DC demands I resign. No fuss, no muss. Nice and clean. If I balk he swears he'll kick me out, and thirty years of service goes down the drain."

"You could take him to court."

"And mudsling the Force? That would undo everything I've worked for up till now. Besides, I can't get around the fact I lied to get in."

"Life won't be easy if you stay. The ranks don't like challenges to our past. The woman who joined the Musical Ride? An obscene photo was taken of her while she was asleep. Another found plastic breasts scrawled with her badge number taped to her desk. And they were both straight."

"I'm not afraid of the bigots. It's losing my pension which scares the hell out of me. I'm too old and lack the training to build another career. In my heart I want to fight, but I guess resignation's the only real choice."

DeClercq owed MacDougall a debt from the Headhunter case. He had retired a hero: the man who brought that raving psycho down. Few people knew about the booze, the pills, and the gun he stuck in his mouth. Jack had kept the squad on track while he was falling apart. Now as he studied this sleep-deprived cop at a crossroads of indecision, he recalled Samuel Johnson's sage advice: *A man, Sir, should keep his friendship in constant repair.*

"Go home and get some sleep, Jack, and leave the problem with me. Phone tomorrow about noon and I may have the answer."

After MacDougall was on his way, DeClercq put the *Moonlight Sonata* back on the stereo. He lit a crackling fire on the living room hearth, then stood before it, warming himself while staring at the mantel. Along it in silver frames were three photographs. One was of Kate, his first wife, playing Rebecca on Broadway in Ibsen's *Rosmersholm*. The shot was taken center stage the night they met. The second photo was of Jane, maybe four years old, sitting in a pile of autumn leaves with sunlight in her curls. The shutter had caught her mid-laugh, head thrown back. The last picture was of Genevieve, DeClercq's second wife, on a beach in Western Samoa during their honeymoon. Her body tanned in contrast to the white bikini she wore, Genny held a large conch shell to one ear. The fire reflected Robert's features off the glass in the picture frame.

Face to face, he eyed himself juxtaposed on the past. Wavy hair rapidly turning gray, aquiline nose a little bonier than before, narrow chin slackening where jaw met throat: time was definitely taking its toll. Still, all in all he felt comfortable with himself—hard to imagine five years ago.

Tuesday, December 28, 1982, 2:00 P.M.

Rain hammered down from an iron gray sky in driving spikes that nailed the ground and pocked the gathering puddles. It dripped from the black umbrellas above the heads of the silent mourners, then snaked around DeClercq's shoes before it trickled into the pit sunk deep in the muddy earth. The Mounted Policeman stood motionless beside the open grave, his feet on the very spot where he would lie one day, and watched his wife's casket being lowered into the hole. "Bless this grave," the priest intoned as clouds boiled in from the sea, hand and sky sprinkling the coffin with holy water, ". . . and send Your angels to watch over it and grant our sister peace . . ." while Robert DeClercq's heart cried a black rain of its own.

"Let us pray."

Commissioner François Chartrand stood on the other side of the grave, concerned that DeClercq was the only one present who hadn't bowed his head. This was the second time Chartrand had witnessed his friend bury a wife, the previous funeral in Quebec twelve years before when Kate and daughter Jane were killed by terrorists. The commissioner vividly recalled that bright autumn morning: sunshine on the maple trees ablaze with color, the smell of smoke adrift in the crisp, hazy air, how small Janie's coffin seemed beside her mother's. It had been dicey whether DeClercq would ever recover from that, so considering the present aftermath of the Headhunter case, Chartrand was worried his friend might go home and eat his gun.

"Amen," the priest said.

"Amen," the mourners echoed.

In turn, those gathered stepped forward to drop a handful of earth on top of the polished coffin. While the priest completed his solemn Catholic prayer—"Let perpetual light shine upon her, O Lord, may her soul and the souls of all the faithful departed through the mercy of God rest in peace"—DeClercq bent down and placed a long-stemmed red rose on the casket lid above Genevieve's stilled heart.

The service over, the mourners congregated in smaller groups. Downhill, an old woman in black brocade leaned on the arm of a much younger man. Here on the slope of Hollyburn Mountain, Capilano View Cemetery overlooked the city. Mother and son were silhouetted against the dismal rain which lashed the waters of English Bay and the forest of Stanley Park. The woman's eyes flinched as DeClercq approached.

"Voulez-vous venir avec moi?" he asked.

Genevieve's mother shook her head. *"Mon fils a une auto. On préfère être seuls."*

Chartrand lingered behind while the other mourners dispersed. In twos and threes they offered their condolences to the widower before drifting away toward the parking lot. Only when DeClercq stood alone by Genevieve's grave did Chartrand approach. *"Viens avec moi, Robert. Il faut qu'on se parle."*

"She blames me, François. So did Kate's mother."

"Neither death was your fault," Chartrand replied, switching automatically to English from French.

"Weren't they?" DeClercq said. "Who brought the killers into their lives?"

The Mounties walked in silence to the commissioner's car. The limousine left the cemetery by Hadden Drive, turning down Taylor Way to descend the mountain toward the crashing sea. Sitting in back with DeClercq, Chartrand lit one cigarette off the stub of another, his mind fine-tuning the proposal he planned to make. Dull afternoon light transmogrified the rivulets worming across the windows into a nest of rain-snakes that slithered about the men. Once the Cadillac turned west on Marine

Drive, DeClercq sought glimpses of Ambleside Beach behind the shorefront buildings. Occasionally a dog would bark as if running after the car, only to be drowned out by the swoosh of puddles beneath the wheels.

When they reached DeClercq's driveway, Chartrand asked the chauffeur to wait.

Here beside the Pacific the storm was worse. Giant firs lining the steep walk down to the house waved wildly in the wind as lights flanking the front door threw convulsing shadows across the wooded lot. The tarmac beneath their feet was a rushing river while the nearly horizontal rain turned Chartrand's umbrella inside out. Both men were soaked by the time DeClercq unlocked the door.

"Scotch?"

"Please."

"Water?"

"Just ice."

"Join you in a minute."

DeClercq went into the kitchen off the entrance hall. Chartrand walked straight ahead to the seaside living room facing English Bay. Right of the ocean view, a greenhouse jutted toward the beach. Inside, the prize rosebushes Robert had hybridized himself were wilting from recent neglect. A Christmas tree half-decorated beside the greenhouse door was scattering dead needles about the pegged-wood floor. Over near the mantel, the grandfather clock had stopped at quarter past nine.

Chartrand had stood in rooms that felt like this before: murder scenes where death had brought time to a halt. The difference here was someone living still moved about. Eyes probing for danger signs, he noticed little things. The tapes on the stereo weren't the classics Robert preferred, but albums someone twenty years younger had liked. Beethoven, Brahms, and Mozart had given way to *Astral Weeks* and Solomon Burke. The mantel was cleared of everything but three photographs—one of Kate, one of Jane, and one of Genevieve. A flower from the greenhouse lay beside each frame, while on the table in front of the hearth was an empty aquarium.

"I found that in her closet," DeClercq said from the hall, "while searching for a dress in which to bury her.

There's a gift certificate to stock the tank with fish. That was to be Genny's Christmas present to me."

Chartrand took a sip from the drink Robert handed him. He was relieved to see DeClercq pour a ginger ale for himself. "What you need are tropicals. Bright, colorful ones."

"Maybe tomorrow I'll get around to that."

DeClercq crosshatched kindling around a Duraflame on the hearth, then added an alder round. As he lit the fire Chartrand said, "Last week I received a call from this Hollywood producer. He planned to revive *Sergeant Preston of the Yukon* for TV. Had this brilliant idea to update the series. Preston, now in his fifties, would mush his dogsled across the Arctic tundra while his sidekick, a nephew on duty with the Alaska police, would use a computer to help his uncle track down crooks."

"One of those who thinks it snows as soon as you cross the border, huh?" said DeClercq.

"The fellow was flummoxed when I told him we could fit the whole Alaska computer system in one corner of our Operations Building. He was incensed to hear we get the Pentagon's latest hardware years before American cops. I didn't tell him we're about to lose that edge.

"We have a problem, Robert. This mess with the Security Service won't go away. The PM's decided to strip the Force of its counterintelligence arm. We're through with spying, and you know what that means."

There was no need for Chartrand to elaborate. In his book *Men Who Wore the Tunic* DeClercq had outlined the benefits the RCMP reaped from its dual enforcement role. In the U.S. and Britain, civil policing and espionage were split. The Americans had the FBI and the CIA; the British New Scotland Yard and MI-5 and -6. In Canada both functions belonged to the RCMP, so not only did the Mounted acquire foreign intelligence, but also the latest advances in high-tech expertise.

"The way of the world," Chartrand said, pulling up a chair. "External security always gets the best hardware first. Years later the internal police get what's cast off."

"You're worried losing our spy function will downgrade the Force?"

"It has to, Robert, if we suffer a sudden network gap. We'll be reduced to begging high-tech handoffs like everybody else. End up like the Brits and Yanks, wasting half our time infighting with the PM's new spies. I'll go down in history as the commissioner who weakened the Force, the man in command when my predecessor's chickens came home to roost."

During the 1970s, in its zeal to ferret out "subversion" in Quebec, the RCMP Security Service had resorted to "dirty tricks." The Mounties stole dynamite to plant on suspected terrorists and issued fake communiqués calling for the violent overthrow of the government. They burned down a barn to prevent a meeting between the radical FLQ and American Black Panthers, then burglarized the office of the Parti Québecois to steal its membership list. Losing the Security Service would be their punishment.

"What I plan to do," Chartrand said, "is strip the company of assets before it changes hands. One out of every ten members now works in Security. Each did several years of regular service before becoming a spy. I plan to create a new unit responsible for investigations beyond our borders. The unit will be Special X—the Special External Section of the RCMP. Those members with the best foreign intelligence links will be offered the top jobs. They'll have the opportunity to stay with the Force rather than enlisting with the PM's new spies. We keep the external contacts we've built up, and Ottawa gets the empty shell to start from scratch.

"Robert, I want you to head Special X."

Outside, the wind whooped and wailed under the eaves. Rain drummed the greenhouse like a military tattoo. As the fire sparked, DeClercq said, "You needn't worry, François. I'll not kill myself."

The commissioner blinked. "Did I say you might?"

"No, but that's the subtext to your therapy of work."

Chartrand drained his scotch and put down the glass. "Special X is not a salvation tool. You're the best man for the job."

"I appreciate what you're doing, but the fact is I'm leaving the Force."

"You haven't been out of retirement more than three months!"

"And I'm going back in."

"To do what? Sit alone and brood all day until you've had enough?"

"No. I'll write."

"You're a cop, not a scribbler. You said so yourself when you took on the Headhunter case."

"I was wrong. And look what happened."

DeClercq took the photos of Kate and Jane down from the mantel. He set them on the table beside the fish tank. "I didn't kill myself when they died," he said. "Instead, these pictures sat on my desk while I wrote. I too believe in work's therapy—depending on the work. Day in, day out, a cop sees the shitty side of life. Before long the job drives wedges into the fissures of your mind. I put the gun in my mouth *because* of the Headhunter case, because leaving retirement resurrected my guilt over what occurred in Quebec."

DeClercq fetched Genevieve's picture from the mantel. "When I met Genny I couldn't believe my luck. Few men find love once in their lives, but I found it twice. She picked up the broken pieces and glued them back together. Now this job has cost me her.

"*Men Who Wore the Tunic* got me through Kate and Jane. The deeper I went into history, the more I forgot the past. François, you've been a good friend, so please understand. What I need is time and space to heal. Taking on Special X would finish me."

DeClercq left for the kitchen to refill Chartrand's glass. He returned with a copy of the book in his other hand. Opening it to a passage marked in blue, he turned on the lamp so his friend could read:

CHAPTER SEVEN

THE LOST PATROL

Wilfred Blake was the finest detective in the North-West Mounted Police. He was the best tracker of all "the Riders of the Plains." An officer instilled with rectitude, discipline, dedication, and self-reliance, the inspector embodied that gung-ho combination of patriotism and "muscular Christianity" that built the British Empire. He was just the sort of warrior the Force required to lay down the law in the Canadian West. How Blake dealt with the fugitive Sioux who crossed into Canada following Custer's Last Stand gave birth to the myth "The Mounties always get their man."

The legend of Blake achieved the status it holds today largely because of the mysterious way he vanished. In the mythology of the Force this perplexing puzzle is known as the Lost Patrol.

Twenty years after Custer perished at the Little Bighorn, the Mounted Police crushed the last Indian resistance to white settlement of the West. Almighty Voice, a Plains Cree, was arrested in 1895 for killing a steer. That same night he escaped from the Force guardroom at Duck Lake, Saskatchewan, so Sergeant Colin Colebrook rode out to track him down. A few days later when Colebrook found the fugitive, Almighty Voice shot him through the neck with a double-barreled shotgun. For the next two years he vanished from sight.

Finally, in the spring of 1897, he was spotted on Chief One Arrow's reserve near Duck Lake. Along with three young companions, Almighty Voice was chased onto a bluff and surrounded. When the thicket was stormed after reinforcements arrived, two Mounted Police and a civilian volunteer were killed. The Indians, who survived the attack, dug in to make a stand.

News of the firefight reached Regina during a ball to see the Force contingent off to London for Queen Victoria's Jubilee. Fearing the Plains Cree might rise in support (twenty years back, they'd joined the Sioux and Cheyenne to battle Custer), Commissioner Herchmer dispatched twenty-five officers and two artillery cannon to the scene. With their arrival the following night, May 29, fifty-two Mounted Police, thirty-four Prince Albert Volunteers, and a dozen other whites encircled the four Cree hidden on the bluff. A nine-pound Maxim gun was set up aiming east. A bronze seven-pound Mark II pointed south. At dawn both artillery cannon shelled the bluff, pounding it with shrapnel till seven a.m. The guns were then placed side by side and the woods were bombarded with high-explosive canister shot.

Later when police stormed the bluff three bodies were found: Almighty Voice, Tupean, and Standing-in-the-Sky. The fourth Cree, Iron-child, had somehow escaped, crawling away undetected during the night. Herchmer dispatched Wilfred Blake to bring him back.

For six months the inspector tracked the young Cree across the prairies and into the Rocky Mountains. The following diagram maps the evidence left behind when Blake vanished in December 1897:

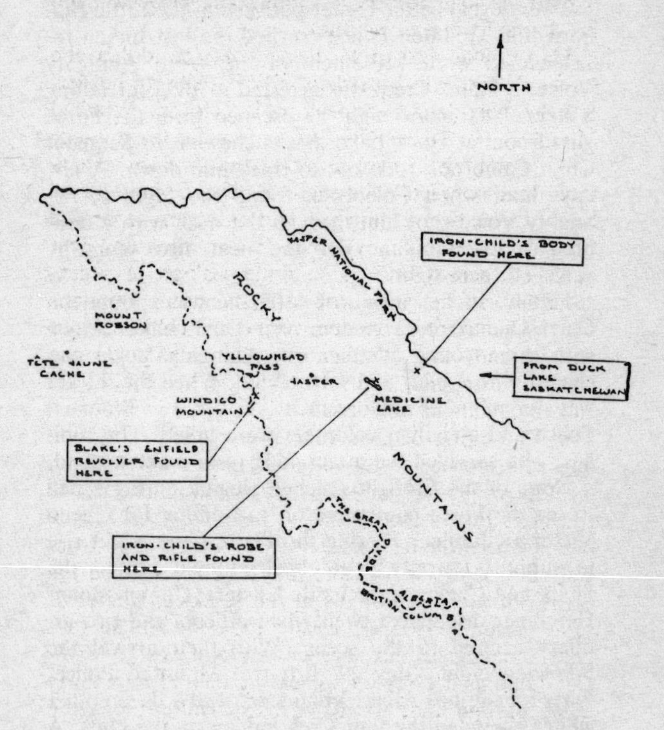

High in the Rockies, Medicine Lake is at the center of what is now Jasper National Park. The Mounties dispatched to hunt for Blake in the spring of '98 found Iron-child's belongings—including his rifle and buffalo robe—near its shore. Since the young Cree would have died of exposure without his robe, we can assume that's where Blake caught up to him. This assumption is strengthened by where Iron-child's naked body was found, half-buried in a snowdrift several miles *east* of Medicine Lake. The Cree had been shot between the eyes with a bullet fired from a .476 Enfield revolver, the service pistol of the Force from 1883 to 1905. His right leg was broken and a second bullet had grazed his head. Near the corpse some of Blake's supplies were cached, those he'd have shed to lighten his load for speed uphill. The inspector and his dogsled were never found.

Thirty miles *west* of Medicine Lake, straddling the Great Divide, which marks the B.C.–Alberta border, juts the most dangerous peak in the Rockies: Windigo Mountain. In December 1897 a massive earthquake split its summit in two, shearing the awesome precipices that now isolate its top. Picture a giant spearhead of rock twelve thousand feet in the air, separated from its lower bulk by a chasm four thousand feet deep. The aerodynamics around the peak are as treacherous as can be, with downdrafts creating vacuums that suck aircraft from the sky. Perpetually covered with ice and snow, Windigo Mountain is an avalanche waiting to happen. Since 1898 the peak has been legally off-limits to everyone.

In the spring of that year, five months after the quake, a prospector recovered Blake's revolver from the foot of a precipice on Windigo Mountain. If one considers the layout of the above map, there's only one explanation for the evidence. Blake shot Ironchild beside Medicine Lake. He then transported the corpse *east* to the foothills of the Rockies, where for some reason he stopped, cached the body and his supplies, then mushed his dogsled *west*. Not west to Medicine Lake as if he'd left something behind, but thirty miles beyond that to the Great Divide. Since the Rocky Mountains in winter have one of the harshest climates on Earth, what might have motivated him to make this grueling trip? That's the unsolved mystery of the Lost Patrol.

Chartrand closed the book and sipped his Johnnie Walker. "Is that what you plan to write about? The disappearance of Blake?"

"The mystery has fascinated me for years."

"Enhanced no doubt by the recent discovery of Blake's trunk."

"You know I have it?"

"Of course. As head of the Heritage Committee, nothing gets released without my approval."

"Want to see it? It's in the other room."

The steamer trunk was of the type popular with British soldiers in the nineteenth century. Four feet long by two feet wide by two feet high, its battered blue sides were reinforced with tarnished brass corners. Chalked around a plaque screwed below the lid were immigration symbols in several languages. The name "BLAKE" was engraved on the plaque.

"It arrived the day Genny was shot, so I haven't gone through it yet. Stacked down one side are several diaries kept by Blake. The one I skimmed is a record of his adventures with the British Army before he joined the Force. The diaries may hold a clue to why he vanished."

"And if they don't?"

Robert shrugged. "I'll write about something else. Butler, Coke, Sleigh, Alexander, and Bonnycastle published their exploits. We intimately know the lives of those soldiers of the realm. Blake disappeared before his memoirs saw print. Using these diaries I'll fill the gap."

Chartrand raised the lid of the trunk for a peek inside. He saw the leather-bound books among dusty red uniforms. By the gray light of the rain-spattered window overlooking the beach, history eerily seemed to seep from the trunk.

"My grandfather had a steamer like this," he said. "I found it in the attic of his house." He tapped the base of Blake's trunk with his shoe. "It had a false bottom filled with naughty photographs."

A few minutes later, DeClercq saw the commissioner to the door. Pausing against a backdrop of rain, François clapped his hand on Robert's shoulder. "By all means write your book, my friend, if that's what you must do. If you need someone to talk to, I'm as close as the phone. The offer to head Special X will wait for you. Mark my words, you'll be back. The Force is in your family."

No sooner had Chartrand departed than a horn honked outside. DeClercq opened the door and squinted up the drive. Through the rain he saw the limo's taillights pull away, then heard insistent barking at his feet.

"Chartrand, you weasel," he groaned, glancing down.

On the doorstep, a puppy jumped up and down in its wire cage, yapping as if to say, *Come on, buddy, lemme outa here.* As DeClercq reached for the note tucked in the mesh, the German shepherd pup licked his hand.

Robert—
I won't say "Happy New Year," just "Life Goes On."
His name's Napoleon.
He'll see you through.

Saturday, March 14, 1987, 11:02 P.M.

Five years had passed since Genevieve's funeral. DeClercq had indeed written his book—*Bagpipes, Blood, and Glory* would be published on Monday—and time, as the proverb says, had healed his wound. Robert was finally ready to accept Chartrand's offer, so the morning after MacDougall's visit ten days before, he'd phoned Ottawa.

"Allo."

"François? Robert DeClercq."

"As I live and breathe."

"You sound terrible."

"I've had the flu. Made me stop smoking. Now I feel worse."

In his mind's eye DeClercq saw Chartrand framed by his penthouse window, the Parliament buildings below him backed by mist off the Ottawa River. Judging by pictures in the paper he'd put on a lot of weight, and his military haircut was iron gray. Hard to imagine François without a Galoise.

"At two packs a day you'll be back on the weed before the end of the week."

"Can't," the commissioner croaked. "I made a pact with God."

"An old sinner like you?"

"Life-and-death decision. My flu flirted with pneumonia till one day I couldn't breathe. Failed Catholic though I am, I actually dropped to my knees. Begged the good

Lord to give me breath while my face turned blue, and damn if my promise to stop smoking didn't open my lungs. 'Fraid if I break it the wrath of God will zap through the roof."

DeClercq chuckled.

"So why the call?"

"Wondering if your Special X offer's still open?"

"Ha! I knew it! The Force *is* in your blood."

"Before you start gloating, there are strings attached."

"Like?"

"I want to work here. Not in Ottawa."

"Don't blame you. Horrible place. A fellow named Goldwin Smith described it as a subarctic lumber village converted into a political cockpit. I couldn't put it better."

"Next, I want Avacomovitch and Chan on my team."

"Whoa. You trying to strip me to my shorts or something?"

"Nice touch, François. Little red hearts."

"Chan's the best software jockey we've got. And Joe, well, you know."

"I'm willing to share."

"That's mighty big of you. Anything else?"

"I want Jack MacDougall as my second-in-command."

Chartrand cleared his throat. "That presents a problem."

"So I hear. I still want him."

"The DC and I go way back. He was passed over when Ottawa gave me this job. I don't want to override his command when he's following policy."

"It's a deal-breaker. No Jack, no me."

"You drive a hard bargain."

"So turn me down."

"Dammit," Chartrand said. "I need a cigarette."

Special X—his Special X—was coming together. Last week Chartrand had shipped the unit's files from Ottawa, and tonight DeClercq was finalizing his roster of personnel. It was another evening of rain on the greenhouse roof, of morose foghorns out on the bay. The file that most intrigued him was that of Zinc Chandler, a Special X inspector stationed in Britain. DeClercq was reading between the lines—trying to imagine what had happened in the lair of the Ghoul—when Napoleon indicated it was time for their walk. Donning a slicker, the chief superintendent followed the dog to the sea.

For half an hour the German shepherd romped along the shore. DeClercq's property sloped down to a log-strewn beach. Atop a knoll beside the ocean stood an antique sundial and a driftwood chair. As Robert sat in the chair above the roiling tide, his finger traced the warning etched around the sundial's face.

Back in the house, unheard, the telephone was ringing.

DeClercq thought, *I need a case to challenge Special X.*

The sundial warning read, *The time is later than you think.*

FIELD NOTES

Valley of the Little Bighorn River,
Montana Territory
Tuesday, June 27, 1876, dawn

Brigadier General Alfred Terry's camp was astir with excitement. Unlike the day before, there wasn't an Indian in sight, while hundreds of turkey buzzards circled the nearby hills. At seven the command moved out in battle formation, scouts fanning farther from the flanks than customary. Rumor ran rife among the troops that Colonel Custer had dealt the redskins a major blow, until a mile downriver they found the deserted Indian camp.

All that remained of the seven circles Custer had attacked were abandoned funeral tepees and debris scattered about: buffalo robes and rotting meat; blankets and cooking utensils; axes, guns, horn spoons, and broken china dishes. A circle of dead horses ringed the tents, while prowling through the camp like wolves, wild dogs snarled at the approaching whites.

A trio of curious soldiers broke rank and cantered ahead. Among the debris one found a pair of bloody longjohns labelled "STURGIS—7TH CAV." While he swung back in the saddle to take the garment to Terry, another staggered ashen-faced from one of the tents. Inside he'd discovered the bodies of five beheaded whites hanging naked from the lodgepole struts. Lashed to the crosspiece were five black balls. Brushing away the layer of flies, he saw they were severed heads. Wired together, the skulls had been dragged for miles behind a horse.

"Search the hills," an apoplectic Terry commanded. "Find the heathens responsible and string them up."

Captain Jericho Sharpe was assigned the task of gathering evidence and mapping the camp. A bundle of tics, tension, and Bible education, Sharpe was a man of effeminate build and fastidious uniform. A pointed nose and thin blue lips dominated his fox-like face, the left eye of which twitched Morse code. He made those around him feel as if ants crawled under their skin.

Sharpe spent an hour in the tent where the tortured bodies hung, conjuring up visions of Hell from the Old Testament. The name "PARKER"stitched on the shorts dangling from one man's foot puzzled him, since no Parker rode with Custer's troops. Mid-morning, a scout came galloping down from the bench land across the river, riding hell-bent for leather toward the camp. He didn't rein in and dismount his horse until he spotted Terry talking with General Gideon Pratt.

"*Sir!*" the scout interrupted, saluting both men. "Lieutenant Bradley sent me down from the bluff across the river. He's counted two hundred bodies up on the ridge."

"Redskins?" Terry asked, glancing at Pratt.

The scout shook his head. "White men, *sir*!"

"Good Lord!" Pratt exclaimed. "Not the Seventh?"

Sharpe watched from the flap of the tent as a column moved out, fording the river, to mount the hogsback ridge. Heat from the sun beating down on the valley warped the retreating image like a desert mirage. Soon word came back that Sharpe was reassigned to the bluff. Packing his gear, he climbed the ridge with an Arikara scout, reining his horse to a halt at the edge of the killing field. "The dead. Dear God, how white they look. How very white," he said.

The massacre site was a scorched waste of eerie desolation. Where the slaughter was thickest atop the hill, a barricade of bloated horses, legs stiff as boards, encircled the rotting cadavers. Dry, porous soil had sucked up all the blood, while swooping vultures fed on the desiccated flesh. The all-pervasive buzzing of flies reminded Sharpe of possum hunting as a boy, trailing his father, the Army preacher, through Tennessee swamps. On reflex he patted his Bible.

Sharpe's new post was in the center of the field. Here he sketched a map on which to log the evidence strewn about the scrub. Later others would use the grid to discern what happened at Custer's Last Stand. Twelve soldiers worked the field, conveying their finds to him.

At noon, a reporter from the *Helena Times* rode up to the bluff. Sharpe was seated on a stump, adding to his map, when the searchers took a break to crowd around the man. "Make sure you spell it with an *e*," he heard someone say.

Sharpe bent down to slap his calf above his cavalry boot. A horsefly had just bit him on the leg. That was how he spotted the notebook in the sage, hidden where it had fallen when Parker was stripped of his clothes. Picking it up, Sharpe leafed through the pages:

"FIELD NOTES"

transcribed to journal / June 25

PROPERTY OF FRANCIS PARKER, YALE UNIVERSITY, NEW HAVEN, CONNECTICUT.

IN CASE OF DEATH RETURN TO PROFESSOR O.C. MARSH OF YALE, ADDRESS ABOVE.

MR CHARLES DARWIN
DOWN HOUSE
DOWNE
KENT, ENGLAND

(WHY TWO SPELLINGS OF DOWN(E)?)

JUNE 21, 1876 – "EUREKA!!!" AT LAST! THE MISSING LINK! NORTHWEST BANK, HIGHEST OUTCROP, CRAZY WOMAN FORK OF THE POWDER RIVER, BIG HORN MOUNTAINS,

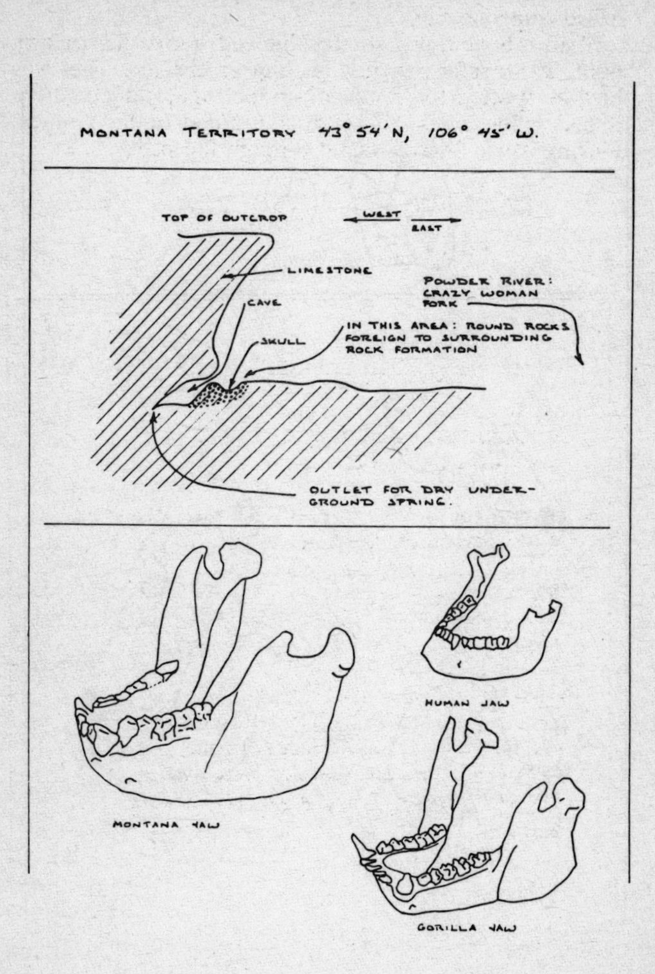
MONTANA TERRITORY 43° 54' N, 106° 45' W.
TOP OF OUTCROP
WEST
EAST
LIMESTONE
POWDER RIVER:
CRAZY WOMAN
FORK
CAVE
IN THIS AREA: ROUND ROCKS
FOREIGN TO SURROUNDING
ROCK FORMATION
SKULL
OUTLET FOR DRY UNDER-
GROUND SPRING.
HUMAN JAW
MONTANA JAW
GORILLA JAW

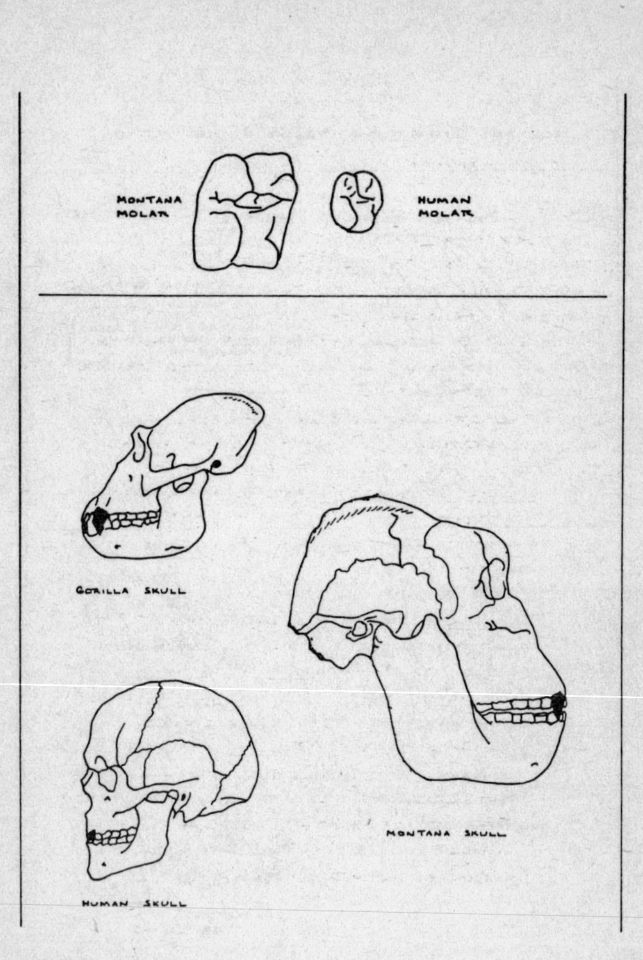
MONTANA
MOLAR
HUMAN
MOLAR
GORILLA SKULL
MONTANA SKULL
HUMAN SKULL

LETTER - DRAUGHT

DEAR SIR, — I DARE SAY YOU WILL BE SURPRISED TO HEAR FROM ME SO SOON; HOWEVER, I BELIEVE I AM THE BEARER OF GOOD NEWS WHICH WILL SPELL THE DEATH KNELL OF YOUR CRITICS. HERSCHEL MAY SAY YOUR BOOK IS "THE LAW OF HIGGLEDY - PIGGLEDY" — BUT I FIND, AS NO DOUBT DO YOU, THE WORDS OF MR HUXLEY COMFORTING:

> "THE GRADUAL LAPSE OF TIME HAS NOW SEPARATED US BY MORE THAN A DECADE FROM THE DATE OF PUBLICATION OF ORIGIN OF SPECIES: AND WHATEVER MAY BE THOUGHT OR SAID ABOUT MR DARWIN'S DOCTRINES, OR THE MANNER IN WHICH HE HAS PROPOUNDED THEM, THIS MUCH IS CERTAIN, THAT IN A DOZEN YEARS THE ORIGIN OF SPECIES HAS WORKED AS COMPLETE A REVOLUTION IN BIOLOGICAL SCIENCE AS THE PRINCIPIA DID IN ASTRONOMY. AND, AS TIME HAS SLIPPED BY, A HAPPY CHANGE HAS COME OVER MR DARWIN'S CRITICS. THE MIXTURE OF IGNORANCE AND INSOLENCE WHICH AT FIRST CHARACTERISED A LARGE PORTION OF THE ATTACKS WITH WHICH HE WAS ASSAILED IS NO LONGER THE SAD DIS-TINCTION OF ANTI-DARWINIAN CRITICISM."

SIR, I HAVE THE AMMUNITION FOR YOU TO STRIKE BACK! AS YOU CAN SEE FROM THE ENCLOSURES WITH THIS LETTER, I HAVE DISCOVERED A SKULL (THE FIRST IN AMERICA, I BELIEVE) WHICH UPON CLOSE EXAMINATION APPEARS TO BE THAT OF AN EARLY FORM OF MAN; THE FOSSIL PREDATES THE SKULL FOUND IN THE NEANDER VALLEY NEAR DÜSSELDORF IN 1856 AND IS NOT SUBJECT TO THE SAME WEAK-NESSES. IT CANNOT BE SAID THAT THIS SKULL IS THE REMAINS OF A DEFORMED MAN, NOR THAT IT IS A SPECIMEN OF APE; FOR THE FEATURES OF THIS SKULL COMBINE THOSE OF BOTH SPECIES, MAN AND APE. ALSO, IT IS A VERY LARGE FOSSIL INDEED.

TWO YEARS AGO WHEN PROFESSOR MARSH WAS HERE IN THE WESTERN BADLANDS SEEKING THE FOSSILS OF DINOSAURS, HE FOUND THE NATIVE INDIANS MUCH EXCITED. TO ME THEY HAVE BEEN OPENLY HOSTILE AND I HAVE FEARED FOR MY SAFETY MORE THAN ONCE. WHEN SPOKEN TO THE INDIANS ACT IN A MOST SULLEN AND MALEVOLENT WAY, FOR THEY BELIEVE ME TO BE PROSPECTING FOR GOLD!

TOMORROW I SHALL SET FORTH FOR CIVILISATION, TO POST THIS LETTER TO YOU. I UNDERSTAND

FROM THE LOCAL TRADERS (A BAD LOT INDEED) THAT A FORCE OF CAVALRY IS EXPECTED SOON TO QUELL THE UNREST OF THE NATIVES. PERHAPS I SHALL BE FORTUNATE TO MEET UP WITH THEM.

YOURS FAITHFULLY AND OBLIGED,

Let God be true and every man a liar, Sharpe thought. He knew of Charles Darwin and his blasphemy. Would this book give succor to that Antichrist?

The captain was pleased to see the others had their backs to him, boasting of their exploits to the scribbling reporter. Unobserved, he slipped the *Field Notes* into his saddlebag.

That night the book was in the hands of General Gideon Pratt.

CHIPPER

Vancouver, British Columbia
Sunday, March 15, 1987, 2:00 A.M.

Pender Street between Main and Gore is the stomach of Chinatown. Selling bean curd sticks and melon cakes and thousand-year-old eggs; selling lychees and loquats and rice candy and sweet almond cookies; selling water chestnuts and enoke mushrooms and dried anchovies a hundred to the bag, these shops are heaven on earth to local epicureans. A bustling hubbub during the day, along this street armies of Asian shoppers lugging giant bags jostle and elbow one another examining what's for sale, shrewd fingers squeezing bulbous vegetables on display: foo qua, mo qua, lotus root, and Shanghai bok choy. In velvet vests and baggy pants too short in the leg, gray hair bunned at the nape of the neck with pieces of mother-of-pearl, women in slippers shuffle down alleys where fishermen hawk oolichans fresh from the net, others with baskets of scurrying crabs held up to attract a crowd. Only with the evening meal does the street wind down.

It was now two in the morning and Pender was deserted.

Half cleaned up, the butcher shop was closed for the night. Though barbecued pork and skewered ducks still hung in the windows, the display counters were empty and scrubbed. At street level a barred vent opened into the cellar, where flickering fluorescent lights succumbed to black shadows. Here links of Chinese sausage and fowl pressed flat as skate aged in drying racks along both walls. Rows of shelves lined with bowls filled with curing beef ran from the vent to the basement's rear. In back a large wooden door sealed the meat freezer. Nailed to it, the skin of a pig was stretched on a circular frame, pompons tipping Slinky springs replacing the animal's eyes. In front of the door a butcher stood over a whirring saw.

Stacked around the man were boxes filled with antlers. The shipment had arrived while he was cleaning up.

Abandoning that dirty task for this more lucrative one, he was shaving the antlers into thin wafers.

Close by, a small table was set with a plate of beef jerky, an apple pear, and a Tsingtao beer.

Each time he finished chipping a rack, he wiped his hands on his blood-stained apron and paused for a bite to eat.

He was eating when the meat cleaver struck him in the mouth.

Under flickering lights the killing seemed like a jerky black-and-white film. Beside and behind the man stood three Asian punks. Each was dressed in black jeans, a white muscle shirt, and a black leather jacket. All three had studs in their left ears and tattoos on their hands. The noise of them breaking in had been masked by the whirring saw.

The cleaver hit the butcher horizontally. Its blade smashed his upper teeth, split his cheeks and his tongue, then lodged in his spine. Below hair that stuck up on top like Woody Woodpecker's, his eyes rolled back in his head till just the whites showed. In a futile gesture he tried to grab the blade. When the punk yanked it out, blood sprayed in twin geysers from the man's face, the cleaver having severed both carotid arteries. The butcher crumpled to the floor, his feet doing a spastic jig as his split tongue flicked like a snake's.

It took the punks fifteen minutes to chop up the corpse.

While one stayed behind to steam-clean the cellar floor, the other two stuffed the butcher into Glad bags and drove the pieces to a Richmond building site.

There a concrete truck was parked beside a stump chipper, its cylinder rotating beneath the watching moon.

One by one the Glad bags were fed to the chipper, spraying bloody pellets into a foundation mold.

The truck then dumped a layer of concrete on top.

DESCENT OF MAN

Downe, England
Friday, October 27, 1876, 11:02 A.M.

The carriage from Down House was waiting at the station. Since the nearest train stop was at Croydon, ten miles away, General Gideon Pratt of the U.S. Army was treated to a drive through the hills of Kent. Passing the carriage windows on this sunny autumn morning were graceful stretches of purple heath and thickets of oak. Bible in hand, Pratt read Genesis on the way.

Down House was in a narrow lane off the Westerham road a quarter mile from Downe. The village population of a few hundred lived in rows of cottages converging in front of a small flint church. A Georgian three-story with bow windows, the house was clad in creepers and embowered by elms. As the carriage pulled up and Pratt stepped down, an elderly woman opened the front door.

"Welcome to Down House, General." Her voice was wary.

"At your service, ma'am." Pratt removed his hat.

"My husband's in his study. Do come in."

A barrel-chested evangelist in his mid-fifties, Pratt exuded the arrogance of a man personally chosen to serve God. Today the general wore his most resplendent uniform, showing more flash than usual since this was the British Isles. A firm vegetarian, his body had weathered well. His long gray hair met a salt-and-pepper beard. He didn't smoke; he didn't drink; but rose each morning before dawn to witness the creation of another day. The scar down his cheek was from the Battle of Bull Run.

"I beg you not to provoke my husband," the woman said, glancing at the Bible in the general's hand. "He's not been well since the publication of his last book. If only his critics knew how much their barbs have hurt him."

Unmoved, Pratt responded with a gentleman's nod.

He followed her through the house to the study door. Opening it, Emma Darwin ushered him in.

The blasphemer sat at a cluttered desk beside a leaded-glass window looking out on the garden. The years of controversy had left their mark. His brow furrowed by deep thought, his shoulders had stooped beneath the weight of harsh criticism. A silver-white beard and bushy eyebrows overcompensated for his balding crown. Floor-to-ceiling bookcases surrounded him, while tacked-up notes covered every patch of wall space. The orange glow of a coal hamper burning on the hearth waxed the globe behind him as if it were the moon. Setting down the beaker and test tube in his grasp, the naturalist stood up as the general entered.

"You honor me, sir," Darwin said, offering his hand. "How fortunate you should wish to see me as much as I do you. I regret my health necessitated your journey to Downe."

The general opened his Bible after shaking hands. *"And God said, Let us make man in our image, after our likeness,"* he read. "Is that passage familiar to you, sir?"

"Of course," Darwin said. "Genesis."

"So God created man in His own image. Does that mean God is a monkey?"

"Permit me to answer your question with a question, General. If the Bible is to be read literally, to whom do the "our" and "us" in that quotation refer? Is God just one of many as the Greeks and Romans thought?"

"I like to know where a man stands from the start. Do you still maintain there is no God and the ape is our Adam?"

"I'm agnostic, General. I hold no theory of God. Nor am I anxious to influence the speculation of others. If *Origin of Species* offends you, the effect is unintended."

The Englishman offered the American a pinch of snuff. A man of no vices, Pratt declined.

"Not once did I use the word *evolution* in that book. I avoided discussing the question of man because the subject is surrounded with prejudice."

The general snorted, raising the Good Book. "Perhaps, but now you've published *The Descent of Man.*"

"Is suggesting species change akin to confessing to murder?"

"Sir, your blasphemous theory should have been strangled at birth."

"Why is that?" Darwin scoffed. "Because it explains too much?"

Pratt's eyes narrowed, piercing the naturalist. "Next I suppose Queen Victoria will knight you for your work?"

"That I doubt," Darwin sighed. "My theory doesn't please her."

"Nor does it please the congregation of Tennessee Baptist Redeemer."

Darwin crossed to the hearth for his snuffbox and walking stick. Inhaling a pinch up his nose, he summoned a hearty sneeze. Eyes watered, he said to Pratt, "Each day before dinner I take a walk. Join me, General?"

The creationist nodded.

Down House was surrounded by eighteen acres of land. Out back, a field of mounds and banks bordered the lawn and vegetable garden. The naturalist had cleared a strip three hundred yards long at this end of the field. He'd planted it with oaks and elms, with limes, maples, birches, and flowering shrubs. Circling this arbor, which autumn had set ablaze, was a grit-covered path he called "The Sand-Walk." As they strolled in silence the trees and bushes around them stirred with wildlife.

Side by side the men were a study in contrast. Rigid-spined, Pratt marched with brisk, purposeful strides, hands behind his back while his eyes and ears ignored the evidence they collected. Occasionally he paused until the scientist caught up. Attuned to every nuance, Darwin bumbled along. His walking stick was shod with an iron tip, producing a rhythmic click each time it struck the ground. A pile of flints was heaped at a turn in the path. With each lap Darwin knocked one off.

"Does the name Francis Parker mean anything to you, General?"

Pratt glanced at Darwin. "Not that I recall."

"What about Professor O. C. Marsh of Yale?"

"The chap who likes to dig for bones in the Western Badlands?"

"Two years back, Marsh explored the Black Hills of

Dakota. He'd heard tales of prehistoric monsters buried there. Marsh returned with two tons of dinosaur fossils."

"The Hills are sacred to the Sioux. Lucky they didn't scalp him."

"Parker was a graduate student studying with Marsh. Last year he wrote me a letter from Yale. Parker was of the opinion, having read my books, that support for evolution might be found near Marsh's digs. Come spring he planned to journey to the Black Hills. I'm told he embarked—but never returned."

"What," Pratt asked, "has this to do with me?"

"We English delight in reading about colonial wars. Our papers have printed a detailed account of your—your recent setback. According to *The Times* you are in London to seek support from Her Majesty's government?"

"We believe the renegades who slaughtered the Seventh Cavalry will try to seek refuge in Canada. Since your government runs the Dominion's foreign affairs, should that occur we want the fugitives returned."

"Were you not with the column that discovered the massacre?"

"My troops joined Terry's the day before."

"We're told your army recovered a body that's unaccounted for."

"Such a body was found, but not on the battlefield. It was strung up in a tent across the river."

"Why was the corpse not identified?"

"The features were mutilated beyond recognition."

"Is it true the man wore civilian underclothes?"

"Yes, but the name tag was cut out."

"Did you see the underdrawers?"

"No, I spoke to Captain Sharpe, who catalogued the camp. The pagans often do that. Some sort of spirit thing."

"If the man was a civilian, who might he be?"

"Perhaps a reporter riding with Custer's men. The colonel, you may have heard, liked publicity."

"We're told a correspondent was killed and later identified. But he was with Reno's battalion and not involved in the slaughter."

Pratt smirked at Darwin. He scratched his nose. "What makes you think the body was Francis Parker?"

"A scientist works from speculation, General. Parker

was a civilian in the Black Hills. He went missing at the relevant time. What if he encountered Custer's troops while fearing for his life? Might he not join them for safety's sake? And if the Last Stand occurred shortly after that, is your mysterious civilian not explained?"

Pratt guffawed. "You are a desperate man. The critics hounding your heels must have drawn blood. No wonder your theories are half-baked if that's what you call logic."

Darwin stopped walking. He glared at Pratt. Because the general was his guest he held his tongue.

"You now know, sir, why I asked you here. Reciprocate by telling me why you accepted."

The creationist fixed the naturalist with a baleful eye. He raised the Bible above their heads. "If your blasphemy takes hold, Man will be reduced to utter degradation. Without the Good Book to guide him, money will be his god. Soon he'll believe what is good for himself is the ultimate goal of life. Before long ethics and morals won't be worth a cent. Greed will be his new master, Darwin, because of *you*. I have come to witness the new serpent in Eden!"

The scientist nodded. "You've not read my books."

"On the contrary, sir, I have read them all."

"Then tell me why God in creating each species made several so alike? Lion, tiger, leopard, jaguar, and common household cat? Surely the answer is because all are descended from common stock. Only natural selection explains why living things have features that are useless to them. Do you think God created meaningless organs for the idle pleasure of doing so?"

"Who are you to question the motives of the Lord?"

"Pratt, you strike me as a rational man. Do you not see how an individual with an advantage over others has a better chance of surviving and procreating his kind? The giraffe with the longest neck reaches the most fruit in the trees. The rodent with ground-coloring is missed by the owl. If the 'fittest' then pass this advantage on to the next generation, those inheriting the trait are more likely to carry on each species than those who don't. In this way natural selection ensures those who best adapt to where they live survive, and over time compounds the traits of the fittest into *new* species. Reptiles become birds. And apes become men."

Pratt grabbed Darwin by the arm and gave him a shake. "Let's quit beating around the bush, Antichrist."

"Unhand me, sir."

"You say man had ancestors ranging from the level of apes to man himself? Where, pray tell, are these transitional forms today?"

"Dead," Darwin said as Pratt released his arm.

"And how is that?"

The scientist backed away, gripping his cane like a sword. "Life is a struggle for food and space. Because they eat the same food and thrive in the same place, competition is fierce among those of the same species. The fittest eventually kill off rivals without the new trait. That's what man did to his transitional forms."

"You miss my point," Pratt said. *"Where are the bones?"*

The Englishman leaned on his cane, struck in his Achilles' heel. "I admit that's the weakness of my theory."

"Weakness!" Pratt chided. "There must be *millions* of bones. Yet you wrote *The Descent of Man* without a single fossil from these ape-men. To advance such heresy without proof is more than unscientific. It's downright reckless and seditious. You're the most dangerous man on Earth, and you will burn in Hellfire for what you're trying to do!"

"There is Neanderthal Man."

"Ah, yes," Pratt said. "The bones from the Neander Valley." His contempt was unbridled as he listed the counter-theories. "Was he an idiot with rickets or water on the brain? A Cossack who perished during Napoleon's retreat from Moscow? An old Dutchman or a relic of the Celtic race? Freaks like that are on display at every carnival."

"There is that debate," Darwin conceded.

"I don't suppose Parker wrote to say he found your 'missing link'?"

"No, just the letter announcing his plans."

"Did he correspond with others?"

"It appears not."

"So your wild hope is he discovered a fossil in his digs, and had the specimen with him at Custer's Last Stand?"

"I admit," Darwin said, "that occurred to me. Do you

admit the fossils we've found represent but a few of the species that once roamed the Earth? Only by chance does any creature leave permanent evidence of its existence. The overwhelming number die without a trace. But each year we discover more."

A smug look of satisfaction crossed Pratt's face. "Human thought is nothing, sir. Revelation is all."

"One fossil, General, and your theory will be smashed."

"Not my theory, Darwin. God's theory, you mean."

Pratt declined Emma's invitation to stay for lunch. As the carriage journeyed from Down House back to Croydon Station, he sat in back smiling to himself.

So Parker's letter to Darwin had remained in draft. It wasn't posted with one of the traders in the Black Hills.

The only two people on Earth who knew of Parker's *Field Notes* were Captain Jericho Sharpe and himself. Both attended Sunday service at Tennessee Baptist Redeemer, where the Army preacher railed at Darwin's blasphemy. Both knew the effect such "evidence" would have on unchristian minds.

Oh, how the disbelievers would rejoice at the "Yellow Skull," clasping Parker's fantasy to their bosoms as proof of evolution.

No doubt his death would promote him to saint of their cause, the missing "missing link" their new unholy grail.

Transcribed to Journal/June 25 Parker wrote on his *Notes,* summoning Satan's crusaders to Unholy Land.

"Find the *Journal,*" they would shout.

"Find the 'Yellow Skull.' "

A heathen chorus intent on drowning out the word of God.

Outside the carriage the miracle of divine creation passed by.

Marveling at it, Pratt thought, *Burn in Hell, Parker*.

Darwin entered the dining room smoking a cigarette. It was a habit he'd picked up among the gauchos of South America while sailing on the *Beagle*.

Dressed in stern black brocade, her wide eyes and ringlets circled by a scarf bowed at her throat, Emma Darwin served a steak and kidney pie.

"Charles, I heard shouting. What was that about?"

"Nothing, Emma. Merely the general justifying his life. Men who make war their vocation need to believe God is on their side."

HOT AND COLD

Banff, Alberta
Sunday, March 15, 1987, 3:57 P.M.

Age, Zinc Chandler thought, pouring a ladle of water onto the sauna rocks. The steam hit him like a monsoon, searing his skin.

Zinc had spent the day skiing Banff's most challenging slopes, one of those crystal-clear days in the Rockies that make an unbeliever believe there is a God, the boundless sky empty except for small clouds asail on its blue, blue depth, the southern sun hot on his face as he wound down the ribbon-like trails, zigzagging between tall stands of mountain fir and pine, soaring over moguls like a hawk on the wing, blazing through virgin powder fields where no one else had been, bending and twisting and gliding above the hushed whisper of his skis, while reveling in the absolute freedom that comes only from high speed and oneness with the terrain.

Then he took the tumble.

Zinc was schussing down Hell's Gate at a breakneck clip, streaking into the narrows that led to the mountain's face, when suddenly a sprawled skier loomed in his path. The unexpected danger sparked an adrenaline high, the chance to prove conclusively who controlled *his* fate, so as his reflexes slammed into overdrive, Chandler coiled, yelled "Do it!" and took the leap.

In a jackrabbit jump his skis left the snow, tips clearing the sprawled figure by an inch or two, leg muscles loosening to absorb the coming jolt.

Whuuump! Shwooooosh! "Yes!" he cried, landing intact . . . then his downhill knee popped, his foot began to wobble, and at God-knows-what speed he caught an edge.

Suddenly Chandler was airborne without doing a thing, life giving him one of those extra free rides it saves for the brave and the foolish, his body performing a snow ballet with arms and legs spread-eagled, one ski up and one ski down until *whaamm*! "Oooph!" "Jesus!" he skidded fifty feet. Facedown, he bumped to a halt and lay half-dead in the snow.

A blue jay watched him quizzically from an overhead pine.

His man-made snowfall began to settle.

"Trying to kill me, hotshot?" the downed skier snarled as he slid by.

"What happened?" Zinc asked the puzzled bird.

Sitting up in the drift to check for broken bones, dusting off his jacket and gathering up his skis, limping down the slope to the rented cabin where he stored his gear and cranked on the heater, shucking his clothes and dragging his battered body into the sauna, Chandler knew exactly what had occurred. He'd come within sight of the Big 4-0, truth be known.

"Age," Zinc muttered. "What a fucking drag."

The sound of the woeful word on his tongue brought memories flooding back.

"*Age, I do abhor thee.* Shakespeare, son.

"*Age will not be defied.* Francis Bacon."

Crabbed age, Zinc thought. *Pop, you taught me well.*

Again he was standing in the farmhouse of his youth, maybe ten, perhaps eleven years old, he and his brother, Tom, dressed for bed. Pop was seated at the table with his drinking buddies, slopping a round of Canadian Club from the bottle in his hand. Fixing his rheumic eyes on Zinc he slurred:

"Even such is time, which takes in trust
Our youth, our joys, and all we have,
And pays us but with age and dust.

"Think lively, son. Name the bard."

"Sir Walter Raleigh, Pop," he replied.

His mother sighed, turning from the sink, her workday far from over while her husband held court. "Run along, boys. And say your prayers."

"Got one for you, Chandler," old MacKinnon said. He owned the farm next to theirs.

"A buck?"

"Two."

"Three."

"Four," the two men wagered.

"A fool and his money . . . y'old fart," his father mumbled.

Ed MacKinnon thumbed through the thick anthology that arbitrated their game. Blinking to focus his bloodshot eyes on the poem, he read:

> "What is the worst of woes that wait on age?
> What stamps the wrinkle deeper on the brow?
> To view each loved one blotted from life's page,
> And be alone on earth, as I am now."

"Lord Byron! *Childe Harold*!" Pop howled with glee. "Pay up, you cheap son of a bitch."

"Shit," MacKinnon grumbled. "Two out of three?"

For hours he listened to them carousing through the bedroom wall, betting who could identify the most obscure poem. Finally the Plowmen Poets were so sloshed they could barely speak, at which point his father began to rant at life. The speech was a standard. He'd heard it before.

First his dad would quote from Wordsworth's *The Fountain:*

> The wiser mind
> Mourns less for what age takes away
> Than what it leaves behind.

Then he'd launch into a wild tirade on the tyranny of time: how life was so unfair because we peaked at twenty-one when we didn't know sweet-fuck-all, spending the wise years of our lives watching our bodies decline, sliding downhill slowly at first but gaining speed rapidly as middle age took hold. "What's the use?" Pop would shout. "Why do we struggle on?" Then he'd turn his vitriol on Zinc's mom.

Oh, how he hated Pop for that. Lying in the bunk beds he shared with Tom listening to the old man berate his wife.

"Would you believe it, boys? Look at her. The prettiest girl in Saskatchewan the day we wed. See what cruel time has done? Left me with a crinkled, gray-haired hag."

As he shivered in the dark, Zinc's heart bled for her. Why did she put up with such abuse? For the sake of her kids? Because she was afraid? Crying himself to sleep, he promised one day he'd make the hurt up to her.

Come morning, Zinc knew what to expect. Hungover and sleep-deprived, Pop would make him run the gauntlet of the bards, hitting him with quote on quote to bring him to his knees, flaring at his mother if she tried to intervene.

"Stand back, woman," Pop would growl. "I'll not raise an illiterate lout.

"Crabbed age and youth cannot live together:
Youth is full of pleasure, age is full of care.

"Think lively, son. Name the bard."

"Shakespeare, Pop."

One day he'd stood up to the old man, told him to his face he didn't deserve a wife like her, someone who'd seen him through drought, famine, near bankruptcy, and his current boozing bouts, someone who not only made him a home but defended him against gossip no matter how big an ass he'd been. Told the old man eye to eye he was a piss-tank bully, but the beating he'd taken in return was so severe it made his mother scream, so he'd never mouthed off like that again to save her pain.

Got the old man back, though, by becoming a cop.

Pop had hated the police since the Depression, when he was clubbed unconscious in the Regina Riot.

Tick . . . tock, Zinc thought. *Time moves on.*

Sweating profusely, he poured another ladle on the sauna rocks. When the blast hit him he slumped along the cedar slats, holding the ladle out like an improvised mirror. From its shiny bottom his reflection stared at him.

For Age, with stealing steps,
Hath clawed me with his clutch,

he thought.

Rugged and sharp-featured, he wasn't bad-looking.

His natural steel-gray hair had been that way since birth, its metallic tint responsible for his given name. Of late the color masked one telltale sign of age, but nothing hid the crow's-feet etched around his gray eyes. Six-foot-two and 195 pounds, his physique was muscled from working the family farm in his teens. Zinc did one hundred fifty sit-ups and pumped iron every day, but naked there were hints the Reaper was sharpening his scythe. Here and there his skin was losing elasticity, while rogue hairs sprouted where they never grew before. The two-inch scar along his jaw was slackening.

The passing years had also wrought change on the Chandler farm. Nine years back, Pop had passed away. The farm had been in the family for over a century, settled after the Riel Rebellion of 1870. Zinc's father had raised two boys to inherit the land, and never forgave his elder son for abandoning it to join the Force. Pop's last words on his deathbed were "At least one turned out a man."

Now, twenty years after donning the red serge, Zinc found himself questioning why he had become a cop.

Was it to "Maintain the Right"—the motto of the Force—or to kick the old man in the balls?

These days he sensed Tom had made the better choice.

Zinc's younger brother had modernized the family farm. With all two thousand acres in continuous cropping, he had a major cow/calf operation on the side. Because Tom ran the business hi-tech all the way (self-propelled John Deere Titan II combine with LED readouts and hydrostatic drive; Air Seeder with radar depth control that planted accurately to one-tenth of an inch) he worked only seven months of the year. Tom's office was a three hundred horsepower four-wheel-drive Case tractor with flotation seats and climate control, modified with a retractable roof and removable sides. Come the good weather of the planting season, he would open up the cab, strip off his shirt, and sun-block his skin. The tractor's stereo would make a headbanger weep: an Alpine CD with amplifiers monobridged at four hundred watts and ten-inch subwoofers crossed over through an EQ adjustable from 80 to 160 hz. With Springsteen or Led Zep cranked to ear-bleed volume, Tom would smoke some primo pot and plow his fields.

The harvest in, it was time for fun. While Zinc put his life on the line with psychos like the Ghoul (holiday time, a few weeks a year), Tom spent five months kicking back in the South Pacific or scuba diving the Caribbean. With the spring thaw he'd return, take over from the hired help, and start the cycle again.

If you wallow in shit, Zinc thought, *some of it's going to stick.*

He wondered if he was going through a mid-life crisis?

Sparked by what?

Arithmetic?

40 x 2 = 80 years, with the average male life span 72?

Or was it the effect of visiting Mom last week?

Tom had two German shepherds: Bark and Bite. Bark was named Bark because his bark was worse than Bite's. The dogs had followed him down the driveway from his rented car, then up the steps to the front porch and the farmhouse door. After his knock it took his mom a long time to respond.

For more than a minute he stood out in the bone-cracking cold. His breath billowed visibly in the sub-zero air. His feet stamped snow from his boots to thaw his toes. Wouldn't you know he'd get a car with the heater on the fritz? As he gazed across the glittering fields he'd romped in as a boy, watching a barn owl swoop down from the silo roof, a sense of innocence lost forever caught in his throat. There'd been a time when this farm was his whole world.

"Hello, son," Mom said, finally opening the door.

"Hi, Mom," he replied, trying to hide his shock.

It had been less than a year since his last visit, but in the interval she had aged a decade. Her hair was now entirely white with streaks of dull yellow, her narrow shoulders rounded into a hump. As he took her hand in his and kissed her on the cheek, the scent of Pears soap reminded him of his youth. He winced at the feel of her swollen knuckles in his palm, and at the stiff gray hairs on her upper lip. Behind wire-rim glasses her aging eyes were clouding with cataracts.

The old man sucked her dry, he thought.

Then he recalled his promise one day he'd make it up to her.

Guilt from not seeing her more often caused him to avert his eyes.

"The cold hurts my bones, son. Are you coming in or do I heat Saskatchewan?"

He stepped through the door and closed it behind him.

"Let's sit in the kitchen. That was always your favorite room."

The farmhouse hadn't changed since he was a kid. Tom had built his own place across the fields, leaving their mother's home caught in a time warp. Same pine kitchen, same wood-burning stove. Same copper pots and pans hooked on the walls. Same preserving jars on the shelf with cans of tea. The only thing missing was his mother's energy.

"Earl Grey, Zinc? You must be chilled."

"Wouldn't mind a cup. But let me make it."

"I've *always* made the tea in this house," she said.

It made him squirm to watch her gnarled hands warm the pot, then struggle to put the kettle on to boil. She looked so exhausted. So frail. So used up. Reduced to fighting day after day to convince her mind her body could still take care of itself. What happened when you awoke one morning to find the war was lost? Was that when you cashed in your will to survive?

Till age, or grief, or sickness must
Marry my body to that dust,

he thought.

"Ever considered moving into Rosetown, Mom?"

"No," she said bluntly. End of discussion.

"You know, during the winter? When Tom's away?"

"What would I do in town, Zinc? My life's here."

"You'd come back in spring, Mom. Tom could pick you up when he—"

"Remember the snowmen you built in the yard? Some days I miss a frozen face as much as I do yours."

"About Rosetown, Mom . . ."

"Son, I'm staying here. You and Tom live your lives. I'll live mine."

"You're not getting any younger."

"Neither are you. Soon you'll be forty and into middle age. Do you realize if you were married and your wife was expecting right now, you'd be sixty when your child was twenty?"

"Well . . ."

"Don't you want children, Zinc?"

"Mom, there's plenty of time for that. We're talking about you."

"No, son. The truth is we're talking about *us*. Is there a woman in your life?"

"Not at the moment." *I blew it,* he thought. *I chose between Carol and Deborah, and lost them both.*

Uncomfortable with this topic, he crossed to the kitchen window. "What say after tea we build one together? You sit here and direct me in the yard?"

"A snowman like old times? I'd love that."

"And I love you," he said, giving her a hug.

His mom filled the pot and snuggled the "brown betty" into a quilted cozy. Moving toward the table, he gave Pop's rocker a shove. Listening to it *creak . . . creak . . . creak,* he thought of Pop smoking a pipe with *The Farmer's Almanac* in his lap. There'd been a time when Zinc was afraid to sit in this chair.

A photo album lay open on the table next to the rocker. Had Mom been leafing through it when he arrived? Glancing down, Zinc confronted a moment locked in time: his father tall and resolute with a proud gleam in his eye, his mother—no more than twenty-five—in her wedding dress.

He looked at the old woman steeping tea.

He looked at the beauty in the photograph.

If only I could turn back the hands of time, he thought.

The ringing of a telephone interrupted his wish.

At first he thought the phone was in the farmhouse kitchen; then he realized it was in the ski chalet.

Leaving the womb of the sauna, he grabbed a towel and padded across the cold cabin to answer the cellular.

"Chandler."

"Inspector, my name is Robert DeClercq. I'm the new commander of Special X."

"Yes, sir," Zinc said. "Welcome back."

"I want you on a plane to San Francisco."

ACUPUNCTURE

Vancouver
8:50 P.M.

A block from the shop where the butcher had disappeared the night before was the store of the man who bought and sold the antlers. Down Pender and around the corner on Gore, the Chinese pharmacy was wedged between a kung fu studio and the Good Luck Restaurant. Biding time until the shop closed in ten minutes, three young punks with studs in their ears and tattoos on their hands stood outside eyeing the drugs displayed in the window. Dressed in black jeans, white T-shirts, and black leather jackets, they called their Asian street gang the Alley Demons.

Chinese characters painted on the glass listed common Taoist cures:

antlers	fertility and general health
crocodile marrow	childbirth and muscular pain
bear gall bladder	heart disease and cancer
python fat	cold sores
lizard livers	abortion
cobra/viper skin	fetal sedative
rhinoceros horn	male sex stimulant
cockroach	blood clots and stomach ache
stinkbug	asthma, weak kidneys, and spleen
carp bile	deafness and blindness
tiger penis	production of semen

A Chinese tael is 1.3 ounces. Displayed behind the window were tiers of porcelain trays. Some contained dried lizards, snakes, bugs, and frogs. Others held the hoofs, tails, and gonads of ungulates. Beet-shaped yellowish-green sacs, bear gall bladders were priced at $650 a tael. Elk and caribou antlers, shaved to wafer-thin flakes, were for sale at $550 a tael. For those who could afford endangered species, rhinoceros horn was available at $2,900 a tael and tiger penises at $1,800 each.

The store beyond resembled a Western pharmacy. The area in front had floor-to-ceiling shelves stocked with commercial health foods and packaged medicines. Here two Asian women in UBC sweaters bought mugwort, knotgrass, and Bengal madder. At back, behind a counter filled with wild animal parts, the pharmacist mixed prescriptions from apothecary jars. Traditional Taoist medicine combines herbal yin and animal yang for a balanced prescription. Acupuncture was performed in a side room.

At five to nine, the UBC students departed. One woman had her arm in a sling.

Two minutes later, the last prescription was filled. The man who purchased it hobbled out.

The punks waited until the pharmacist was alone, then entered the shop when he was in the acupuncture room.

A shadow on the wall opposite the door made the druggist turn from the acupuncture table.

Wide-eyed with alarm, the Asian opened his mouth to summon help, but one of the punks rammed a gleaming needle into his eye.

The acupuncture tool drew a squirt of ocular fluid before it pierced the retina and jabbed into his brain.

The next day a noise complaint was made to the Richmond RCMP.

After building hours permitted by the local bylaw, a stump chipper and cement mixer worked at the new factory site.

ZODIAC

San Francisco
Monday, March 16, 1987, 11:04 A.M.

Canadian Pacific Flight 51 from Calgary connected with 241 in Vancouver to fly him to San Francisco. Waiting in Vancouver to board the plane, Zinc noticed a shopkeeper unpacking DeClercq's new book. He purchased *Bagpipes, Blood, and Glory* to read in the air, and was at the opening of Blake's trunk when the 737 touched down in California. *Myth bites the dust,* he thought.

At six-foot-two, Chandler didn't look up to many men. But the pair of giants at the gate were the size of Hulk Hogan. Facing them, Zinc felt like a dwarf.

"McIlroy," the redhead said, crushing Chandler's hand.

"McGuire," the blond said, finishing the job.

"Call me Mac."

"Me too."

"Easy to remember."

McGuire craned his bullish neck. "Where's the horse?"

"Don't be silly," McIlroy said. "It's in cargo. You think the Mounted let their beasts fly first-class?"

"I know you," McGuire said, cocking a finger at Zinc. "You were in *Missouri Breaks* and DePalma's film."

"Shirley Temple was a Mountie."

"So was Alan Ladd."

"Nelson Eddy."

"Tom Mix."

"And Gary Cooper."

"Wrong," Chandler said. "He played the Texas Ranger."

"Someone call me?"

A woman's voice behind.

"Take it easy, boys. No fisticuffs in the airport."

Zinc's heart skipped a beat.

His throat went dry.

"Hello, babe."

"My God."

Palms sweating, he turned.

McIlroy looked at McGuire.

McGuire shrugged. "Must be Old Home Week," he said.

Special Agent Carol Tate was a six-foot amazon, born and raised in Texas. Blue-eyed, blond-haired, cheeks sprinkled with freckles, her down-home good looks could grace a Kellogg's Corn Flakes box. Large-boned figure taut from daily aerobics, she moved with the confidence of an expert in the martial arts. In aura she reminded Zinc of Daryl Hannah. The first time they had made love in Rhode Island, she almost broke his spine.

"You get around," Chandler said. "Thought you were in Boston."

"I was till they shipped me out last night."

"To baby-sit me?"

"One way to put it. This Murdoch kill has Washington spooked. Foreign judge shot in the States is bad enough. Foreign judge shot addressing the Bar is worse. Foreign judge shot at the A.G.'s party goes over the top."

"Ah," Zinc said, catching on.

"The Bureau wants no holdbacks on this. When word came down it was you being sent, the computer linked me and you. I'm to squeeze you dry of everything you've got."

Tate blew him a kiss. Her lips were straight Bardot.

McIlroy looked at McGuire.

McGuire shrugged. "It ain't fair, Mac. Mounties get their man and our women."

"Must be the spurs."

2:55 P.M.

Police work is governed by the Two Rules of Jurisdiction. Rule One: when a cop takes on a case as his own, he doesn't appreciate other cops nosing in. Rule Two: before a cop takes on a case as his own, he doesn't mind another cop assuming the burden. Rule One is a question of Hey-buddy-I'm-up-to-the-job. Rule Two a matter of Why-suffer-if-you-don't-have-to? Mac and Mac had hoped to activate Rule Two, and indeed the Murdoch case was wrenched from their hands, but not by the FBI and Mounties as planned. Instead the sniping was usurped by the SFPD's defunct Zodiac Squad. Mac and Mac were still on the case, but low on the totem pole. Who said life was fair?

Zodiac remains the arch nemesis of the San Francisco Police. Not since Jack the Ripper vs. Scotland Yard has a killer so taunted and bested the cops. Twenty years later he's still on the loose.

The extent of Zodiac's killing spree is a matter in dispute. Though some put his score at forty-nine victims, conservative opinion holds that between December 20, 1968, and October 11, 1969, he killed five people and wounded two.

August 1, 1969, two San Francisco papers and the *Vallejo Times-Herald* received the first letters bearing the zodiac sign:

Written in blue felt pen with lines of code, they described four lovers' lane shootings with details only the killer would know. When the code was cracked it read:

> I like killing people because it is so much fun it is more fun than killing wild game in the forrest because man is the most dangeroue anamal of all to kill something gives me the most thrilling experence it is even better than getting your rocks off with a girl the best part of it is thae when I die I will be reborn in paradice and thei have killed will become my slaves I will not give you my name because you will try to sloi down or atop my collectiog of slaves for afterlife ebeorietemethhpiti

August 7, the killer wrote again. The new letter began "This is the Zodiac speaking . . ."

September 27, 1969, police were called to the shore of Lake Berryessa. There they found Bryan Hartnell bleeding profusely and Cecelia Shepard stabbed twenty-four times. Hartnell described the killer as wearing a black executioner's hood emblazoned with a white cross over a circle. Threatening them with a gun, the man pulled a knife. "I'm going to have to stab you people," he said.

October 11, the following month, taxi driver Paul Stine was shot in the head. Three days later, the *Chronicle* received a note in blue felt pen:

> This is the Zodiac speaking I am the murderer of the taxi driver over by Washington St & Maple St last night, to prove this here is a blood stained piece of his shirt. I am the same man who did the people in the north bay area . . . School children make nice targets, I think I shall wipe out a school bus some morning. Just shoot out the front tire & then pick off the kiddies as they come bouncing out.

The end of 1969, other letters arrived. One included a diagram for a school bus bomb. Another, to lawyer Melvin Belli, enclosed a piece of Paul Stine's shirt. The Zodiac killings, however, seemed to stop.

This afternoon those letters from the sixties were projected on a screen in the makeshift Zodiac Room at the Hall of Justice on Bryant. They were arranged around a letter from this morning's mail. Carol, Zinc, Mac, and Mac were seated in front of the screen, surrounded by other cops discussing the Murdoch case. Above them cigarette smoke curled through the projector's beam like ghosts.

"*Clew, kiddies,* and *boughten,*" McIlroy said. "Same Brit phrasing as the earlier notes."

"*Kill rampage* and *come out of cover,*" McGuire said. "Military terms he's used before."

"Same misspellings of *bussy, victoms,* and *Paradice.*"

"Same three-stroke *k* and checkmark *r.*"

"See how the *i*'s dotted with a circle?"

Enclosed with today's note was a .300 Winchester Magnum casing like the one recovered from the Carlton Palace roof. Ballistics confirmed both cartridges were discharged in the same gun, the Walther WA2000 dropped in the alley. The note read:

This is the Zodiac speaking back down among you. I have boughten a new gun so the cops have som bussy work to do to keep them happy, to prove this here is a clew for the pigs to match. I have made a little list of new victoms Sty. was the 1st. Soon it will be time for me to come out of cover again to go on a kill rampage. I shall torture all of my slaves that I have wateing for me in Paradice. Some I shall tie over ant hills and watch them scream & twitch and squirm. Others shall have pine splinters driven under their nails & then burned. Others shall be placed in cages & fed salt beef untill they are gorged then I shall listen to their pleass for water and I shall laugh at them. Others will hang by their thumbs & burn in the sun then I will rub them down deep heat to warm them up. Others I shall skin them alive & let them run around screaming. By the way, let the police be haveing a good time with this new code. Tell them to cheer up; when they do crack it they will have me.

Yours truly:

⊕ - 53

SFPD - 0

"Tokuno," McGuire said. "Spearheads the Squad."

Zinc glanced left toward an opening door. Silhouetted against fluorescent light in the office beyond, a stocky man entered the darkened theater. A dozen cops milled about the adjoining room, some in shirtsleeves talking on the phone, others washed green by desktop computers. The far wall had a map of the Bay Area stuck with colored pins.

Closing the door, Tokuno limped to the projection screen. The images cut his features into Picasso wedges. Mid-fifties, with a brushcut turning gray, the Asian-American wore a blue shirt cinched with a shoulder holster. The butt of a .357 Colt Python caressed his armpit.

"Listen up, people. Will someone get the lights?"

A moment later, the room lit up.

"Napa?"

"That's us."

"Solano?"
"Present."
"Benicia?"
"You got it."
"Vallejo?"
"Right."
"San Mateo?"
"Here."
"Marin?"
"In the john."
Tokuno checked the jurisdictions off his list. "Locals accounted for. Who else we got?"
"The Bureau," someone said. "Eight of us."
"Post Office."
"A.G."
"Highway Patrol."
"Naval Intelligence." A woman at the back.
"Psych."
"Handwriting."
"The Mounted," Zinc said.
Satisfied, Tokuno folded the list. "Y'each got a file as you came in. It's a summary of where we stand. Handwritten statements from those at the hotel Saturday night. Forensic and police reports. Zodiac's history. Here are a few points to consider.
"The gun used to kill the judge was stolen in Belgium. Interpol's checking to see if it hit the black market.
"Casing mailed with the letter came from that gun. Since the gun was abandoned at the scene, the killer must have kept the shell to authenticate the note. Same MO as the taxi driver's shirt.
"No hairs, fibers, or fingerprints recovered. Not on the roof. Not from the gun. Not from the letter. No saliva with DNA on the stamps."
Tokuno turned to the screen.
"Document techs say the note's either from Zodiac or a world-class forgery. Same felt pen and cramped writing style. Again the lines trail to the right. Few contractions and odd punctuation. Final report will take a day or two."
Using a pointer, Tokuno tapped the letter center-screen.

"Eight lines of code, seventeen symbols each. A mix of Greek characters, weather signs, Egyptian hieroglyphics, navy semaphore, and the Cyrillic alphabet. The Morse dots-and-dashes are international, not American. Cypher expands on the code from the sixties."

The pointer tapped symbols on the other letters.

"Your turn," Tokuno said. "Comments, anyone?"

First to speak was the Vallejo rep. "Whoever whacked Murdoch is a crack shot. While chasing Jensen, Zodiac put five slugs in tight formation into her back."

Next up was the shrink, a Freudish-looking gnome. "The letter fits Zodiac psychologically. *Cheer up* and *happy* are manic depressive, combined with the size of the script and how the spacing varies."

Someone else: "A long letter's usually genuine. Forgers like to keep them short."

"Outlandish nature of the sniping meshes."

"Both killers love to taunt and one-up the police."

"The rifle used on Ferrin and Mageau in '69? It was a 9-mm Browning FN. Manufactured in Canada for the Canadian Army."

"Good point," Tokuno said. "The Northern Connection. Our friend from the Mounted, please take note. The victim's a Canadian judge. The taunt has British spelling. Zodiac used a Canadian gun. And today's letter says *back down among you*. The Haight was Mecca to freaks from all over in '68 and '69."

McIlroy stood up.

"The perp didn't flee the hotel roof by chopper. None was seen and none was heard."

McGuire joined him.

"He'd have to be Batman to reach the nearest building. Streets and lanes surround the hotel on all sides."

"A fire escape runs from the roof to the alley, but a couple of rubbies were at the bottom that night. Though drunk, they were sober enough to swear no one came down."

"As near as we can tell, the hotel was sealed before anyone got out."

"Meaning the killer was trapped inside."

"Prob'ly came down the fire escape and entered one of the suites."

"Since everyone in the hotel that night gave a written

statement, what say we compare them to the Zodiac notes?"

"Same misspellings . . ."

"Or writing style . . ."

"And we got the fucker."

CHAMBERS OF HORRORS

Vancouver
9:35 P.M.

Trent Maxwell stared at the envelope, then went back to the section.

Section 21(2) of the *Criminal Code* read:

> Where two or more persons form an intention in common to carry out an unlawful purpose and to assist each other therein and any one of them, in carrying out the common purpose, commits an offence, each of them who knew or ought to have known that the commission of the offence would be a probable consequence of carrying out the common purpose is a party to that offence.

The section presented a problem:

Suppose two men decide to rob a jewelry store. Both enter the shop with loaded guns, and one of them on impulse shoots the clerk. Under this section, both would be guilty of murder because the one who didn't fire ought to have known that murder could result from their agreement to rob with loaded guns.

But say two men decide to murder *X*. One then goes out on his own and commits *that* crime. Is the man who wasn't present caught by this section, or does it only apply where one crime is planned and a *different* offense occurs?

Riding on the answer were two million taxpayers' bucks.

At bar in Trent Maxwell's court was a massive Colombian drug trial with twenty-one counts on the indictment and nine accused. Appeal Court judges across the country were split fifty-fifty over what this law meant. Some would convict the absent killer, others wouldn't. Section

21(2) of the *Code* was currently before the Supreme Court of Canada in another case, but that judgment wasn't expected for months. Meanwhile Maxwell had to charge a jury tomorrow, and if his summing-up was later found to be at odds with what the SCC ruled, the verdict would be quashed by the Court of Appeal. A retrial would cost two million dollars.

Puzzling over the section, Maxwell tapped his *Criminal Code*.

Say I fill in the abstract parts with a concrete example? he thought.

After scribbling a few notes, the section read:

> Where two or more persons form an intention in common to murder John and to assist each other therein, and one of them in murdering John commits the murder of John, each of them who knew or ought to have known that the murder of John would be a probable consequence of murdering John is a party to that offence.

Maxwell scratched his temple.

Where was the problem?

You'd have to be pretty thick in the head to think Parliament intended gibberish like that.

Sometimes he wondered if the legal system was a mammoth self-perpetuating make-work project for incompetents.

Tomorrow he'd omit Section 21(2) from his charge.

Glancing at the envelope, he rubbed his tired eyes.

Trent Wellington Maxwell was one of those phony Anglophiles so prevalent in the law. Perhaps it was the "British" in "British Columbia" that nurtured them here, but whatever the reason the judge was a prime example. Maxwell drove a "pre-owned" Jaguar XJ6. He lunched each day at The Wig and Pen. Conspicuously he read his mail-order *Times,* rooting for Oxford in the soccer scores. In court he spoke with a cultured English accent despite the fact he was born and raised in Vancouver.

Waiting at home beside his bed was *British Ghost Stories:* a collection of hoary favorites like Blackwood's "The Willows," James's "The Mezzotint," and Le Fanu's "Green Tea." Nights like tonight—dark, wet, and blustery—Maxwell indulged his belief in ghosts. This inclination sprang from his conviction that ghosts were a venerable British institution, enhanced by the fact Sam Newton had hanged himself from the ceiling fixture. The ceiling fixture above Maxwell's head.

The senior judges all had their favorite Newton stories. Justice Claude Doumani, the only other jurist in chambers tonight, called his anecdote "Pigeons from Hell." It went back to the days of the Old Courthouse down the street, a columned edifice with two stone lions guarding the front steps.

For years Sam Newton had been a troubled soul. During World War II his ship was sunk in the South China Sea. By the time the crew was rescued twenty hours later, all but four had been eaten alive by sharks. According to Sam, he still heard their shrieks in his dreams.

That Sam was walking the borderline was known to his brother judges. Early one Sunday morning in 1978, Claude Doumani was in his chambers proofreading a judgment when Sam called him on the phone. "Claude, you've got to help me. It's Sam Newton. My chambers are full of pigeons and they're shitting all over the place!"

Doumani rolled his eyes. *Why me?* he thought. "Sam," he said evenly, "here's what you do. Hang up and breathe deeply for ten minutes, then if you *still* see the pigeons I'll come up."

Ten minutes later, the phone rang.

"Claude, you've got to help me. My chambers are full of pigeons and they're shitting all over the place!"

"Hold on, Sam. I'm on my way."

Newton's chambers were high in the peak of the old West Wing. All the way up three flights of stairs Doumani mulled over how to handle this. Best if the chief justice had Sam committed.

"I didn't bother to knock," Doumani recounted later. "Just pushed open the door and walked in. To my surprise Sam *was* surrounded by pigeons shitting all over the place. Someone had neglected to close the window Friday afternoon."

Four months ago Sam had finally snapped. Every half hour he'd recess his court, retiring to the chambers where Maxwell now worked. Here Sam kept a police radio, and during the break he'd scan its bands to check if any killers he'd sentenced had escaped. His fears quelled, he would return to court, fidgeting until it was time to check again.

Sam hanged himself the day his radio broke down.

And Maxwell took Sam's place on the bench.

Twenty minutes ago, Claude Doumani had popped in to say he was going upstairs to read the riot act to his deadlocked jury. "They're afraid to convict an Asian gang," he grumbled.

Now Maxwell sat alone in Supreme Court Chambers, listening to the wind hurl rain against the Law Courts.

The judge had to piss.

Scowling at the envelope, Maxwell pushed back from his desk. As he crossed to the bathroom en suite, he glanced out the windows at the lights of Theatre Row. One block over, and several floors down, the Orpheum's sign shimmered in puddles splashed by passing cars. There he'd hand over the envelope at ten, and hopefully that would end this nightmare.

Maxwell emptied his bladder and washed his hands.

One foot in the bathroom, the other in his chambers, the judge felt a palpable presence in the room.

Sam? he wondered, just before a gloved hand grabbed his chin, wrenching back his jaw to expose his throat.

The gleaming razor sliced him ear to ear, cutting carotid arteries and jugular veins. It slit Maxwell's pharanx and esophagus, the steel scraping the bone behind his Adam's apple. Bursts of silver light exploded in his brain as the killer grasped him by the hair and propelled him across the room. Gurgling, gasping, and drowning in blood, Maxwell clawed empty air while Cutthroat used arterial spurts to spray-paint the walls.

The last thing the judge saw before his mind shut down was a black mask reflected from the windows.

His own cut throat was a raw, red grin.

LET THE DOGS BARK

10:10 P.M.

Robert DeClercq was at RCMP Headquarters in Vancouver when his editor called.

"Burning the midnight oil, are we, Kirk?"

"I'm in Los Angeles, not New York. So being a cop really is a twenty-four-hour job?"

"We're moving Special X from Ottawa to Vancouver. A mound of paperwork setting it up."

"Congrats on your pub date. The dogs have started to bark. Critics love *Bagpipes*. Scientists don't."

"Anthropologists are a fractious lot. They hate established theory challenged unless they're drawing the blood."

"Good for sales."

"So let the dogs bark."

"Reason I'm calling is one malcontent is going for your throat. He's convinced *Parker's Journal* is a fraud. Likens it to the Piltdown hoax of 1912, and plans to expose you in the *L.A. Times*."

"Who is he?"

"Professor in Arizona. Book editor of the *Times* told me tonight."

"This detractor? What's his allegation?"

"That someone cooked the Yellow Skull. He says it's impossible for a *Gigantopithecus* jaw to mesh with an *Australopithecus* cranium."

"I didn't say the skull's Australopithecine."

"His allegation's based on shape."

"Why would I cook the skull?"

"To rack up sales. Who cares if the fraud's discovered once the money's banked?"

"Tell that to Clifford Irving or *The Hitler Diaries* folk."

"Too bad the Yellow Skull wasn't found with Blake's gun. Any luck with your inquiries?"

"Not so far. I sent a computer request to all detachments in Alberta and B.C. It expands on the one I sent last month. Again I asked them to search their files back ninety years, and look for mention of a corpse found with a second skull. I followed up the computer request by mailing each detachment a Xerox of Parker's drawings."

"I wonder what happened to the *Field Notes* mentioned in the *Journal*."

"Anybody's guess, but I'll tell you one thing. This Arizona prof is on very shaky ground. *Parker's Journal* was hidden away for almost a century. The drawings in it predate discovery of both *Gigantopithecus* and *Australopithecus* after 1920. How could Parker have combined two species that weren't even known in his time?"

"Assuming the *Journal* is genuine."

"It has to be, considering where it was found."

"What if the prof says that's a lie?"

"Then Fourier Transform Infrared will prove the *Journal*'s age. Joe Avacomovitch is in Colorado, but when he returns I'll have him FTIR the book. Send the results to the prof and threaten a lawsuit."

Historically this building was known as the Heather Stables. The West Coast trek of Special X had caught E Division in a space bind. With no room available at 37th and Heather, MacDougall had suggested the training academy down the street at 33rd. Special X had now usurped the offices once occupied by the Headhunter Squad, and DeClercq's room was an airy, high-vaulted loft in the Tudor building. His windows faced Bloedel Conservatory atop Queen Elizabeth Park.

Three Victorian library tables placed to form a horseshoe were the chief superintendent's desk. High-backed with a barley-sugar frame, the crest of the North-West Mounted Police crowning DeClercq's head, his chair was an antique from the Force's early days. Contemplating his editor's call, he sat back thoughtfully, then reached for a copy of *Bagpipes, Blood, and Glory*. He flipped to the chapter that reproduced *Parker's Journal*:

CHAPTER THREE
THE IMPERIALIST

In 1857 Blake was stationed on the Ganges, and during the Sepoy Mutiny was besieged at Cawnpore. For weeks he slept through the screams of soldiers nailed to makeshift crosses, then flayed alive, and saw the well near the Bibighar filled to overflowing with the severed heads, trunks, and limbs of British women and children. The following year the Highlanders wreaked revenge at Lucknow, where kilted and bloodstained and shouting "Cawnpore" as his battle cry, Blake spiked countless mutineers with his bayonet, taking no prisoners as the bagpipes drove him on.

From 1847 to 1854, Lord Elgin was Canada's governor-general. During the China War of 1856, Elgin was sent to Peking to express the Queen's displeasure at Chinese obstructiveness. Blake served with Elgin's troops in 1861 when they torched the Summer Palace of the Emperor as "a well-placed blow to Tartar pride."

During the Riel Rebellion of 1870, Blake fought in Canada with Viscount Wolseley's men. After the Metis and Cree were defeated, he and William Butler crossed the Canadian prairie by dogsled in winter to assess conditions in the West. Their recommendations led to forming the North-West Mounted Police.

The British had been on the Gold Coast for two hundred fifty years. They had built a string of forts along the African shore, first as slave depots, then for general trade. The Ashanti living inland threatened Cape Coast Castle, and in 1825 had beheaded Governor Sir Charles Macarthy when he ventured into their realm. Each year Macarthy's skull—now used as a drinking cup by the Asantahene—was paraded through Comassie on a stick. In 1872 London ordered Wolseley to settle the score.

Blake commanded the firing line at the Battle of Armoafo as wave upon wave of Ashanti attacked the British Imperial Army. Three rows deep and outnumbered five to one, the "squares" followed his order "Fire low, fire slow" as a mountain of African dead piled up in front of the Black Watch rifles. Triumphantly the Highlanders stormed Comassie, where Blake desecrated the Death Grove of the Asantahene, kicking over the Golden Stool kept wet by the blood of 120,000 sacrifice victims. The Queen awarded him the Victoria Cross.

In 1874, Blake left the army to join the North-West Mounted Police. In my book *Men Who Wore the Tunic* I wrote this of him:

> Wilfred Blake was the finest detective in the North-West Mounted Police. He was the best tracker of all "the Riders of the Plains." An officer instilled with rectitude, discipline, dedication, and self-reliance, the inspector embodied that gung-ho combination of patriotism and "muscular Christianity" that built the British Empire. He was just the sort of warrior the Force required to lay down the law in the Canadian West. How Blake dealt with the fugitive Sioux who crossed into Canada following Custer's Last Stand gave birth to the myth "The Mounties always get their man."

The time has come to reconsider Blake's legacy.

From 1882 to 1920, Regina's "Depot" Division was Headquarters of the Force. In 1920 (the year the Royal North-West Mounted Police became the RCMP) Headquarters moved from Saskatchewan to Ottawa. Today "Depot" Division houses the training academy, the RCMP Museum, and one of the crime labs. Heritage buildings such as the chapel, "A" Block, and the riding stables remain.

"Depot" Division has 1,640 acres of land. Beneath it run numerous tunnels that once carried heat from the steam house to other buildings. Over the years, as structures came down, their tunnels fell into disuse, and several converted to storage were lost from memory. Occasionally during construction a tunnel will reappear, which is how the museum curator found Blake's trunk in 1982. It was left in Regina while the inspector chased Iron-child toward Windigo Mountain. The trunk was stored—then forgotten—awaiting his return.

Writing my first book, the museum curator and I became friends. He offered me the honor of opening Blake's trunk, which is how it arrived at my residence that December. . . .

West Vancouver
Wednesday, December 29, 1982, dawn

The day after Genevieve's funeral, DeClercq awoke at dawn. His new friend, Napoleon, was jumping on the bed. *Come on, buddy,* the puppy seemed to say. *Let's get this show on the road.*

While the German shepherd romped along the beach, DeClercq sat in the driftwood chair. The rains of the day before had passed, but the sky remained overcast. The sunlight filtering through the clouds was dirty pink, and too weak to tint the whitecapped waves.

Back in the house, while brewing coffee, he spotted Chartrand's note on the empty kennel. *I won't say "Happy New Year," just "Life Goes On."* Cup in hand, he stood at the entrance to the living room, noting the skeletal Christmas tree, the thirsty greenhouse roses, the vacant fish tank. *Pull yourself together,* he thought.

Room by room, he spent an hour cleaning up, then after breakfast sat down beside Blake's trunk. The lid was open from Chartrand's peek.

As Blake's possessions touched his hands, history came alive before DeClercq's eyes. Uniforms, medals, diaries, pipes, and photographs: item by item he unpacked the trunk. Near the bottom was a grainy photogravure, a portrait of the inspector astride his horse. Blake's uniform was more ornate than those today, with lots of gold braid tied in Austrian knots. His holster was backward, butt to the front, a white pith helmet replacing the Stetson. DeClercq studied Blake's eyes: cold and arrogant.

As he began to repack the trunk he remembered what Chartrand said about "a false bottom filled with naughty photographs." When he tape-measured the trunk's depth inside and out, he found a difference of six inches.

The wood was chipped along one edge of the bottom.

Probing with a knife point, he sprung the catch. The fake bottom popped up like a jack-in-the-box.

Packages wrapped in tartan were hidden within the secret cache.

A note tied to each bundle explained what was inside.

In Blake's words, the Trophy Collection was gathered "from colored heathens I redeemed to God."

One by one, DeClercq unwrapped the packages.

The first fetish was an idol of the Hindu demon Kali Ma. The statue was a she-ogre naked to the hips, wearing a necklace of snakes and a girdle of human skulls. Kali Ma, according to the priest from whom it was seized, was consort to Shiva and black mother of the Brahmanic Dharma. Blake had "redeemed" the priest by hammering short nails into his brain.

The next package held a Chinese amulet engraved with the Cosmic Mirror. On it "the four directions were marked by the four mountains formed from the body of P'an ku, first man on Earth." Blake had lifted its owner up to spike his neck on a hook, leaving the man to thrash a foot off the floor.

The third fetish was a Maori feeding funnel of carved wood. It was used to keep food from soiling the lips of a cannibal chief as he was tattooed in the sacred state of *tapu*. Stuffing the New Zealander's body orifices with hemp, Blake had cleansed his "pagan spirit" by igniting the caulking.

The fourth souvenir was an Ashanti kuduo box filled with crocodile teeth and elephant-hair *gris-gris*. Blake had disemboweled the African witch doctor who used it in funeral rites, feeding the man's intestines to a lion while the "heathen" watched.

In the next package was a Netsilik talisman belt. Hung with talons and bird skulls, it joined the Inuit wearing it to Koodjanuk, the spirit who healed the sick. Blake had dragged the Eskimo behind his dogsled until, half-skinned, he froze to death.

Among the remaining tartan packs, one was square and larger than the rest. Unwrapping it, DeClercq uncovered a leather-bound book. At first he was puzzled how the book fit in, for unlike the other trophies it wasn't a memento mori of some vanquished pagan religion. Reading it, however, the link became clear:

for location of find and background
see my <u>Field Notes</u>

<u>THE JOURNAL</u>
of
FRANCIS PARKER

"WHIT TE CO..... the DEVIL." Might this be the ancestor of Man? What I am about to relate is astounding indeed.

In the year of our Lord, 1876, I set forth from Yale University to the Bad Lands of Western America to seek the Missing Link which would support Mr Darwin's theory of the Descent of Man. My destination was determined by the discovery two years ago of giant dinosaur fossils in the same area by Professor O. C. Marsh. Might the bones of early Man be preserved as well?

As Professor Marsh informed me the native Indians were in a much excited state – a hostility to which I can presently attest – I studied their cultural customs before departure so as not to make a wrong step. The way matters have unfolded, certain information is now pertinent.

As early as 1636 the Jesuit missionary Paul Le Jeune wrote to his Superior in Rome of a monstrous Demon the Indians feared would eat them alive. This creature they called the Atchen

In his vocabulary of Cree and English words (1743), the trader James Isham of York Factory on Hudson's Bay gave it another name. "The Devil.... WHIT TE CO" he wrote.

Another trader EDWARD Umfreville recorded this account of an Indian belief in 1790:

> "They further say there is an evil Being, who is always plaguing them; they call him Whit-ti-co. Of him they are very much in fear, and seldom eat anything or drink any brandy without throwing some into the fire for Whit-ti-co. If any misfortune befalls them they sing to him, imploring his mercy. They frequently persuade themselves that they see his tracks in the moss or snow and he is generally described in the most hideous forms."

Six years later DAVID THOMPSON, the pioneer surveyor wrote:

"It is usual when the Natives come to trade to give them a pint of grog; a liquor which I always used very sparingly; it was a bad custom, but could not be broken off: Wiskahoo as soon as he got it, and while drinking of it, used to say in a thoughtful mood "Nee weet to go" "I must be a Man eater." This word seems to imply "I am possessed of an evil spirit to eat human flesh"; "Wee tee go" is the evil Spirit, that devours humankind."

Then Edwin James, M.D., in 1830:

"Weendegoag, Cannibals. This last is an imaginary race of giant dimension."

And Paul Kane, the artist, in 1846:

"They were, as I afterwards learned, considered to be cannibals, the Indian term for which is Weendigo, or "One who eats Human Flesh."

And so on. The accounts are numerous and all the same. Many are the monsters that haunt the northern woods, yet none is more feared by the Plains Tribes than the Windigo.

On June 21, 1876 (four days ago) I uncovered a giant fossilized skull and jaw of amazing proportions. This discovery occurred on the Northwest bank of the Crazy Woman Fork of the Powder River in the Big Horn Mountains of the Montana Territory. The brain cage was buried in a cave among rocks foreign to the surrounding land. It is yellow in colour.

That the Yellow Skull is the Missing Link supporting Mr Darwin's theory I have little doubt. The features of this fossil (as illustrated below) combine elements of both Man and the ape. The brain cage itself is larger than a gorilla's, yet more akin to the shape of a Man's. The molars are like ours, but three times the size.

Since this discovery I have been on the move. The local natives grow more agitated every day and eye me with increasing hostility. A force of cavalry is expected soon to quell the unrest, so my hope is to encounter them for protection. I fear the Yellow Skull will be my undoing.

This unease results from my own foolishness. Yesterday I encountered a native family while watering my horse. I was examining the

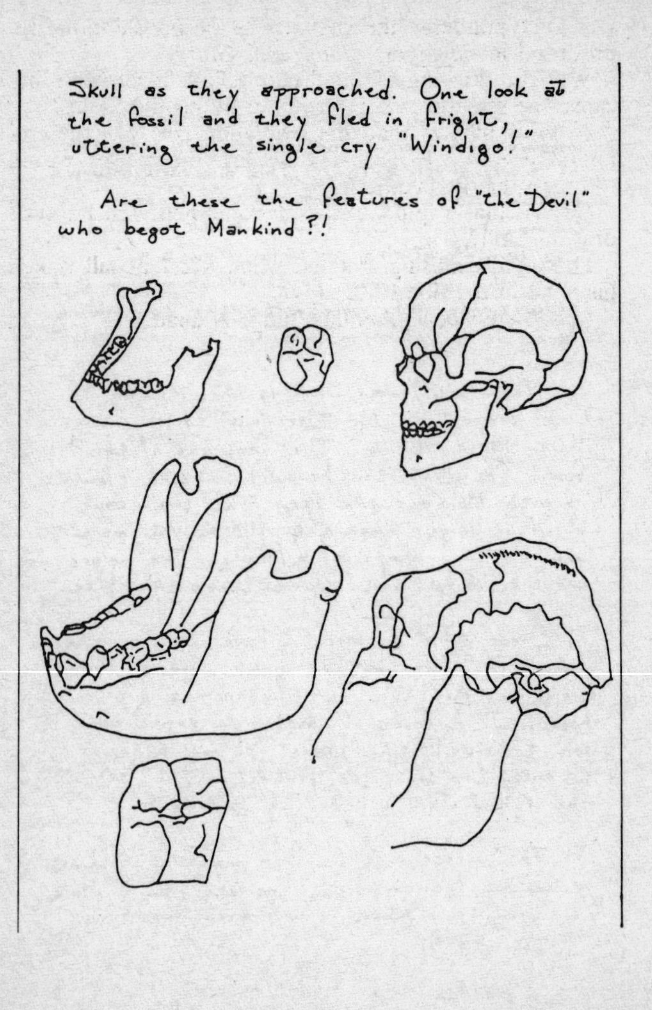

Skull as they approached. One look at the fossil and they fled in fright, uttering the single cry "Windigo!"

Are these the features of "the Devil" who begot Mankind?!

Vancouver
Monday, March 16, 1987, 10:22 P.M.

DeClercq pondered the last page of *Parker's Journal* reproduced in *Bagpipes, Blood, and Glory*.

Was the drawing of the Yellow Skull incomplete because the scientist was interrupted by hostile Sioux?

If the Skull was that of *Gigantopithecus,* was the cranium *Australopithecus*-shaped because the species was on the path that evolved into us?

Or was that a quirk of nature combined with Parker's drawing skill?

DeClercq's musing stopped when MacDougall poked his head in the door.

"Grab your coat. Another judge is dead."

CHIMO

San Francisco
9:05 P.M.

Carol ordered sautéed prawns.

Zinc, cracked crab.

"Soup or salad?" the waitress asked.

"Bowl of clam chowder."

"Make that two," Zinc said.

"And a glass of white wine."

"The same," Zinc said.

"Coming right up."

They were in Sabella and La Torre on Fisherman's Wharf, having spent the day with the Zodiac Squad. "If It Swims We Have It" the menu claimed, but neither cop felt adventurous.

"Penny for your thoughts," Carol said.

Zinc shuffled the witness statements spread out on the table. "I was mulling over Tokuno's comment about the Northern Connection, in light of what Mac and Mac said about the fire escape. Read these statements and tell me what *you* think."

Carol perused what Arnie Smolensky, Lotus and Martin Kwan, and Chuck Fraser had told the police. When she was finished, Zinc passed her a photograph.

"I've been searching the file for Canadians at the hotel when Murdoch was shot. Smolensky's Canada's liaison to the American Bar. He arranged for Murdoch to speak. Smolensky's suite was on the top floor. The *X* on the photograph is his bathroom window. See how the fire escape outside runs one story up to the roof and down to the alley?"

Carol studied the exterior of the hotel.

"The drunks in the alley swear no one came down. Assuming they're believable, that means the sniper fled into the hotel. The doors to the roof were locked and the elevator downstairs, so the killer must have used the fire escape. The first window he reached was Smolensky's bathroom."

"Smolensky has an alibi," Carol said. "He missed Murdoch's speech to bed Lotus Kwan."

"In her statement Kwan says she nodded off between fucks. What if Smolensky left the bed while she was asleep, locked the bathroom door as if to use the facilities, then climbed to the roof and shot Murdoch? Discard the gun, zip downstairs, and get back into bed."

"If he and Lotus were in it together, each alibi's no alibi."

"Another alternative," Zinc said, "is Lotus was the sniper. She used the bathroom and climbed to the roof. Or was there someone else involved? A third participant? An accomplice of Smolensky or Kwan?"

The wine arrived, so they both took a sip.

"The third man shoots Murdoch and descends the fire escape. He might have been on the roof for hours. Smolensky or Kwan had unlocked the bathroom window. When they're caught in flagrante delicto by the news, they go downstairs while the killer enters the room. He escapes into the hotel."

"Who's the third man? Martin Kwan?"

"He's the only Canadian without an alibi. Martin says he was looking for Lotus at the time of the murder. After discussing business with Fraser, he checked the bar and the mall. I can't find anyone—Fraser included—who was with him when Murdoch died."

"Did either Kwan's room adjoin the fire escape?"

"No, both faced the front street."

"What about the other rooms off the fire escape?"

"Smolensky was the only Canadian occupant."

The chowder arrived, so they cleared the table. Chandler stuffed the statements back into the file. "All this assumes the motive's Canadian."

"Which," Tate said, "is a long bow to draw. Say the motive is up north and Zodiac's not the trigger. An 'accident' in Vancouver would mask the killer and be much easier. Why go to all this risk and *still* be suspected?"

"Stranger crimes have happened."

"When I hear the thunder of hoofbeats, I think horses,

not zebras. My vote is the killer's a local psycho. Murdoch just happened to be the one at the podium."

"Zodiac would be what now? Forty or fifty? Besides, the MO's different. The moon's not full and the kill's away from water."

"We all change as we grow old," Carol said.

After dinner they returned to his room at the Hyde Park Suites. Earlier Zinc had packed a bottle of Chardonnay in an ice bucket to chill, so they took the wine, a corkscrew, and glasses up to the roof. Here above the intersection of North Point and Hyde, Golden Gate was to the left, Alcatraz ahead, Telegraph Hill to the right. Below, the Hyde Street cable car clanged up Nob Hill, heading for Chinatown, Union Square, and Market Street beyond. The night was balmy, the sky full of stars.

"Tell you a story," Carol said as Zinc uncorked the wine.

"The year is 1851. The city San Francisco. Firemen rescue a little girl from a raging hotel blaze. From then on Lillie Hitchcock Coit, eight years old, runs beside the fire engines on emergency calls. When she's sent away to school by her wealthy parents, separation from the fire hall makes her physically ill. In the end she's allowed to resume her mascot duties, becoming a San Francisco legend as time goes by. Adult Lil's a toughie who smokes cigars and wears fireman's garb. She promotes boxing matches in hotel rooms. When she dies, age eighty-six, in the twenties, San Francisco firemen throng her funeral. Today," Carol said, pointing at Telegraph Hill, "Coit Tower is her monument. The tower represents a firehose nozzle."

"You're a walking guidebook," Zinc said, passing her a glass of Chardonnay.

"I honeymooned here," Carol said. "Stories like that stick."

"You were *married*? First I've heard."

"Lots about me you don't know, Zinc."

She raised her glass.

"Cheers," she said.

The Hyde Park Suites was a cozy hotel. Big, fluffy pillows in every room, newspaper on a breakfast tray in the morning. Since checking in, Zinc had nursed a hot fantasy: returning here this evening with Carol on his arm, sipping wine and flirting while their libidos heated up, then rolling about on the pillows having torrid sex till dawn.

"*Chimo,*" he said, getting things underway. Raising his glass, he rubbed his chest with his other hand.

"Is that a Canadian toast?"

"An old Inuit greeting."

"Meaning what?"

"Basically, 'Are you friendly?' "

"Why the circular motion?"

"Performative act. Like knights of old shaking hands."

"*Chimo,*" Carol said. "What do I do?"

"I'll show you," Zinc said, taking her hand. Guiding it in a circle, he caressed her breasts. "The second Eskimo is saying, 'Yes, I'm friendly.' "

"What are you saying?"

"Your nipples are erect."

"Just the cold," she said, stopping him.

Sprouting wings, Chandler's fantasy flew away.

"My husband and I split in 1984. After I caught him fooling around. The woman I caught him with wasn't my competition. He was messing with her to make his *girlfriend* jealous. He told me I didn't fill his needs. I wasn't 'soft' enough."

Carol moved away from Zinc, distancing him.

"After the divorce, I requested a transfer. Left Texas for Rhode Island and a new start. When you came along I thought, *Here's the man for me. Someone who respects me for what I am.* Gave myself completely because we had so little time. Only to find you're fucking Deborah behind my back. What'd she give you, babe, I haven't got?"

"The chance to be a rescuer, I suppose."

"Sir Galahad, huh?" Tate shook her head.

"I'm sorry, Carol. I was a fool. I've always been a sucker for a damsel in distress. Around the vulnerable, we knights-in-tarnished-armor feel strong."

"Not 'soft' enough for you, eh?"

Zinc reached across the distance and touched her cheek. "The problem's me, not you," he said. "I've lived too long ignoring the sand in the hourglass. Time runs out on other men, not me. For years I've indulged myself as if I were my own child, ducking obligations with consummate skill. Suddenly I find I have to realign myself, because my past behavior won't keep me afloat. The problem with living for today with no thought of tomorrow is tomorrow inevitably becomes today. My blindness toward you was a symptom of that disease."

"Do not pass Go," Carol said. "Do not collect two hundred dollars. The dice are yours, babe. Start at the start."

They took the bottle of Chardonnay back to his room. Kicking off her shoes, Carol curled up in a chair. Zinc turned on the radio and twizzled the dial. He stopped when he found the Jarmels' "Little Bit of Soap."

"Let's dance."

"Here?"

"You can dance, can't you?"

"Of course I can dance," Carol said.

"The old Zinc Chandler watched women dance to find good lovers. A klutz on the dance floor is a klutz in bed. Somehow I got things backward with you."

Carol's body next to his revived the emotional turmoil he had felt at the airport. His mind said *Take it easy,* but his palms were sticky, his throat dry, his heart a triphammer. Zinc felt as giddy as on his first date, a barn dance with Lynn Miller in grade eight. Carol's body was rock-hard except for her breasts and the soft swell of her hips near his groin. Her chin on his shoulder, they danced cheek to cheek, driving home what a bloody fool he'd been. Zinc's limbic brain and rational brain were at war.

"Start at the start," he whispered, nibbling her ear. The Jarmels gave way to the Stones' "You Can't Always Get What You Want." "What was Carol like as a kid?"

Hips against his, she arched back. In the move a button popped, exposing her cleavage. "A tomboy," she said, watching if he'd peek. Would looking mean he was attracted to her, or didn't see her as a person? Sex was a mine field. He kept his eyes on her face.

"The boys in Amarillo wouldn't let me play guns."

"Damn right!" Chandler said with mock outrage. "Girls could never make the proper *KHHHwuh-pwuhrrss pingggg!* of a Buntline Special slug ricocheting off a rock. They always sounded like they were gobbing on the sidewalk."

"I used to go off by myself and play Apache brave. Stripped to a breechclout—just a towel—with war paint on my body."

"I assume this predates the shape you're in today?"

"I was eight and flat as a board."

Nudged, Zinc's eyes didn't sink to the bait. Was he passing the test, or blowing it?

"Sonny Twigg lived up the street. He was a jerk who chased me with snakes. I made this bow from a branch and a piece of string. One arrow, no feathers, just a notch in the end. I painted a ring around it with nail polish.

"In our yard we had this big leafy tree. I'd hide in its branches, pretending to ambush the Texas Rangers. One day Sonny whizzed by on his two-wheeler, after our neighbor had washed his car.

"I didn't aim to hit him, but to miss him by a mile. Without feathers, the arrow veered through his front spokes. Sonny flipped over the handlebars like an acrobat.

"Soon the ruckus brought our neighbor out. There was Sonny bawling in a wallow of mud. The only evidence was a broken stick with a painted circle. No one saw me up the tree. I'd have got clean away if my dad hadn't driven up as I was sneaking down. He put two and two together, and thrashed me with his belt. Kept hollering girls who played like boys got whupped like boys. My dad was very big on 'ladylike behavior.' That night he burned my jeans and sentenced me to three years wearing a skirt. Deep down I'm a cop because packing a piece is unladylike behavior."

Déjà vu, Chandler thought. *My female dopplegänger.*

"Who's your favorite cowboy?" he asked.

"You ask the weirdest questions."

"I have this theory the world went to shit when the Western went out of vogue. Every Western makes a moral statement, though sometimes not the one intended. How you feel about them says a lot about you."

"Good guy or bad guy?"

"Both," he said.

"Good guy: Gary Cooper. Stole my heart in *High Noon*. Bad guy: Henry Fonda. *Once Upon a Time in the West.*"

"Hmmmph. That's a good one. Forgot about him."

"Bet your favorite's a singing cowboy. Roy Rogers? Gene Autry? Hopalong Cassidy?"

"Give me a break! Good guy: Paladin. *Have Gun Will Travel*. Bad guy: Jack Palance. Wilson in *Shane*."

"That explains it. Why you wear black."

"Black goes with my hair, smart ass."

The Stones gave way to U2, "I Still Haven't Found What I'm Looking For."

"We had this dog, my brother and I, a collie named Jet. He died the last day of school when I was eight. Tom, two years younger, was really broken up. So Mom took us to the States for Stallion 38s.

"In those days the guns in Canada were the pits. Wimpy reproductions that fired rolls of caps. Across the line, you could buy the real McCoy: six-shooters where you put a round cap in each cartridge and loaded the cylinder."

"Age eight in Texas, we shoot real .22s."

"The store in Great Falls, Montana, was a kid in the fifties dream. Tom came home dressed like Lash LaRue, entirely in black. I had this flowery cowboy shirt and white Stetson hat, with Acme boots, spurs, and a holster tied to my leg.

"Our pop had these whiskey shot glasses rimmed with gold. Mom tended bar with a bottle of Orange Crush. Glass in hand, Tom sat at the kitchen table.

"The guy in white, I bowlegged in and sat down. 'Howdy, Wilson. Hear you're fast.' Tom was supposed to say, 'Hear you're fast too,' but instead the little twerp picks up his Orange Crush and throws it in my face. Hat ruined, shirt stained, pop dripping from my chin, I coulda killed him then and there. 'Just like in the movies, huh, Zinc?' he said. Now *I* wear black 'cause it masks the stains."

"Allegory of your life?" Carol asked.

11:12 P.M.

Zinc was in bed alone when the telephone rang.

It was DeClercq.

BLOODBATH

Vancouver
11:12 P.M.

DeClercq called San Francisco from the Barristers' Lounge, using the phone next to the Robing Room. Canadian lawyers wear the full court regalia of an Old Bailey gladiator minus the wig. Nothing squeezes odor from pores like asking a stupid question that tubes a million-dollar case or setting a psychopath free because the indictment is faulty. As Zinc and Robert conversed, the stink of a thousand lockered robes assailed DeClercq's nose. He was thankful to hang up and escape to fresh air.

The Old Courthouse where Sam Newton had fought the "pigeons from Hell" was up the street. The new Law Courts—in use since 1978—resembled a piece of cheese. Thirty-five courtrooms on five tiered levels were stacked up the right angle of the glass wedge. Greenery spilled from each level like the Hanging Gardens of Babylon. On sunny days the Great Hall beneath the sloping glass sizzled lawyers in a Death Valley fry. Nights like tonight the Great Hall became a freezer, explaining why Jack MacDougall's breath billowed while he rubbed his cold hands.

"This how the killer got in?"

"Looks that way."

DeClercq joined MacDougall in front of the lowest tier.

"The door's kept locked and rigged to an alarm," Jack said. "You can touch it. The techs are through."

The Great Hall of the Law Courts served a dual function. When court was in session, the public used it as a waiting room. After hours, the legal profession held parties here: lavish dinners and Calls to the Bar. On such occasions the door in question gave Her Majesty's judges access to the Great Hall from their chambers behind the stacked courts.

DeClercq examined the lock.

Left of the door frame was the access pad. It resembled a pushbutton phone:

1 2 3
4 5 6
7 8 9
* 0 #

Those who knew the access code punched in a sequence, then hit the # button to release the door. The * button canceled out mistakes. Those who didn't know the code were locked outside, protecting the judges from public harm.

"VPD clocked in the squeal," MacDougall said. He consulted his notes. "At 9:54 an alarm sounded in Court Security. This lock's on a thirty-second delay. If it doesn't reengage, the alarm trips. A night guard came to investigate.

"The same time as Security found the door ajar, Justice Claude Doumani returned to chambers where Maxwell was dead. Their offices are side by side in the Supreme Court wing. Doumani had been in Court 53 recharging a jury. He called the VPD at 9:58. Within a minute the first blues arrived."

"Anyone else around?"

"Not in Supreme Court Chambers. An appeal court judge and the cleaning staff were up on the C.A. floor, but the wings aren't connected."

"Why was Maxwell here?"

"Jury to charge tomorrow."

"Type of case?"

"Colombian drugs."

"What about Doumani?"

"Asian gang. Jury's out deliberating on the fifth floor."

"The Hall was open to the public when Maxwell was juked?"

"Yeah, street access through that door." MacDougall pointed to the Nelson Street entrance. He looked better now that the deputy commissioner wasn't gunning for him.

His back to the judge's door, DeClercq surveyed the Great Hall. To his left the Nelson entrance was guarded by several blues. To his right stood Themis with her blindfold and scales. Instead of the sword the statue should carry, someone had commissioned a scroll. DeClercq thought that apt considering how the courts had weakened the law.

Above him, the glass roof sloped to Hornby Street. In front of him, across the street from the wedge's toe, loomed the B.C. Hydro building. Hornby was a circus of flashing lights.

"That side structure attached to Hydro? If you were on its roof with 4,500mm lens, think you could make out the code being punched in here?"

"Probably," MacDougall said. "If the glass didn't refract and warp the view. A safer bet would be a random-access device. Latest ones run through every lock combination in minutes."

"Who has access to the code?"

"Just the judges. No support staff."

"Do you need the code to open the door from inside?"

"Yep. Both ways."

DeClercq ran through the permutations, counting them on his fingers. "The killer's a judge who knows the code. Or someone who got the code from a judge. Or someone who intercepted it visually. Or someone with a random-access device.

"The killer entered with the public through the Nelson door, then used the code or device when no one was looking. Shutting the judges' door, he made his way to chambers and cut Maxwell's throat. He escaped the same way but left the door ajar, vanishing before the alarm went off. Out the Nelson exit, he fled up the street."

"Big risk," MacDougall said. "Must have nerves of steel."

"Murdoch in San Francisco was high risk too. Audacity's an MO common to both crimes."

From the judges' door the Mounties wound their way along a concrete tunnel deep in the bowels of the Law Courts. Here and there were traces Ident had tossed the route: fingerprint powder, H & F scrapings. A three-way fork led to staircases marked with plaques: "APPEAL COURT" and "SUPREME COURT" up, "COUNTY COURT" down. They took the middle stairs.

"The DC called on Friday to apologize," Jack said. "Someone must have reamed him out."

"Let's be magnanimous and say he had an ethical insight."

MacDougall laughed. "Thanks anyway."

The staircase opened into a scarlet-carpeted hall. In alcoves down the left were secretarial stations; the judges' chambers were along the right. Cops and personnel from the Body Removal Service clustered outside the fifth door from the end.

In this city, the VPD investigates murder. Under Section 17 of the Police Act, each municipality with over five thousand people must provide its own police. Some contract with the RCMP to supply their cops, while others organize their own departments. Vancouver, since 1886, has had its own police.

Inspector Mac Fleetwood (no relation to the pop group; no relation to Mac and Mac down south either) was in charge of Major Crime. Like his American counterparts working the Murdoch case, he leaned toward the Second Rule of Jurisdiction: before a cop takes on a case as his own, he doesn't mind another cop assuming the burden. Major Crime had its hands full investigating disappearances in Chinatown, so knowing of the Murdoch kill, Fleetwood had called Special X.

"Mac."

"Robert. Jack. Thought you should see this."

The city bull followed the Mounties into Maxwell's chambers.

"If there's a link to Murdoch, it's your realm. Personal motive, we'll take charge. Till we know the score, share the work?"

"Fine by us," DeClercq replied.

Fleetwood had a face only a mother could love. Too many years of policing a heroin port had left their mark. An ugly scar damaged his cheek. On Welfare Wednesday a few years back, he had busted a junkie in the Moonlight Arms. "Shit, fuzz," the hype said, resigned to his fate. "Gimme a sec to butt my weed." The punk then stubbed his cigarette out on Fleetwood's cheek, and now was a paraplegic from "resisting arrest."

Maxwell lay dead on his chambers floor. The pool of blood around his headless corpse had stained the red carpet brown. Exposed in the gory stump of his neck, a vertebra peeked from a mess of sliced tubes. The judge's head was spiked on a coat stand nearby, joining a furled umbrella, bowler hat, and coat. The killer had yanked Maxwell's tongue from his mouth, leaving it to dangle like a pendulum of flesh. Both eyes rolled back, only a sliver of pupil showed.

Bob George—Ghost Keeper—was already at work. Using an instrument like a wrench with a dial on its clamp, he was calibrating blood spots on the windows. The sergeant was a hefty man with black hair, bronze skin, and wide cheekbones. His faded Levi's matched a denim shirt with Cree designs, a gift from his mother when he left the reserve. Known in the Force as "The Tracker" and "The Human Vacuum Cleaner," George was Avacomovitch's favorite tech.

"Ghost Keeper," Jack said. "Meet Robert DeClercq. The sergeant worked the acid bath with Zinc last year."

George rounded the desk to shake the chief superintendent's hand.

"Bad one, eh?" DeClercq said, eyeing the walls.

"A nut case," the Cree replied.

Blood accounts for nine percent of body weight. Since murder by violent means usually sheds it, and plasma, like all liquids, spatters according to physics, Bloodstain Pattern Analysis will reconstruct the crime.

When blood drops vertically onto a flat surface, it leaves a circular mark with crenated edges. Such a pattern indicates the victim was stationary at the time of the wound. How far the drop fell is determined by its circumference. A two-foot fall produces a circle that's intact, but as the height increases, spines and tiny droplets radiate out in a burst. By measuring these with calipers—the wrench-like instrument in George's hand—scientists compute how far the drop fell.

Blood from a moving source or projected from a wound leaves an oblique stain like an exclamation mark. The "." of the "!" reveals direction of travel; the length and width of the mark, angle and speed of impact. Applying math formulae to the shape of the stain, not only can techs determine where the assault occurred, but often the type of weapon and the blow involved.

"The judge was attacked as he left the can," George said. He pointed to the door of the bathroom en suite.

"The mist pattern on the carpet fans into this room. Stains like that we call a 'medium velocity impact spatter.' First spurt from a cut throat spews in a mist. Then the wound gapes open and squirts in gouts."

"Find the weapon?"

"No, but it's a razor."

George crossed to the wall left of the bathroom door. "The killer entered and waited here. He slit the judge's throat as he returned to this room. The attack came from behind because the mist on the carpet has no gaps. If the slash was front-on, there'd be a patch where the killer blocked the spray."

With his right hand George pretended to cut his own throat. Sweeping left to right, he outstretched his arm. "The stain beside me on the wall is a 'cast-off pattern.' See the razor outlined in blood? The killer's hand hit the wall following through on the cut."

"Did that behead Maxwell?"

"No, slit his veins. The judge should have dropped like a stone in the doorway. That he didn't turns things weird."

The Cree approached the wall opposite the bathroom door. At each stain on the carpet he paused. " 'Footwear transfer patterns,' " he said. "The smeared edges indicate the judge was half-dragged. The killer had him by the scruff of the neck, marching him around the room with his head yanked back. See how the blood ring undulates? Maxwell's heartbeat painted the walls. When the ring was finished, the killer beheaded him."

DeClercq followed the wavy line across the judge's Daumier prints, photo of Lord Denning, and meager Wall of Respect. The blood across the windows rained down on the city beyond.

"Why no blood in the hall?" MacDougall asked. "Did the killer clean up in the john?"

"Body sheath," George said. "That's my guess. Torched before he left the room."

The Cree retrieved an evidence pouch from his exhibit kit. In it was a piece of carpet cut from near the door. "Burnt low-molecular-weight polyethylene." He indicated nubs of gunk adhering to the fibers. "I found similar traces by the door to the Great Hall."

"Two sheaths?" DeClercq said. "One was a bib? The other a mask?"

MacDougall made a note to check with San Francisco for the same MO.

"The killer was after something," George said. "Slitting Maxwell's throat sprayed his desk with blood. See the clean square where something was removed? It's about the size of a manila envelope."

DeClercq examined the bloodless square, then glanced at the wall.

There a symbol was scrawled in blood:

THE EAST/WEST ROOM

11:33 P.M.

The East/West Room of Fankuang Tzu Pharmaceutical Inc. occupied the top floor of the city's tallest building. The East Window faced west, the West Window east, for Hong Kong minds had designed this room. Beyond the East Window beckoned the Orient, across English Bay, Vancouver Island, and the black Pacific. Beneath the West Window Canada lay at their feet, Gold Mountain kowtowing in fealty. The windows were aligned to adhere to *feng-shui,* see-through so "the dragon could bathe in the harbor." The East Wall was hung with Chinese watercolors, the West Wall with paintings by the Group of Seven. Between them stretched a carpet of pure silk, on which stood the boardroom table and eight chairs. On the table was a model of the factory presently under construction on the bank of the Fraser River. The center of the carpet bore the Taoist yin-yang sign:

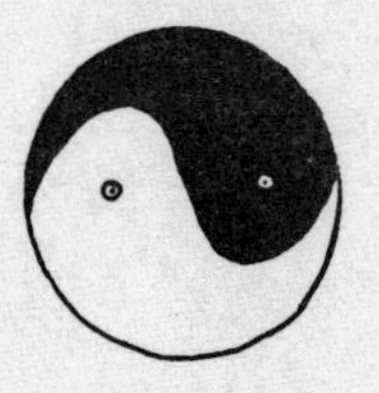

Tadpoles 69ing each other, some whites said.

Under the West—the Yin—Window, the sloping glass roof of the Law Courts glistened like an opaque skin. Amorphous movement beneath the runoff indicated life.

Red-and-blue police lights circling the court clashed with the garish neon of Theatre Row.

Martin Kwan watched from the West Window.

Beside him stood his brother.

THE-ONE-WHO-TIES

Pinto Horse Buttes,
North-West Territory
Monday, May 28, 1877, 10:10 A.M.

General Sheridan had stripped every U.S. Army post from Canada to Texas of all available men. Since shortly after the Last Stand, his cavalry had chased the Sioux around the Montana and Dakota territories south. For the past eleven months the "moccasin telegraph" had kept the Mounted informed, its riders traveling the three hundred miles between Fort Walsh in Canada and the Black Hills. In April word arrived the Sioux had crossed the Missouri to follow the White Mud Creek. The next report had them southeast of the Cypress Hills. Then the day before yesterday a scout burst into the fort with news that Sitting Bull was near the Pinto Horse Buttes. If that was true the fugitives had crossed the "Medicine Line," challenging the authority of the Mounted Police. Within the hour, Walsh and six men rode out at a gallop.

Today the sun had dawned on a fine spring morning. It blazed high overhead in a cloudless sky. As red-tailed hawks circled the confrontation, Walsh and his lancers breached the pickets that marked the Indian camp.

Women pegging hides to dry in the sun stopped work. Boys with toy tomahawks interrupted play. Old men crouched in the shade of tepees mumbled epithets. And warriors watching their horses graze leaped to their feet.

Before the intruders reined to a halt, a tense crowd gathered.

"Dismount," Walsh ordered, swinging down from the saddle. While the escort assumed lance positions, he dusted his uniform. "Do as I do," he said, standing ground.

Superintendent James "Bub" Walsh looked like a musketeer. A man of arrogant temperament and swashbuckler's grooming, he was Custer's equivalent in Canada. The difference between them was British reserve: thin red line, white man's burden, servant of the Crown. Today Walsh wore a Norfolk jacket trimmed with gold braid, white cord breeches with gauntlets to match, and the white cork helmet of the North-West Mounted Police. His face was overpowered by a bushy black mustache, while a tiny tuft of beard graced his chin. Among Indians he liked to stand with one hand on his hip, the other on the pommel of his cavalry sword. This had been the stance of Wellington at Waterloo.

Soon the crowd parted to let three painted warriors through. The scalps on their weapons indicated they were chiefs of importance. "Ask this one his name," Walsh said to Louis Leveille.

The scout put the question and translated the answer. "I am Spotted Eagle of the Sans Arc Tetons. You are in the camp of Sitting Bull."

Walsh ordered his men to unfurl and pitch their tents. "Tell him I wish to speak to the Chief of Chiefs."

Before Leveille could translate, two men came through the crowd. Sinewy and bare-chested, the first wore his hair in braids. He carried a scythe-like tomahawk with three blades. "I am The Lung," Leveille interpreted. A dozen scalps hung from his belt.

The second was older and walked with a limp. His sun-baked face was cracked and wrinkled. Cheekbones high and prominent, thin lips resolute, the skin beneath his jaw was taut despite his age.

"Yep," Leveille said. "Ol' Sit himself."

"What are they doing?" Barking Wolf asked his sister.

"Quiet. Bull is speaking," Sun-fire said.

Thirty feet from the tent flap where the two Cree watched, Sitting Bull touched the eagle feathers in his hair.

"Are we not *Shaganosh*?" he asked rhetorically. "Did the Great Father not welcome us when we fought the American *Wasichus* in the Revolution? Did King George not give us medals to seal the peace?

"Yesterday, White Forehead Chief . . ."

He turned to Walsh.

". . . white men hunted me like wild animals after my blood. Today . . ."

Sitting Bull addressed the crowd.

". . . white men erect their lodges next to mine. Do the *Shaglashapi* defy me in my camp? No . . ."

He returned to Walsh.

". . . because the White Forehead Chief offers his hand in peace. Today my heart is both glad and sorrowful. Glad because I have met white men whose word I trust. Sorrowful because they relieve me of my powers.

"Lakota," Sitting Bull said to the crowd, "the grass of the *Shaganosh* is not stained with blood. To honor this, I buried my weapons across the line.

"White Forehead Chief," he said to Walsh, "know my heart is good except with the *Mini-hanskapi*. We left the other side because we could not sleep. The Big Woman is good to her children and keeps them in peace. We have come so *our* children may sleep without worry. Tell us of your laws that we might obey. I will ask The Lung to prepare a pipe of peace. The Lakota wish nothing more than to walk the good road to the day of quiet. Let us smoke together so there will be only good between us."

Wily old bugger, Walsh thought.

The Buffalo Calf Pipe was sacred to the Sioux. The bison carved on its bowl represented the Earth from which all life springs. Twelve eagle feathers hung from its stem, symbolizing the Sky with its twelve moons. The bowl and stem were joined together with grass-that-never-breaks, so friendship sealed by its smoke would last forever. Custer had once puffed from this pipe.

Barking Wolf and Sun-fire watched from the tent. The superintendent sat on a blanket ringed by the crowd, talking with the chiefs as the pipe passed back and forth. Red willow bark smoke curled about his helmet.

"Your presence here creates problems for Queen Victoria. My chief, Commissioner Macleod, is duty-bound to protect *all* her children. You are camped where the Blackfoot, Blood, Peigan, and Plains Cree hunt. There can be no war among you over the buffalo herds."

To signify agreement, the Lakota puffed.

"Only a few Americans wish you harm. It would be better if you returned to the other side. They merely seek to ensure once the buffalo are gone the Lakota will carry on."

At this suggestion, Sitting Bull scowled. "I have made much meat in my time. The Creator made me an Indian, not an *agency* Indian. I will not become one."

"You cannot make war on Americans, then return to Canada for sanctuary. We are ready to defend our position here. Obey our laws and the Great Mother will keep your children safe. Break our laws and you must leave British soil."

As Walsh stood up with a flourish of Imperial domain, White Owl rode into the camp leading eight horses.

"Who comes?" Barking Wolf asked his sister.

"My husband," Sun-fire said.

Walsh had one foot in the stirrup when Leveille approached. Buckskinned and fiftyish, the scout had worked for the Mounted Police since 1874. Their paths had crossed at Old Wives Creek during the Great March West.

"Why does he call me White Forehead Chief?" Walsh asked.

"The peak of your helmet shelters your brow from the sun. Did you see the brave ride in as you finished speaking? Solomon thinks three o' the horses belong to Father Decorby."

"He's the one the Cree call The-Priest-Who-Speaks-All-Tongues?"

"Same fella," Leveille said. "Keeps a horse or two for them in need."

Walsh released the stirrup and eyed the thief. Surrounded by Sans Arc warriors, White Owl boasted of his crime.

"Yankee Sioux?"

"Plains Cree. One o' them that crossed to fight Custer's men."

The superintendent summoned his second-in-command. "That buck in the circle? Arrest him for theft. Let's give the Sioux an observation lesson."

"Aye," the Scot replied.

Wilfred Blake was a tall man with a firm, unflinching glare. He too was dressed in the scarlet tunic of the North-West Mounted Police. Chest, shoulders, neck, and arms corded with muscle, his spine was straight as a ramrod down a rifle barrel. Weather-beaten from decades of fighting around the globe, his ruddy face seemed older than its forty years. Below a square-cut forehead and flanking pale eyes, the skin of both temples was raw and scabbed. His eyebrows looked as fierce as his ragged mustache.

Shoving the Sans Arcs aside, Blake grabbed hold of the Cree. "Come along, laddie. Dinnae give me trouble."

White Owl stared in amazement. Arrested here with his friends? Seven whites against the tribes? He laughed in Blake's face.

The swiftness of the Scot's reaction stunned the Sioux. Grabbing a braid, he jerked the Cree's head to one side, then chopped him beneath the ear with his open palm. Sun-fire shrieked as White Owl dropped.

The Indians fingered their weapons in agitation. A white who boxed with an open fist was something new. When two Sans Arc braves moved to intervene, Walsh snapped, "You and you are also under arrest." A constable fetched three pairs of shackles from the pack horse.

Blake cuffed White Owl's wrists behind his back, then did the same to both Sioux. He strode to the tent and pushed Sun-fire aside.

"No!" she cried when Barking Wolf drew his knife.

Blake whipped the Enfield from his Sam Browne. "Drop it, laddie, or yer gonna die."

The youth backed off.

"Cree, are ye?" Blake said, attempting their tongue.

Sun-fire nodded, eyes on the gun.

"Why'd ye scream, lassie? During the fight?"

"You hit my husband."

"Bonny woman. So this is his tent?"

To Blake, most Indian squaws were ugly hewers of wood and scrapers of hide, but this one was comely in a pagan way. Eyes dark as midnight, hair black as coal, there was mystery to her face. Six months pregnant, her fine-boned figure dressed in quilled deerskins bulged at the belly. Blake thought her twenty. She was fifteen.

The tepee was made of buffalo hides, tanned and stitched together. Mats covered the prairie grass which was its floor. Willow wicker rests tied with thongs served the purpose of a white's armchair. On one of the rests Blake found a hide-bound book. The words *Parker's Journal* were tooled into its cover.

"A wee bit out o' place, lass. Yer buck's a busy lad. He may ha' more than theft t' answer."

Confiscating the *Journal,* he left the tent.

The crowd surrounding Walsh was in a hostile mood. Braves hefted tomahawks while old men, chins in hand, glowered at him.

"Understand, Sitting Bull, I mean what I say. Disobey our laws and you will be my enemy. The Cree who stole the horses comes with us. The interveners I leave with you. If your tongue is not crossed, they'll be here when I return."

Gabriel Solomon rounded up the stolen mounts.

"Kill The-One-Who-Ties," White Owl shouted as Blake dragged him to a horse.

The Sioux turned to Sitting Bull, who held up his hand.

Unimpeded, Walsh and his men rode out of camp.

The American press would dub Walsh "Sitting Bull's Boss."

Of Blake, the first headline read "THE MOUNTED POLICE DON'T SCARE WORTH A CENT."

In the next edition that was changed to "THE MOUNTIES ALWAYS GET THEIR MAN."

The headline stuck.

Blake cinched a rope around White Owl's ankle. He looped his lariat over the head of the prisoner's horse.

"Take him to the fort," Walsh said. "We'll wait here to see if the reds behave."

Blake and the Cree left the group.

They stopped to water their horses in the *Mauvaises Terres* named by French voyageurs in the last century. It was now late afternoon and the setting sun cast long shadows to the east. Ahead, the White Mud Creek snaked along a valley, but here both riverbanks were perpendicular walls. The White Mud—the "Shining River" to the Indians—had mica deposits embedded in its banks. Now as the blood red disc of the sun hurled rays into the canyon, crystals in the rock walls winked at them.

Blake rubbed his temple.

He picked the scabs.

Parker's Journal was open in his lap.

"Where's the skull, laddie? The one in the book? Dinnae be coy with me. Yer gliff betrays ye have it."

Blake cocked his head as *the pipes began to play. "Pibroch o' Donuil Dhu." A bonny tune.*

"Did ye scalp him, laddie? Did ye eat his heart?"

One by one, skeletal fists burst through the rock.

Around him the banks of the river gave up the Fallen Lads, bone white fingers clawing through the walls. M'Pherson and M'Gregor, killed at Lucknow. Grant and Stewart, who stopped Ashanti spears. M'Naghten and Campbell, cut down in the China War. Munroe, with his glorious pipes, slaughtered by the Maoris. Flesh-hung skeletons draped in tartan gathered around.

"What ha' we here?" M'Gregor asked, his voice an echo through the crack in his skull.

"Be it a colored heathen?" M'Naghten asked, maggoty guts spilling down the front of his philibeg *kilt.*

"One fer the Trophy Collection?" said Grant, the broadsword in his bony grasp rusted orange, a five-tailed sporran tangled in his ribs.

"A pounding will loosen his tongue," suggested Campbell, his worm-chewed bonnet caked with dust, his doublet home to spiders fiddling with prey.

"Aye," agreed the Fallen Lads. "Give him a pounding, Blake."

The Mountie's eyes roamed from one death's head to the next, meeting sockets as empty as holes blown by a double shotgun.

"A pounding it is," he said.

Wrists cuffed behind his back and sitting astride his horse, White Owl frowned as the white man talked to himself. Blake dismounted and tossed the ankle rope over a tree, one branch of which extended from the riverbank. Here the White Mud Creek was squeezed by the canyon walls, churning angrily in its channel beside the narrow path. The branch over which the rope was looped reached across the stream. The cord's loose end coiled around Blake's wrist.

"Where's the skull, laddie? Where are the *Field Notes*?"

White Owl didn't answer, so Blake spurred his horse. Bucking, the animal bolted, throwing the Cree from its back. Blake pulled hard on the rope, hoisting White Owl upside down by one leg. As he looped the line under a root to fashion a pulley, the Indian's feather and hair braids dunked in the stream.

"Up kilts, out cocks," the Fallen Lads yelled, broadswords raised and dirks drawn. "Give the colored heathens a taste o' Highland steel!"

Blake slammed his fist down hard between White Owl's legs.

"Atholl Highlanders" sang from Munroe's pipes.

A howl of excruciating pain burst from the Indian's lips as both testicles were crushed against his pelvic bone. With a jerk the Cree jumped like a puppet on a string, free leg thrashing about in the air. His belly muscles bunched in knots, his spine curled like a fishhook. The sinews in his neck snapped taut as his eyes rolled back in his head.

"The skull, laddie?" Blake said, pounding again. Blood ran down his cheeks from the temple scabs.

Hyperventilating, the Cree hung limp. Blake played out the rope until his face was submerged. White Owl splashed frantically to keep from drowning, but his spastic muscles wouldn't respond. Each time his lips surfaced, the fist came down again. Again and again as *the phantom pipes wailed.*

Sun-fire knelt on the tepee floor, the child in her belly kicking. She folded back one of the mats to expose the grass below. Using Barking Wolf's knife, she dug in the ground.

"Why must we leave?" her brother asked.

"Because we cannot trust the Sioux. We must return to our own people until White Owl is released."

She lifted the buried medicine cloth from its hiding place. When she unwrapped it, Barking Wolf stared at the Yellow Skull.

"What is that?"

"My husband's trophy from the Greasy Grass."

"But what *is* it?" he asked, amazed by the size.

"Windigo," she said.

THE CRUNCH

Vancouver
Tuesday, March 17, 1987, 6:02 A.M.

UBC crowns this city's finest real estate. Spread across the cliffed plateau of Point Grey, it juts west like a tongue French-kissing Georgia Strait. To the south, Richmond chokes the mouth of the Fraser River, while English Bay and the Coast Mountains are to the north. Across the strait from the tip of the tongue lies Vancouver Island, and beyond that unbroken sea all the way to Asia.

As usual, the chemist arrived before dawn. He perked a thermos of coffee in the university lab, then left the building, bundled up, for Wreck Beach. In the summer the beach was a nudist haunt because of its isolation, but now it was deserted except for the birds. The chemist descended the cliff path until he reached the towers.

Graffiti-covered, the towers had once housed big guns. During World War II they had guarded the harbor from Japanese attack. Today the abandoned emplacements were cracked, chipped, and covered with seagull shit.

The chemist strolled down the beach around the tip of the tongue. To his left the cliffs rose to UBC above. When he reached the south side he stopped for a lid of coffee. Steam swirled around him like wisps of morning fog.

Across the Fraser River, Richmond was waking up. Early flights took off and landed on Sea Island. Car lights on the bridges were strung like electric pearls, already gridlocked with the morning rush. The site of the factory was a black hole on the shore.

Staring at the construction site, the chemist scowled.

Stopping that insanity was his obsession. The current government would do anything for investment, including waiving pollution standards if the price was right. Fankuang Tzu had offered the right price, and consequently it pulled the puppet strings.

For months the chemist had lobbied about hazardous effects. A drug factory on the river could mutate salmon stocks. When people ate the salmon, they were polluted too, with growth hormones, sex hormones, God knows what. The hormones in meat already affected the onset of puberty. Soon girls would start their periods at age eight.

Fankuang Tzu Pharmaceutical Inc. has no plans to discharge effluent into the Fraser. The proposed factory will create thousands of jobs. This is a win/win business deal for all involved, the kind of Asian investment this government seeks to promote. Thank you for your letters, which will remain on file.

The Greenpeace movement had begun in Vancouver. To date the chemist had kept his concerns low-profile. This afternoon, however, he planned to see a lawyer, one who'd won several environment lawsuits. The tests in the chemist's lab would provide evidence.

Bang! . . . *Bang!* . . . *Bang!* . . . The logs slammed each other.

The mouth of the Fraser was used for lumber storage. Side by side, floating booms lined Wreck Beach. The rains of the day before had ceased, but not the wind, chopping the water and tossing the booms like galleons in a gale. The chains linking some of the logs were too slack.

The punks who grabbed the chemist took him by surprise. As he was propelled across the boom abutting the shore, iron fingers gripping his upper arms, the assistant prof glimpsed black leather above black jeans. Chinese tattoos adorned his captors' hands, while tiny studs pierced their ears.

Bang! . . . *Bang!* . . . *Bang!* . . . The booms bashed one another, the gap between them opening and closing like a mouth.

When the logs parted, the punks threw him in, holding the chemist by the wrists waist-deep in the water.

It took only one crunch to fracture his ribs, the splintered bones piercing his organs like spears.

The force of the collision cut the prof in half.

Food for the fishes, both halves slipped under the logs.

THREE BRAINS, ONE MIND

Approaching British Columbia
8:51 A.M.

Carol looked down on the shark's teeth of the Northern Cascades. She could see the Olympic Peninsula, Seattle, and Mount Rainier. The snows of Canada were visible ahead.

In 1962 her family had camped in the Rockies: Banff, Lake Louise, Yoho, and Jasper. Driving home, they had stopped in the Okanagan, spending a night at the Dew Drop Inn on Skaha Lake. The local kids had built a fire on the beach and were roasting marshmallows on sharpened sticks. They were scaring each other with Bigfoot stories.

"Hi," Carol said.

"Hi." A chorus.

"Mind if I sit down?"

"Someone give her a stick."

A skinny runt with acne passed her his.

"Where ya from?" Acne asked.

"Amarillo, Texas. What ya doin'?"

"Playin' a game."

"Can I play?"

"Got any money?"

"A dollar."

"Okay."

"What's the game called?"

"How Smart Are You?"

"How do you play?"

"Y'in?"

"Yeah."

"Then cough up yer buck."

She took the crumpled bill from her pocket and dropped in into a jar. One of the Canadians held the pot.

"My dad says our schools are better than yours," Acne said. "Ten times better, my dad says. He says you stand around with yer hand over yer heart, starin' at yer flag and thinkin' yer better than everyone else. He says yer a bunch of empty-headed ice-lationists."

"What's an ice-lationist?"

"What you are, dumbo."

"That's not true. We got good schools."

"Yeah? Let's see. How Smart Are You?"

Wary, Carol gave him back the stick.

"Washington was yer first president. If they don't teach you squat in school, name our first PM."

She didn't know.

"This time for the money," Acne said. "You got fifty states, we got ten provinces. Bet I can name more states and their capitals than you can ours. Five times more. That's fair odds."

As Acne rattled off the names, the other kids kept score. He missed Concord, New Hampshire, for a total of ninety-nine.

"Okay, Texas. Yer turn," he gloated.

When Carol got nine out of twenty, everybody laughed. Places like Fredericton and Charlottetown she'd never heard of, and she thought Calgary was the capital of Alberta.

"Wanna do the kings of England?" Acne asked.

The next day her family checked out as a family from Utah checked in.

Carol overheard the local kids making plans.

They didn't call the game How Smart Are You?

They called it Dumb Yankees.

"You're awfully quiet."

"Thinking," Carol said.

"About what?" Zinc asked.

"The last time I was here."

The plane had crossed the border and was into its descent. As it banked out over the Strait of Georgia to approach Sea Island from the sea, she told him how Acne had bushwhacked her twenty-five years ago.

"Probably studied an atlas," Chandler said. "Lucky if I could name five U.S. capitals."

"The thing is, it still bugs me today."

"In school I was bullied by a guy named Scott. I hope one day to clean his clock."

"Snooty little xenophobe."

"Get used to it. Canadians are never as happy as when they're complaining about the Yanks. If you're not coming for our land, it's our oil or water. The history of this country rides on fear of the States."

The landing gear beneath them thumped into place. The wings skimmed over the Gulf Islands and the Fraser Delta.

"Don't take it personally. That's just Canada. We're a nation riddled with self-hate. The French loathe the Anglos. The English despise the Frogs. The East abhors blacks. The West the Chinese. Our greatest tragedy, of course, is the Indians. We're the Miscellaneous Country. We don't know who we are. You can only describe a Canadian by stating what he's not. We take that insecurity out on 'aliens.' "

"I can describe a Canadian," Carol said. "A funny-speaking logger in a red-checked shirt."

"Try someone who drinks Brazilian coffee from an English cup and eats Italian food with French bread while sitting on Danish furniture watching American TV. You're right. We're limbic xenophobes. A nation of cannibals eating themselves."

"Limbic?" Carol said.

The plane hit the ground, bounced once, and let out a whine. As the engines died, Zinc doodled on his breakfast napkin. He passed the sketch to Carol:

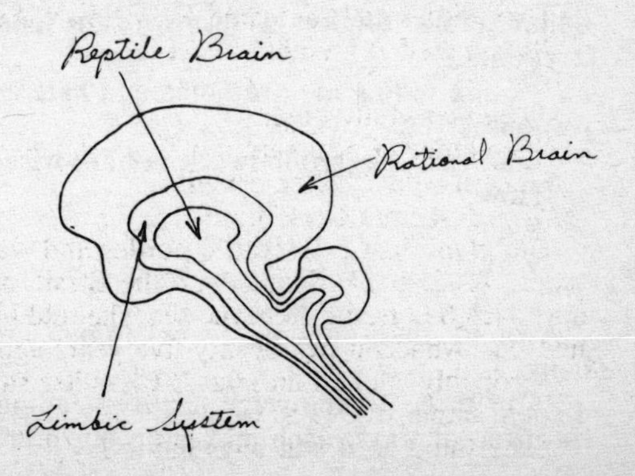

"This a masterpiece from your abstract period, Rembrandt?"

"That, student, is a cross-section of your brain."

"Who says?"

"Avacomovitch."

"Who's he?"

"This Russian defector who runs our labs. Joe's best friends with DeClercq. Got the Order of Lenin before he jumped ship. *Time* called him 'the Renaissance tech.' Joe eats, breathes, and dreams forensics."

"Okay," Carol said. "Let's tour my brain."

"The human brain," Zinc said, "is three brains in one. All three parts feed our mind. The reptile brain—the oldest part—tops the spinal cord. Scientists call it the R-complex, says Joe. Here we store instincts like self-preservation and survival of the species. Body language and territory are reptile thoughts."

"I loathe reptiles," Carol said.

"The rational brain is the outer part. It folds over the inner brains like a thinking cap. The cerebral cortex makes us human through forethought and reason. It was the last layer to evolve."

The plane turned off the runway toward the docking bay.

"The limbic system is our middle brain. It controls the four Fs—feeding, fighting, fleeing, and sexual intercourse. Our emotions spring from here. Sex, violence, and xenophobia are limbic thoughts. The limbic brain thinks in terms of us and them. It's irrational."

"You're telling me prejudice and hate aren't learned responses?"

"Like sex, the groundwork is hard-wired in."

"How?"

"Evolution."

"Why?"

"DNA."

Around them people were unbuckling their seat belts.

"The three brains wage a never ending tug-of-war. In different ways, each makes up our mind. As we endeavor for rational thought, the limbic system floods us with disruptive emotions. Love, hate, guilt, fear, lust, etc.

"I'm a good example of the brains out of sync. Hearing your voice at the airport, my limbic brain kicked in. It remembered what you were like in bed. While my palms sweated, my heart pounded with passion for another go. My rational brain, however, observed civil niceties. It knew I had blown my chance with you and accepted the fact.

"Even as we sit here discussing physiology, the erection in my pants has a mind of its own."

"Shhhh!" Carol said, looking around. Granny across the aisle cocked an ear.

"The point is what we feel is often at odds with what we know. The limbic system is part of every human brain. For proof, take a look at the daily news. We're all inclined toward xenophobia. Tolerance becomes hate. Fear, aggression. Survival, destruction.

"The limbic system is why Catholic priests bugger orphan boys. Why the third-stage male is a feminist fantasy. Why blacks wild out of Harlem, and the Irish blow each other up. Why the Germans followed Hitler, and the British conquered the world. Why Acne bushwhacked you, and you still feel the hurt."

"I thought we were born with a brain like a blank slate?"

"Not the inner layers, according to Joe. They're the 'collective unconscious.' Genetic memory. Not the rational brain either, given its structure.

"The rational brain has right and left hemispheres. The right is creative, imaginative, perceptive, and spiritual. It sees whole things and overall patterns. The left gets down to nuts and bolts. It's logical, analytic, and scientific. It sees facts, details, and goals. Indians think mainly with the perceptive side of the brain. Whites think mainly with the analytic. Through twenty thousand years, Indians left this land unscarred. Look what we've done in a century. That, Joe says, is why the cultures were doomed to clash."

"I doubt his theory's politically correct."

"Political correctness is at odds with evolution. It replaces facts with what interest groups want. The politically correct are the new creationists."

The plane reached the docking bay and its engines shut down. Passengers around them gathered coats and hats.

"Women tap one hemisphere while thinking with the other. Men don't have that ability," Zinc said. "We see the crossover on brain scans, a process we once called female intuition. Should we deny the fact to be politically correct?"

"Men and women are different species," Carol said. "They happen to be sexually compatible."

"Compatible?" Zinc said.

They shared a laugh.

"What good is the limbic system to DNA? Why retain such a destructive influence?"

"Our most powerful driving force is the need to ensure survival and reproduction of our *own* genes. It combines self-preservation and survival of the species. Xenophobia protects DNA. It encourages us to keep our gene pool 'clean.' Our rational brain developed to make better weapons. Civilization is a mere side effect. Evolution doesn't care about 'correct' behavior, but wants us to turn out exact replicas of ourselves. This instinct predates our rational brain, which is why bigotry and racism never go away. To get rid of them we'd have to core every human head.

"I told you about Caradon? He worked the Ghoul case with me?"

"He's the fellow who saved your bacon last year?"

"Bill's a video freak who collects old films. He was present when Joe told me about the three brains. Caradon's theory is monster movies are limbic flush films. *Frankenstein, Alien, War of the Worlds, Them,* and *The Thing*. The monster's just a stand-in for real-life 'aliens.' We sit in the darkened theater and throw our hate at the screen. Behind the alien's mask the monster is xenophobic us. That's why horror films are popular. They allow us to kill the Outsider by proxy."

Zinc held out the sketch and tapped the three layers.

"Visceral brain, emotional brain, rational brain," he said.

"Dr. Jekyll . . ."

His finger moved from the outer brain to the limbic system.

"Meet Mr. Hyde."

BIGWIG

Vancouver
10:00 A.M.

The chief justice of British Columbia was not a man to be taken lightly. For twenty-six years Calvin Cutter had clung to his Seat of the Scornful, going to the bench an already conservative maritime lawyer, then veering right as criminal cases hardened what little elasticity there was in his brain. A brain the defense bar dubbed the "Black Hole of Cal Cutter"—so dense good arguments that went in never came out in his judgments.

The defense bar of this country (of any country using the adversarial system of law) contains its most disrespectful citizens. A prosecutor runs into a snag, he's got the public purse and the police to back him up. Defense lawyer hits a bump, you hear the clanging of bars.

Judges get to be judges by pleasing politicians, and politicians stack the courts with those who think the "right way." From a defense lawyer's point of view the game is Russian roulette, losers being assigned to the Streamliners' courts. The Streamliners are a Crown-minded clique obsessed with order, who know how a case should be decided before it gets to trial. Every volume of case reports used as precedent has judgments out of whack with both common and legal sense. Invariably such rulings involve a horrendous set of facts—child murder, rape–murder, crimes like that. The trite expression for what went wrong is "Hard cases make bad law." The defense lawyer's version: "Witness the Streamliners' work."

Counsel who feel aggrieved can take "a swim with the Great White Sharks." Unlike Ontario, which represents the liberal wing, the Court of Appeal in this province is conservative. Crown and defense alike call it the Court of Apples ("every barrel has one or two rotten ones"). Who are the rotten apples depends on your point of view, the common candidates being "Limelight," "Wrong Way," and "Mr. In-Between."

Wrong Way got his name the day he tottered into court and pronounced a ruling written by three of his brother judges. The case involved a drug hit in which a snitch was iced. When Wrong Way announced the appeal was allowed, the appellant's buddies whooped from court to pop champagne. By mistake, Wrong Way had read the last line of the *dissenting* judgment. The majority had sentenced the hitman to death.

The Court of Appeal sits with an uneven number of judges. This ensures there's never a tie. When judgment is given from the bench as opposed to written reasons, the justice presiding states his opinion, followed by the others who say "I agree with my brother" or voice a dissent.

His first day on the bench, Mr. In-Between (who drafted wills in practice) failed to grasp this simple concept. Come the end of the first case, the justice presiding said, "I allow this appeal." The next senior judge said, "I dismiss this appeal." Mr. In-Between—not one to ruffle feathers—appeased them by saying, "I agree with both my brothers."

Then there was Cutter, in a class by himself.

The CJ had so many pet names it was hard to keep track of them all. "Rum, Sodomy, and the Lash," "The Iron Fist in the Iron Glove," "The Smiling Viper," "Moon Face," the list went on. Lately the bar had dubbed him "Mr. Catch-22." This grew out of his logic in court:

> Appeal Number One:
>
> "Mr. Peabody, did your client give evidence?"
> "No, M'Lord Chief Justice. But then he didn't have to."
> "Quite, quite, Mr. Peabody, we all know the law. A trial judge cannot comment on a prisoner's failure to testify. We, however, are a Court of Appeal, and for my part his failure to take the stand is telling indeed. There was a case to answer which the prisoner didn't meet. Appeal dismissed."

Half a minute later, Appeal Number Two:

> "Mr. Peabody, did your client give evidence?"
> "Yes, M'Lord. He did."
> "Ah, but he wasn't believed, or you would not be here. A trial judge is in a unique position to assess credibility. There was a case to answer and the prisoner put up a phony defense. For my part that is sufficient to conclude the matter. Appeal dismissed."

The bar's respect for Cutter knew no bounds. A lawyer departing the mainland for Vancouver Island arrived at the ferry terminal as his ship was leaving the dock. Hundreds of people were onshore, hundreds on deck. Recognizing a fellow attorney on board, the stranded lawyer cupped his hands to his mouth and yelled, "Hear the good news, Frank? The CJ suffered a massive heart attack." Cutter, however, survived and was back on the bench.

"Enter," he ordered when the usher knocked.

DeClercq, Chandler, and Tate stepped into the CJ's chambers. The usher closed the door, blocking their retreat. The room was an eclectic mix of Danish Modern and marine salvage. Expansive corner windows overlooked False Creek. A ship's steering wheel was mounted in front of the glass; beside it a brass telescope aimed down at the yachts. The walls, painted deep blue, were hung with galleon prints, while boats in bottles crowned the stacks of blue appeal books. "Rum, Sodomy, and the Lash," was a nautical man.

"The CJSC will sit in," Cutter said, nodding at the woman seated in front of his desk.

The chief justice of British Columbia helms the Court of Appeal. The chief justice of the Supreme Court oversees trials. As Elizabeth Toussaint rose and held out a graceful hand, Tate gave her a woman-to-woman scan. Toussaint was dressed in Assize Court robes: black silk gown with scarlet trim, vest to match above a plain black skirt, white wing collar with upside-down *V* tabs. Tate assessed her as a woman of deep reserve, and wondered what she had sacrificed to rise this high by fifty? Above patrician's eyes and a reticent smile, Toussaint's auburn hair clashed with her robes.

"Let's not waste time," Cutter said. "I have work to do."

The CJ was a roly-poly man with sphincter-like lips. The bar called him "Moon Face" because his features resembled your behind. He looked as if someone had blown him up with a pneumatic hose. He could pass for the Pillsbury Doughboy or Mr. Michelin.

"Well?" Cutter asked. "Is there a psycho loose?" He didn't invite the cops to sit down, so they didn't.

"The Zodiac sign is troubling," said DeClercq. "Two judges killed with the same symbol linked to both murders. My gut reaction is a serial killer's at work, based on the MO common to both crimes. Still, we can't discount the fact yesterday's papers reproduced the San Francisco note. The killer last night could be a copy cat."

"Someone using Murdoch as a smoke screen?" Toussaint asked.

"Maxwell's trial involved Colombian drugs. His tongue was pulled out in a 'Colombian necktie.' I understand he was to charge a jury today. Maxwell's death effectively brings that case to a halt. A retrial will cost several million dollars. Perhaps the Crown will take a deal it wouldn't take before? Plea-bargain the case away to avoid another trial? The Zodiac sign hides that motive."

"In which case," Tate said, "the murders aren't connected. Unless Murdoch was killed first to set up the blind. Coke money would explain the high-tech equipment involved. A Walther WA2000 and random-access device are expensive toys. Both are common to Medellín cartels."

"Is that how security was breached? An access device?" Cutter asked.

"Most likely," DeClercq said. "It's the surest means. A mini-computer electronically springs the lock. It taps into the circuitry, then runs through every combination. When it hits the access code, the door pops open."

"The alternative," Chandler said, "is a 4,500mm lens. We use it for surveillance with surprising results. Watching a suspect in a telephone booth a mile away, we can read the number he dials. With the lens we videotape his end of the conversation, so later lip readers can tell us what he said.

"The other possibility is an inside job. Someone who knew the code himself, or gave it to an accomplice."

"A judge?" Cutter said.

"Who else knows the code?"

"If a judge were involved, why kill in chambers?"

"Because he wanted whatever was stolen from Maxwell's desk, while making it look like an *outside* job."

"If the murders are connected," Tate said, "the obvious link is Zodiac. But if the Zodiac connection is a blind, and if one killing doesn't screen the other, isn't the best motive a case heard by both judges? A trial before Maxwell which was then appealed?"

Toussaint shook her head. "That's impossible. Maxwell was killed while trying his first case. It hadn't gone to the jury yet, let alone to appeal."

"What about preliminary motions to suppress?"

"We don't have your system here, Special Agent. No rulings go to appeal until the trial's completed."

"How about bail?"

"That's done in Provincial Court. All the accused in Maxwell's case were released."

"There's another flaw," Cutter said. "Not only did none of Maxwell's rulings rise to our level, but our court sits in corams of three. What good would killing Murdoch do? There'd still be the other two."

"How long was Murdoch on your bench?" Tate asked.

"Eight years," Cutter said. "Appointed in '79."

"Was he elevated from a lower level?"

"No, Murdoch came straight from practice. A lawyer of his caliber will only take my court."

Carol noticed Toussaint register the slight. "Maxwell was a judge how long?" she asked.

"Three months," the CJSC replied.

"Did Maxwell appear in Murdoch's court when he was still a lawyer?"

Cutter sniffed with haughty disdain. "Until his elevation, Maxwell was an in-house lawyer employed by Immigration. Not once did he argue in Supreme Court, let alone the Court of Appeal."

"How long did he work for the federal government?" Chandler asked.

"Twenty-odd years. Since he was called to the bar."

"What did he do there?"

"Adjudications. Sat on deportation hearings, I believe."

"Why," Tate asked, "would Ottawa appoint him a judge? A low-profile lawyer, a quasi-bureaucrat?"

"It happens," Toussaint said, nodding subconsciously toward Cutter. "There are two avenues to the bench. One is legal excellence, the other political clout. Trent's grandfather was Sir Montague Dean Maxwell, a senator."

"Did Maxwell's deportation orders go to Murdoch's court?"

"Immigration matters are handled by the Federal Court of Appeal. Like you, we have a dual system of courts."

"What about personal enemies? Either judge?"

Cutter removed a file of clippings from his desk and handed one to her:

CHOCOLATES POISONED

NEW YORK—A former head of the New York University anthropology department pleaded guilty Tuesday to mailing poisoned chocolates to a federal judge. John Buettner-Janusch's career was destroyed by a drug conviction in 1980. He mailed poisoned chocolates to the judge who sentenced him, Judge Charles Brieant. Brieant's wife became ill after eating four of them.

"A judge makes enemies with every case," Cutter said.

"I was thinking more of enemies within the profession?"

"A lawyer with a grudge?"

"Or a judge. Perhaps someone with separate grudges against both men. Someone who's slipped over the edge and is out to settle scores."

"For that you'd have to weed through six thousand people. Stepping on toes is part of the job."

"No one comes to mind," Toussaint said.

"Did Murdoch and Maxwell socialize?" Chandler asked.

"Bench levels don't intermingle," Cutter said. "My court kicks too much ass."

"Both men were unmarried? By late middle age?"

"*I'm* unmarried," Cutter snapped. "That doesn't mean I'm gay."

" 'The law's a jealous mistress,' " Toussaint said tactfully.

"Murdoch was a rake in practice," Cutter huffed.

"Had every tootsie in the office, rumors I've heard. When he was appointed to my court we had a little talk. Told him I'd have his badge if I heard another story like the glass table."

Carol looked at Zinc.

Zinc looked at Carol.

"Glass table?" Tate asked.

"Next question?" Cutter glowered.

"Did Maxwell womanize too?" DeClercq asked.

Toussaint smiled. "He lived in Shaughnessy with his eighty-year-old mother. Read her ghost stories at night, I'm told."

"Was Murdoch as fine a judge as his reputation?"

"Far too liberal for me," Cutter said. "My court holds the line against anarchy. Murdoch wasn't a team man, always on the dissent. Artsy-fartsy types admired him, of course, and that's why he spoke to the American Bar. Hutton Murdoch's idea of a holiday was to take the latest legal texts to his Gulf Island retreat and read. He was writing a definitive annotation of criminal law."

The CJ rose from his chair and lumbered to the washroom. As he opened the door, Carol saw a counter lined with cologne bottles and a Styrofoam head draped with a horsehair wig. *Thinks he's the Lord High Chancellor,* she thought.

"Anything else about Murdoch we should know?" DeClercq asked.

"Hutton was a practical joker," Toussaint said. "He instinctively sensed a person's Achilles' heel. Made him a deadly cross-examiner."

"Got an example?"

"One slushy March three of us were stranded in Ottawa: Hutton, myself, and the late Thetford York. The Supreme Court of Canada's list fell behind, bouncing our appeals to the following Monday. Thetford—Ted—was a legend in the profession, a man for whom form was more important than substance. He hired a chauffeured Cadillac to tour the capital, and when Hutton said the Prague Spring had the best Czechoslovakian cuisine in town, Ted suggested we dine there at eight the following night.

"Hutton and I arrived at seven for an aperitif. He told me the restaurateur had barely escaped with his life when the Russians invaded in sixty-eight to crush Dubček's government. We were seated by the door as Ted's limo pulled up. Wife on his arm and resplendent in a black fur coat, silk scarf, and white kid gloves, Ted swept into the restaurant in his usual grand style.

" 'Mr. Yorkski?' the owner asked, meeting him at the door.

" 'Yes, my good man,' York replied, probably thinking the added *-ski* a quaint Czechoslovakian custom.

"Whereupon the owner grabbed him by the scruff of the neck and seat of his pants, bum's-rushing Ted back out the door to toss him in the gutter.

"Hutton had told the restaurateur to expect an important guest: Comrade Thetford Yorkski, military attaché to the Soviet embassy."

The cops were grinning when Cutter, smelling of Chaps, rejoined them. From the look on his face he thought the group was laughing at him.

"Any idea what was stolen from Maxwell's desk?" DeClercq asked. "It was the size of a manila envelope."

Both chief justices shook their heads.

"If you think of anything, give me a call."

The usher opened the door so the cops could leave. As they crossed the threshold, Cutter said behind them, "When you catch this bastard, don't screw up the evidence. Fixing a faulty case might hurt my good reputation with the defense bar."

ELECTRICITY

6:35 P.M.

Chandler and Tate spent the rest of the day buried in Drug Section files, combing the Medellín cartel in Maxwell's trial for clues. At dinnertime they returned to Special X, where a woman hailed Zinc as they stepped through the door.

"Carol Tate. Katherine Spann."

Shaking hands, Tate thought she was looking in a mirror. Spann was the same height and of similar build. Both women had blond hair and blue eyes. Both made the men of the squad take a second look.

"Nice outfit," Tate said. "You wear it well."

"I've been giving evidence," Spann replied. She wore the red tunic and a dark blue skirt. "Guy I put away has no use for these. Threw them at me as the sheriffs took him off to jail. Here, Zinc. Take your friend on a date."

Spann handed him an envelope and turned on her heels.

Carol watched her ass as she sashayed away.

"What are you, babe? Catnip to women?"

"Kathy?" Zinc said, blushing. "I barely know her. She was wounded a few years back and has been on extended leave. Only returned to duty a couple of months ago."

"Nice butt," Carol said.

"I hadn't noticed."

In the envelope were a pair of tickets to this evening's AC/DC concert.

"Well?" he said.

"Why not?" she replied.

11:20 P.M.

The elevator stopped at Carol's floor. Zinc's hotel room was three stories up.

"See you tomorrow."

They stepped into the hall.

"What?" she said, cupping her ear. "I can't hear a thing. I think my hearing's permanently damaged."

The two of them were jittered and throwing off sparks. The boys from Australia had electrified their nerves.

"That man Johnson's got a throat of steel. Any idea what 'Jack' is?"

"VD, I think."

Carol was bouncing off the walls, a bundle of energy. "When Angus Young mooned the crowd, I thought they'd riot. Does he always wear that schoolboy uniform?"

"His trademark, I believe."

"How many decibels you think?"

"God only knows. Has to beat The Who *Live at Leeds*."

"The crowd gets younger every year," Carol said. She searched her pockets for the key.

"I think time's expanding the other way," he said. "We're getting older as the crowd rejuvenates."

"I feel recharged," she said, opening the door.

"Let's see how your ringing head feels tomorrow. Remember the limbic system?"

"Sure," she said. "Feeding, fighting, fleeing, and sexual intercourse."

"Joe says the limbic brain is why we age. Have a good sleep." He turned to go.

"Zinc?" she said.

He turned back.

Carol grabbed him by the lapels and backed him against the wall.

"Party time, babe. Shake me all night long."

BREAK-IN

6:45 P.M.

DeClercq spent part of the afternoon at damage control. Today he was to kick off the Blake promotion tour, flogging *Bagpipes, Blood, and Glory* to the fourth estate. His last minute no-show because of the Maxwell murder burdened eleven media outlets with "dead air." For the sake of his publisher he mended fences on the phone.

The last call he made was to the *L.A. Times*. Kirk put him in touch with the book editor, and Robert guaranteed him *Parker's Journal* was genuine. Intent on cutting the Arizona prof off at the pass, he made a note to bring the book to Special X. The moment Avacomovitch returned from Colorado, he promised to perform the dating tests.

By the time DeClercq left for home, he was exhausted. It had been two days since he'd slept, having worked round-the-clock at the Law Courts the night before. Coat in hand, he called the vet's to check on Napoleon, hospitalized on the weekend with severe stomach cramps. "He won't be home tomorrow," the kennel nurse said. "Check with the vet in the morning for an update." It would be a lonely night without the dog.

On the drive home he fed one of Genevieve's cassettes into the tape deck. Passing through Dundarave along the West Van shore, he listened to The Temptations' a cappella version of "Ol' Man River." At the end of the shopping district he parked by 29th Pier, then walked back to buy a Lean Cuisine. Nuking was the only cooking he felt up to tonight.

DeClercq was about to enter the store when a child cried, "Daddy!" Paralyzed, a stark vision flashed through his mind.

In the Shakespeare Garden of Stanley Park stand two trees. "Comedy" was planted by the actress Eva Moore;

"Tragedy" by Sir John Martin Harvey. Since the 1920s each has grown into its name, "Comedy" lush as you like it and "Tragedy" as stunted as Richard III.

Between their trunks, arms outstretched, Janie runs toward him, her frightened voice crying, "Daddy!" plaintively.

No matter how hard she runs, she draws no closer to him.

"You okay, Chief?"

"Huh . . . ? Hi, Charlie. Just overtired," DeClercq said.

A man beside him scooped the little girl into his arms, carrying the child into the store.

"Too old to miss a night's sleep," said DeClercq.

"Tell me about it." Charlie rubbed his hands. "I'd give my right arm to be napping in Hawaii."

Charlie was a war vet who'd lost both legs at Normandy. As long as DeClercq could remember, the crippled seventy-year-old had sold lottery tickets here. Rain or shine, he sat in his booth outside the store, passing the time of day with passers-by. DeClercq always bought a ticket or two so Charlie could have the commission. Not once had he checked to see if he won.

"Pick me a winner, Charlie."

"Coming up, Chief."

DeClercq paid for the ticket and stuffed it into his wallet.

"You better get some sleep, Chief," the old man said. "When dreams show up in the daytime, it's a warning sign."

"I will, Charlie. You dream of those hula girls."

Near Lighthouse Park, he parked the Peugeot off Marine Drive, then descended the path to his home. Behind the house the timeless sea sucked at the shore as, boneweary, he unlocked the front door.

A glass of wine, the Lean Cuisine, *Carmen,* and bed—or at least enough of the opera to hear the Habanera.

Stepping into the hall, he switched on the light.

Damn, he thought.

Whoever had ransacked his home had done a thorough job.

Empty drawers.

Upended furniture.

All his books pulled out.

Half an hour later, the West Van cops arrived. By then he knew the thief had stolen *Parker's Journal* and his notes on Blake.

BAGPIPES, BLOOD, AND GLORY

Medicine Lake, Alberta
Thursday, December 9, 1897, dawn

He awoke with a start.

His muscles tense.

His mind alert.

His nervous system taut like a bowstring at full draw.

Under the blanket he used as a pillow, Blake's right hand closed on the Enfield's grip and his thumb eased back on the hammer. There was a click as the pistol cocked, but the sound was smothered and lost among the frozen folds of the blanket. As Blake drew the gun beneath his head into the bitter cold, he lay stock still in his buffalo robe. Silent. Listening. Waiting.

The night was cold and moonless. To the north the aurora borealis flickered across the landscape, fading in and out with that weird tremor the Indians say is the "Dance of the Dead Spirits." Above his head countless stars pierced the black sky, while to the east, in the vault of space, rose-colored streaks from a meteor shower stabbed the first faint smudge of dawn. The time was 6:00 A.M.

During the hours Blake had slept, an Arctic storm had buried this valley beneath a weight of snow. Now frost came down from the cruel sky to shroud his camp with ice, and all the world seemed to sleep in savage desolation. But in his gut, his primal core, he knew something was out there.

Enfield in hand.

Breath held.

Slowly he rose from the ground.

Blake was camped a few hundred feet from the shore of Medicine Lake. Here, as dawn began to stain the jagged peaks east, he crouched in the lee of a clump of pine, listening to the silence.

From far away, at intervals, came the lonely hoot of an owl.

Lake water lapped at the ice ring creeping from the shore.

A passing breeze caused the firs to whisper like conspirators.

Then—as happens in the mountains—the wind changed direction. A zephyr barely strong enough to turn smoke or twist a feather puffed from the west. Instantly the dogs awoke and turned in that direction. The huskies were curled up near the sled fifteen feet from Blake.

Iron-child, the Mountie thought, whirling on instinct.

The youth churning through the snow was barely a man. He wore the winter dress of his tribe, which offered little protection against the elements. The buffalo robe slung from his shoulder covered a bare chest. A breechclout of leather hung from his waist, augmented by leggings ankle-to-groin. His moccasins were stuffed with grass for extra warmth, and on his head was a horned cap adorned with weasel skins. In both hands he clutched his Winchester like a club. *He's out of shells,* Blake thought.

A jolt of adrenaline hit the white man's blood. This was when he was most alive and knew it most completely. Raising the Enfield, Blake sighted Iron-child down its barrel. But when he pulled the trigger, the gun didn't respond. Either its mechanism was frozen or it was jammed.

A war whoop shattered the brittle mountain air. Having burst from a thicket forty feet west, the Cree clawed his way through drifts of snow. Thirty feet . . . twenty feet . . . he closed the gap.

Biting his mitt with his teeth, Blake wrenched the glove from his hand. Both fists gripped the Enfield as he yanked the trigger. The wood of the handle was cold to his touch, the metal a curl of ice.

Iron-child, discarding his robe, was naked above the waist. He stumbled and faltered as his breath billowed in white clouds. The rifle grasped in both hands was high above his head, but when he saw the Enfield jerk he dropped to his knees.

The muzzle flared yellow, then came the shocking explosion. The pistol lurched in Blake's hands as the blast filled the empty solitude. Mountain echoes bounced back repeatedly. The errant bullet missed. It passed over the Cree's head and hit the breech of his rifle, splintering into several ricochets. One fragment grazed the youth's temple, slashing his cheek, then lodged in his shoulder as his arm went numb. The force of the bullet hitting the rifle threw him back. Iron-child's leg snapped. Then he passed out.

The Cree emerged from the shock of his wounds to find himself staring down the barrel of a gun.

"Aye," Blake said in English. "I see yer alive. Are ye in pain, lad?"

The Mountie stood between Iron-child and the flaming ball of the sun, shafts of glory silhouetting him like an aura. His hand rubbed his temple absentmindedly, the scabs on his forehead picked raw. Now sixty, his mustache, hair, and eyebrows were white, his pale eyes as cold as the winter landscape.

"One dinnae fight because there is hope o' winning, lad. It is much finer to fight when it is nae use. Cyrano de Bergerac. Be thet yer philosophy?"

Iron-child didn't understand a word Blake spoke. Sensing it would be suicide to make a sound, he watched the Mountie squat on his heels, the muzzle of the Enfield four feet from his head.

"Ye dinnae understand English? Or be it the clour to yer brain? Dinnae matter to me, lad, for we must have a wee talk while we have the time."

One of the huskies trotted over to sniff the Cree's face, tongue licking the blood that trickled down his cheek.

As numbness claimed his muscles, the Indian lay still. The sun reflecting off the snow warmed the air, so Blake—still rubbing his temple—loosened his buffalo coat. In the *V* below his throat, Iron-child glimpsed the scarlet uniform.

"I've been trackin' ye fer a long time, lad, so I want ye to know the trouble ye and yer red brother Almighty Voice ha' caused. A wee bit o' trouble indeed.

"Now I can see how ye Cree on Chief One Arrow's Reserve dinnae like bein' boxed into sixteen square miles. Nae when ye once had thousands o' miles o' prairie t' roam. But, laddie, thet's the price ye pay fer backin'

Riel against the government. Ye cannae stop the settlers from comin'.

"This *Kah-kee-say-man-e-too-wayo,* this Almighty Voice, he was a piss-poor leader t' follow in yer escapade. Wha'd ye three young Cree think? He'd drive the whites from yer land? It's *our* land now, lad. A lesson fer yer learnin'."

As Iron-child shivered, his broken leg bones rattled against each other. The pain, the cold, and loss of blood weakened him. Listening to the meaningless words roll off the Scotsman's tongue, he was mesmerized by the rumbling Gaelic burr.

"I'm nae sayin' Sergeant Colebrook was the best o' officers. His record marked, he'd been up fer breaches o' discipline. But when he caught up with Almighty Voice as he was breakin' camp, Colebrook dinnae draw a pistol bead on him. Saskatchewan is nae Tombstone or Dodge City, lad, and the Mounted are nae Yankee barbarians. So tell me why yer heathen friend had t' shoot Colebrook through the neck with a double-barreled shotgun?"

The question hung in the air as Blake picked his temple sores. With the barrel of his gun he scratched his brow. "Aye, the tunes o' glory, lad. How bonny Munroe plays."

Without warning, he grabbed the horned cap from the Cree's head. Smearing blood across his palm, he licked it clean. His eyes lost focus.

"True, the public pressured us, as ye'd expect. But the real pressure came from within. 'Cause no one, Cree—red or white—murders one of our own."

His tongue licked the last drop of blood from his mustache.

"Nae much of a trophy, yer noggin cap. Nae like my scalp would ha' been. Brings ye pride among yer people, takin' a gray-haired scalp?"

Striking out with the Enfield, Blake smashed the Cree in the mouth. With a sickening crack, teeth shattered into chips of enamel. The youth's cry of shock and pain rang down the valley. By the hair, Blake jerked his head off the ground to meet him eye to eye.

"Yer mistake was nae killin' Colebrook, an' it was nae killin' the others. Yer blunder was proddin' Herchmer t' put me on yer tail. Some say I'm excessive, but there's nae mark on my record. 'Cause, laddie, the Mounted Police need me more than I need them. When there's a job o' trackin', it goes t' me. I'm the one thet gets the ones thet ought t' get away. A legend is born when a man beats the probabilities o' life. So, Cree, the legacy o' this Force will be the legacy o' me!"

Releasing his hair, Blake threw the Indian back on the ground. Iron-child heard a click as the Enfield cocked. Standing, the white man lowered the pistol until its bore glared into his eyes. A glint of sunlight danced along the barrel.

"Dead or alive," the Scot said. "It's the same t' them. Bu' I tell ye, laddie. It's nae the same t' me."

Blake shot Iron-child between the eyes.

As the blast from the Enfield sullied the glorious dawn, the Mountie drew the muzzle close to sniff gunsmoke into his lungs. The phantom pipes played on.

Blake turned from the corpse and trudged across to the unhitched dogsled to forage a meal. Rummaging through his dwindling supplies, he found the cache of food, then built a fire, put snow in the kettle, and brewed some tea. While he ate biscuits and pemmican, the dogs ate dried moose meat. Smoking a pipe, he waited for the drone in his head to abate.

For years the pipes had plagued him when alone on a hunt—but only if his quarry wasn't white. Chase a white and the Fallen Lads would rest in peace, but corner a colored and they clamored from the grave. There was vengeance to extract for colonial deaths, and the regiment's Trophy Collection to enhance. On and on the pipes would play until the heathen was dead; then called to a higher service, the Lads would retreat to the grave.

Iron-child was dead.

So why did the pipes play on?

Face buried in one hand, Blake slammed his skull with his other palm. Clawing at his temples, he scraped flesh from the bone. The shrill whine of the bagpipes drilled into his mind like a spike hammered into his brain. The melody wouldn't stop. Something was wrong.

Gripped by impulsive madness, he kicked the fire. Sparks hurled across the pristine snow. A whistle brought the huskies bounding to the sled, jumping on one another in play. As he hitched them to the dog train, tangling traces, back bands, and collar straps into knots, Cerfvola and Spanker fought for the lead.

Striking camp, Blake tramped to the corpse. The slug had sprayed a red halo about the Cree's head. By both hair braids he dragged the body to the sled, lashing it to the platform with cross-hatched straps. He mounted the rear runner blades and flicked a whip at the dogs. With a jerk, the train began to move.

For hours the huskies panted as they hauled the heavy load, biting mouthfuls of snow to quench their thirst. In the wind howling through the overhead peaks, in the squeak of the ice crust crumbling beneath the sled, Blake heard bagpipes calling him. At times inanimate objects moved at the corner of his eye, but when he turned to face them, reality held. The jack pines didn't stalk him; the fissures had no teeth; the cliff faces didn't stare with malevolent eyes.

At midday, a thick blanket of cloud settled over the mountains. When it began to evaporate late that afternoon, he found himself flanked by the spurs of the Rockies.

This was it. He'd reached it. The Indians' "Bridge of the World." That hinge where the Great Divide confronts a thousand miles of prairie.

Tugging on the dog train, he slid the sled to a halt.

Beyond the rift in the mountains the mist had burned away, laying bare an expanse so vast and bleak that every hill and hummock seemed flattened to one continuous level. Glittering here and there across the endless sheet of snow, blue lakelets marched over the far horizon.

In a long, slow switchback, the sled descended the mountain. Everywhere he looked, all he saw was snow. Snow on the humps of the foothills, snow on the peaks behind. Snow on the trees around him, snow on the plains ahead. Then *he heard the wheeze of a windbag drawing air, followed by the melody of "Amazing Grace." One by one, the Fallen Lads were rising from the snow.*

"Wha' ha' we here, Blake?" M'Gregor's voice.

"One o' the colored heathens?" Campbell's burr.

"Nae thinkin' o' keepin' him fer yerself, denyin' us Picts a laugh? Y'are gonna spine him, aren't ye, Wilf?"

Blake rubbed his temple.

He shook his head.

"Aye," he said, reining in the dogs.

They looked like frozen zombies rising from the grave, clawing their way out of the snow with fingers white as bone. They broke through the ice crust in their rimed tartans, staring at Blake with crystalline eyes. Icicles thick as dirk blades hung from their hair and beards, the only color about them their blood red wounds.

"Spine him, Wilf," Stewart said. "Like the juju man."

"Wind's a-blowin'," M'Naghten said. "String 'em from a tree."

"Aye, let's hear this heathen's music," Grant laughed.

The last colored he had spined was in the Ashanti War, the day they found the Death Grove of the Asantahene. As he pulled the dirk from his boot and leaned over Iron-child's corpse, he recalled the delicious rip of steel slitting alien flesh. He'd filleted the African stem to stern, exposing the ivory vertebrae down his back. While Munroe played the pipes they danced the Highland fling, circling the bones strung from the tree on a strip of tartan. The African's spine clinked like a Chinese wind chime.

Aye, Blake thought. *The Lads did like their fun.*

Dragging the body from the sled, he stretched it out in the snow. With his dirk he cut the breechclout and leggings to strip the corpse, then grasped one moccasin and tossed it aside. Removing the other moccasin, something fell to the ground: a square of leather hidden inside. Dusting the snow, he unfurled it to find three black symbols painted on the hide:

The moment he saw the pictographs, the memory struck like a clock.

Parker's Journal had come from White Owl's tent.

Somehow he'd missed the Yellow Skull and Parker's *Field Notes*.

White Owl's squaw was pregnant with a bairn of the Plains Cree.

Be they father and son: White Owl and Iron-child?

Did the son fall heir to the Yellow Skull? The skull drawn on the hide in his hand and the book hidden in his trunk?

Was that why the lad had led him on this merry chase West? To take the skull to the mountain where the Cree said the Windigo lived?

Was the skull an idol? A juju? A fetish?

Was that why it and the hairy beast were painted on the hide?

What about the mountain?

Was the hide a map?

The night before the bluff had been shelled to kill Almighty Voice, the Cree of Chief One Arrow's Reserve had climbed the surrounding hills. The mothers of the renegades had sung their death songs, urging them to stand fast against the redcoats. One begged her son to save his father's "medicine," not to let it become a trophy of the whites. The Mounted had no idea what she was wailing about.

The skull, Blake thought. *You missed it again. Iron-child attacked from* farther *West.* "Ye dinnae check his camp, man. Ye must go back."

While Blake lightened the load on his sled, the Lads gathered round.

"Ye smashed the niggers' Golden Stool," M'Pherson said.

"Ye smashed the chinkies' Monkey God," Stewart added.

"Now smash the redskins' Windigo," the Fallen Lads chimed. "It's one fer the Collection. Find the Yellow Skull."

Friday, December 10, 1897, 4:10 P.M.

Late the following afternoon, Blake reached Medicine Lake. As no snow had fallen since the Cree's attack, he tracked Iron-child's footprints to his overnight camp. There, beyond the thicket from which the youth had emerged, he found the Yellow Skull at the base of a tree.

Blake had the fossil in his hand when he sucked in a breath, for there to the west, miles away on the ridge of the Great Divide, sunlight coruscating off its ice-capped peak, wisps of cirrus cloud caressing the pyramid of its summit, jutted the mountain painted on the hide.

Munroe's pipes began to wail as he mushed toward the peak.

Part Two

BRAIN

The belief in a supernatural source of evil is not necessary. Men alone are quite capable of every wickedness.

—Conrad

WARLORD

Kowloon, Hong Kong
Wednesday, March 18, 1987, 11:50 P.M.

Hong Kong sits like a boil on the rump of China, a festering colonial monument to greed.

Born of the opium trade in 1841, the island was seized from China by Captain Charles Elliot as compensation for twenty thousand chests of British "foreign mud" confiscated in Canton. So enamored was London with having this "barren island with hardly a house upon it" added to the realm that Elliot ended his career as consul general to Texas.

From that inauspicious beginning until the countdown of today, the colony has existed exclusively for profit. Hong Kong is a jungle where commerce takes precedence over humanity, designed to provide everything the acquisitive heart desires. Traffic in Bengal opium nurtured the first trading *hong*, and set the swashbuckling tone of its business ethics. Pirates, exploiters, smugglers, con men, criminals, and the corrupt engaged in capitalism without restraint. Relentless pursuit of money transformed that "barren rock" into what it is today, while the clash of the cutlass, the whiff of the musket, the buccaneer swagger remain. The pirate of old became the cutthroat of the boardroom.

Hong Kong is a colony without an elected government. Its academic record is next to nil. Here it is wealth, not background and breeding, that makes the man. "How much money do you have?" is the yardstick of human worth. Pride, avarice, arrogance, greed, envy, luxury, and gluttony give "face." Vices elsewhere are virtues here.

The game is not to keep up with the Chanus and the Lis, but to overtake them in a gaudy show of wealth. For straight-up, out-front arrogance, no one flaunts better than the colony's elite. Chauffeurs in pink uniforms drive pink cars for women in pink minks. His-and-hers Rolls-Royces purr up the Peak, where status comes from living higher than everyone else. Christie's and Sotheby's come here to auction priceless antiques, aware that Hongkongers who want something want it regardless of cost, if only to keep it from others who want it too.

Not long ago the nouveau riche were tailors, beggars, duck farmers, and other dispossessed. Now every street hawker dreams of the day when he'll wear monogrammed shirts from Italy and silk ties from France.

The colony lives on borrowed time in a borrowed place.

As the clock ticks down to 1997, apprehension grows.

A desperate get-it-while-you-can panic has taken hold, so everyone, high and low, screws every cent out of every second left.

As refugees flood in, the wealthy emigrate, moving their money overseas to buy up foreign lands.

The Middle Kingdom in exile.

The New Colonialists.

The Boxer Rebellion sought to reverse the course of history. Since the Opium Wars of the 1840s and '50s, foreigners in China had done much as they pleased. At the end of the nineteenth century, drought, famine, floods, and war gripped the Middle Kingdom. The Boxers formed in Shandong Province as a peasant-backed uprising against the empress. To prepare for battle, they took the "boxer's stance" common to the martial arts. In Chinese, their name meant "Righteous and Harmonious Fists."

The slogan of the Boxers was "Overthrow the empress; destroy the foreigner." Aliens were blamed for angering the spirits and displeasing the gods. In October 1899, the Boxers suffered a defeat by government troops. The empress saw the rebels as a way to kick foreigners out of China, so in the final days of the century the Boxers and the government formed a xenophobic alliance.

As they burned churches and ripped up railroads, the Boxers massacred missionaries and other aliens. In 1900 they laid siege to the foreign legations' compound in Beijing, while the empress declared war on Britain, Russia, Germany, France, the United States, Japan, and Italy. The colonial powers responded by sending troops, and once again, humiliated, China was defeated.

One of the missionaries killed in the rebellion was an American named Gideon Pratt. While he and his wife endured the Thousand Cuts, their church—Tennessee Baptist Redeemer—was burned to the ground. Among Pratt's possessions, the Boxers found a notebook stored with items from his military days. Spoils from the mission were shipped to Beijing for use in imperial propaganda. That's how Parker's *Field Notes* concerning the Yellow Skull fell into the hands of the Warlord of the Fankuang Tzu.

Today those *Notes* were on a table in the Kwans' Ancestral Hall.

The Hall was part of the Inner Sanctum surrounded by the drug complex near the Walled City of Kowloon. Here, in porcelain spirit jars, the Kwans preserved the mortal remains of their ancestors. The jars lined the wall behind the sacrificial altar, on either side of which hung the yang knives and beheading swords of previous warlords. Adorned with clay, cloisonne, lacquer, and ivory, the altar bore Chinese symbols for longevity. The Bat and Peach. The Three Fruits. The Crane and Stag. A tortoise—denoting long life—crawled around the floor.

Two cushions lay on the tiles before the altar. On one kneeled the present Warlord of the Fankuang Tzu. On the other kneeled his grandson, the Cutthroat Becoming. Four times they kowtowed in family respect, banging their heads on the floor three times with each prostration. The Warlord offered a libation with the sacrifice, splashing wine on the altar around the severed head. Rising to face east, they keened in lament, then the Warlord read a funeral ode. "Sons respect your fathers, brothers your elder brothers, and generation to generation honor your ancestors." As Cutthroat lit incense and cracked the skull, the Warlord burned the funeral ode. One side of the glistening brain was a yang knife. On the other, silver chopsticks.

The Warlord ate.

Opposite the altar, halfway across the room, was the table with Parker's *Field Notes*. Flanking the *Notes* were other items related to the Search: the Oracle Bone which first prescribed the Yang, Zhamtsarano's map detailing where Almas could be found, and *Parker's Journal* stolen from DeClercq's home.

"Is the expedition ready?" the Warlord asked.

"It will be in a few days."

"Can the white monkey's notes be read?"

"That's a problem. His handwriting's bad."

"Then you know what to do. Drain the source."

"Yes, Warlord. When I return."

Suddenly, for no reason, the old man laughed. The shrill, inappropriate giggle pleased Cutthroat. Kuru disease was terminal. Soon Fankuang Tzu would be his.

"The man in the Pit? What damage has he done?"

"We think he sent DeClercq's map to the Gong An Ju. Indications are he's the minister's son."

The Warlord glowered. "Qi breached the Inner Sanctum?"

"The woman you summoned was the man's lover. That's how he stole the map from the Ancestral Hall. She took it when you asked her to be inseminated."

"Qi's son?" Kwan said, savoring the thought. "Then let's give special attention to his questioning."

Cutthroat approached the table spread with Parker's books. He pushed a button behind one leg, sliding back a trapdoor in the floor. Lighting a torch, he led the Warlord down to the Pit.

Forty feet below the Ancestral Hall, a subterranean tunnel ran to the Labs. The door to the Pit was at the foot of the stairs, an oak slab that creaked as it was unlocked. The Warlord giggled out of control.

MIDNIGHT OIL

Thursday, March 19, 12:02 A.M.

It is so cold in the underground morgue he fears his eyes will freeze, fears he'll be frozen staring forever at this atrocity. Before him lies his mother, stiff in an autopsy tray, her body naked, her flesh blue, her breasts transparent. Embarrassed that strangers who enter the morgue can see her sex, he averts his attention to what is left of her head. Facial muscles locked in a rictus of abject terror, the top of her skull is sawn open and she is missing her brain. Severed arteries and veins poke into her cranial vault.

His father, flown down from Beijing, stands at his side. Expression as hard as the terracotta statues at Xian, the minister stares angrily at both autopsy trays. "Look and remember," his father says, guiding his tear-stained face back whenever he turns away.

His brother Wai lies dead in the second tray: also naked, also blue, also robbed of his brain. Condensation films the table supporting both trays, which he absently smears with one fidgety hand. The image revealed on the stainless steel should be that of a boy, so he's perplexed when his reflection shows a grown man.

I must be dreaming, *he thinks with relief as he hears his father say, "I know who did this—"*

(laughter)

"—seen similar deaths before. In the Tien Shan Mountains at the Battle for Chingho."

(distant laughter as)

Shivering, he awoke.

For a moment Qi Fang-pei didn't know where he was, a split second of elation because the nightmare had passed. He wondered vaguely why he felt unrefreshed by sleep, then realized he'd been out only a minute or two.

He could tell from the size of the blood pool on the floor.

The Little Ease was a cross-hatched cage of diabolic design. Four feet long by three feet wide by two feet high, its dimensions stripped a man of what made him a man. No matter how Qi contorted he couldn't straighten his spine, reducing his level of evolution to that of a hunched ape. The Little Ease, like drips on the forehead, worked psychologically.

Naked, Qi lay in a fetal position, hands cuffed behind his back. Nearby, a brazier of coals heated a small pot. Occasionally the pot spit bubbles of oil toward the cage, spattering the table of surgical instruments between. Transparent, the floor was a sheet of glass with phosphorescent liquid swirling underneath, a yellow river emitting an eerie green glow. Luminescent phantoms shimmered up through the glass, sheening the black curtains flanking the only door. The specters tinted the mummy cases lining the other walls.

Eyes vacant or plucked out, some just human parts, the mummies surrounded Qi while blood dripped down on his cage. Icons of flesh, fetishes, monstrous travesties, his was a captive audience of genetic oddities. A skeleton with rickets and one glass eye. A two-faced fetus floating in a tank of formaldehyde. A woman with a third breast between her natural pair, nipples tattooed with swastikas. A man with a second penis growing from his navel, straddling a six-fingered hand displayed on Belgian lace.

Madcap laughter filled the Pit as the door swung open.

Straining against the bars of his cage, Qi saw two shadows. As they entered, the Kwans glowed green. The Warlord was dressed in conjuror's robes once worn by ancestors who had served the Forbidden City. His long, draping sleeves touched the floor while a ruby the size of an eyeball shone at his throat. A *shou* signifying longevity circled his scrawny chest, and leather straps branded with Taoist symbols hung from his waist. Each strap was tipped with a large yellow tooth.

Cutthroat was dressed in unisex black. Black boots. Black slacks. Black gloves. Black jacket. Black full-face mask. Slits were cut in the hood for his eyes and mouth, revealing dilated pupils and pearl white teeth. Qi had no idea who was behind the mask.

"Are you the minister's son?

"Did you send him the map?"

Cutthroat touched the top of the cage, causing an electric hum. Qi's feet began to move toward his head. Inch by inch the Little Ease shrank claustrophobically, pushing his knees against his chest and crooking his neck. The flesh of one cheek bulged through the cross-hatched squares.

"Are you the minister's son?

"Did you send him the map?"

Cutthroat selected an enema syringe from the surgical instruments. Dipping its tip in the bubbling oil, he filled the tube. Rubber bulb held gingerly, he crouched beside the cage.

"I always start with the genitals, for triple effect. First you try to protect yourself, dreading what's to come. Then the pain is horrific during their destruction. Finally, there's the castrato's lament for manhood lost.

"Now you're a man."

He squeezed the bulb.

"Now a eunuch."

The screech was so loud it drowned the Warlord's tittering. Qi lay on one side with his knees under his chin, genitals exposed by his jackknifed rump. The oil fried his scrotum as he thrashed within the cage.

"Are you the minister's son?

"Did you send him the map?"

It was some time before the hollering died to a moan. The virus drew giggle after mirthless giggle from the Warlord as he played with the pair of beads strung on his Fu Manchu mustache. Cutthroat crossed to the curtains and yanked one back.

"Your life or death is not in issue. Just how you die. Do I destroy you piece by piece or grant you quick release? Answer my questions and your pain will end."

Cutthroat gave the Little Ease a push. It swiveled around so Qi could see the shelf behind the curtain. On it were two large apothecary jars filled with murky liquid and two gray lumps. Opening one, Cutthroat withdrew a jellied mass.

"Your mother's brain," he said, squatting by the cage. "Your brother's brain is in the other jar."

Qi's eyes flew wide with horror as the lump approached his face. The odor of formaldehyde was suffocating. The slits in the black mask descended to his level, then Cutthroat pulsed the brain against the bars. Push . . . ease . . . push . . . ease . . . It throbbed like a heart, gray squares bulging in at Qi. Up close, the green glow revealed its cord-like humps.

"Have her," Cutthroat said, shoving the brain until it was diced into oblong squares. Worm-like chunks plopped onto Qi's skin.

"Are you the minister's son?

"Did you send him the map?

"Does he know about DECO and the Search?"

On entering, Cutthroat had stuck the torch in a bracket on the wall. Retrieving it, he held the flame high above his head. Arms and legs on meat hooks dangled from the ceiling, raining drops of blood on the cage.

"Recognize her?" he asked, drawing the other curtain.

Qi took one look at his lover and gasped. He cringed when he heard the syringe take another gulp. Cutthroat inserted the tube through the bars above his eye.

"During the French Revolution, the guillotine wasn't the end. The human brain can survive for a minute on its oxygen supply. One out of ten aristocrats survived the blade, their still living heads held out to the crowd for ridicule. Technology has advanced since then. Behold this marvel of the Labs. Blink and I'll sear your eye."

The head sat on a platform above an array of machines. Wires attached to the cranium fed an EEG. Blood tubes connected it to a heart–lung pump, while a hemodialysis machine removed metabolic waste. Glass columns of poison-absorbing chemicals acted as a liver, another apparatus maintaining fluid around the brain. Amino acids and nutrients were added through other tubes. Qi let out a cry when his lover's eyes moved.

"There! Do you see it? She recognizes you. The bars shadowing your face . . . I warned you not to blink."

Qi began confessing before the first drop hit his eye, the words coming so fast they jumbled up and slammed one another like a derailed train. Syllables alternated with shrieks until he was wrung dry, while the Warlord stroked his mustache with one-inch fingernails.

A lull in the storm followed, a quiet time of whimpers and the hum of high-tech machines. Blind, Qi heard his tormentor's voice, though he didn't see the mallet and four-foot barbecue spit in his hands.

"I promised you release, and you'll have it the Syrian way. Embrace the black slave," Cutthroat said.

SKELETON

Vancouver
Wednesday, March 18, 4:15 P.M.

Carol's ears were still ringing the day after the concert. She was also sleep-deprived from having made love with Zinc most of the night. By two in the afternoon, her energy was gone.

Chandler and Tate had spent the morning searching Maxwell's home. Having had no luck the day before with the Drug Section files, they hoped for a clue as to what was in the manila envelope stolen from his desk. Again they struck out.

At noon, both cops returned to Special X. Eating lunch, they reviewed reports filed by others working the judges' case. At two, Carol left Zinc and cabbed to her hotel. There she blubbed in the hot tub and swam in the pool, then treated herself to a revitalizing massage. By four-fifteen, she was back to work.

Using the hotel fax machine, she sent her report to Bureau headquarters at Ninth and Pennsylvania. Then sipping coffee in her room, she dialed the Zodiac Squad.

"McIlroy."

"Hello, Mac. It's Carol Tate."

"Hey, Mac. Grab the extension. The tourist's on the line."

"Hi, Tate," McGuire said, munching some sort of food. "Moose, mountains, and Mounties agreeing with you?"

"Weather's the pits."

"That's to be expected. Rain, rain, and more rain in the Northwest. Hope you packed your gumboots and umbrella."

"You get the Redcoats' report on the carpet sample? The Horsemen think their killer wore a body sheath. The residue's low-molecular-weight polyethylene. Same down there?"

"Hairs and fibers came up negative," McIlroy said. "Techs redid the roof of the Carlton Palace. All those choppers, no wonder there's no trace."

"Perp may have torched the sheath in the hotel," McGuire said. "After he came in off the fire escape. Maids would have cleaned up the residue. Unless he washed it down the drain."

"What about the letter?"

"A clever little fraud. Note's a world-class forgery."

"You like puzzles?" McIlroy asked.

"What kinda puzzles?"

"Forensic shit. Egghead stuff like how you show 'Zodiac' is a blind."

"Give her a clue, Mac," McGuire said.

"Ever heard of—and I'm reading here—a micro-anatomical examination of wood-pulp cells?"

"Possibly," said Tate.

"How 'bout a microscopic search for dead planktonic fossil deposits in the surface mineral loading of paper?"

"Doesn't ring a bell."

"According to the techs—I'm still reading—paper is made by chemically or mechanically breaking wood down into its individual cells. The resulting pulp makes newsprint or is mixed with flax and cotton—"

" 'Rag' to the trade." McGuire's color comment.

"—to make paper of better quality. This involves depositing a web of rag and pulp on a wire-mesh screen. A sheet forms when liquid suspending the fibers drains away. As pulp alone is porous and not suitable for ink, spaces between the fibers are filled with a loading of some type. Got that, Tate?"

"Got it," she said.

"First thing the techs did was track down the pulp. Using alkali solution—don't ask me what that's for—they determined the kind of tree and where it grew. Then they checked the loading to see if it was kaolin, chalk, or silica. Chalk was formed eons ago by the sedimentation of plankton, so the little critters' skeletons are preserved as fossils in chalk loading."

"Let me guess," Carol said. "The paper's different?"

"*Au contraire,*" McIlory said. "The paper's the same. Even the watermark matches the 'dandy' on the wire screen."

"The techs did beta radiographs," McGuire added. "Beta rays are electrons ejected during the decay of isotopes like carbon-14. When they checked the film, the techs found—"

"Christ, McGuire! I get the picture. What kinda paper was used?"

"Eaton-watermark Monarch-cut bond."

"Same as the Zodiac letters?"

"Yeah, Murdoch matches."

"Here's another clue," McIlroy said.

Carol slumped back on the bed. This could take awhile.

"Consider the ink," McIlroy said. "Thin-layer chromatography and X-ray spectroscopy separate ink dyes into—"

"What kinda pen?" Tate said.

"Blue-felt Staedtler."

"Same as the other notes?"

"Yeah, it matches the sixties' letters."

"Fine," Carol said. "It must be the writing."

"Girl's a go-getter, Mac. But no cigar. Handwriting matches Zodiac's, Tate."

"The style's the same? The paper's the same? The ink's the same?" she said. "How in hell do we know the letter's a fake?"

"What's the one thing the sniper couldn't discover? The single fact about Zodiac's letters beyond his reach?"

"I hate puzzles," Carol sighed.

"Every book on Zodiac mentions paper, ink, and reproduces writing style. Only one detail requires the *original* letters. Sorry, Tate, but I gotta get technical again."

Carol heard McIlroy flip pages on the phone.

"Says here an electron microscope accelerates atom particles through 30,000 volts to produce X rays. X rays have shorter wavelengths than visible light, so they magnify a paper surface 100,000 times. Because the microscope has a boggling depth of field, it reveals the skeleton of what's been written. With it you can determine—"

"The order in which crossed lines were inked on paper?" Tate said.

"The image shows one pen stroke on top of another—"

"And the strokes on our letter aren't like Zodiac's?

One draws the circle, then adds the cross. The other draws the cross, then adds the circle."

"Close," McGuire said.

"Someone's gone to a lotta trouble to fool us poor dumb cops," McIlroy said. "My gut tells me the perp's got a motive to hide. If the Zodiac sign on the wall up there is ass-backward too, dollars to donuts the motive's Canadian."

"*Au revoir,* Tate," McGuire said. "Send a postcard of the Musical Ride."

MISSING LINK

4:40 P.M.

Robert DeClercq was nine when he fell heir to his father's collection of lead soldiers. The figures depicted the Norman Conquest of England. That Christmas he received a medieval fort and a miniature cannon that shot tiny shells. Hours, then days, he spent holed up in his room, knocking the soldiers off the castle battlements. One by one he gunned them down with the cannon, readjusting the trajectory after every shot. A single soldier, well placed, once took him two weeks to hit. This was back when imagination, not lawsuits, designed toys.

Two days before his tenth birthday, Robert's mother died. His aunt gave him her present: a book of battle plans. Marathon, Agincourt, Culloden Moor, the Plains of Abraham, and Waterloo were a few. Robert pinned the maps to the wall of his new room, using them to organize the soldiers on the floor. Since then—like during the Headhunter case or when he plotted a book—DeClercq habitually arranged his thoughts visually. He was doing that now as MacDougall trudged in.

With a thump the inspector dropped a heavy carton near the door.

"What's that? A box of bricks?"

"Adjudicators Rota. I asked Immigration to send us a list of Maxwell's deportations. They sent their rota going back twenty years."

"See that pile," DeClercq said, pointing to his desk. "Those are Murdoch's judgments on the Court of Appeal. I read for a couple of hours and didn't make a dent."

"Find anything?"

"Nothing relevant. But American precedent has replaced British since we passed the Charter of Rights."

MacDougall studied the spreading collage. Ceiling to floor, the office was walled with corkboard sheets. The left half surveyed the Murdoch case: aerial photographs of the Carlton Palace Hotel, one showing the fire escape descending to the lane; blow-ups of the murder slug and cartridge casings; lists of lawyers at the convention and hotel patrons; the Zodiac letter, forensic reports, shots of the corpse, etc. The right half surveyed the Maxwell case: a blueprint of the Law Courts and a drawing of his chambers; photos of the body, severed head, and blood marks on the walls; a list of those in the building that night, and various other reports. Colored threads tied to pins zigzagged between the cases.

"So?" Jack said. "What's the missing link?"

"Damned if I know," Robert said. "Nothing but dead ends."

"Same with me. We're running out of leads."

MacDougall opened his notebook to a paper-clipped page. "Forensics came up with little but the residue on the carpet. We can't find any motive among those with the access code. Drug Section knows nothing beyond the obvious about the Colombians. And neither chief justice has any idea what was in the envelope. Nothing's missing from the file of Maxwell's only trial."

DeClercq approached the blueprint of the Law Courts. "What about the people in the Great Hall?"

"The jury trial on the fifth floor involved two Asian gangs. The spectators milling around were Asians too. Chan interviewed those who'd speak to us, but they saw no one suspicious the night Maxwell was killed."

"*Two* gangs, you say?"

"The trial grew out of a fight."

"So there were two groups of spectators? One for each side?"

"No love lost between them, that's for sure."

"Say the killer came in with the public that night. If the spectators were all Asian, a white would stand out. But if the killer was Asian too, he'd be camouflaged. Each side would think he was with the other."

"If it's an Asian," Jack said, "the motive could be deportation." He indicated the carton he'd dropped near the door."

"What about Doumani? The other judge in chambers?"

"Clean as a whistle. Stalwart of the bench."

A knock at the door interrupted them. Chandler entered. "I just spoke to Carol. The Zodiac note's a fraud. The forger strokes his letters differently."

Zinc reversed and straddled a chair, cradling his arms along its back.

"Even more interesting, Maxwell's killer does the same. The circle and cross on the Murdoch note and Maxwell's wall are juxtaposed opposite to Zodiac's sign. Unless the judges are connected, that's one hell of a coincidence."

"Who wants coffee?" Jack said, glancing at his watch. "There's a call I have to make."

Zinc held up his hand. He scanned the collage.

"Make it three," Robert said. "And do me a favor? Napoleon's still sick and at the vet's. Have someone call and ask when he'll be home."

"Do it myself," Jack said. "What's the number?"

DeClercq opened his wallet and removed a lottery ticket. "Number's on the back." He handed Jack the slip.

MacDougall left as Chandler said, "They've got to be connected. Two Canadian judges linked to the Zodiac symbol. The killer's *not* Zodiac, and Maxwell wasn't juked by a copycat. If the same guy drew both symbols, the same guy killed both judges."

"What gets me," DeClercq said, "is the MO of these murders. Both are high-tech and audacious, way beyond what's required. Why kill Murdoch in San Francisco with all that risk? Why not stage an accident in B.C.? Why breach chambers to slit Maxwell's throat? Surely the envelope could be obtained by safer means. It's almost as if alien thinking is behind both crimes. The judges are linked. My gut says so."

"The motive must be tied to law. The envelope is the key."

"So what was in it?"

"Papers. Documents from a case."

"What case?" DcClercq said. "Bounce the options."

"It can't be the Colombians. Nothing was appealed."

"It can't be an appellate case. Maxwell didn't argue in court."

"It can't be a deportation. They go to Federal Appeal."

"Unless . . ." DeClercq said.

Zinc snapped his fingers. "The case goes back *ten* years."

"Murdoch became a judge in 1979."

"Maxwell judged deporation hearings from 1966 until recently."

"So what if Murdoch defended a case between 1966 and 1979?"

"An immigration matter. Someone being deported."

"Someone who now wants the facts permanently forgotten."

WHERE MONEY BUYS EVERYTHING

4:51 P.M.

Three floors down from the East/West Room, the Californian paced the Hall of the Future at Fankuang Tzu. At least once a minute he glanced at the clocks on the wall, the left tracking Vancouver time, the right the time in Hong Kong. In Asia it was almost 9:00 A.M. the following day, while here dusk gathered its shawl around the city. Impatiently he crossed to the bank of video screens.

> "Should your heart or kidneys fail, will lack of a suitable donor mean your death? Fankuang Tzu Pharmaceutical, using nuclear transplantation, will soon clone duplicates for you. By replacing an embryo's nucleus with one from your cells, genetically matched organs will be harvested from our surrogate mothers. The clones will be frozen in our Labs for future need, solving problems of availability and tissue rejection. Organ donors will be obsolete."

On-screen, a ward of patients languished near cardiac monitors and dialysis machines. As Beethoven's *Emperor* concerto rose on the soundtrack, they left their beds and support systems behind. Through French doors, they strolled out to a glorious new dawn.

Scowling at the clocks, the Californian moved to the next video. There were audio buttons for English, Mandarin, Cantonese, Japanese, and French. He punched English.

> "As you watch this video, your brain cells are dying. Each dead cell is never replaced. Instead of diminishing tissue working 100 million times slower than a computer, would you not prefer to have the mind of

a god? Fankuang Tzu Pharmaceutical will soon test the Biochip—a supercomputer of organic protein for implant in the brain. All the world's knowledge will be stored in your head, and because you will "live" in the Biochip instead of your brain, when your body dies we'll move it to a new host. Emperors have long dreamed of immortality. You'll be one of the first to enjoy an immortal soul."

On-screen, a group of scholars wandered about the Library of Congress discussing Einstein's theories.

The Californian was watching the next video when Martin Kwan entered the room.

"Are the aches and pains of old age getting you down? Fankuang Tzu Pharmaceutical is developing Dynorphin, a synthetic endorphin that stops pain before it is felt in the brain. Worried your sexual prowess is not what it used to be? Fankuang Tzu Pharmaceutical has developed a drug from the sap of the *Coryanthe yohimbe* tree. Mixed with naloxone, it binds with receptor molecules in the sperm ducts—"

"Sorry I'm late," Kwan said, punching the off button. "A business call from Hong Kong kept me on the phone."

"Quite an operation," the American said. "How many floors are your company's?"

"We own the building. At present we use eight. Once the transfer is complete, we'll occupy the rest."

"And that?" Jackson said, indicating an architect's model in a case.

"Our new factory under construction here. Original plans called for a thousand employees. Recent developments have tripled that estimate. The photograph beside it is our complex in Hong Kong. It currently employs thirty thousand people."

Kwan led the Californian to his corner office.

"Tea or coffee, Mr. Jackson?"

"Coffee," the businessman said.

"Costa Rican or Turkish espresso?"

"Either," he replied.

When Kwan snapped his fingers, a beauty in a tight

chong-sam materialized. The Asians spoke Cantonese and the woman disappeared.

The lawyer's office was decorated with pre-Columbian art. Thick Oriental carpets graced the parquet floor. The room commanded a breathtaking view of the harbor, Stanley Park, and the North Shore peaks. Skiers performed lazy *S*'s down the Cut on Grouse, while choppers flew the well-heeled over the mountains to Whistler.

"So," Kwan said. "Shall we get down to business? I understand Chuck Fraser referred you to me?"

"He said you met in San Francisco at the bar convention. He said the two of you struck a 'finder's deal'?"

"That we did. What do you need?"

"A heart and a kidney for my son."

Both men wore the power suits of the corporate elite, but Kwan's, tailored in Hong Kong, was a better fit. The Asian exuded confidence with energy to spare: his slickness that of a man who can smell money a mile away. The American, however, had gone to seed: a lethargic, atrophied sad sack who'd seen better times. Each man personified his economy.

The beauty entered with coffee in Royal Doulton. Unobtrusively she passed each man a cup. Jackson waited until she left the room.

"Time is of the essence, Mr. Kwan," he said. "If I don't find the organs soon, my only son will die."

With manicured fingers Kwan raised his cup. "Are there no donors in the States?" he asked through its steam.

"Ten thousand Americans need kidney transplants. The number requiring new hearts is as daunting. My boy has complications and can't wait in those queues."

"There are other means."

"I hired an organization to steal the organs from funeral homes. The deal fell through when the FBI arrested the group. An organ-procurement agency bought me a kidney from a derelict. It turned out he had AIDS. I was considering murder when Chuck told me about you."

"Where's your son now?"

"In L.A. with his mother."

"Can you fly him to Hong Kong?"

"I have a company jet."

"The price is two million dollars. Including the operation."

"It can be wired today."

"There are . . . requirements. Safety precautions."

"I don't care. I'll do *anything*."

The lawyer put down his coffee. "Then we have a deal."

"You have the organs?"

"Donated as we speak. In Hong Kong, the market is unfettered by rules. Survival of the fittest governs needs. Why should life-saving commodities be wasted on the poor, on those unfit to survive in the marketplace? Fan-kuang Tzu will meet your needs. Welcome to Hong Kong, Mr. Jackson. Money buys everything here."

"Here?" the American said, glancing out the window.

"By 1997, there won't be any difference."

BLACK SLAVE

On the Pearl River, People's Republic of China
Thursday, March 19, 1:30 P.M.

They were hunting snakeheads, these Red Chinese police.

Three weeks before, a customs official in Hong Kong had pulled over one of the seven thousand trucks that travel daily between China's Guangdong Province and the New Territories. Inspecting the cargo of crates bound for the colony, packed inside he found nine frightened girls. Two weeks before that, marine police patrolling the colony's outer harbor intercepted an inbound launch. Cowering in the hold were a dozen crying girls. Eight days before that, a routine sweep of the marshlands between Hong Kong and the Chinese border turned up a sampan floating in the reeds. Huddled together beneath an oilcloth stretched across the stern were five drenched girls six to eight years old. Four snakeheads were arrested.

The child-smuggling trade of South China began for laudable reasons. The People's Republic grants seventy-five one-way permits a day to those who want to live and work in Hong Kong. To make sure dollars earned there are spent in China, Beijing allows just one child per family to leave. Inevitably this policy spawned a criminal racket, so for a fee of $2,000 or more, snakeheads will smuggle a child from Guangdong Province to its parents waiting in Hong Kong.

In rural China the birth of a girl is considered a curse. Despite economic advances, Chinese peasants are rooted to feudal ideas. Confucian tradition honors men and despises women. The government aggravated this bias by decreeing each family could have but one child. With prenatal sex tests, China's abortion rate has soared to nine million a year. Most terminations are among women expecting girls. Crimes of female infanticide are common, usually by suffocation with a wet towel.

Supply and demand control every market, including the black. China has millions of girls nobody wants, while the noveau riche of Hong Kong have sexual needs to fill and toilets to be cleaned. Both sides pay well in this human traffic, so they were hunting snakeheads, these Red Chinese police.

It was now mid-afternoon and the Pearl was crammed with boats.

No other country has as many ships afloat on its territorial waters as China. All the main rivers and coastal ports have a floating population with no other home. The number of junks and sampans alone exceeds the rest of the world's shipping combined.

A city of almost four million people with fifty million more out in the countryside, Canton—Guangzhou—straddles the apex of the Pearl River Delta seventy miles north of the South China Sea. Downstream, where river and ocean meet, sits Hong Kong.

From Shamian Island city center to the container port of Huangpu fifteen miles away, a yawing, bobbing, creaking armada tossed on the brown-capped waves. Buffeted by a warm wind out of a stifling sky, freighters and tankers and ocean tramps and chugging public ferries, barge trains and gunboats and leaking sampans with kitchen pots clanking, passenger liners and hydrofoils and cargo tugs moving goods ship-to-shore and ship-to-ship, rocked back and forth on the river tide. While beggar boats hung around the waste chutes of steamers, and *fa-shuen* flower boats attracted singsong girls, Amoy trawlers, bulging with fish, tacked around a junk. Out of control, the red slipper junk plowed into a dock.

The police boat turned.

Window-trimmed on three sides, it was open like a corvette. The drab gray bridge was armed with a .50-caliber machine gun. As one cop, Mongolian, primed the gun, his Han partner veered the launch toward the junk.

Onshore, the collision had caused a stir. Behind silver fishnets strung to dry, cabbies and coolies and kids in jeans gawked at the wreck. Crushed amid the splintered dock were gooey kegs of black tar and crates of oyster paste. Laughing children and yelping dogs scampered across the decks of boats moored nearby. While hampers of ginger and lotus root surfaced in the water, the launch pulled up alongside the junk. A faded black eyeball painted on its bow glared at the muddy river and demolished dock.

High-sterned, square-bowed, flat-bottomed with no keel, junks are the workhorse of China's merchant marine. Though all junks are shoe-shaped, the red slipper is most shoe-shaped of all. Legend is the shipwrights of P'oyang Lake were told by the emperor to build a new boat. Bored with the meeting and wanting it to end, the empress kicked off her slipper and said, "Design it like that."

Eyes squinted beneath the red star on his cap, the Mongol grabbed hold of a notch in the bulwark cut to house a cannon last century and pulled himself up the port side. As the deck above him rose and fell with the chop, brown batwing sails banged against the masts. Several horizontal battens had snapped, tattering the matting, which flapped in the wind. Fatter, with wary eyes in wire-rim specs, the Han cop followed on his heels.

The deck was a mess.

Heaps of litter, clumps of mud, pools of oil-slicked water fouled its planks. Amidships, the remnants of a meal lay strewn near the cabin: chicken bones, beer bottles, tangerine skins. Foot-long rats with swishing tails abandoned rancid pork to hide from the cops. Rattan baskets had tipped in the collision, scattering hunks of maggoty meat about the cabin door. The door banged in time with the slapping lugsails.

Guns drawn, they entered the amidships cabin.

Dark and murky inside, the stench was nauseating. The Han cop lit a match so they could see, prompting strident squeals from deck-level mouths. The body of a naked man hung from the ceiling, gravity making the fly-infested flesh sag from his bones. A four-foot barbecue skewer hammered into his anus had pierced intestines, stomach, and heart before cracking out through his head. Both ends of the horizontal spit were hooked to ceiling chains, so his limbs dangled inches from the deck. Feasting rats had stripped his toes and fingers of meat.

The Han cop found an oily rag which, wrapped around a stick, he ignited.

While the spit swayed to and fro with the chop, they circled the body, noting wounds.

Not only had the brain been removed from the skull, but the eyes and scrotum were severely blistered.

The Mongol was looking at cross-hatched bruises purpling the skin when his partner drew his attention to the far wall.

There, written in blood, were Chinese characters:

有一個人，他有

兩個兒子…

CASELOAD

Vancouver
Thursday, March 19, 10:46 A.M.

Though Hutton Murdoch had changed lovers as often as he changed socks, he'd kept the same secretary for seven years. Stern-faced, with mousy hair in a bun and wearing sensible shoes, Faith Peters reminded Zinc of the prairie schoolmarm who had cracked his knuckles for throwing spitballs in class. She was the kind of no-nonsense assistant who made a boss look good, which no doubt explained why Cutter had commandeered her as his own.

"Let's make this snappy," Peters said. "I have a judgment to type."

Murdoch's chambers reflected a man of refined taste. Originals by Gathie Falk, Philippe Raphanel, and Gordon Smith hung on the walls. The furniture was from the shops along South Granville, law books and papers spread across a black walnut desk. Zinc picked up the nearest text and glanced at its title: *Champagne Cork Injuries to the Eye.*

"Americans," Peters said, sniffing with disdain. "We put the law of torts in a single volume. They devote an entire book to that."

She thinks I'm a Mountie, Carol thought. *Or she's Acne's mother.*

"Did Murdoch ever mention Trent Maxwell?" Zinc asked.

"Not that I recall."

Peters removed the book from his hands, returning it to the desk. She set it down in perfect alignment with one corner.

"Who was Murdoch's secretary when he was in practice?"

"Jane Forsyth. Alzheimer's disease."

Scanning the shelves, Carol asked, "Are his court diaries here?"

"The current one. The rest are at home with his closed-out files."

Peters straightened the papers on the desk. They had looked straight to Carol before she fussed with them.

"A cluttered office reflects a cluttered mind," Peters said. "I made sure we didn't drown in litter from the past. At the end of each month I packaged up his closed-out files. Hutton removed them from chambers along with his diaries. He was writing a book. A text on criminal law."

"His files from practice? Were they destroyed?"

"Discard a client's file and a lawyer can be sued. Both practice files and bench files he kept at home. He used his cases as examples in his book. His diaries were an index to the files."

"Where did Murdoch live?"

"West Vancouver."

Zinc opened his notebook.

"What's the address?"

West Vancouver
12:15 P.M.

Atop the British Properties, Murdoch's home clung to the slope of Hollyburn Mountain. Below its outdoor hot tub and rock swimming pool, the city of Vancouver was a hazy welcome mat. As Zinc picked the lock with a skeleton key, Carol watched the tugs and freighters bob on English Bay. West of Lions Gate Bridge and Stanley Park, a sullen armada of nimbus clouds approached the coast. "After you," Zinc said, springing the door.

The house was an architect's maze of cedar and glass. Four wings encased a central court like steps around a shaft. In a loft crowning the highest wing they found the closed-out files, alphabetically arranged along three walls. The fourth side was solid glass behind a free-standing fireplace.

"Jesus," Tate said. "Must be five thousand files. We'll be retired before we're through them all."

"See the diaries in your search?"

"No."

"Neither did I."

"Could be in his car."

"They're not in the report. It was found at the airport and searched."

"Someone burned a file," she said, crouching by the hearth. Tate plucked an Acco fastener from the ashes.

"Probably Murdoch."

"Or someone else."

"Someone who burned the file *and* the diaries?"

"Not enough ashes for it to be both."

"Think he took them with him?"

"Then why not take the file? Why burn one and not the other?"

"Suppose he found the file but not the diaries."

"Then where are they?"

"Murdoch's retreat. Remember Cutter's comment about the judge? 'Hutton's idea of a holiday was to take the latest texts to his Gulf Island cabin and read.' "

"Where's Gulf Island?"

"Islands, Carol. They're in the Strait of Juan de Fuca. We flew over them."

Approaching Pender Island
3:52 P.M.

The JetRanger's shadow flitted across the angry waves. Through the bug-eyed cockpit of the Bell 206, Carol saw the brooding hump of North Pender Island. Wind whipped the trees that cloaked its rocky cliffs, behind which a darkening sky heralded a storm. As the helicopter hovered above a rugged beach, its whirling blades threw up gritty clouds of broken shell. "Move fast," the pilot shouted over the noise. "If the storm gets any worse, we'll spend the night here."

A zigzag staircase scaled the cliff to Hutton Murdoch's "cabin." On a thirty-foot bluff overlooking the strait, the cedar tepee was three stories high. Roof indents created a series of pointed gables, and a stained-glass window was set into the southern slant. *Must have done a lot of drug work,* Tate thought.

As the chopper set down, a killer whale breached in

the channel. A bald eagle flew over the whupping blades. Carol and Zinc, scrambling out, headed for the staircase. Halfway up, the first rain began to fall.

Zinc burgled the door with his skeleton key.

Once inside, they split up to save time. As Carol tossed the upper floors, Zinc searched the main level. In a fridge in back of the bar he found a chilled bottle of Dom Perignon Brut. At $79.95, he didn't taste it often. *If I were murdered and two cops were hunting* my *killer, I'd bequeath them bubbly as an incentive reward.* He found two glasses and carried the Dom to the second floor.

The stained-glass window was a mosaic of Christ with the words "AND THE SON OF GOD" beneath his feet. Murdoch had shared a trait with DeClercq, in that both organized their thoughts on the wall. A long sheet of paper ran around the room. On it was drawn a time line of thirty-six years. Case names like *R.* v. *Sinclair* and *Wright* v. *The Queen* were penciled at points along the graph. On a table near Carol were thirty-six diaries.

Zinc popped the champagne.

"If the killer burned the file, he overlooked these. Bet he didn't know Murdoch had this place."

"No record of it in West Vancouver," Zinc said. "His tax papers are probably at his accountant's."

A crack of lightning sounded overhead.

"To us," he said, passing her a glass.

"And to Murdoch," Carol said. "May these find his killer."

"Hungry?"

"Famished."

"Then let's pack up and leave. Your choice. Sushi, Italian, or Chinese?"

"Let's get our fortunes told," she said.

FORBIDDEN CITY

Beijing, People's Republic of China
Friday, March 20, 8:01 A.M.

North of Tiananmen Square, the Gate of Heavenly Peace guards the Forbidden City. Built in 1651, it's one hundred ten feet tall. From its top the emperor's edicts written on scrolls were flung to his officials humbly kneeling below. Five doors pierce the gate and seven marble bridges span the stream in front. Only the emperor could use the central bridge and door. Transgressors were summarily put to death.

Mao proclaimed the People's Republic from the gate's parapet in 1949. Today a giant portrait of Mao hangs from its rostrum. Behind the gate stretch the palace grounds. Here in Zhongshan Park is the Altar of Land and Grain. Each of the altar's sections was filled with a different colored earth to symbolize that the emperor owned all land. A tiny pavilion resembling a lantern is next to the park. If an official made a mistake, his cap was placed in the pavilion before he was executed.

Farther north is dull red Meridian Gate. Reserved exclusively for the emperor's use, its gongs and bells announced his coming and going. Here the Son of Heaven reviewed the Imperial Guard, passed judgment on prisoners, and watched his ministers flogged. Those who entered without permission were decapitated.

Beyond Meridian Gate, which spans the palace moat, meanders the Golden Stream, shaped like a Tartar bow. Across five bridges reflected in its water, two immense bronze lions flank the Gate of Supreme Harmony. The courtyard behind this gate holds one hundred thousand people, a square dominated by the Three Great Halls of the Forbidden City. High on a marble terrace approached by three flights of stairs, the Halls were "the Center of the World" to the Middle Kingdom.

Here in pomp and luxury, the emperor lived in nine thousand rooms served by one hundred thousand eunuchs and ten thousand concubines. The Palace of Heavenly Purity, the Tower of Propitious Clouds, the Caves of the House of Fairies, and many more were his. The name of each concubine was on a jade tablet in the royal chambers. By turning one over, the Son of Heaven made his request for the night. The eunuch on duty then scurried off to find the chosen lady. Stripped so she was "weaponless," the foot-bound female was piggybacked to the royal boudoir and dumped at the emperor's feet. Before leaving, the eunuch recorded the date to legitimize any heir.

The Eunuch Clinic supplied the palace with men who survived the chop. Castration was done with a sharp knife while the candidate sat on a chair with a hole in its seat. Half those who endured the chop bled to death. Those who survived to serve carried their severed ornaments around in a silk pouch. Mutilation of any kind was a bar to the afterlife. They hoped the pouch would deceive the spirits into thinking them whole.

The Hall of Supreme Harmony was the most important building. A turtle-shaped incense burner out front entreated longevity. Until the last emperor fell in 1911, the lacquered hall within was China's holiest of holies. Here beneath a pillared ceiling embossed with a gold dragon, Mount Xumi carved behind to signify paradise, veils of smoke creeping up its yellow-carpeted stairs, the statues on either side a pair of cranes, towered the seat of the emperor: the magnificent Dragon Throne.

In silk, the Son of Heaven sat with the known world at his feet. While gongs bonged and wind chimes tinkled, those before him kowtowed in respect, banging the floor nine times with their foreheads. His word would send one hundred thousand men to war. Disturbing his serenity meant beheading on the spot. The emperor's power was absolute, for he controlled all things.

Except the man who controlled him.

The Warlord of the Fankuang Tzu.

East of the red wall around the Forbidden City, headquarters of the Gong An Ju face Beichizi Dajie. Sunlight deflecting off the roof tiles of the palace crossed the wall and the street to gild its upper windows. Behind the sheen of gold sat Minister Qi.

In his eighties, Qi Yuxiang was crippled by a stroke. His blue Mao jacket hung loose on his withered frame, his body eaten by liver cancer. The sun scars on his pinched face were from the Long March, for he'd helped forge the party sixty years before. The photos on the wall beside him showed a vibrant man: Qi with Mao and Chou En-lai, Qi with Richard Nixon, Qi with Deng Xiaoping, Qi with Margaret Thatcher. His health gone, he now had a few months to live.

"Minister?"

Qi looked up from his desk.

"The fax is sent," his secretary said.

"I'll be with my doctor if there's a reply."

On his desk were three snapshots and a map. One was of his wife and sons in 1962. Hair and clothing whipped by wind that later became a typhoon, they stood near Canton's Temple of the Six Banyan Trees. In the second photograph, from 1963, their bodies blue against the steel of autopsy trays, his wife and younger son lay in a morgue. Their skulls were cracked open and missing brains.

The final photograph was taken the day before. It showed his elder son skewered on the junk, head cut open and minus its brain.

Behind the body, Chinese characters were scrawled in blood.

"There was a man who had two sons . . ." they read.

Vancouver
Thursday, March 19, 4:01 P.M.

Special X had its own communications room. The member wiring it was Inspector Eric Chan. Chan was present when the Beijing fax came through. He stood by the machine as it emerged.

REQUEST INFORMATION CONCERNING FANKUANG TZU PHARMACEUTICAL COMPANY OF HONG KONG. OWNER:

CROWN COLONY RESIDENT KWAN KOK-SU. PLEASE INTERPRET MEANING OF THIS MAP.

The sender, Qi Yuxiang, was the minister in charge of the Gong An Ju.

The Gong An Ju was China's Public Security Bureau. Its police.

The map was of the mountains around Jasper National Park.

"To the Expedition" was written in Chinese down the left.

Windigo Mountain was circled in black.

An arrow ran from the circle to the right margin.

There, four Western capitals were lettered.

D E C O, they read.

CHINATOWN

5:12 P.M.

Chinatown.
East and West.
Confronting in no man's land.

They came to find gold and work, but they found hate instead.

The first Chinese immigrants to settle in B.C. swept north from the California mines in 1858 when gold was discovered along the Fraser and Thompson rivers. Once news of the Cariboo Gold Rush echoed back to China, hundreds more quit the Middle Kingdom with its wars, overcrowding, and famine.

The next wave of immigrants came to build the CPR through the Rocky Mountains. Hired because Asian coolies worked cheaper than whites, and because they didn't balk at hazardous jobs, between 1881 and 1884 the Canadian Pacific Railway imported fifteen thousand Chinese. While little English girls skipped rope to this refrain:

> Chinky, Chinky, Chinaman
> Sitting on a rail,
> Along came a choo-choo train
> To snip off his pigtail

the coolies said a Chinese died for every foot of railroad. This, of course, was an exaggeration. It only cost a Chinese life for every quarter mile.

Chinatown was founded on an act of fraud. Coolies hired in Asia were told their return fare would be paid once the job was done. When this promise wasn't kept, they found themselves stranded in a hostile land. To survive they had to work as houseboys, gardeners, cooks, and fishermen for whites. Beaten regularly by marauding thugs, they settled together in "Shanghai Alley," a low-lying, unhealthy part of False Creek. The main road—Dupont Street—they shared with the whores.

Many whites considered "the yellow menace" a threat. Secretive and inscrutable, they were "an emotionless race." They babbled a singsong language grating to "civilized" ears, and had the nerve to eke profits from abandoned mines. Worst of all, the Chinese worked for lower wages. Many a factory hung the sign "NO ENGLISHMEN NEED APPLY."

As Chinatown grew in size, so did the colonists' hate. Between 1878 and 1913, twenty-four anti-Asian statutes became law. Chinese were denied the vote and barred from government jobs. Banned from the professions, they couldn't attend white schools. Chinese women could immigrate as mistresses for whites, but Orientals couldn't hire European women. A head tax was imposed on new arrivals: $10 in 1886, $50 in 1896, $100 in 1900, $500 in 1904.

Finally, in 1907, violence broke out.

The Asiatic Exclusion League was formed that year. A rally it sponsored drew an ugly crowd. Harangued by racist speakers, a mob five thousand strong stormed Chinatown, damaging $25,000 in property and goods. The Chinese retaliated with a general strike, which effectively closed the city's hotels. White hatred grew.

In 1923, the Exclusion Act was passed. It barred all Chinese immigration. The law was not repealed until 1947, and the population of Chinatown reflected its success. In 1921 there were 6,500 Asians. Thirty years later, there were 8,750.

Pro-communist riots rocked Hong Kong in 1967. They sparked a new wave of Chinese immigration. Fearing their newfound status and wealth in imminent jeopardy, the colony's "yacht people" dispersed relatives overseas. When Britain agreed to give China Hong Kong in 1997, what began as a wave grew to a tidal flood.

Today, 150,000 strong, the Chinese make up twenty-three percent of Vancouver's population.

This may explode to forty percent before the colony dies.

Bursting at the seams, Chinatown has changed.

* * *

Zinc parked the car at Pender and Carrall. Popping umbrellas, they stepped into the rain. "See that building? On the corner?" he said. "It's in *Ripley's Believe It or Not.*"

Carol eyed the two-story with big bay windows. "I don't see why," she said.

Umbrella cascading rain, he led her up the street.

"Unbelievable," she said, viewing it from the side. "Three feet wide and people work in there?"

"Four feet eleven inches, actually. The Sam Kee Building is the narrowest in the world."

"There must be a story?"

"In 1910 the city widened Pender Street. All Chang Toy's land except this sliver was expropriated. The city refused to compensate him for the remaining strip, so his neighbors in Shanghai Alley thought they'd get it for a song. To spite them, Chang built the narrowest building in the world, using tunnels and bay windows to maximize space."

"I like guys who won't be pushed around," Carol said.

As the purple veil of twilight masked the dragon's face, the neon lights of Chinatown lit its eyes. Pausing here and there, the cops strolled up the street, while rain gurgled in the gutters and splashed their feet. Past *The Chinese Times,* which still used handset type, and Dr. Sun Yat-sen Gardens with its ancient rocks, they crossed Columbia to approach Main. Carol gazed up at the dripping facade of an elegant green building, red filigree balconies lining its front. The year 1909 was gilded below its roof.

"The Chinese Benevolent Association," said Zinc.

"The balconies are all recessed. They're not in San Francisco."

"Unlike yours, our Chinese are mostly from Guangdong. That's the province around Hong Kong. Eric Chan—you'll meet him—says inset balconies are unique to South China."

"Pagoda phone booths. Nice touch."

The narrow shops were crammed with Asian bric-a-brac: wigs and fans and tea sets and multi-armed jade idols; ivory Buddhas and mandarin chessmen and lacquered cabinets; chops and cookware and wicker and porcelain panda bears. Red lanterns burned in some of the stores to bring good luck, while the pungent smell of incense wafted into the street.

"Is gambling legal here?"

"No," Zinc said.

Carol drew his attention to a rundown barber shop. Through its grimy windows and behind a row of plants, men with fists full of dollars paced a smoke-filled room. One shouted guttural Cantonese while another repeatedly banged a mah-jongg tile on the table. A third in a dirty undershirt tallied the score.

"The VPD has six Chinese-speaking cops," Zinc said. "Proportionately there should be two hundred."

"Good planning," Carol said.

"Typical," he replied. "Only recently has the Force begun ethnic recruitment. Chinatown's an unpoliced no man's land."

Main Street is home to the derelict, the loser, and the lost. It cuts the throat of Chinatown north and south. As they crossed Main heading for Gore, a black Trans Am "boom car" screeched down the street.

"Bet this was an opium den in years gone by," Carol said. They stopped in front of a deserted butcher shop. A sign in the window announced the space would soon be occupied by Fankuang Tzu Medicinal Meats. From an alcove beside the shop a set of stairs ascended to a pair of swing doors. Beyond the doors, a sagging staircase disappeared above. Three punks in black leather jackets, white T-shirts, and black jeans descended the steps. When they saw the round-eyes, they paused and sneered.

"They look friendly," Carol said. "Wicked tattoos. Must be their clubhouse upstairs?"

"Who knows," Zinc said. "Can't keep track of the gangs. New ones form every week."

"Refugees, huh?"

"Most of them. One hundred twenty-four thousand claimants have yet to be processed. The gangs recruit them right off the plane."

"The problem with immigrants," Carol said, "is they don't arrive with our values. To some, democracy means a haven to run amok. Tolerance should stop when the drive-by shootings start."

"We busted this kid," Chandler said, "for knifing a gang rival. He'd escaped from Vietnam with his mother, crammed in a small fishing boat with a hundred others. Two days out of port the engine stalled, leaving them adrift on the open seas. When food ran out, the crew pulled guns on the refugees. They were forced to draw lots to see who'd become meat. The kid's mom lost the lottery, so she was shot. He watched her butchered and consumed piece by piece. No wonder he arrived with no respect for rules."

The Kuomintang Building is at Pender and Gore. Along Gore was their destination, the Good Luck Restaurant. Beside it was a Chinese pharmacy. Recently the name on the window had been changed. It now read Fankuang Tzu Pharmaceutical Inc.

"Man, this riles me," Carol said, gazing in the window. "How many animals were killed to get these 'drugs'?"

"Each beet-shaped sac cost a bear," Zinc said. "The Air India flight that exploded in 1985? The one from Toronto? Went down in the Irish Sea? Reported lost with the plane were two suitcases weighing thirty-five pounds each. The shipper claimed the luggage contained the dried gall bladders of one thousand Canadian bears. His out-of-pocket loss was $125,000. Had the bladders reached the Orient, they'd have been worth a million bucks."

Chandler pointed to the antler rack on display. Wafer-thin flakes cut from it were in a tray below.

"Last year an exporter called the Northwest Territories Wildlife Service," he said. "The Asian asked if it was true by treaty Indians could hunt caribou out of season. If so, he wished to place an order for one hundred metric tons of antlers in velvet. He said he'd front the Indians fifty dollars a pound if they stacked the racks on the tundra so his firm could pick them up by helicopter. The order meant slaughtering 22,000 caribou. The Indians would get $11,000,000.

"See that?" Zinc said. "It's a tiger's penis. And that over there's rhinoceros horn."

"What's the 'medical' theory behind killing endangered species?"

"Don't know exactly," he said. "It's some sort of yin-yang thing."

BUSINESS DEAL

5:24 P.M.

As Carol and Zinc moved up the street, the Alley Demons entered the butcher shop. Locking the door behind them, they descended to the cellar under Pender Street. Waiting, they talked about the money they'd be paid that night, until a car engine sounded in the lane.

Someone entered the back door.

Footsteps on the stairs.

A man in a business suit.

"Where is he?" asked Martin Kwan.

The punks opened the freezer and disappeared inside. The round-eye they dragged out could barely stand. His hands were tied behind his back, and his eyes darted with fright. A gag secured the racquetball wedged in his mouth. Breathing through his nose had coated the gag with ice, while the tears down his cheeks were streaks of rime.

"Mr. Lee," Kwan said. "About your land?"

One of the punks started the slicing machine.

"Our factory will be three times as large as planned. We need your real estate to expand."

The rotor saw whirred, picking up speed.

"You'll not sell to Taiwan. You'll sell to me. It's merely a question of how much encouragement you need."

The punks untied the white's hands, then pulled him toward the machine.

"You may not have reached the airport, thanks to my friends, but your ticket to Taipei is being used. People vanish in Taiwan all the time."

As one of the punks moved Lee's hand toward the blade, Kwan produced documents from his briefcase.

"The other hand," Martin said. "He writes with that one."

Back and forth, back and forth, Lee's fingers caressed the machine, shaving off thin-sliced circles like fine corned beef.

"After your fingers, my friends will run your penis across the blade. Tell me when you're ready to sign, Mr. Lee."

Though Lee was screaming behind the gag, only mewling came out. Kwan placed the transfer deed on the table with a gold pen. Lee's head bobbed up and down so fast he whiplashed his neck.

"It would have been easier if you had just accepted my deal. Please be careful not to get blood on the forms."

After the round-eye had sold his land—the document backdated to launder the transaction—the Alley Demons finished the job.

"Chip him into the foundation," Martin said, piling a bundle of cash on the table.

"When do we meet the Red Pole?" one punk asked.

"He returns from Hong Kong tonight."

"Have we proved ourselves?"

"Yes, he is pleased. One more job and you'll be his 49s."

Kwan placed an address on the table.

"When?"

"This evening. Bring DeClercq here for questioning by the Red Pole."

"And if there's trouble?"

"Kill him," Martin said.

FAMILY TREE

Richmond, British Columbia
5:25 P.M.

As the plane roared down the runway, Cutthroat awoke. He shook his head to clear it of the vivid dream. The dream went back twenty years.

Within the Kwans' Ancestral Hall surrounded by the drug complex near Kowloon's Walled City, a passage runs between the Room for Singing Merits and the Sacrificial Altar. Two trees in small gardens flank this corridor, where a marble bench is set between the pines. On the bench, the boy is fascinated by the yellow teeth that tip branded straps hanging from the Warlord's waist. The Warlord is dressed in his magnificent robes, yang knife in one hand, beheading sword in the other. The boy too is dressed in the clothes he must wear, garments he cannot remove without permission.

"Who are the Fankuang Tzu, Grandfather?" he asks.

The Warlord sheathes the yang knife and sits beside the boy. Blade down, he rests his hands on the hilt of the sword. "To ask that, Cutthroat Becoming, is to ask, Who are we? Do you wish me to tell you the history of our family?"

"Yes, Grandfather."

"The trees on either side are bristlecone pines. They are the longest-living form of life on Earth. Some of the trees on Methuselah Walk in the White Mountains have survived forty-nine hundred years."

"Where are the White Mountains?" asks the boy.

"In the land of the white monkeys across the great sea."

The six-year-old laughs, picturing the apes.

"Our family, Cutthroat Becoming, is like the bristlecone pine."

The Warlord points to one of the trees.

"See how new growth grows on old growth each generation? Just as 'grandfather' and the 'ancestors' are the trunk

of the pine, so am I the Warlord of the Fankuang Tzu. The 'father' layer, you will note, is hollow and dying. Likewise your own father is no more. Yet see how the 'son' grows to renew the pine, just as you, Cutthroat Becoming, will carry on our line? To you will fall the Dragon Throne when I am gone, and you will advance the Ways of the Fankuang Tzu."

The Warlord spreads his flowing sleeves like a conjuror.

"Twelve thousand years ago," he said, "a race of giant men seven feet tall reached the Middle Kingdom. Where they came from no one knows, but soon they attracted local followers. Because their clothing shone with the solar glare, they were called the Fankuang Tzu—the Sons of Reflected Light.

"The Fankuang Tzu taught us skills unknown before. The lessons went on so long the first disciples died, leaving it to their families to carry on. Finally, after centuries, the giants disappeared, and nothing has been heard from them since. Those who learned were left to build on what they were taught, as families dispersed throughout the Middle Kingdom. Different areas were suited to different arts, so the families developed different skills. One perfected the I Ching. *Another* Feng-shui. *While we advanced the healing arts."*

Reaching into one sleeve, the Warlord withdraws a carved bone.

"What is that?" the boy asks.

"Chia-ku-wen. *The Oracle Bone that first prescribed the Yang."*

"Yang, Grandfather?"

"The Yang of Immortal Life."

Sacredly, the Warlord passes the bone to the boy. His grandson traces the ancient symbols carved on the fossil.

"Can you guess who gave our family this?"

"The Fankuang Tzu? The Sons of Reflected Light?"

"Five thousand years back, Cutthroat Becoming, Emperor Shennong tasted herbs to learn their effect. This he did in the mountains near our home in Xian. Shennong's Materia Medica *is the world's oldest book on drugs. We have a copy here in the Ancestral Hall. But older than writing on paper are the Oracle Bones,* Chia-ku-wen *like the one you hold in your hand. Such bones were passed down from the Fankuang Tzu."*

"May I taste the Yang?" Cutthroat asks.

"Not in its potent form. That is the quest of the Search. But you may taste weaker Alma Yang."

"When, Grandfather?"

"Now, if you harvest it. The time has come for you to tap the cold part in your mind."

The Warlord leads the boy to the Sacrificial Altar. Through the hole in the floor, they descend to the Labs. Approaching the Donor Farm, the Warlord hands the boy his yang knife. Beheading sword against the wall, he unlocks the cell.

So much blood.

Outside the window of the plane, lights streaked by. Beyond the engines, Vancouver spread to the mountains. DeClercq's book protruded from the seat pocket in front of him. A first-class ticket marked Cutthroat's place:

CHAPTER NINE

THE HUMAN FAMILY TREE

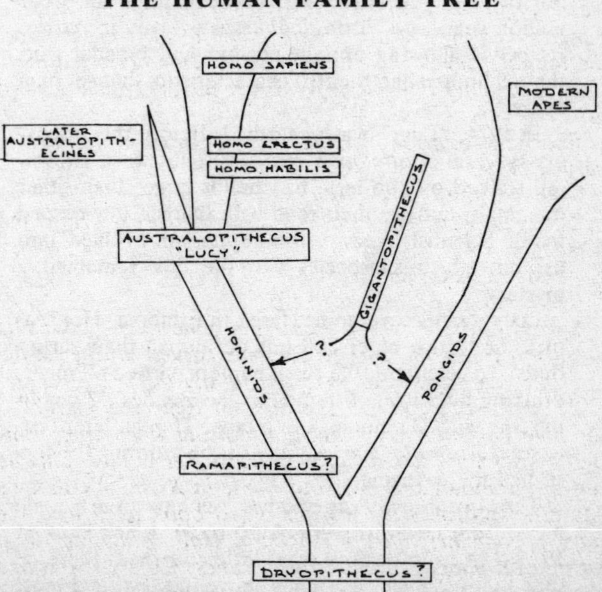

Four to nine million years ago, the last common stock of apes and man split. From then on, the branches evolved separately. Though we know the split occurred in Africa, few digging sites cover the relevant time. We still have little evidence of the forking process.

Anthropologists are a quarrelsome lot. There is no consensus on which species was the "last common stock." So far the most popular candidate—based on skeleton and dental structure—is the ancient ape *Dryopithecus*. This primeval giant roamed the forests of Africa, Europe, and Asia until it disappeared eight million years ago.

Whatever species was the trunk of our family tree, scientists agree on the result of the split. One branch—the pongids—became modern apes. The other branch—hominids—evolved into us.

Who was the first hominid is another disputed question. Ape-like *Ramapithecus* periodically falls in and out of favor. In any event, between three and four million years ago, *Australopithecus* evolved in Africa. Its pelvis allowing upright posture and bipedal gait, this subhuman had the two characteristics that set man apart.

In 1974, "Lucy" was unearthed. Before this discovery, several *Australopithecus* subspecies were known. All walked on two legs, had brains larger than other mammals, and ate their food with flattish, low-cusped teeth. Scientists knew *Australopithecus* evolved into us, but which subspecies was the link remained a mystery.

Lucy was discovered at Hadar in Ethiopia. Her features are much older and less developed than earlier finds. To celebrate, the fossil hunters partied all night, drinking beer while listening to the Beatles' "Lucy in the Sky with Diamonds" on a tape. Though later designated *Australopithecus afarensis,* by morning the fossil had its nickname.

The *Australopithecus* question remains an academic mess. Each new discovery—such as the Black Skull in 1985—seems to destroy what little consensus there is. One theory, however, stands above the rest, and most likely explains how we evolved.

Australopithecus afarensis developed into us. Lucy is the mother of all later hominids, both Australopithecines and the first man. This split occurred about three million years ago, after which the branches lived side by side. Later the Australopithecines died out.

Homo habilis ("Handy Man") was discovered in 1964. Unearthed by Louis Leakey in Tanzania's Olduvai Gorge, he was most likely the first man. Leakey named the species for its use of stone tools.

One and a half million years ago, shortly before the Australopithecines died out, *Homo habilis* was replaced by *Homo erectus*. With brains almost double the size of the Australopithecines, Peking Man and Java Man belong to this group. *Erectus* was the hominid who migrated from Africa to settle Eurasia. Only within the past 500,000 years did he give way to Archaic *Homo sapiens,* who in turn evolved into Neanderthal Man and us.

Forty thousand years ago we first appeared on the scene.

Homo sapiens sapiens.

Modern Man.

Who or What Was Gigantopithecus?

In China, the teeth of "dragons" are thought to have curative properties. . . .

BRAIN CAGE

Vancouver
5:27 P.M.

DeClercq was about to call it a day when MacDougall walked in.

"Chan's unable to get through to Minister Qi."

"What time is it in Beijing?"

"Nine-thirty tomorrow morning."

"If Eric connects, have him call me at home."

DeClercq stuffed the Gong An Ju fax into his briefcase. A gust of wind hurled a torrent against the windows. Donning his coat, he turned the collar up.

"Feeling lucky?" Jack asked.

"Not especially. But you look like the cat who ate the canary."

MacDougall held up a lottery ticket and waved it in the air.

"How much did you win?"

"Not me. *You.* It's the ticket you gave me with the vet's number on back. I checked it with the paper. You won $10,000."

"I'll be damned," DeClercq said. "And I throw them away. How will you spend your third, Jack?"

West Vancouver
6:23 P.M.

DeClercq stopped in Dundarave to buy fondue fuel. As always, Charlie huddled in his tiny booth. "Wet enough for you, Chief?" the war amp asked. "Give my right arm to bask in Hawaii."

"Pick a winner, Charlie."

"Coming up." The old man eyed his lottery tickets, choosing one.

Along with the price of the ticket, DeClercq gave him a check.

"Careful, Chief. This belongs to you."

DeClercq waved the check away. "That's for you. I won $10,000 in the lottery. A third for the man who picked it. A third for the man who saved it. A third for the fool who threw it away."

Charlie was dumbfounded.

He stared at the check.

"Why'd you give the extra dollar to me?"

"Send a postcard, Charlie. I want to see if those hula girls are as pretty as they say."

DeClercq made another stop.

Then he went home.

7:35 P.M.

The black Barracuda passed DeClercq's home.

"There it is," the driver said in Cantonese.

The punk in front checked the address against Martin Kwan's note.

"Turn here," the punk in back said.

The Barracuda left Marine Drive for the beach. They parked the car in a lovers' lane by the sea. This time of night, the spot was deserted. As each zipped up his leather jacket, the Alley Demon took a balaclava from the bag.

The driver slammed a clip into his Ingram MAC-10.

The punk in back loaded the trank gun and stuck a .45 in his belt.

The punk in front got a .44 and sledgehammer from the trunk.

"Let's get him," the driver said.

7:38 P.M.

"Hey, buddy. Got enough light?"

"Yes," said the fare.

The cabbie glanced at his passenger in the rearview mirror.

"I can turn on the overhead, though I ain't s'pose to drive that way."

"No need," the fare said. "My penlight's strong enough."

"Don't get sick, huh? Readin' in a car?"

"No," he said, returning to the book:

Who or What Was Gigantopithecus?

In China, the teeth of "dragons" are thought to have curative properties, so since the Han Dynasty (206 B.C. to A.D. 220) Asian druggists have sold *lung ch'ih* as medicine. In actual fact these "dragon teeth" are fossils of any kind, so G.H.R. von Koenigswald, the paleontologist who discovered Java Man, made it a practice to visit Chinese pharmacies.

In a Hong Kong drugstore in 1935, von Koenigswald purchased a giant fossil tooth. Larger than the molars of any living ape, this tooth was three times the size of a man's, yet exhibited a human cusp pattern. Obviously from a primate unknown to science, he named it *Gigantopithecus blacki* in honor of Davidson Black, who co-discovered Peking Man. Armed with a proper prescription and the appropriate Asian name, von Koenigswald purchased similar teeth in Hong Kong and Canton.

During World War II, a scientist named Weidenreich, who analyzed the teeth, concluded *Gigantopithecus* was a hominid ancestral to us. Based on the decrease in tooth size from *Homo erectus* to modern man, he theorized the trend had persisted for some time. Since the cusp pattern of the fossils matched ours, *Gigantopithecus* evolved into us.

By 1952, von Koenigswald had eight teeth. He too linked the primate to "the human group." Matching stains on the teeth with those on known fossils, he determined they came from caves in South China. . . .

7:42 P.M.

Mushroom, dill, garlic, curry, plum, and herb. DeClercq removed the Handi-Wrap from the sauces and placed them on a tray. Closing the fridge with his foot, he carried the tray through to the dining room table. Uncorking a bottle of Châteauneuf-du-Pape to breathe, he lit the pair of candles and the fondue burner.

Tray in hand, he returned to the kitchen for wild rice.

7:45 P.M.

Crouched behind the beach knoll, the punks cased the house. DeClercq, framed in the dining room window right of the greenhouse, set a rice pot on the table and disappeared. The punks pulled the balaclavas over their heads.

"Here's what we do," Trank Gun said. "I go around to the front of the house and hide by the door. Wait five minutes, then break in here. When the round-eye flees through the door, I shoot him with a dart. Then we take him to Chinatown."

"What if he doesn't run?" Sledgehammer asked.

"Wing him or kill him. I don't care."

"Take him alive," MAC-10 said, "and the Red Pole will be impressed."

"Let's do it," Trank Gun said, circling the knoll.

He vanished behind the driftwood chair and antique sundial.

The cab passed Willow Creek, heading for Lighthouse Park. *Snik-snik-snik* went the wipers, deluged by rain. The cabbie studied his passenger in the rearview mirror. *Bohunk,* he thought. *Judging by the accent.*

First sight of the fare at the airport, he'd done a double take. Six-foot-four giant in a ten-gallon hat. Had to remove the Stetson to fit in back, and even now was hunched down to keep from bumping the roof. Not every day you picked up a Slavic John Wayne.

Below albino white hair, the ski-tanned face was covered by the book.

Seeing the word *Blood* in its title, the cabbie assumed the fare was reading something by Stephen King:

> With Davidson Black, Pei Wen-chung co-discovered Peking Man. After the Communist Revolution in

1949, Pei asked the central pharmacy in Beijing to examine incoming "dragon teeth" for *Gigantopithecus* bones. By 1956, Pei had fifty teeth, all from caves in South China.

That same year, a farmer named Chin Hsiu-huai, out collecting "bone" to fertilize his field, found a fossil on Lountsai Mountain west of Canton. Leng-Chai-Shan cave, in which he discovered the jaw with teeth, was three hundred feet above the surrounding terrain. When Chin tried to sell the teeth as medicine, the fossil was sent to Pei Wen-chung. Pei dispatched an expedition to the cave, where, in 1958, two more jaws and one thousand *Gigantopithecus* teeth were found.

The spring of 1968, a team from Yale uncovered a similar jaw in the Siwalik foothills of the Himalayas. Dug from sediment five to nine million years old, the Indian primate predated its Chinese cousin. Yale named the subspecies *Gigantopithecus bilaspurensis*.

Recently scientists from the University of Arizona examined a fossil trove from the mountains of North Vietnam. Combined in the same rock formation were teeth from *Gigantopithecus* and *Homo erectus*. . . .

7:47 P.M.

Squatting in front of the stereo, he flipped through his compact discs.

Shostakovich, DeClercq decided.

7:48 P.M.

The setup was too good to resist.

DeClercq's house dated from the days when people didn't lock their doors, let alone bar them. The door was solid planks of oak with no flanking windows or paranoia peephole. The city was adjusting to its new "world-class status," where urban predators were free to stalk the streets, but hadn't reached the point of bunkerizing every home. Lucky for Trank Gun. Too bad for DeClercq.

The punk changed plans.

Scaring DeClercq out the front door had its risks. What if he grabbed his gun at the sound of the break-in? What if, being a cop, he made a stand? What if he barricaded himself in one of the rooms? What if he dialed 911?

Surely the better plan would be simply to knock on the door. DeClercq couldn't see who was outside without opening it. Aim for the crack where door met jamb, then tranquilize him. If he asked who was there, say, "Federal Express."

The punk knocked on the door.

"Okay, buddy. You're home."

Avacomovitch switched off his penlight and paid for the cab. Before he stepped into the downpour and popped his umbrella, he closed the book on the passage that was causing such a stir:

> Until the Yellow Skull drawn in *Parker's Journal, Gigantopithecus* was known solely from jaws and teeth. The shape of its cranial vault remained a mystery.
>
> From the fossils discovered before I opened Blake's trunk, anthropologists agreed on certain facts. *Gigantopithecus* evolved in the Himalayas, then spread east. Chinese *Gigantopithecus* descended from the Indian form and was a contemporary of man until 500,000 years ago. The species exhibited a curious mix of ape and hominid characteristics. In addition, fossils of *Dryopithecus*—arguably the "last common stock" of ape and man—were discovered near all *Gigantopithecus* sites.
>
> From the shape of the jaws, the primate was probably twice the size of a male mountain gorilla. Weighing six hundred pounds, it stood nine feet tall. In all other aspects, the species shuffled in the realm of myth, disconnected, disembodied, lost in time.
>
> Where did he/it come from?
>
> Where did he/it go?
>
> Some anthropologists believe *Gigantopithecus* was a large, now extinct ape.
>
> Others consider the species a giant unplaced hominid somehow ancestral to man.

Still others hold the creature is alive today, surviving in remote areas as the Yeti of the Himalayas and Sasquatch of the Rockies.

Whatever, the Yellow Skull appears to place it here:

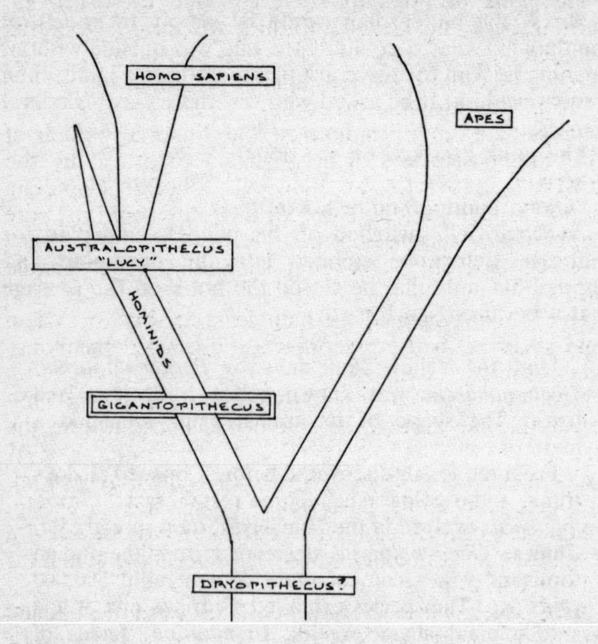

7:49 P.M.

Right on time, DeClercq thought, hearing the knock at the door.

He walked down the hall, thumbed the lock, and turned the handle.

Footsteps approaching from the other side.

Trank Gun aimed the dart pistol where DeClercq would first appear.

The lock was thumbed and the door began to move.

Too late to react, DeClercq saw the bore of the gun.

He knew he was gone.

* * *

"Hey you!" Joe shouted from halfway up the path.

Trank Gun turned.

A giant in a Stetson descended from the road.

The punk dropped the dart gun and drew his .45. Turning back, he kicked the door to expose DeClercq completely.

"Die," the punk snarled, aiming for his head.

"Kill," the Mountie ordered.

Fangs bared in a brindle face, one hundred pounds of purebred muscle and agility, trained to attack by the RCMP Dog Service at Innisfail, Alberta, Napoleon sprang through the door. Before the punk could fire, the shepherd tore out his throat.

"Back, Joseph!" DeClercq shouted. "We'll handle this."

The Mountie opened the hall closet for his .38. When glass smashed in the greenhouse, he doused the house lights.

Napoleon spit out the punk's throat, growling ominously. He ran around the side of the house toward the sea.

Down the hall and past the candles in the dining room, DeClercq reached the greenhouse as the punks broke in. Silhouetted against the lights across the bay, one had a sledgehammer, the other a MAC-10. DeClercq aimed for the punk in front.

As Sledgehammer drew his .44, the Mountie opened fire. Three shots, arm extended in a rising sweep. The first slug caught the punk in the groin. The second in the stomach. The third in the heart. Sledgehammer arched back, hindering MAC-10.

The Asian with the automatic stepped back to avoid the corpse. He was now just outside the greenhouse door. Targeting the muzzle flashes from DeClercq's gun, he crouched and aimed, using the falling body as a shield. He heard a bark, and a blur appeared at the corner of his eye. Napoleon was in the air when he saw the bloody fangs.

The German shepherd bit through his arm as the MAC-10 exploded. A line of holes ripped across the eaves of the house. The Asian shrieked as the dog gnashed his throat, cutting the cry off in mid-scream. As rain poured down from the eaves trough holes, blood fountained up from his severed arteries.

By the time Joseph rounded the house, tree branch gripped like a club, DeClercq was on his knees nuzzling the dog.

"King had nothing on you, pal," the Mountie said.

DECO

10:29 P.M.

Joseph Avacomovitch enjoyed nothing more than a puzzle. This DeClercq had learned with their first case.

On a snowy night in November 1965, an MP had left the House of Commons to visit his mistress. In the lot near Center Block where his car was parked, someone caved his skull in with a bottle of cheap wine. Wallet beside him, the MP died on a bed of shattered glass, for the snowdrift into which he fell was already littered with shards from an earlier auto collision. Off to see *his* mistress, another MP found the body.

DeClercq was called in.

At two in the morning, several hours after the crime, Ottawa cops checked a drunk passed out in the gutter. In one pocket of his overcoat they found $90 in cash. The neck of a broken bottle was recovered from the other.

Avacomovitch had defected recently. He was in Ottawa teaching an Ident course. When DeClercq reached the murder scene at six that morning, having just flown in from Montreal, the Russian was bagging the snow within a twenty-foot circumference of the corpse. It was loaded on a truck destined for the lab, where, by late the next afternoon, he'd gathered a thousand shards of glass through evaporation.

"Well?" DeClercq said, placing the bottle neck on the lab table. "Without the rest of it, our case is shaky."

"Hard request," Joe said, scratching his jaw. "Cheap wine comes in cheap bottles that disintegrate. Reintegrating a bottle is itself a daunting task, but here the fragments are mixed up with a shattered auto headlamp."

He held the bottle neck up to the light.

"Leave it with me," he said.

Six weeks later, DeClercq returned to the lab. The bottle—831 shards glued back together—sat on the table beside the bottle neck. Joseph lowered the piece recovered from the drunk onto the reassembled part for a perfect fit.

"How?" DeClercq asked.

"Glass is made by mixing sand and soda-lime. The *amount* of soda-lime determines the angle at which a piece of glass bends light. Stand waist-deep in a swimming pool and gaze at your feet. The reason they appear close is water refracts light. Light refracts on passing from one medium to another because it changes speed. Different glasses bend light at different angles.

"First I inked a black dot on a sheet of paper. I focused a microscope on it and noted the setting. Next I placed a shard dug from the victim's skull over the dot. Refocusing the microscope, I got a second reading. Knowing the thickness of the glass and the difference between the settings, I was able to calculate the shard's index of refraction. The index is the speed at which something transmits light compared to the speed of light in a vacuum.

"Trimethylene dichloride has an index of 1.446. The index of chlorobenzene is 1.523. The average index for glass—1.46—lies between, so by mixing the liquids I obtained a solution with the same index as the shard from the MP's skull.

"Next I dunked the fragments from the parking lot in this solution. Those with the same index as the bottle disappeared. Why? Because they bent light at the same angle as the solution. The headlamp shards, however, could still be seen because their soda-lime content produced a different index. Once I had the fragments from the bottle, I 3-D microphotographed each piece to scale and interfaced the surfaces like a jigsaw puzzle. That took time."

"Not as long as someone I know will do in Kingston Pen."

Over the years, Robert and Joseph had become friends. They shared an aptitude for unraveling Gordian knots, one by tactics and intuition, the other by forensics. When Robert's second retirement had ended their joint cases, they made a point of meeting for monthly soirees. "My Dinners With Joe" DeClercq dubbed them, after the Louis Malle film.

It was ten-thirty before they were left alone to salvage the meal. Outside, the West Van police were searching the grounds. Cops with flashlights and tracking dogs combed the beach. The Alley Demons were en route to the morgue.

"I need a drink," Robert said. "And wine won't do."

He fetched a bottle of Moskovskaya chilling in the fridge, filled two shot glasses, and downed his.

"*Na zdorovie,*" Joe said, gulping the vodka.

"*A votre santé,*" Robert said, pouring another hit.

"What was that about? Your uninvited guests?"

"I'm not sure. The skull, I think. Someone chasing myths."

"Connected to the break-in?"

"Possibly. Last night they stole the *Journal*. Tonight they came for me."

"Why?" Joe said.

"The motive baffles me. But whoever sent them is deadly serious. I suspect it has something to do with this."

From his briefcase near the kitchen sink he removed the fax from the Gong An Ju. Joe read the first page:

> REQUEST INFORMATION CONCERNING FANKUANG TZU PHARMACEUTICAL COMPANY OF HONG KONG. OWNER: CROWN COLONY RESIDENT KWAN KOK-SU. PLEASE INTERPRET MEANING OF THIS MAP.

The second page was a map with Windigo Mountain circled in black.

"The fax is from Beijing's police," Robert said. "It arrived this afternoon. What's most perplexing is the map is *mine*."

"Yours?" Joe said.

"Months ago my publisher sent proofs of *Bagpipes, Blood, and Glory* out for advance reviews. The backlash in one of them warned of the controversy coming with publication, so I sent an internal computer request to all Force detachments in Alberta and B.C. It asked that they search their files back ninety years for any mention of a corpse found with a *second* skull. Blake's bones might have been discovered without us knowing it. The second skull could be Parker's fossil.

"Nothing came of my request, so I sent a follow-up with Parker's drawings of the skull and a map. Again I got no reply from my internal query, then weeks later the map comes back by way of Beijing. Someone in the Force sent it to Asia."

"Any idea who?"

"Chan's investigating. He says the fax is from China's minister of police. Eric hasn't been able to contact him."

"What's your theory?" Joe asked. "A spy in the Force?"

"Someone tracking my progress with the Yellow Skull."

"For whom? This drug company?"

"Looks that way. I write a book about *Parker's Journal* and Windigo Mountain. Someone in the Force sends my map to Asia. *Parker's Journal* is stolen in a break-in at my home. The map comes back with a Chinese request asking what it means to an Asian company. Hours later, three Asian thugs lurk outside my home. The address is unlisted. Our spy again?"

"What interest would Windigo Mountain hold for a drug company?"

"That, my friend, is a puzzle worthy of your brain. Between my computer request and publication, Fanku-ang Tzu applied for a research permit to go to Windigo Mountain. Ottawa turned them down because the peak's off-limits."

The three of them—dog included—ate the fondue. Above its sizzle, Shostakovich was backed by the rain. One of the cops searching the beach sat down in the driftwood chair. They watched him smoke a cigarette, red tip pulsing in time with the lighthouse beacon.

"So?" Robert said. "How was the convention?"

"Anthropologists came from around the world. Some brought exhibits from their favorite trials. Colorado State U. resembled an undug graveyard before we were finished."

"What did you take?"

"Liese Greiner's pelvis from the Headhunter case."

"Bet that pleased U.S. Customs."

"They gave me the third degree. Being born in Russia didn't help."

Joe withdrew a letter from his sports coat. In Cyrillic

print, it looked official. The seal of the Soviet Union was on the letterhead.

"A friend of mine, Dmitri, came from Russia. He's head of Moscow's Darwin Museum. Before I defected, we were both students of Gerasimov, the reconstructionist who inspired *Gorky Park*. Dmitri brought this from the Kremlin. Seems I can return anytime I want."

Joe fed Napoleon a cube of steak.

"Your book caused a furor at the convention. Consensus was the Yellow Skull upsets the status quo of human evolution. The one defense is to brand *Parker's Journal* a fake."

"Some professor in Arizona has done just that. I promised you'd prove the *Journal* authentic on your return. Now with the break-in, I'll have to take my lumps."

"Fossil fever is a virulent disease. I know anthropologists who *sleep* with certain bones. Perhaps the Yellow Skull destroys a life's work. Motive for the theft?"

"I'm inclined to think someone wants a fossil. The break-in was to gather everything I know. That wasn't enough, so the trio came for me. Why the tranquilizer gun if I was to be killed?"

"Let's hope whoever sent them doesn't try again."

Avacomovitch had spent his youth in a Moscow orphanage, for his parents were killed in the Nazi push on Stalingrad. As a boy he amused himself with acrostics, riddles, and anagrams. His interest in forensics grew out of his skill with puzzles—his defection out of a quest for the perfect adversary. Only freedom breeds a Moriarty.

His home was a houseboat moored on False Creek. Crosswords were tacked to the galley walls. Conventional, three-dimensional, and computer-as-opponent chessboards were in play. A blackboard over the bathtub was scrawled with algebra. Beside his bed, four whodunits were marked with changing guesses: Berkeley's *The Poisoned Chocolates Case,* Queen's *The Greek Coffin Mystery,* Carr's *The Three Coffins,* Christie's *And Then There Were None.*

The puzzle of Windigo Mountain had him hooked.

"The *Journal* is nothing but lines on paper," Joe said. "Everyone's focus is the Yellow Skull. What do we know about it? Let's do a Follow-Through."

Follow-Through was a game of theirs akin to verbal

chess. By thrust, parry, and counterthrust, it was their technique for whittling at puzzles. The object was to trace a problem back to its source, then follow subsequent twists and turns through to the present. Often a solution was found along the way.

"According to Parker," Robert said, "he found the Yellow Skull on sacred Indian land. He connected the fossil to the myth of the Windigo, a monster the Plains Cree linked to the Rocky Mountains. One peak, Windigo Mountain, was named by them."

"According to Blake," Joe said, "Parker was at Custer's Last Stand. White Owl seized the *Journal* from him and brought it to Canada. Blake took possession here and hid it in his trunk. Query? Did White Owl have the skull which Blake overlooked?"

" 'Windigo' pops up twenty years later," Robert said. "According to witnesses at Almighty Voice's stand, White Owl's widow sang of a 'great medicine' bequeathed to her son. She urged him not to let the 'Windigo' fall into white hands. Iron-child escaped and fled across the prairies. Blake, dispatched to bring him back, disappeared. No skull was found with Iron-child's body."

"Query?" Joe said. "What drew Iron-child to the Rockies?"

"Insanity," Robert said. "He was chasing myths.

"Iron-child suffered from Windigo psychosis. The symptoms were described by members of his tribe. According to Dr. Ruryk, it's a mental disorder unique to Indians. Cree youths sought a spirit helper through their dream-quest, a vision induced by isolation, fasting, and meditation. Iron-child sought the Windigo as his spirit helper, believing himself possessed by the monster's craving. Ruryk says there are seventy documented cases. It's a classic example of myth breeding psychotic behavior."

"Iron-child fled to the Rockies to take the 'Windigo' home," Joe said. "He was pursuing his quest to *become* Windigo. Query? What locked Blake firmly on his tail?"

"He was a paranoid schizophrenic," Robert said. "That's obvious from his Trophy Collection. Blake served twenty-three years with the North-West Mounted Police. He joined as an inspector and vanished with the same rank. Repeatedly he refused promotion to stay in the field, always on a manhunt and always hunting alone. Now we know why."

"Did Blake find the skull, carry on to the peak, and die in the Earthquake of '97?" Joe asked. "Was the inspector also chasing myths? Linked trophies from father and son. What a Collection coup. Did curiosity—or madness—get the better of him?"

"I find the *Journal*," Robert said, "and show it to you. You connect the jaw to *Gigantopithecus*. The *Australopithecus*-shaped skull places 'Windigo' on the hominid branch."

"Okay," Joe said. "Where do we stand?"

"The Yellow Skull equals Windigo," Robert said.

"Windigo equals Windigo Mountain," Joe said.

"Therefore, the Yellow Skull equals Windigo Mountain."

"*Gigantopithecus* equals the Yellow Skull."

"*Gigantopithecus* equals Windigo."

"Therefore, *Gigantopithecus* equals Windigo Mountain."

"Why would that interest a drug company?" Robert asked.

"Because the company hopes the myth is true," Joe said.

The Russian flipped the fax to the map and laid it on the table. "What do the Chinese characters down the left mean?"

" 'To the expedition' Eric says."

Joe pointed to the letters D E C O penned on the map.

"DECO is an acronym for the Decreasing Oxygen Consumption Hormone. It's a chemical produced by our brain. Burning calories generates heat to give us energy. Excess heat escapes through our skin to keep us cool. As time goes by, skin loses its cooling ability. If we didn't have another way to regulate heat, our brain would soon cook to death. DECO slows the rate at which we burn calories. Some say the process brings on age. We pay the price of lost youth in order to survive."

"What has that to do with Windigo Mountain?" Robert asked.

Joe shrugged, palms up. "Leave it with me."

THE CONNECTION

Vancouver
10:23 P.M.

They began their search in 1979 with Murdoch's first day on the bench, then worked back through his diaries and the adjudicators rota. The rota listed the deportations heard each day, plus the rooms to which the aliens were assigned. Who sat in which room wasn't on the rota, so to find the judge Carol had to flip to Appendix A. Matching this with the rota didn't guarantee that judge heard the case, for if an adjudicator bogged down, the rest of his list was switched to a room where work had finished early. Case transfers were noted in Appendix B.

"December 13," Carol said, suppressing a yawn. "Maxwell did Crawford and Phan Van Doa . . . No, wait a sec. Phan went to another room."

Zinc scanned the chart on the floor and checked the diary. "Murdoch defended Walter Shugg that morning."

"December 12," Carol said, flipping a page. She was curled up in an armchair with the rota in her lap. "Maxwell did Trout, Leschuk, and Truong Minh Ba."

Zinc checked the diary and the chart beside the bed. "Murdoch flew to Ottawa for José Silva."

"December 11," Carol said, yawning again. "Maxwell did Hluchnik, Ho Hing Houng, Kessler, and Tsalginof."

"Sure would be easier," Zinc said, "if Murdoch had noted the court. Then we could isolate the deportations at a glance."

"I've had enough," Carol said. "I'm falling asleep. How 'bout a Jacuzzi, then crawl into bed?"

Zinc marked his place in the diary and rolled up the chart. "Last one in's a rotten egg," he said.

Carol stared at the bathroom mirror while Zinc brushed his teeth.

"Mine are not the tits of an eighteen-year-old," she sighed.

"So, you're not eighteen," he said, rinsing his mouth. "They look pretty damn good to me."

"I think they're starting to sag," she said, turning sideways.

Zinc moved behind her, cupping both breasts. "Worry solved." He kissed her neck.

"I don't get as many wolf whistles. And fewer men make passes."

Chandler shrugged. "I thought you abhorred such behavior."

"I did," she said. "Until it stopped. Then I started wondering what's wrong with me."

" 'There are two tragedies in life,' " he said. " 'One is not to get your heart's desire. The other is to get it.' "

She kissed him back. "My philosopher."

"Oscar Wilde, actually."

They left the bathroom, crossed the hotel room, and climbed into bed.

"Light on or off?" he asked.

"Off," she said.

The wind outside wailed like a banshee on an acid trip, while inside they held each other for shelter from the storm. The masts of the boats on Coal Harbour rang to the lash of their riggings, rocking on the ebbing tide of passing time.

"Yesterday, by the pool, I overheard a teenage girl tell her mom to suck her gut in. The look on her mom's face said it all. 'My gut *is* sucked in,' she replied. Around the pool were other women beset with minor waffles, wrinkles, and stretchmarks. I wondered why they let themselves go like that? Then I noticed a twenty-year-old look at me the same way. Now when I see myself in the mirror, everything's half an inch lower than it used to be."

"You're exaggerating."

"Not by much. Seen Jane Fonda lately? Those cords in her neck? And look at the effort she puts in to defeat age. I'm not ready for time to run out on me."

"Even King Canute couldn't hold back the tide. Last year my high school had a reunion. Four people in our class were already gone. One dropped dead doing the twist practicing for the reunion! Our president had a shiny pink dome pushing his hairline back to the nape of his neck. Time to accept we baby boomers are no longer young. More of us should read *The Picture of Dorian Gray*."

"I keep having this dream," Carol said, "where I wake up one morning to find I'm no longer me. Sometimes it frightens me, babe, facing life alone. I often wonder, *How long have I got left*? Whatever I joined the Bureau for has long since disappeared. What about the part of me that wants a child and a home? I don't want to end up a lonely old wretch knocking on heaven's door."

Zinc ran one finger gently down her forehead. It crested her nose, touched her lips, and rounded her chin to her throat. "I can't turn back the hands of time, but I can ease your worries. Marry me, Carol, and I'll shoo them away."

She rose to one elbow. "Is that from the heart?"

He eased her head toward his lips and whispered in her ear:

"When, in disgrace with fortune and men's eyes,
I all alone beweep my outcast state,
And trouble deaf heaven with my bootless cries,
And look upon myself, and curse my fate,
Wishing me like to one more rich in hope,
Featured like him, like him with friends possessed,
Desiring this man's art and that man's scope, With
what I most enjoy contented least;
Yet in these thoughts myself almost despising,
Haply I think on thee—and then my state,
Like to the lark at break of day arising
From sullen earth, sings hymns at heaven's gate;
For thy sweet love remembered such wealth brings
That then I scorn to change my state with kings."

"Mmmm," she murmured, straddling him, slipping him inside. "Who's that?"

"You know. Sonnet Twenty-nine."

"Know any others?"

"You got all night?"

"Depend upon it, sir," Samuel Johnson said, September 19, 1777, "when a man knows he is to be hanged in a fortnight, it concentrates his mind wonderfully."

They ravaged each other as if the gallows were waiting at dawn, fucking face to face and alternating who was on top. For an encore they turned on all the lights and angled the bureau mirror toward the bed. On hands and knees, rump in the air, Carol watched Zinc mount her from behind, moaning as one hand played with her clit and the other kneaded her breast. Like a pair of jungle cats in heat they rocked and rolled the bed, until someone in the next room banged on the wall. Zinc came with such force his teeth drew blood from her shoulder, then a moment later Carol let go. The contractions of her orgasm almost bucked him off.

"Good Lord," Zinc said, dripping sweat and gasping for breath. "Mine's not the heart of an eighteen-year-old either."

"A year of this, day in, day out, and I'll whip you into shape. I could stay here forever, locked in your arms."

"You'd get hungry after a while."

"The answer's yes."

"Yes what?"

"Yes, I'll marry you."

Friday, March 20, 7:02 A.M.

"Zinc!"

"Uh?"

"Wake up! I found it, babe."

Chandler rubbed the sleep from his eyes. Face flushed, hair mussed, bathrobe gaping, Carol leaned excitedly over the bed.

"Hear me? I found it. The link between Murdoch and Maxwell. They did a case together in 1978."

Chandler threw back the covers and got out of bed. "How long you been up?" he asked as she pulled him toward the window.

"One, two hours. I lost track."

An armchair and table half-blocked the city view. Above Stanley Park an eagle circled, hunting breakfast. The rising sun stained the downtown core pink.

"Note," she said, pointing to the adjudicators rota. On the page for November 17, 1978, the name Evan Kwan was circled in red. "Maxwell heard the case," she said.

Carol laid Murdoch's diary for 1978 on top of the rota. She opened it to November 17. The name Evan Kwan appeared on the page.

"There's more," she said, thumbing back in Murdoch's diary. A diagonal line was drawn across the page for October 5. Along the line was written Kwan Kok-su, Hong Kong.

"Remember the witness statements we discussed in San Francisco? That brother and sister at the Carlton Palace Hotel?"

"Yeah. Martin and Lotus Kwan."

"Could be a connection."

"Let's find out."

TOTEM POLE

9:31 A.M.

Stanley Park, like the RCMP, owes its origin to Canadian fear of the States. A one thousand-acre peninsula sheltering the harbor, it was a Coast Salish settlement until whites arrived. On Deadman's Island off Brockton Point the Indians buried their elders, while the Squamish village of Whoi Whoi occupied what's now Lumberman's Arch. When the British settled Burrard Inlet mid last century, they kicked the natives off the land to have it for themselves. In 1859 the States annexed the San Juan Islands, raising fears the U.S. Army planned to take B.C. For defense, the site became a military reserve, saving it from the grasp of land developers. In 1888 Stanley Park was born, which soon had a cricket pitch and lawn bowling green. Ever sensitive to native traditions they displaced (a fact displayed daily in London's British Museum), the colonialists stole totem poles from villages up the coast, reerecting them near Hallelujah Point. This morning, Russ Barrow was using these totems to backdrop his shots.

"That's it."

Click. Click.

"Open the coat."

Click. Click.

"Stroke the fur."

Click.

"Break and reload."

While Barrow fed his Hasselblad 120 film, Lotus Kwan wandered among the totem poles. The rain clouds of the day before had blown east, clearing the sky for another storm expected from the Pacific. Meanwhile, the sun blazed behind the mythic carvings, hurling orange rays through the trees. Warmed, the ground exuded an unearthly mist.

"Okay," Barrow said, slinging the camera about his neck. "This time we juxtapose the coat, Tsonoqua, and you."

"Which one's Tsonoqua?"

"The Monster of the Forests. It's that carving over there."

Wispy white tendrils curled around the forty-foot cedars, veiling the Nhe-is-bik Totem and Sisa-Kaulas Pole. The sun shone behind their crests like an aura.

"How do you read a totem?" Lotus asked.

Barrow fiddled with his lights, moving the reflectors. Half Danish, half Welsh, he was a ladies' man. Ice blue eyes and sun-streaked hair complemented cream corduroy slacks and a chocolate bomber jacket. He wore his paisley scarf rakishly.

"See that carving? The Nanwaqawe Pole? Like a European coat of arms, it tells a story symbolically."

"How do you read the story?"

"You have to know the myth. The seven Pacific totem tribes—the Tlingit, Tsimshians, Haida, Bella Coola, Kwakiutl, Nootka, and Coast Salish—preserved their legends through cedar art. They had no writing."

Russ walked Lotus back until they stared up the pole.

"The crests, top to bottom, are Thunderbird, Killer Whale, Wolf, Wise One, Hoxhok, Grizzly Bear, and Raven. The Wise One's Nanwaqawe, a legendary chief from the abyss of time. Chief Wakias, his descendant, paid three hundred fifty blankets to have this totem carved in 1899. Before the pole was moved here, it served as a door post in Alert Bay up the coast. Wakias was chief of the Raven clan of Kwakiutls, so the door to his longhouse was a hole beneath the Raven's beak."

Barrow indicated the pole's bottom crest.

"Why's the Wolf biting the Wise One's head?" Lotus asked.

"To give the chief wisdom to fight the Great Cannibal. As lord of the land, the Wolf symbolizes cunning."

"The Great Cannibal? You mean the Windigo?"

Barrow raised an eyebrow. "A woman who knows her myths?"

"I'm reading this book about a Mountie named Wilfred Blake."

"*Bagpipes, Blood, and Glory*?"

"I'm at the Windigo part."

"The myths are different. The monsters similar. The Windigo was the cannibal spirit of the Plains tribes. It haunted a triangle from the Atlantic to the Arctic to the Rocky Mountains. A ten-foot carnivore, it shoved trees from its path. The demon had a monstrous head and fangs in a twisted mouth.

"When Europeans sailed here in the 1700s, the Kwakiutls had a cult that ate human flesh. Hamatsas—the cultists—worshiped Baxbakualanuxsiwae, the Great Cannibal. His name means He-Who-Is-First-to-Eat-Man-at-the-Mouth-of-the-River. By legend, he lived in a spirit house atop the Rocky Mountains, where his chimney billowed blood red smoke night and day. He was a giant whose body was covered with gnashing mouths, and he danced around a smoke-filled room chanting "*Hap! Hap!*" Eat! Eat! A fabled bird named Hoxhok guarded his door. The bird cracked open each victim's skull to gobble up its brain."

Barrow pointed to the six-foot beak on the Hoxhok crest.

"A totem tells its story symbolically. The Great Cannibal isn't present, but his symbol is."

A zephyr swirled the morning mist about their feet.

"Back to work," Barrow said, "before the rains come."

BUSINESS CONFERENCE

10:10 A.M.

The Nine O'Clock Gun is a Vancouver institution. It fires every evening at—you guessed it—nine o'clock. In the 1890s the blast was set off by William D. Jones, the Brockton Point lighthouse keeper. Back then it was necessary for sailing ships in tidal waters to check their chronometers, so at nine each night Jones tied a stick of dynamite to a pole and exploded it by means of a wire running back to his hand. After several complaints to City Hall about his working conditions, in 1894 the gun arrived. A twelve-pound naval cannon cast in Woolwich, England, it dated from the time of Waterloo. Jones positioned the gun on the point so its muzzle aimed at the mayor's office across the inlet. He stifled the political urge to stuff its barrel with rocks. When pranksters later did just that, lobbing stones at the Texaco barge moored in Coal Harbour, the gun was moved along the shore to Hallelujah Point. Once a pioneer homestead known as Johnny Baker's Clearing, the new site was renamed when the Salvation Army held revival meetings there. Martin Kwan was leaning against the gun when Lotus crossed the park drive from the totem poles.

"Another magazine?"

"Business Woman."

"How many's that?"

"Six so far."

"You and that real estate agent will be the most photographed Chinese in town."

" 'The Asian Invasion' is currently big news."

"Risky, don't you think? Hardly low profile."

"Fankuang's move is too big to hide. This photographer wants to shoot you. Don't worry, the problem will be solved before any photos see print."

"Next they'll want Grandfather's picture. Imagine that."

"He'll be dead before then."

"I wish he were dead now."

"Don't we all."

They found a secluded park bench and sat by Coal Harbour. A cruise ship was docking at B.C. Place as float planes buzzed the water. Another wave of storm clouds darkened the west.

"You get my message?" Martin asked.

"He launched the expedition."

"Worse. They hit a blizzard. Calgary lost contact."

Lotus frowned. "The chopper crashed?"

"By now it's out of fuel. Unless they landed on the peak, the expedition's gone."

"If so, we launch another."

"That'll take a week."

"Maybe laughing sickness will kill him by then."

"That's what you said about the judges. Do it his way. The Way of the Fankuang Tzu could have got us caught. He thinks the methods of feudal China still apply today, that a killing should terrorize others as it wipes out the immediate threat. It's like we're haunted by a nineteenth-century ghost."

"A ghost who owns a hundred percent of Fankuang's shares."

"Each step forward, he drags us two back. I say we kill him and seize control."

"The Inner Council would condemn us for that. The Code of Succession says the Warlord must die naturally. Break the rule and the heir forfeits the throne. Some of the council members predate Chingho."

"*Ayeeyah,*" Martin said, slamming his palm with his fist. "How do we conduct business with a madman in control? I loathe being Grandfather's puppet."

"Take the long view," Lotus said. "It's only a matter of time. Kuru disease will kill him any day. The Zodiac note effectively masks our involvement in San Francisco, and he's content with the fearless audacity of both crimes. Let him think the killings have the *gweilo* in a panic, and view the risks as a test to hone our skill. Soon we'll be legitimate, and such thrills will be rare."

The harbor waves roughened, tossing whitecaps here and there.

"Aren't you worried he'll ruin us with his insanity?

First he summons Qi's lover to inseminate her. The result: she steals the Windigo map which could be in Beijing. Next he sends the minister's son home on a junk. That's like waving a red flag at an angry dying bull. Third, by having the judges killed in such a brazen way, he taunts the Mounties and FBI as well as the Gong An Ju. Were it not for his obsession concerning details about the Yang, the Alley Demons wouldn't have died trying to kidnap DeClercq. Now he's launched the expedition in a raging storm, destroying any hope he'll taste his precious Yang. Grandfather's self-destructing. What will he do next?"

Overhead, the sky turned gray, smothering the sun. Gulls flew in from the sea, a foreboding sign.

"The glass is half-full, Martin. Not half-empty. With the butcher and druggist gone, Fankuang Tzu controls local Taoist medicine. In time, we'll control North American distribution. By then Asian wildlife will be extinct. When we control the wildlife here, supply and demand means we control Asia. The DECO experiments in the Labs are most promising. If they succeed, our company will patent the result. With it, we'll control the round-eyes too. Business couldn't be better."

Martin reached into his jacket for a sheet of fax paper. "Do you really think we can afford to wait until he dies?"

Passing the sheet to Lotus, he watched his sibling read. The Chinese characters on the fax were written by the Warlord:

LOTUS AND MARTIN—FLY TO HONG KONG AT ONCE
EVAN—STAY BEHIND AND KILL THE PROFESSOR

XENOPHOBIA

10:46 A.M.

Immigration Canada was a fort under siege.

Carol and Zinc were halfway between the public waiting room and the area manager's office when the bureaucrat guiding them stopped in his tracks. Hoarse shouting reverberated through a closed door. "He's on the phone," the bureaucrat said. "You'll have to wait."

Cooling their heels in this part of the building the public didn't see, they took in the tense confusion surrounding them. The in-basket on every desk was ten times as high as the out, while swamped clerks sapped of all morale worked apathetically. Coffee cups were everywhere, a sign of caffeine addiction, as cigarette smoke hazed the air.

A bulletin board lined the wall to Carol's right. "KNOW THE PITFALLS," its banner blared, "AND DON'T TALK TO THE PRESS." She scanned the clippings pinned below:

> WE'RE NOT EXPLOITING FEAR OF 1997, OFFICIAL SAYS
>
> With the Red Chinese takeover just ten years away, more and more people are thinking of leaving Hong Kong. This year Canada will issue 23,000 immigrant visas to colony residents, 72% to the financial elite. . . . .
>
> CITIZENSHIP FOR SALE
>
> What's a Canadian passport worth? The answer seems to be $250,000, the price Hong Kong businessmen must pay to march to the head of the queue that will allow them and their families to live here permanently. For most colony businessmen that amount is spare change. . . .

ASIAN INFLUX STARTLING

Next year thousands of immigrant children will register for Vancouver schools, where 20% of the students already speak a foreign tongue. . . .

RICH FLY HERE TO DELIVER CANADIAN BABIES

Hong Kong women are flying to Canada in the last month of pregnancy to deliver babies who will later sponsor their parents as immigrants. A child born in Canada is a Canadian citizen with rights under the Family Reunification Program . . .

OTTAWA PAVES THE WAY FOR CRIME BOSSES

Among the immigrant investors Canada welcomes with open arms are Hong Kong gangsters and Triad bosses. Canada's immigration laws are an invitation to bring your money . . . no questions asked. . . .

COURTING POLITICIANS SAY CITY MUST ADJUST

Vancouver must accept changes in its racial makeup if it's to become a major Pacific Rim player, visiting MPs told the Asian Businessmen's Association yesterday. "You can't say Hong Kong money is welcome, but the people aren't. . . ."

RACIST BACKLASH PREDICTED

More than 50% of Canadians are bigots, a recent poll suggests. Half those canvassed want no more immigrants, while those who do favor candidates from European countries. . . .

A nation of immigrants that hates immigration, thought Tate.

Casey Grigg's office was a claustrophobic box with a glimpse of gray Lost Lagoon in gray Stanley Park. The area manager's ashen face resembled leftover meat covered with Saran Wrap. His bloodshot eyes had black bags and raw eczema spread down his chin. Carol noticed a well-thumbed copy of Joyce's *Ulysses* on his desk, a sure sign the man was on the verge on a nervous breakdown.

"Sorry," Grigg said, his voice croaky from shouting. "One of the forty-odd harassment calls I get a day."

He popped a pill and washed it down with Maalox.

"Woman wouldn't stop yelling, 'What the fuck are you doing?' Said her son's school picture was a joke. Said there were only six white faces in his class because we've turned the East Side into Little China. 'Get a boat and send 'em back. They don't respect our culture.' Asked if we knew the damage we had done? 'Whites founded Canada. That's why it's so peaceful. All those riots in Britain once they let niggers in.' Kept saying we were reducing Canadians to a minority in their own land. Said we'll end up Occidentals serving a Chinese raj."

Grigg's pupils dilated. Spittle mottled his lips. His cheeks sagged lower than Nixon's during Watergate.

"See that piece in the paper? 'Buying Up Their New World.' Any idea how many calls I got after that?"

Words slurring, he washed a lethargic hand down his face.

"Ever thought you might get lynched?" Grigg asked. "I did. Last night. Concerned Citizens' Meeting. This fellow approached with a rolled-up paper and bashed me on the head. 'Asshole,' he shouted, and the crowd cheered. 'Thirty years I've lived here and can't afford a house 'cause all your Asian cocksuckers have driven up the price. What cost $185,000 a year ago now costs $260,000 because of you.' "

"Mr. Grigg—"

"Christ Almighty. See what I'm up against? One hundred twenty-five thousand refugees in backlog. Add one hundred fifty thousand immigrants a year. Ottawa's beckoning, 'Bring your bucks and come on in,' while cutting my staff to trim the deficit. They're arriving so fast we can't keep up, and you guys wonder why crooks slip through? The only ones we can control are those we've deported!"

"One of whom is why we're here," said Zinc.

Hawksworth of Enforcement—the man Grigg summoned to find the Kwan file—had chins on his chins and a beet-red face. His baggy blue three-piece with gold fob chain was soiled by lasagna and Big Mac stains. While the elevator descended he ate a sausage roll, burping rye fumes as he finished. Tate considered him an Alfred Hitchcock look-alike.

"Kwan, huh?" Hawksworth said. "Would have guessed. If it ain't the ragheads, it's the slants."

The theme of *The Twilight Zone* played in Carol's head.

"What'd he do? The usual? Dope?" Hawksworth asked.

"Don't know," Chandler said. "That's why we need his file."

The door slid open on a sign: "RECORDS ROOM." Under which an arrow pointed left. Moving down the hall Hawksworth tripped on his own foot.

"Easy," Carol said, steadying him.

"Early retirement party. Last day on the job. Little hair o' the dog, that's what I need."

Hawksworth stopped at a fire station near the Records Room. From behind the extinguisher he withdrew a mickey of Seagram's VO. Carol and Zinc declined his offer of a swig.

"Hate this job," Hawksworth said. "Kowtowing to slants. Money, money, money is all they understand. Vancouver today. Hongcouver tomorrow. Slant baby's born with an abacus in its hand."

"About that file?" Zinc said, guiding him down the hall.

"Robsonstrasse," Hawksworth said. "One fine street. Quaint European shops until the slants elbowed in. Billion dollars in real estate gobbled up overnight. Forty-three years of hard work, they priced my dad off the block. Now Robsonstrasse's so slick you gotta wear cleats to keep from slipping and sliding all over the place."

As they entered the Records Room a Haida woman emerged from the rows of shelves. Hair in braids, she wore a sweatshirt and blue jeans. The sweatshirt bore a black-and-white print of Skidegate totem poles.

"Shake a leg, Wilma. We need a file. Year?" Hawksworth asked.

"Nineteen seventy-eight."

"Kwan, right?"

"Evan. November 17."

"Hear that, Wilma? Evan Kwan."

The native woman disappeared into the labyrinth of

files. Draining his mickey, the bureaucrat slouched on the counter. *Limbic Man,* Carol thought, watching him.

Wilma returned with a skimpy file which she passed to Hawksworth. Fumbling it, he spilled the contents on the countertop. He retrieved a form and said, "Section 27(2) based on Section 19. Kwan arrived that May with a 1208."

"Twelve-oh-eight?" Tate said.

"Student authorization. Visa to study at a named institute."

"UBC?" Chandler asked.

"Where else?" he sneered. "University of a Billion Chinks."

"Where'd he get the visa?"

"High Commission, Hong Kong."

"Date?"

"May 15. Good for a year."

"The visa bear his picture?"

"Not in '78. Today it would," Hawksworth said.

"Why the deportation?" Carol asked.

"Misbehaved himself after he arrived."

A black ring binder was chained to the counter. *Immigration Act, Selected Regulations, and Immigration Appeal Board Rules* read its spine. Thumbing pages, Hawksworth said, "Seventy-eight was the first year of the new act. Look at Section 19 (1)(a) and (d)."

Carol and Zinc perused the legislation:

Inadmissible Classes

> 19 (1) No person shall be granted admission if he is a member of any of the following classes:
>
> (*a*) persons who are suffering from any disease, disorder, disability or other health impairment as a result of the nature, severity or probable duration of which, in the opinion of a medical officer concurred in by at least one other medical officer,
>
> (i) they are or are likely to be a danger to public health or public safety . . .
>
> (*d*) persons who there are reasonable grounds to believe will
>
> (i) commit one or more offences punishable by way of indictment under any Act of Parliament. . . .

"Section 19 lists who can't get in," Hawksworth said. "To get a visa, Kwan passed the test in Hong Kong. He arrived in Canada with a clean slate. No criminal record or sign of mental impairment."

Turning three pages, he found another section:

> ***Removal After Admission***
>
> 27 (2) Where an immigration officer or peace officer has in his possession information indicating that a person in Canada, other than a Canadian citizen or a permanent resident, is a person who
>
> > (*a*) if he were applying for entry, would not or might not be granted entry by reason of his being a member of an inadmissible class . . .
>
> he shall forward a written report to the Deputy Minister setting out the details of such information. . . .

Tate said, "Someone complained Kwan violated Section 19 here?"

Hawksworth waved a paper from the file. "Don Voice confirms that in his report. Kwan was a nut case and a criminal."

"Who's Don Voice?"

"C3PO. Used to work in our office."

"C3PO? *Star Wars*?" Tate said.

"CPO, actually. Case presenting officer who prosecutes aliens. I call 'em C3POs 'cause they act like robots."

"Where's Voice now?"

"Dropped dead jogging. Don escaped this shitty job by emigrating to Heaven."

Zinc read the prosecutor's report to the deputy minister. "Voice repeats the words of the act, then refers to 'attached psych reports' for the facts. I don't see any psych reports."

"File's been stripped," Hawksworth said. "Leaving bare bones. Everything's gone—passport included—that reveals who Kwan was or what he looked like."

"There a duplicate file?"

"Not with evidence. Just name and outcome in our data banks."

The envelope missing from Maxwell's desk, Zinc thought. "Who has access to these files?"

"Anyone who works here."

"Including past employees?"

"If they have loose ends to tie up."

Carol turned to Wilma. "Is there a sign-in book?" The Haida woman passed her a thick binder. Starting with the present, the special agent skimmed back to Monday afternoon. Sure enough, the day he was killed, Trent Maxwell had signed in.

"What happens when the deputy minister gets a report?" asked Tate.

"If approved, he authorizes a deportation hearing."

"Where does the report go then?"

"It comes back with a Direction for Inquiry."

"Who took the complaint against Kwan?"

"Don Voice, the CPO who prosecuted him."

"Who adjudicated?"

"Trent Maxwell, rest his soul. Worked here till he was appointed, you know."

"What if someone deported under Section 27 later wants back in?"

"Guy's shit-out-of-luck under Section 19. The deportation order puts him in an inadmissible class."

"Maxwell deported Kwan?"

"Nope. No deportation."

"Why?"

"Because the day of the hearing the case was adjourned. According to Don's note on the file, that night Kwan left voluntarily for Hong Kong."

"Meaning what? The allegation died?"

Hawksworth nodded. "In '78 the deportee had to be physically present. When Kwan left Canada, the file was closed."

"Why an adjournment?" Tate asked. "Instead of deportation?"

"Probably a tactic by Kwan's lawyer. Under Section 32, a deportation hearing has one of three results. The adjudicator can deport, can issue a departure notice, or he can dismiss the application. If necessary, he can adjourn from time to time. Kwan's lawyer must have thought it best to keep the matter in limbo."

"Do I have this right?" Tate said, holding up three fingers. "One, if Kwan's deported, Section 19 bars him from entering again. Two, a departure notice . . ."

"Has the same effect."

"Why?"

"Because the allegation is upheld."

"But three, adjournment and exit is like the case was dropped? Meaning Kwan could return at any time?"

"Technically, yes. Practically, no. A reference to the file is stored in our computer. If Kwan tried to enter, we'd check his file. The '78 complaint would activate Section 19."

"What if the file was stripped? There'd be no evidence."

"Then we'd contact those involved. A hearing takes place in private, eh? Adjudicator, CPO, alien, and his lawyer. No interpreter here means Kwan spoke English. If any one of them confirmed he was a nut or prone to crime, he'd be barred under Section 19."

"What if all participants were now dead?"

"Except him, you mean?"

"Except Kwan."

"Then he shows up at the border and we have no reason to keep him out. Kwan beats the system. Hell, he could immigrate."

While Tate questioned Hawksworth, Chandler examined the file. "This name on the back cover. Who wrote that?"

The bureaucrat glanced at the writing. "Prosecutor," he said.

"Who's Nicole Daniells?"

"No idea."

"Hazard a guess?"

Hawksworth shrugged. "Person who made the complaint?"

IN THE LAB

11:35 A.M.

A telephone number was scribbled beside Nicole Daniells' name on the back of the Kwan file. While Hawksworth was off buying a chocolate bar from the vending machine, and probably having a nip from another secret stash, Zinc dialed the number from the Records Room.

"Department of Zoology."

"Nicole Daniells, please."

"The professor is giving a lecture and won't return until noon."

Zinc glanced at his watch.

"Address, please."

12:12 P.M.

They parked the car near Fraternity Row as circumpolar winds launched an all-out attack. A pledge in a bathing suit cavorted on one of the frat house lawns.

"I'm sorry," the receptionist said, "but Dr. Daniells has left. She didn't return from her lecture to the Vancouver Institute."

"Where's she gone?"

"Couldn't say. She flew in from Africa yesterday, so probably to sleep."

"The doctor's a faculty member?"

"On extended leave. The past year she's been in Tanzania, researching at Lake Tanganyika. Tomorrow she leaves for a year at the Davis Primate Center."

"Where's that?"

"California."

"More research?"

"Here's Dr. Yan. He may know where she went."

Yan, a man in his late twenties, wore a lab coat and

carried a sheaf of papers under one arm. As the cops introduced themselves, he studied them over thick glasses. "Nothing serious, I hope."

"Routine," Zinc said. The routine reply.

"Terrific lecture. Too bad you missed it. Why Man Makes War: Chimps Develop Our Ways."

"Daniells teaches zoology?"

"In a manner of speaking. She's accredited in Psychiatry, Faculty of Medicine, cross-appointed to Anthropology, Faculty of Arts, associated with Zoology, Faculty of Science. We're all interdisciplinary these days."

"Where's the professor now?"

" 'Visiting old friends.' She said she'd call in for messages at five."

"Why *does* man make war?" Tate asked.

"You've heard of Jane Goodall's colony of chimps? The Gombe Colony in Tanzania?"

"Wasn't she murdered?"

"That's Dian Fossey. Everyone thought Goodall's chimps coexisted peacefully in separate territories. Then suddenly apes from Kasakela invaded Kahama domain. They killed the males, raped the females, and seized territory. The attack was the first-known *planned* aggression by non-human primates against their own kind. For a year Dr. Daniells has studied the colony, concluding the chimps' behavior parallels ours. They mirror human evolution. They've developed war."

"That's an achievement?"

"Objectively," Yan said. "In the past 3,400 years, only 268 have seen relative peace. The world now spends two million dollars a minute on weapons. Our brain evolved to build weapons, thereby ensuring survival and reproduction of our own genes. Darwin thought thwarting genetic competition the most powerful driving force in man. Dr. Daniells' research supports him."

Déjà vu, Carol thought. *The Russian's limbic theory.*

Zinc left his number at Special X with the receptionist. "Have the professor call me. It's important," he said.

West Vancouver
1:36 P.M.

They drove up Hollyburn Mountain to Hutton Murdoch's home. As rain fell in drenching sheets, pounding the roof and gushing down the gutters, they checked the name tags on the judge's files.

"No Evan Kwan," Carol said. "And no Kwan Kok-su."

"No Martin Kwan or Lotus Kwan either."

"That's because the file's in the fireplace."

Vancouver
5:39 P.M.

Carol and Zinc were sharing a pizza at Special X when the telephone rang.

"Inspector Chandler?"

"Professor Daniells?"

"You asked I call?"

Sharp enunciation. Straight to the point. Zinc imagined her about fifty years old.

"The FBI is checking the background of Evan Kwan. His name cropped up in a California case. I believe you know him?"

"*Knew* him, Inspector. Evan did graduate work with me in 1978. I haven't seen him for ten years."

"Kwan arrived from Hong Kong?"

"Yes, a foreign student."

"To study what?"

"Molecular biology."

"Can you be more specific?"

"He hoped to build on Sarich and Wilson's work concerning Eve."

"Eve?" Zinc said.

"Your ten thousandth-great-grandmother. Mine too," Daniells said. "And that of every other human alive today."

"I thought her name was Lucy."

"Wrong species, Inspector. But I doubt you want a lecture in evolution."

"On the contrary," Zinc said. "Kwan's field of study may be relevant."

Daniells covered the mouthpiece and conversed in a muffled voice. Zinc caught the words "SRV samples." A moment later she was back on the line.

"Has Evan done something?"

"Not that we know. Routine inquiry for the FBI. We're checking several leads."

Most people are reticent when questioned by the police. It's usually best to approach a subject laterally. To get the person talking freely is job one.

"Does *Australopithecus* mean anything to you?"

"That's the hominid species that evolved into us."

"Lucy was an Australopithecine three million years ago. She's an example of the species that evolved into us. She's not the individual from whom we all descended."

"And Eve was?"

"Eve was a *Homo sapiens* of the Archaic type. She lived two hundred thousand years ago, maybe much later. Eve wasn't the only human on Earth at the time, but she was the most fruitful in that everyone alive today carries her genes. She *was* the individual from whom we all descended."

"So Evan researched our literal mother?" Chandler said. "Why haven't I heard of Eve before?"

"You will when the popular press tunes into what's going on. Eve has rekindled the oldest human debate: Where did we come from? Who begot mankind?"

"Eve answers that?"

"In two ways. Not only did we inherit her genetic code, but evolution from Archaic to Modern Man took place in her family."

"This occurred in Africa?"

"Probably. Though some place Eve's home in South China."

Again Daniells covered the phone. This time Zinc overheard "Retrovirus tests." "Am I interrupting something?" he asked.

"We're almost finished," the professor said. "I'm a primatologist, you no doubt know. For years I studied the monkeys in the local zoo. The curator asked if I'd test the greens for Simian AIDS. It's a good excuse to visit old friends."

"We were discussing Evan and Eve."

"Evan was fascinated by mitochondrial DNA. DNA, I'm sure you know, is what transfers genetic characteristics. Genes line the DNA strands in the nuclei of our cells, for they're the building blocks of heredity. Nuclear DNA is a mix of genes inherited from both parents. It determines our physical traits. But there is another type of DNA in our cells, stored *outside* the nucleus in the mitochondrian. Mitochondrial DNA comes solely from our mother, so it isn't scrambled every generation through sex. Because it changes only through mutation—random errors in copying the genetic code—scientists use it to trace family trees.

"Mutated DNA is as distinct as a fingerprint. Laws of probability tell us DNA mutates two to four percent every million years. By comparing mitochondrial samples from around the world, we've traced our genetic code back to a single woman. That's why she's called Eve."

Zinc said, "Lucy was a subhuman three million years ago. She was one of the type that evolved into man. One of those later humans was this Eve. Two hundred thousand years ago, *she* evolved into us. That's why Evan studied her?"

"Precisely," Daniells said.

"What happened to Eve's contemporaries? Other Archaic humans?"

"They died out through Darwinism. Eve endowed her offspring with a genetic advantage that made them superior to other men. Sometime between her lifespan and ninety thousand years ago, her descendants fanned out around the world. They replaced other humans through survival of the fittest."

"Why was Evan fascinated by Eve?"

"Supergenes are genes that control other genes. He thought there was a supergene controlling age. The average life expectancy in North America is 74.7 years. That's the length of time you'll probably live. But your MLSP—the maximum life span potential programmed in your DNA—is approximately 110 years. Something gyps us out of 35.3 years, preventing us from living a third of our lives. Evan thought that was because we inherited a defective supergene from Eve."

"That's illogical. We'd be *less* fit."

"Not if the defect kicked in after reproductive age. With the advantage we got from Eve we'd still be fittest in our prime."

"Do you accept that?" Zinc asked.

"Evan studied Sacher and Cutler's work. Sacher noticed longevity increases across primate species when there's an increase in brain-to-body size. The larger the brain compared to its body, the slower a species ages. He concluded the brain controls longevity.

"Cutler tied Sacher's theory to extinct species as well. Comparing the skulls and bones of subhumans with ours, he found longevity shot up the closer he got to us. Then for some reason the increase stopped."

"Longevity ceased evolving with us?"

"No, Neanderthal Man."

Daniells covered the phone and said, "Thanks. I'll clean up."

Uncovered: "A minute more, Inspector, then I must call a cab. It's cold and wet out here, and I'm used to African heat."

"You were saying Neanderthal Man lived longer than us?"

"The Neanderthal brain was larger than ours—1,470 cc compared to 1,370. True to Sacher's theory, his lifespan was greater too. Cutler postulated there were hominids with superbrains compared to their bodies. If so, perhaps they held the key to longevity. Evan thought that key their non-defective supergene."

"How long did Kwan study with you?"

"About four months. He helped with research in my private lab. We had a falling-out and he returned to Hong Kong."

"You complained to Immigration?"

"You know about that?"

"Evan wasn't deported?"

"No, he left on his own."

"What prompted your complaint, Dr. Daniells?"

The professor hesitated, weighing her reply. Then she said, "I love animals. That's why I research. My lab contains equipment for surgery. I only use it in beneficial ways. Vivisection is abhorrent to me.

"In the fall of 1978, I was asked to speak at a New York symposium. While gone, Evan would mind the lab and monitor our research. My flight to New York was at six a.m. Packing my suitcase, I realized I was missing some notes. At two a.m. I drove to the lab.

"The light inside was burning when I arrived. It irked me Evan had neglected to turn it off. Using my key, I entered and surprised him conducting an obscene experiment. I ordered him out. He threatened me. I called Immigration from New York and never saw him again."

"Did you appear at the deportation?"

"No, it was adjourned. His lawyer advised him to leave and that's what he did."

"What was the experiment? The gist will do."

"My favorite patient was a chimp named Tarzan. Evan had cut off his head and mounted it on a plate. Plastic tubing ran to the neck of a second immobilized ape, supplying life support to keep the head alive. As the anesthesia wore off, Tarzan looked around. I walked in while Evan was taunting the chimp with its headless body."

"Sounds like science fiction," Zinc said skeptically.

"The first experiments were done two decades ago. A head at Case Western University lived for thirty-six hours. Science has advanced a lot since then."

"Why would Evan do that?"

"He was psychopathic. I did the psych report for the deportation. Also, he was high on drugs and dressed bizarrely. Coming here, he suffered culture shock. The experiment revealed his lust for money."

"How's that?"

"His motive was cryonics."

"The freezing of human bodies at death so they can be thawed when there's a cure for fatal diseases?"

"Keeping a head alive is the first step. If the body's too far gone, just the head is preserved. Even when the body's preserved, only the head matters. By then we'll have replacement robots."

"So longevity was Evan's obsession?"

"Everyone's obsession as they grow old. Evan aimed to market the Fountain of Youth."

"Where in the zoo are you, Professor?"

"With the green monkeys, near the harbor seals."

"Wait twenty minutes, I'll pick you up."

MAN-EATERS

6:17 P.M.

Lord Stanley, the governor-general of Canada and the man responsible for hockey's Stanley Cup, threw his arms heavenward in 1889 to dedicate Stanley Park ". . . to the use and enjoyment of people of all colors, creeds, and customs for all time." The year before during the Ghoul case, a psycho had tried to skin Zinc alive near the Brockton Point totem poles, so now whenever he entered the park he wondered if that was one of the "uses" Lord Stanley had in mind.

Past the Vancouver Rowing Club, a Tudor manor on pilings slapped by the churning sea; past the statue of Robbie Burns streaked with pigeon shit; past Queen Victoria Monument, speckled pink with blossoms blown from branches overhead; past Theatre Under the Stars and the President Harding Fountain, the unmarked police car circled the park.

"Zoo's in here," Chandler said, driving into the lot. Umbrellas popped as they reluctantly climbed out into the squall.

"One thing we haven't discussed," Tate said, "is where we're going to live."

"Don't let the rain sour you on Vancouver. Forecast is the sun should return by June."

Carol grinned. "Poor animals. Bet they wish they were trapped by Californians."

"Knowing Californians, I doubt it," Zinc said.

Rushing up-inlet, a chill wind shrilled among the cedars and maples overhanging the path. Rain pummeled their umbrellas, flapping the fabric. As each gust rippled the pond to their right, a hungry bear up ahead growled for its dinner.

"Canada has three pluses over the States," said Carol. "Few guns, so there's less chance we'll be shot. Less crime, so it's a safer place to raise kids. And the fact I look great in red."

"You'll have to shed your citizenship if you plan to join the Mounted."

"Why's that?"

"Because Americans are barred by law."

Zinc had long accepted the fact he'd never understand women, but Carol's reaction took him by surprise. Head hidden behind the umbrella shielding her face, she turned to say something when the wind blew it inside out. The force of the gust tore the umbrella from her hand. Immediately she reached out and gave him a shove. Caught off balance, he fell to the ground. "Roll!" she yelled as a pair of slugs chipped the pavement near his eyes.

The cops were halfway across a pedestrian bridge that angled left to the polar bear pit. "You!" Carol shouted, drawing her Colt. "Police!" she added, and broke into a run.

Squinting through the downpour, Zinc scrambled to his feet. The bear pit was sixty feet ahead. A chain-link fence around the grotto kept spectators back, but now the zoo was deserted, closed since dusk. The circular wall of the pit was topped with metal teeth, beyond which the cavern dropped to a subterranean moat. The moat surrounded a mountain of platformed rocks, its summit crowned by a green pool and fountain spraying mist. Pool to platform to platform to moat, runoff tumbled freely, while something below attracted the bears. A masked figure by the edge of the pit took shots at Tate.

Dodging bullets, ducking for cover, crouching as she ran, Carol couldn't tell the gunman's sex. Head to toe the shooter was sheathed in polyethylene, with a bulky parka overtop. The black full-face hood had slits for the eyes. The gun in the gloved hand was a Glock 17.

Cutthroat bolted from the pit along a narrow path. Hemmed in by a fence and shrubs, he sprinted toward the harbor seal–green monkey exhibit.

As Carol chased the gunman, Zinc vaulted the chain-link fence around the grotto. The sound of crunching bone echoed from its depths. A sign at Zinc's shoulder read:

DO NOT FEED THE BEARS. PERSONS THROWING ANYTHING INTO THE GROTTO ARE LIABLE TO PROSECUTION.

The tawny thousand-pounders were tearing a woman apart. One had Daniells' crushed skull clamped in its jaws. Another gnawed her leg while a third ate her arm. If and when the killer was caught, there'd be the Parks Board to answer.

Nearing the far end of the path, Cutthroat whirled and emptied the Glock 17 at Carol. Hitting the ground, she tore both sleeves of her jacket. She rolled against the fence as slugs cleaved the rain beside her face.

Throwing the Austrian gun away, Cutthroat darted right. He vanished beneath the corrugated roof and dripping awning of a concession stand. Carol followed.

Back at the grotto, Zinc took up the chase. He high-jumped the chain-link fence as scavenging seagulls dive-bombed the pit. He reached the path a moment before Carol disappeared behind the concession stand.

Ahead, beyond her silhouette, the seal–monkey exhibit was lit up. It faced the open area at the end of the path. The seals sought safety in their horseshoe swimming pool, while the monkeys, shrieking from the shots, frantically swung hoop to hoop in their abutting cage. When the machine gun opened up, Zinc's heart lurched.

Tate rounded the building to find Cutthroat waiting in ambush. Sneaking up on Daniells near the green monkey cage, he'd left his weapons valise beside the stand. Casting the Glock aside had been a trap for Carol, who, thinking the killer unarmed, dashed around the corner to keep their quarry in sight. Slugs from a Mini Uzi greeted her instead.

Only six pounds and fifteen inches long, the Uzi is the commando weapon of the Israeli Army. With an effective range of 500 yards, it spits 950 9mm Parabellum shots a minute. The pistol grip in Cutthroat's hand fed a 32-round clip. As he triggered the Uzi, barrel slits vaporized the raindrops to fine Scotch mist. The slugs hit Carol before she could react.

Like slaps on leather, the *blap! blap! blap!* drove the monkeys crazy.

The first slug punched a hole through her palm, grazing the side of her hip.

The next blew blood like red exhaust out the back of her arm.

The third slammed her shoulder, spinning her around. It nicked the bone, hurling her to the ground.

Carol hit the pavement hard and let out a yelp.

The puddles turned crimson.

Knowing she was dead if she didn't keep on the move, Tate rolled once, twice, and gained her feet. The seal–monkey complex had three parts: the swimming pool near the end of the path, a wire enclosure where the apes romped outside, and a house with a swing door so they could escape the rain. Windows along the right side exposed the interior, with a spectator area bounded by a low stone wall. Head first, she dived behind the wall as the Uzi burped again.

Blap! blap! blap! . . . ping! pingg! pinggg! . . . bullets raked the stone, ricocheting up toward the glass. The windows exploded one by one as bewildered apes hooted hysterically. Carol curled up in a fetal ball when guillotines of glass knifed down around her.

Suddenly she was grabbed by the hair and punched about the eyes. Her new assailant jerked her head back and forth. Between blows she glimpsed a black face fringed with cream fur, and a two-and-a-half-foot tail behind bared fangs. As she raised her arm to protect herself, the ape bit her hand, flashing the thought *AIDS*! through her mind. The last thing she saw was a pair of blue balls as the monkey sprang for the roof.

Tate passed out.

Halting at the concession stand, Zinc whipped off his bomber jacket and flicked it around the corner. A line of splintered holes ripped through the wood in front of his eyes. Crooking his hand around the corner, he squeezed off three shots. Then hearing fleeing footsteps, he exposed his head.

The black-masked killer had disappeared. Carol's Colt lay abandoned on the ground. A trail of blood led to the low stone wall.

Crouched like a crab to shrink him as a target, .38 fanning the rain in front of him, Zinc sidestepped to the primate house. Carol lay sprawled behind the wall, bleeding so profusely he thought she was dead.

Carol!

Carol!

"Carol!"

She opened her eyes.

A concerned face hovered above.

". . . less chance we'll be shot . . ." she muttered.

"You need a doctor."

"Just my arm. Don't let that bastard out of your sight."

"Later."

"Now! I'll get help. There's a phone over there."

When Zinc hesitated, she urged, "Go! If I was going to die, I'd want to be in your arms."

Scooping up the Colt, he resumed the chase.

Tate sucked in a ragged breath and struggled to her knees. Stumbling toward the phone, she wondered, *Is it 911 or 999 in this town*?

Gun in each hand, Zinc searched the zoo. Swans, ducks, and a peacock waddled out of his way. Left of the otter slide, the Uzi barked again. The six-shot burst sent the otters diving for their pool.

Cutthroat stood near Bill Reid's carving of a Haida killer whale. He fired through the fountain in front of the aquarium. One of the aquarium's doors was propped open with a pail.

As Zinc dodged the muzzle flash from the one-inch barrel, a janitor mopping the entrance hall stepped out to investigate. He stood in the doorway squinting at the sky, wondering why no lightning accompanied the thunder. A blast from the Uzi blew his head apart.

Cutthroat entered the aquarium.

Both guns blazing, Zinc jumped the turnstile and dived for the Clamshell Gift Shop. Halfway down the hall to the Sandwell North Pacific Gallery, Cutthroat turned. Glass panels separated the gift shop from the hall. As Zinc crawled back to the doorway, the submachine gun snarled. The panels shattered in a line, hurling shards at the tourist souvenirs. Flat on his belly, the Mountie got off two shots. The Smith & Wesson clicked empty in his hand. As Zinc flipped open the Colt to find two live rounds, Cutthroat ducked right into the Tropical Gallery.

Decision time.

A mistake could cost his life.

How many shots had the Uzi fired?
Almost thirty-two?
More important, did the killer have backup clips?
How long until the VPD arrived?
Was there a patrol in the park?
How would they know where he was unless they heard shots?
Wait a minute.
He looked around.
There it was. On the wall. Partway down the hall.
He sprinted from the gift shop to the Tropical Gallery door. Passing the fire alarm, he yanked its handle. The aquarium filled with urgent clanging bells.
Zinc poked his head around the door frame. Huge iridescent tanks bubbled in the gloom. To his right, the Uzi flared again. The volley made the tanks shimmer, scattering the fish. The bullets tore chunks of wood from the jamb, exploding the doors behind him that led to the whale exhibit outside.
Frightened by the commotion, a gray beluga breached. One slug hit the mammal's fin as others strafed the Killer Whale Habitat beyond. Torpedo-shaped, black-and-white, twenty-two-feet-long, Hyak sounded beneath his pool. Water sprayed in waves as the gunfire ceased.
Instinct told Zinc the Uzi was out of rounds.
Were those fleeing footsteps, or his mind playing tricks on his ears?
Amid the alarm's cacophony it was impossible to tell—but trusting intuition he stepped through the door.
Arms fully extended in a marksman's stance, he swept the Colt back and forth in a two-handed arc. The empty Smith was tucked in his belt.
A beady-eyed manta ray hung suspended overhead. In front of him swam the most colorful fishes he had ever seen, the tank a treasure of glittering South Seas jewels. Spooked by movement to his right, he ducked behind a glass case for protection, squatting face to face with a preserved coelacanth.
Ahead, the doors to the Graham Amazon Gallery were shut to keep it acclimatized. What Zinc had glimpsed was a door closing as someone passed through, so rounding the coelacanth display, he dashed for the entrance. He cocked the Colt as the fishes of China—

spotted scat, fingerfish, calico bubble eyes—watched unblinkingly from their tanks. Staying clear of the line of fire, he yanked open the door.

To his left were hanging gardens and the crocodilian pool. A half-submerged cayman gnashed its teeth and thrashed its tail. A huge tank straight ahead brimmed with neon tetras and discus fish. A maroon cord to his right blocked public access, beyond which the gallery circled around to the Open Jungle in back. Footprints marred the mop-wet floor in that direction.

Zinc ducked under the cord.

Bisecting the Open Jungle, a boardwalk zigzagged through the dense palms and ferns. The only illumination was light from the piranha tank opposite the exit. The rain-spattered glass roof was gloomy gray. As Cutthroat fed the Uzi another magazine, two-toed sloths in the pepper trees stirred from slumber. Near where the killer waited in ambush, a yellow-billed cardinal ruffled the fronds of a Swiss cheese plant. A scarlet ibis flitted from banana palm to strawberry guava, while a furtive iguana scurried around the Asian's feet.

When Zinc appeared at the exit—his silhouette black against the piranha tank beyond—the Uzi erupted. Deep within the Open Jungle, a fiery-yellow tongue licked in his direction. On its tail came the *blap! blap! blap!* of death. Zinc's shoes slipped on the mop-wet floor as he cut the corner too sharply, his feet flipping out in a pratfall as the tank behind him burst. Another hail of shards rained about his body, then a gush of water alive with teeth engulfed him.

One . . . two . . . three piranhas bit into his hands.

Instantly, Zinc knew his luck had run out. Lower jaws prognathic with upper teeth forward and bottom teeth back, their tiny faces resembling W. C. Fields, piranhas—though only a foot long—can strip a skeleton of flesh in minutes. Not only was Zinc the next course on the menu, but shocked by the rupture of the tank he'd dropped the Colt. Footsteps on the boardwalk meant the killer was coming to finish him off.

Submerged among the flipping, flopping, snapping carnivores, Carol's gun had disappeared. Chandler scrambled to his feet and ran for his life. Adrenaline hit his pounding heart like a wooden stake, powering his sprint for the gallery doors. Flinging the last tenacious piranha from his hand, he burst through the exit as the Uzi barked again.

Black carp and rice eels swam beneath Chinese lanterns . . .

The coelacanth stared vacantly from its glass cage . . .

The door beyond the hanging manta ray beckoned . . .

As Zinc ran like Jesse Owens and Carl Lewis combined.

The doors behind crashed open with Cutthroat in hot pursuit. Zinc imagined a bull's-eye painted on his back. Lights turned on by the janitor to mop the hall lit up the exit like a shooting arcade. Sensing he was a dead duck if he chanced that route, Zinc angled right for the north wing of the Tropical Gallery. A moment later, he saw his mistake.

At the far end of the passage he chose, so large it occupied the entire wall, was a massive aquarium filled with nurse, lemon, and sand tiger sharks. No option left but to run this gauntlet of cold blood and scales, the passage lit by dozens of tanks along both sides, a slimy-sacked octopus suckered to the one he now passed, Zinc ran toward the flesh-tearing teeth dead ahead. Would the shark tank withstand an Uzi blast?

Let it hold! his mind implored as he raced beneath a hammerhead guy-wired to the ceiling, the soles of his shoes squeaking across the metal-ribbed floor. . . . *Let it hold!* as the gunman's reflection appeared on the glass ahead, the Uzi gripped waist-high to brace the weapon. . . . *Let it hold!* as he flying-tackled the rest bench in his path, a swan dive unparalleled since he'd been a skinny-dipping kid at the Rosetown swimming hole, the bench legs scraping the floor like fingernails on a blackboard. . . . *Let it hold!* as deep in the tank looming ahead, gill slits flapped behind ripsaw teeth. . . . *Hold, goddammit!* as the Uzi spit lead, the bench slamming the tank in a wild toboggan ride, bucking Zinc to the floor as he begged, *Let it hold! Let it hold! Let it—*

It didn't hold.

A spider's web of cracks fanned across the glass. The area in front of the tank was *T*-shaped. Other aquariums formed the *T*'s underarms, the passage down which he had fled its stem. Zinc filled his lungs to capacity and rolled to the right as the pressure of 32,000 gallons blew out the glass. A flash flood akin to Moses releasing the Red Sea threw him against the sea turtle tank along one underarm. Water pinned the half-drowned Mountie to its face as the tide from the rupture surged along the stem. Thrashing within this deadly gush, an armada of sharks, sawfish, and eels engulfed the killer. Inundated, Cutthroat fired desperately, triggering the Uzi at every dorsal fin that broke the surface.

When the flood waned, Zinc pushed away from the turtle tank. He waded knee-deep along the *T*-arm. Hitting the exit crossbar as hard as he could, he escaped into the night. He hid until the killer emerged and ran for Lumberman's Arch.

Wailing sirens competed with the insistent alarm. Chandler followed Cutthroat as far as the Seawall. There, outlined by lights across the inlet, the killer discarded the Uzi for an oxygen apparatus. Stuffing the harmonica-shaped device in the mouth area of the mask, Cutthroat dived into the sea.

Zinc ran back to find Carol and alert the harbor police.

CHINESE PUZZLE

9:17 P.M.

When Eric Chan was ten years old, his father had sat him down for a man-to-man talk. They were on the porch of their Strathcona home, less than a block from Chinatown. The family next door was painting a dragon for the New Year's parade.

"Son," the elder Chan said, an abacus in his hand, "four secrets lead to success in Gold Mountain. One"—he flicked across a bead—"be pragmatic. If you wish to prosper, you adapt. Two"—he flicked another bead—"be self-reliant. Earn your own way. Don't expect handouts. Three"—a third bead clicked—"be industrious. To succeed, you must work hard. Four"—he pushed the beads back—"be discreet. The ghosts despise a wealthy Chinese."

He pointed to the phallic towers in the ghosts' part of town. "See how each strives to be taller than its rivals? That's the ghosts' game. Play and they'll hate you."

The antique calculator of wood and brass passed from father to son.

"Your great-great-grandfather worked the Cariboo mines. He was a British Columbian at the start. Not once in five generations have we left this land, surviving and thriving through hard work and the long view. The time has come, youngest son, for you to join the business, so where in our grocery does your future lie?"

"I want to be a Mounted Policeman," Eric said.

His father choked.

Only through "the long view" did Chan survive. The Chinese consider police work "the dishonorable profession," so Eric's nose was bloodied weekly in school. Finally, when he rapped on the door, the Force didn't want him either, for traditionally red serge enhanced a *white* face. If not for burgeoning heroin traffic from the Orient, his application would have been denied. Of sixteen thousand members today just ten are Chinese. Eric Chan was the first non-white.

While training at "Depot" Division in 1961, he was nicknamed "Charlie" by the ghost recruits. Ostracized, one afternoon he bussed to the library, where he read Earl Derr Biggers' *The House Without a Key*. Charlie Chan was the hero of the book, a great detective fond of prophetic proverbs. *Fresh weeds are better than withered roses,* Chan thought.

Eric's most embarrassing date was his first Red Serge Ball. Sally Fan, now his wife, flew in for the dance. As they entered the banquet hall, conversation hushed. Chan wondered why until he found their table: sixteen chairs and only two name tags. "It doesn't matter," Sally whispered. "Pretend it's a restaurant." A few minutes later a couple approached from the head table with their plates and cutlery. "Mind if we join you?" the man asked. "We're Kate and Robert DeClercq."

Chan worked hard to become the Force expert on Triads and heroin. When the RCMP began selecting members for college degrees, he studied random processes and probability at UBC. Mastering computers fed the Asian stereotype, but Eric figured, *Fuck 'em*. He'd take the long view.

Corporal, to sergeant, to inspector: his foresight paid off, so now with the Force computerized and the exodus from Hong Kong, Eric Chan was doubly indispensable. These days the taunts were saved for Sikhs who asked to wear their turbans on duty.

Alone in the Computer Room at Special X, Chan punched his keyboard and analyzed the screen. Overlaying the green print was his reflection: fox-like face, balding, with quizzical eyes. To information already collected on Fankuang Tzu—prompted by the fax from the Gong An Ju—he added Zinc's report on Evan Kwan's deportation.

Finished, he printed a copy:

THE FAMILY KWAN

1. Fankuang Tzu Pharmaceutical is a Hong Kong-based corporation owned by Kwan Kok-su. He is the sole shareholder on record.

2. Kwan Kok-su has two surviving relatives: granddaughter Lotus and grandson Martin. They run the business day-to-day, with Martin head of their Canadian subsidiary. There is no mention of Evan Kwan in company records.

3. Martin Kwan is Canadian by birth. His mother flew here pregnant in 1962, returning to Hong Kong after he was born. Martin attended U of T for a law degree, residing in Canada on and off since.

4. Lotus Kwan is a recent immigrant. She was sponsored by her brother. Until this year, she had never been to Canada.

5. Kwan Kok-su was born in China. During the Communist Revolution, he fled to Hong Kong. Martin is sponsoring him as an immigrant. Kwan Kok-su is eighty-four.

In the beginning, Triads weren't crime societies. They were secret orders formed to drive out the Manchus. Three hundred years ago in 1644, Mongol barbarians crossed the Great Wall to conquer China. The Manchus replaced the Ming Dynasty with their own rulers, so Triads formed to return the Mings to power.

The Triad symbol is an equilateral triangle. The three sides signify the Chinese concepts of Heaven, Earth, and Man.

*Triad leadership is triangular too. Control is vested in the Dragon Head (*lung taus *in Cantonese). He is served by the Red Pole and White Paper Fan. The Fan (or "415") is the businessman, tracking money and financial affairs. The Red Pole (or "426") is the enforcer, executing those who get in the Triad's way.*

6. Fankuang Tzu Pharmaceutical markets both modern drugs and ancient Taoist cures. The company made a fortune supplying Hanoi during the Vietnam War.

7. The parent corporation is abandoning Hong Kong. All assets are moving to its subsidiary in Canada. A new factory is under construction in Richmond on the Fraser River.

8. No Evan Kwan has applied to immigrate.

Incited by the Triads, the Taiping Rebellion of 1850 caused twenty million deaths. Suppressing it, the Manchus killed a million people by beheading, live burial, slow strangulation, and the Thousand Cuts. So many Triad members fled to Hong Kong that soon three-quarters of the populace belonged.

For money, the Triads in exile turned to crime. Piracy, smuggling, extortion, gambling, vice, and drugs became their trade. The Chinese invented organized crime. Triad heroin earns more each year than the value of U.S. currency in circulation.

In 1941 the Japanese occupied Hong Kong, destroying police files and criminal records. When the British returned in 1945, the Triads controlled the docks, transportation, and labor. Decimated by the war, the RHKP was rebuilt from scratch, enabling Triad recruits to infiltrate. Soon corruption was rampant throughout the Royal Hong Kong Police.

When China fell to Mao Tse-tung in 1949, Hong Kong opened its borders to refugees. Three-quarters of a million people—Triads included—entered the colony for sanctuary. Today Hong Kong is home to fifty Triad gangs. None of their three hundred thousand members plan to be there when China takes over in 1997.

Chan was the cop who drove the Five Dragons from Vancouver.

In 1973, Police Commander Peter Godber fled to England from Hong Kong to avoid prosecution. His subsequent conviction prompted the Independent Commission Against Corruption to investigate RHKP bribes. Five hundred files were open within a year, including those on five cops with the Anti-Triad Bureau who were 14K Triad members. Hundreds of millions of dollars in payoffs had fattened their bank accounts.

In November 1974, the five flew to Vancouver. Their Five Dragons Corporation purchased a local office building for $60 million. Lui Lok, their leader, was known as "the six-hundred-million-dollar man." The amount referred to his illegal wealth. When Chan moved in, the Five Dragons fled to Taiwan, currently the refuge of forty millionaire ex-Hong Kong cops.

In January 1983, North American Triad affiliates met

in the colony. The RCMP learned of the meeting through their Asian Gang Squad and Crime Intelligence Service. Within weeks, Triad assets were moving to Vancouver, the bulk being laundered through local real estate. Had the city been chosen as the Triads' future base?

What worried Chan greatly was the spy within the Force. He could be any one of the recent Asian recruits. The Triads had rotted the RHKP from within, undermining the law until it served them.

The spy tracking DeClercq for the Kwans used the same tactics.

Was Fankuang Tzu a Triad on the move?

10:01 P.M.

The Mounted were closing ranks.

They met in DeClercq's office—DeClercq, MacDougall, Chan, Chandler, and Avacomovitch—where they stood in a group facing the collage. The judges' case had expanded to include the Kwans' interest in Windigo Mountain. There were now so many connecting threads, the overview resembled a road map. Earlier, Chan had swept the room for bugs, attaching "hummers" to the windows to defeat vibration laser mikes. The equipment the Kwans had used so far—Walther, forgery, access device, Mini Uzi, and Glock 17—was state-of-the-art. Down the hall, two guards watched the closed door.

"How's Carol?" DeClercq asked.

"Bullet chipped the bone. St. Paul's may have to operate," Chandler said.

"How are you?"

"Scratch or two." His hands were bandaged and his clothes were torn. The look in his eye was stark as he read the printout on the Family Kwan.

Each took awhile to study the collage. Eventually DeClercq said, "Here's where we stand. Murdoch, Maxwell, and Daniells were killed so Evan can immigrate. In the past, he may have come and gone under an alias, but he couldn't settle permanently. With the deportation participants dead, now he can."

"Question," MacDougall said, pointing to the photo of the blood-spattered desk. "If Maxwell was bribed to ensure the outcome of the deportation, why did he adjourn instead of dismiss?"

"Daniells was too strong a witness," Chandler said. "Dismiss her allegation and questions would be asked. The Kwans had to settle for second best."

"The family took the long view," Chan added. "They set him up for ten years down the line. In 1978 the payoff was easy to earn, but a decade later he was forced to strip the file. By then *Justice* Maxwell had too much to lose."

DeClercq indicated the pages from Murdoch's diary. "During the deportation, Murdoch flew to Hong Kong to confer with Kwan Kok-su. Kwan Kok-su and Evan are linked somehow. Evan's identity is the key to the murders."

Avacomovitch approached the collage. He touched Parker's drawing of the Yellow Skull. "Evan studied molecular anthropology with Daniells. Robert's theory concerning Blake sparked his interest. Before that, Windigo Mountain was a hunk of ice. Now the Kwans seek to explore the peak. They were denied a research permit to land, but sent a helicopter anyway. It disappeared this morning."

"All flights in and out of Alberta are grounded," MacDougall said. "The weather office predicts the Rockies will sock in for a week. If the chopper reached the mountain, they'll freeze to death."

"Someone in the Force sent my map of the area to Asia," said DeClercq. "It made its way back to us through Beijing. The Chinese police want information on Kwan Kok-su. Night before last, someone stole *Parker's Journal* from my home. Last night three Asian punks came after me."

"I've had no luck contacting Minister Qi," Chan said. "And no one there is authorized to speak on his behalf. Qi's request appears to be a personal one."

"If Murdoch, Maxwell, and Daniells were killed so Evan can immigrate, why now?" Chandler asked. "His interest in Windigo Mountain?"

"Fankuang Tzu is on the move," said Chan. "Perhaps the time is ripe to quash the obstacle in Evan's way. Beijing's say in the colony grows every day. If the company's a Triad afoul of the Gong An Ju, now's the time to get out."

"Martin and Lotus were at the hotel when Murdoch was shot. Was Evan there," MacDougall asked, "under an alias?"

"Triads kill to gain 'face,' instill fear, and silence witnesses," said Chan. "If Evan's psychopathic, that's a powerful mix. Perhaps it explains the audacity of these crimes."

"I should have asked Daniells two more questions," Chandler said. "Who wrote the other psych report on Kwan? And what ritual did he perform in the lab?"

"Eric," DeClercq said, turning to Chan. "This spy in our midst must be found. Meanwhile, try to reach Minister Qi. Why does Kwan Kok-su interest the Gong An Ju?

"Jack," he said, facing MacDougall. "Find that chopper and search the expedition.

"Joe," he said to Avacomovitch. "Link Windigo Mountain to the Kwans' business. Once the weather clears, we land on the peak.

"Zinc," he said to Chandler. "Pack your bag. Next flight out, you leave for Hong Kong."

Part Three

LIMBIC SYSTEM

When first my way to fair I took
  Few pence in purse had I,
And long I used to stand and look
  At things I could not buy.

Now times are altered: if I care
  To buy a thing, I can;
The pence are here and here's the fair,
  But where's the lost young man?

—A. E. Housman

FRAGRANT HARBOR

Kowloon, Hong Kong
Sunday, March 22, 11:50 A.M.

Hong Kong hit him like a sledgehammer in Arnold Schwarzenegger's hands.

From the moment the 747 roared by the apartment blocks crowding Kai Tak's runway, the washing that flapped on bamboo poles almost touching the wings, the faces of people inside the flats so close Zinc saw their moles, he was slammed into sensory overload. Outside the airport the heat and humidity stuck his clothes to his skin, as if he'd opened a laundry dryer before its cycle was through. On the anthill of Hong Kong Island and here across the harbor in the beehive of Kowloon, half of six million people live in less than nine square feet of space. Packed seven to a room in the densest place on Earth, they literally can't all go out in the streets at once. Sitting in a police car inching south, Chandler was convinced this morning they tried. Nathan Road, the spine of Kowloon, called the "Golden Mile" because it picks tourists' pockets, ranks as one of the colony's widest avenues. Elbow to elbow and fender to fender, it swarmed with hostile traffic, pedestrians elbowing one another as red double-decker buses belched fumes and vied for space with seventeen thousand taxis. Honking horns and squealing brakes added to the clamor, chaos, and stress. To his left the Marlboro Man stared into the car, hands cupped around a cardboard cigarette. Fish ogled him from a tank truck to the right, air pumped in to keep them fresh until chosen from the menu. A forest of glass and steel lined the road, pneumatic pile drivers on dozens of sites thumping to build more. Up wobbly bamboo scaffolding covered with nets, spidermen raised sixty-story skyscrapers overhead. So frantic was the construction pace that not only were the old colonial buildings all gone, but little remained of the 1950s. The human theater on Nathan Road bustled at double time. Even the escalators descending to the MTR zipped at twice the speed of those elsewhere. Under neon signs stacked ten high, a duty-free trade in gold, jade, diamonds, pewter, ivory, watches, cameras, chops, rugs, candles, linens, silks, cottons, tables, cots, cribs, pots, paintings, and whatever else three million tourists will buy raged on. Street hawkers jammed every nook and cranny, flogging T-shirts, *shar'pei* puppies, erotic carvings, and barbecued chicken feet. The streets off Nathan Road had their specialties. Down some were enough sweatshop tailors to clothe the world, while others dealt in bird's-nest, ginseng, or snake wine. The Red Lips Bar and Bottoms Up served the bare-breast crowd. The bird markets of Hong Lok sold cockatoos, parakeets, thrushes, and finches. The restaurants all had ceiling racks on which to hang cages so owners could air them, show them, compare them, and listen to them sing. Everywhere Zinc looked something caught his eye. Japanese tourists followed guides bellowing through bullhorns. A new business opened to firecrackers and a prancing dragon. Slaughtered pigs were piggybacked along the sidewalk. Calligraphers and fortune-tellers did brisk trade. The hiss of fritters in a wok mixed with the smell of salted squid. Businessmen on cellular phones cut deals while they jostled. Traffic drove on the left like it did in Britain. Crosswalks were marked the same as on the cover of *Abbey Road*. The diesel stench in the air reminded him of London. Then as the car neared the last vestige of old Hong Kong, the brick and sandstone Clock Tower marking the eastern terminus of the Orient Express, a pungent whiff of incense assailed his nose.

Off Nathan Road, the car stopped at a red door.

Joss sticks burned in a small shrine beside the entrance. The Chinese markings read "FANKUANG TZU LONGEVITY RESTAURANT."

The Chinese word for a place like this is *renao*—"hot and noisy." The cavernous room was a hullabaloo of clicking chopsticks, mingled voices, and exotic aromas. To the Chinese, food is a religion, the restaurant its shrine. Ambience is measured by how many people are packed in, great-grandma to babe in the womb crowding every table. Into a decor of gold serpents coiled around red pillars, giggling children darting between the family groups, Zinc wormed his way toward the only vacant chair.

A Chinese kitchen is an ark of doom. Confucius said, "Enjoying your food is first among pleasures," to which were added the later canons, "If it has four legs and isn't a table, put it in your mouth," and "If its back points to Heaven, you can eat it."

Chinese cooking is famine cuisine. Nothing is wasted, inspiring such dishes as duck's feet, bird saliva, and fish lips with eyeballs. "Dragon's duel tiger" is cat and snake. "Three squeals" is named for the sound rat fetuses make when squeezed with chopsticks. "Ingredients should be as fresh as the new day," so Zinc passed tables where fish were served scaled and filleted with their hearts still beating. When Peking duck was first made, the ducks weren't killed. They were locked in an iron cage over a charcoal fire. As the heat increased, the thirsty fowl drank from a bowl of vinegar, honey, malt, and ginger. As each expired, it was sliced and served on a tray.

Monkey brains scooped live from the skull are a Chinese delicacy. The British—dog lovers by and large—banned dog meat, so it's consumed secretly. Recently Chinese chefs invented "drunken prawns." Served live and twitching in a covered glass bowl, they're doused with red wine poured in through a hole in the lid. The prawns leap about getting riotously sloshed, then are spooned out and dropped into boiling soup.

The man who sat facing the vacant chair was enjoying a thousand-year-old egg. Not long ago a Canadian writer tried this delicacy and died from a bone fungus that ate his skeleton. Zinc didn't mention this to his host.

"David Ong," the man said, wiping his hands on the tablecloth.

"Zinc Chandler," the Mountie said, exchanging grips. The back of his chair was to the door. Poor Asian etiquette.

"Pardon my not meeting you at the airport as planned. The Sun Yee On and Wo Hop To had a dispute. The argument spilled out into the street and a passer-by was shot. I spent the night ordering lights up, everyone's ID on the table, right now if you please. Triads don't like losing money and face. Best I watch the door. Duck if I shout."

Chandler felt indigestion coming on.

Superintendent David Ong was an Anti-Triad "hard-man" with the Royal Hong Kong Police. His close-shaved skull and pitted face topped a stout body developing a paunch. He picked his teeth, pearly whites, with an ivory toothpick once he finished the egg. Navy blue with a burgundy pouf, his suit was of the finest cloth Wing On Street produced. The jade ring on his signet finger caught Zinc's eye.

"Mo," Ong said, making a kung fu fist. "God of war and the martial arts. Patron of police and rogues alike."

"Dead," Zinc said, flashing his ring. The engraving was a bird with an arrow through its chest.

"I booked you a room at Blackfriars Hotel. Your fax did say 'shabby genteel.' Fallout from last night has shortened time for supper. I ordered without you. Here it comes."

The waiter set a dish down between the men. Reversing his chopsticks, Ong served Zinc. " 'Food is medicine. Medicine is food.' " He translated the Chinese characters glazed on the plate. Turning his chopsticks right way around, Ong popped a morsel into his mouth.

The appetizer crunched between Zinc's teeth.

"Special black ants from Northeast China," the Asian said. "Fried in oil with sesame seeds, then packed around walnuts. Ants prevent arthritis."

The next dish arrived.

"Colorful shredded snakes," he said, serving his guest. "Snakes aid the blood, dispel wind, and cure rheumatism."

That's lunch? Zinc thought, watching the waiter vanish. He wished Triad gunmen *would* burst in. Shot full of holes, he'd have an excuse to flee.

When bear's paw braised in brown sauce neared the table, his Adam's apple caught in his throat.

Ong was frowning, deeply hurt, his hospitality flouted by this *gweilo* with no respect. Then he burst out laughing as the waiter veered. "Enough," he said, calling for their actual meal.

Chandler grinned. "Ice broken," he said. Then because men have braved such tests for thousands of years, he reached out with his chopsticks and ate another ant.

They dined on quail (good for the lungs), pineapple deer (muscles and kidneys), and stone-cold rice with barley (a healthy complexion). This they washed down with a ginseng drink.

"We have no record of Evan Kwan. No birth certificate, passport, or other documents. You're sure someone of that name lived in the colony?" Ong said.

Chandler nodded. "We tried to deport him in 1978. Our file was stripped last week, removing all trace."

Ong held a rice bowl to his chin and shoveled its contents. "Kwan Kok-su is quite the opposite. He's one of the greatest successes of modern Hong Kong."

The Asian pointed to the wall on the far side of the room. Chinese markings and Taoist symbols covered it ceiling to floor.

"Kwan's *zong pu*. His family tree. His line goes back two thousand years to the Court of Qin Shihuang. Qin united China and built the Great Wall. Kwans served the imperial throne until 1911."

"Uninterrupted? All that time?"

"Qin, Han, Sui, Tang, Mongol, Ming, and Manchu—they survived them all. Qin Shihuang was obsessed with death. The Kwans had herb collectors throughout the known world. Qin commissioned them to find him an elixir of immortality."

Setting down the rice bowl, Ong spread his arms. "Longevity has always been the Kwans' specialty."

"Everybody wants a long life, eh?"

"Don't you, Inspector?"

From his jacket Ong removed a cigarette case of mother-of-pearl. Pushing his meal aside, he offered Zinc a smoke. When Chandler declined, he lit a Benson and Hedges. As he spoke he jabbed the air with his cigarette.

"After the last emperor fell in 1911, the Kwans served the Kuomintang of Sun Yat-sen and Chiang Kai-shek. In 1945 they fled from Communist troops, and near here were ambushed by a Red Army patrol. Kwan's father, mother, wife, and son were killed in the attack. Just he and his elder son reached the colony."

Zinc withdrew his notebook, jotting while Ong spoke.

"The Kwans arrived with nothing but their *zong pu*. They used their reputation as imperial pharmacists to build this restaurant. Every dish cures some ill."

"Year?" Zinc said.

"Nineteen forty-six. A decade later, Fankuang Tzu Pharmaceutical was formed. By then Kwan's son had changed his name to Stephen Kwan. The Asian community here bought their herbal drugs while he researched Western medical techniques. Today the company makes millions off both markets."

The waiter cleared the table and brought them tea.

"In 1960 Stephen married a Mainland refugee. The following year, she gave birth to Lotus Kwan. Martin, the only son, was born in 1962. There is no Evan Kwan in the family."

The superintendent passed the Mountie a birth certificate. "Lotus was born here. Martin in Canada."

Smoke swirled about them like mist on the Peak in spring. Zinc had snuffed the monkey during the Ghoul case. Each whiff of the sidestream made him crave a drag.

"Tragedy struck Kwan Kok-su in 1963. Stephen and his wife were bombed here in the colony. The device was wired to their Rolls."

"Anyone charged?"

Ong shook his head. "It may have been a Triad shaking them down. Or a rival losing business to their company. By then they'd built a huge factory in Kowloon.

"Kwan blamed the Communists for Stephen's death. After 1949, the family was condemned for counterrevolutionary crimes. 'Loyal running dogs and their lackeys,' remember? Kwan thought the Reds were out to execute him. He hasn't left the factory in twenty-four years. He lives like a hermit in a fort."

"Does he run the company?"

"Not anymore. Kwan's over eighty and in poor health. He amassed a fortune from Vietnam. Sold both the Yanks and Hanoi drugs. The Americans hate him, but here he's respected for his business acumen."

"The kids took over?"

"Yes," Ong said. "They grew up in the factory. Locked away with the old man, they were tutored privately and learned the trade. Kwan feared the Reds might assassinate them too, so neither stepped outside until their teens."

"Might the company be a Triad front?"

"If it were, I would know."

Ong stubbed his cigarette and lit another one. "The Triads fought the emperor, while the Kwans prospered by serving his court. The Triads undermine us, while the Kwans grow rich selling legal drugs. Taoist medicine serves a billion people. And that's just *half* their world market."

At the next table, the diners ate an owl. Its beak lay on the platter as a garnish.

"How does eating wildlife promote longevity?"

"To understand, you must fathom Taoist beliefs."

Ong rolled the toothpick across his lips as if to illustrate a point.

"Everything in life must maintain a balance between yin and yang. This includes the body, if we're to have good health. Imbalance causes sickness, leading to death.

"Yin represents all things negative. Yin is cold, thin, contractive, dark, and feminine. Yang is the opposite: all things positive. Yang is hot, fat, expansive, light, and masculine. Since death is contractive and life expansive, serious illness moves from yang to yin. Taoist drugs act to restore the balance."

The toothpick stopped in the middle of his mouth.

"Pathways of energy line our bodies. These 'meridians' start in the organs and surface under our skin. *Ch'i*—life energy—circulates along these paths. When yin and yang are balanced, *ch'i* flows freely. When they are out of harmony, death occurs. Disease signifies an imbalance is underway.

"Have you ever been to an acupuncturist?"

"No," said Zinc.

"Acupuncture needles stimulate the paths. Drugs pass through them to reach internal organs. The paths carry a drug's effect throughout the body. To seek balance is to seek the Way. The Way—or *Tao*—is the order behind life."

The waiter brought them pitted lichees on ice. Zinc had trouble lifting the slippery fruit with chopsticks. Finally he speared it, barbarian-style.

"Aging leads to death, so it is yin contractive. Longevity is prolonged life, so it is yang expansive. Yin effect is overcome by yang influence. So with the right yang drug, life extends."

Zinc stabbed another lichee and popped it into his mouth. "I wish to meet Kwan Kok-su. Can that be arranged?"

"Possibly. Depending on his health."

"Oww!" Zinc yelped, jumping in his seat. "Damn!" he muttered, spitting out half a tooth. A chunk of lichee pit dropped into his palm.

"Are you—"

"Ouch! The nerve's exposed."

"I'll take you to my dentist." Ong flashed his pearly whites.

Not yet forty, Zinc thought, *and already I'm falling apart.*

The fish, stout and five feet long, had eight fleshy fins and a square, toothy jaw. It lay on a bed of ice in a silver tray. Unchanged for sixty million years, it was called "the living fossil" by ichthyologists. The man in the wheelchair was a fossil too. He'd paid a king's ransom for the fish. With *joss,* the spinal fluid of the coelacanth would prolong his life.

They were in a private room off the restaurant. Special orders were served here. Kwan pierced the fish's back with a silver straw. "Suck," he said in Cantonese to the old man. The cripple slurped as someone rapped on the door.

Kwan excused himself and left the patron to his meal.

A few minutes later, he approached Zinc.

"I'm told you suffered an injury from our food."

Zinc took in the impeccable suit and Cupid's-bow mouth.

"Have your dentist send his account to me."

The Asian handed Zinc a card, then left the restaurant.

The name on the card was Martin Kwan.

MEDICINE THAT KILLS

3:10 P.M.

When the New Territories were ceded to Britain in 1898, China excluded the Walled City from the lease. To this day the Kowloon area is a no man's land where fifty thousand squatters live in a maze of squalid hovels, four-foot alleys, and open sewers. Colony health and licensing laws don't apply, nor do the police bother to patrol. Untrained dentists and drug peddlers prey openly, while sweat-soaked wretches eke a living from plastic flowers, soles for shoes, wontons, and puppets. Human rats and real rats breed side by side.

The drug complex near the Walled City was an enclave too. As the chauffeured Rolls-Royce approached its brick walls, the razor wire on top gleamed in the sun. The car was cleared by the Perimeter Intrusion Detection System, geophones recording Martin's voice within while a computer compared it to his voiceprint on file. Before the guards electronically opened the outer door, sensors checked for explosives and stowaway's breathing. Vetted, the limo entered the complex.

Inside, the Rolls skirted the hydroponic herb farm to park between the hospital and the Inner Sanctum. Martin cleared Security to enter the building—EyeDentifyer reading the veins on his retina, Identimat measuring the geometry of his hand—then made his way to the Kwans' Ancestral Hall.

The hall's front gate was guarded by armed sentries, the red door studded with nine rows of bolts. Another gate flanked by stone dragons secured the court within. In the Room for Singing Merits across the yard, Chung Chong sat at a table forging documents. Dressed like the Warlord in nineteenth-century style, his dangling mustache two thin strands, he was erasing all trace of the boat people used for the DECO tests. As Martin approached, the old man put down his calligraphy pen.

"How is he?"

"Slipping. The doctors are with him now."

"Is the Donor Farm well stocked?"

"Spares arrived this morning. The snakeheads also brought fresh Alma Yang."

"The Warlord will be pleased," Martin said. "Tell him another expedition leaves for Canada soon. With luck he'll have his Immortality Yang."

Beyond the third gate, a passage ran between two pines to the Sacrificial Altar, off which was the Ancestral Shrine. As Martin pushed the button that opened the trapdoor in the floor, tittering laughter echoed inside.

By flashlight he descended the stone steps to the Pit, then walked the subterranean tunnel to the Labs. Decoding the security door that sealed the research center, he entered opposite the Cryonics Freezer. The walls of the metal chamber dripped condensation as blue light shimmered behind triple-glazed windows. Inside, shrouded by swirling mist, a hundred naked bodies hung upside down in tubes, individually frozen in liquid nitrogen. Smaller containers preserved as many heads, severed from bodies beyond future use. The fee to await resurrection was five million dollars.

To Martin's right, the latest DECO test was underway. "Well?" he asked, entering the lab.

A Chinese in a white coat gazed, clipboard in hand, through one-way glass. His face was disfigured by a purple birthmark. Behind the glass, five naked men hung chained by their wrists. They sat on exercise bikes, pedaling frantically. The bike seats had wire jocks that cupped their genitals, with power cables plugged in the wall. Electrodes were taped to each man's skin. A blindfold and microphone masked each face.

"Left to right, the dose was doubled for each injection. The needles went in at the base of the skull for an intracranial test."

Lab Coat monitored an array of LEDs.

"Each man's metabolism is tracked by computer to ensure they burn calories at the same rate. Those who pedal too fast or slow are given a jolt. The results so far are similar to those from rats."

Five sets of digital instruments glowed below the glass. Each was equipped with stereo speakers and a VDT. "Shall we see how they're faring?" Lab Coat asked.

He cranked the audio volume for the subject on the left. The room filled with heavy breathing and soft moans. "Low dose. Cool brain. Some rejuvenation." He recorded data from the LEDs.

The next set of speakers produced sobs. "Higher dose. Hotter brain. The readouts change. Heart flexibility, lung capacity, white cell count are up."

The scream from the third subject raised hackles on Martin's neck. Whatever the drug was doing to his brain, the man's metabolic rate was promising indeed. By blocking DECO they were turning back the hands of time.

"How much younger is he?" asked the businessman.

"From these figures, about ten years. Only youth's resilience could endure such stress."

Suddenly there was convulsing beyond the glass. The man to the far right stopped pedaling. Sparks and gray smoke shot from his groin. His chest heaved wildly as he thrashed against his chains. His heart was trying to burst through his ribs.

As blood gushed from the man's nose, Lab Coat turned up his speakers. The only sound was a strangled hiss.

"Overload," the scientist said. "His vocal cords have torn. Without sufficient DECO, he's fried his brain."

Now the man second from the right was in trouble. His genitals sparked as gibbers howled from his speakers. Both legs twitched like a galvanic frog's.

"See how his metabolic rate is on the rise? This subject has shed twenty years. Blocking DECO allows the cells to properly use thyroxine, another hormone of the pituitary gland. Thyroxine burns calories, raising the temperature of the brain. A sudden return to youth is the side effect. Heart, lungs, and immune system rejuvenate."

The man to the far right hung limp in his chains. His LEDs showed he was dead. The man next to him shuddered as his heart exploded in his chest. His LEDs jumped erratically, then leveled out. The gibbering from his speakers died to a gurgle.

"Where next?" Martin asked.

"Find the DNA. Blocking DECO isn't enough. To market youth, we need the supergene."

Martin left the viewing room as the third man died. The corridor to his right led to double steel doors. Again his palm was cleared by an Identimat, then the doors opened like a prison gate.

The Donor Farm resembled a penitentiary. Around an open central core were tiers of cages, each home to one of the refugees the snakeheads smuggled in. A team of doctors moved from cell to cell, hunting the best transplant source for the Californian's son. Jackson's boy wasn't a high rejection risk, so the heart and kidney could be harvested from several spares. Martin was irritated by their pathetic whimpering.

Near the steel doors was an isolated cell. The plaque beside its peephole read "ALMA CAGE." Inside, Martin saw what looked like an ape curled up on the floor. Its arms were long, its shoulders broad, its knees semi-flexed. Five feet tall, the primate was covered with reddish hair.

As he watched, the creature stirred.

Protruding jaws and a flattened brow turned toward the door.

The head was conical-shaped.

The face was human.

TURN BACK THE HANDS OF TIME

Vancouver
Sunday, March 22, 6:10 P.M.

He knocked on the door of the houseboat and waited in the rain. Beneath his feet the deck rose and fell with the tide, while out on the water a foghorn moaned. The smell of chili cooking hung pungent in the air.

"Be it ever so humble . . ." Joseph said, inviting Robert in. His finger provided a bookmark in *Trent's Last Case*.

"Delicious aroma," DeClercq said, his tone not so sure. The Russian's culinary skills were notorious.

"The meals at Chez Moi are now haute cuisine. Ruth—she rents the boat next door—is out of work. I help with the overhead and she fattens me. Uvalde Chili tonight. Corona?" Joe asked.

Robert shucked his raincoat and hung it by the door. A cheery gas fireplace warmed the cabin, the voice of Billie Holiday luring him in. Beside Joe's reading chair was a half-done jigsaw puzzle, its picture a crossword not completed. *Two puzzles in one,* he thought, noticing the books on the arm of the chair.

Joe emerged from the galley with uncapped beers. A wedge of lime was stuck in each bottle's neck.

"Those them?" Robert asked, nodding at the chair.

"Yep," Joe said, handing him a beer. "Fascinating passages the Kwans have marked."

MacDougall was in Calgary, hunting the expedition. The weather in the Rockies had yet to clear, thwarting any search for the missing chopper. He had, however, tracked down the expedition's base, a motel between Calgary and Edmonton. Jack had tossed the rooms on the pretext of launching a rescue attempt. The books were under a table with a mah-jongg set. Aware of Joe's assignment, he'd sent the books to him.

Robert crossed to the chair and thumbed through the volumes. *Bigfoot or Bust: A Cryptozoologist's Handbook* read one spine. *Still Living? The Yeti/Sasquatch Enigma* was the other.

"I think I know what the Kwans are doing," Joe said. "The map from Beijing, what Daniells told Zinc, and these books are clues. Remember Dmitri?"

"Your friend at the convention?"

"He and I have been having the most interesting talks."

Joe searched the bookcase behind his reading chair. He flipped through several anatomy texts, then showed Robert a picture. It was a magnetic resonance image of the human brain, an eerie green cross section taken from the side.

"The brain stem," he said, running his finger up the spinal cord. It was capped by a half-ring that looked like a doughnut nibbled at the bottom. "The limbic system," Joe said, "and pituitary gland. DECO is secreted here." Wrapped around the inner brains was the cerebrum, a nest of worms atop a vertical snake.

Billie Holiday gave way to *The Divine Miss M*.

"First question," Joe said, "is, *Why do we age?* What controls longevity? The Kwans think the answer is our brain. That's why DECO is written on the map. A change in brain chemistry affects the whole body, for everything below the neck is a supporting organ. Their belief that DECO causes age makes sense, begging the question: *What controls the pituitary gland?*

"Daniells said Evan thought there was an aging supergene. Supergenes are genes that regulate and control. The pituitary secretes the hormones of growth, puberty, and sex, ensuring DNA will pass on to the next generation. DECO sees us through reproductive age, then kills us off when we're no longer of use to DNA. A supergene controlling our DECO level makes sense."

They moved to the galley to give the chili a stir.

"Evan thought we inherited a defective DECO supergene from Eve. If he could find it and engineer a correction, we might live the full one hundred ten years of our MLSP, instead of the seventy-four years of our life expectancy.

"Searching for a particular gene is like trying to find

that needle in a haystack. Human DNA has one hundred thousand genes, only eight hundred of which have been identified. Most of those are genes that cause genetic defects, like cystic fibrosis and muscular dystrophy. They're found by comparing the 'mutant' sample with 'normal' DNA—but how do you find a mutant gene common to everyone?"

They served themselves in the galley and moved to the dining nook, a table with two benches under a porthole in the wall. Rain rapped the window as brine lapped the hull.

"Our closest living relative is the chimpanzee. It shares ninety-nine percent of our genes. Skeleton to cells, both species are the same, so what makes us man and it ape must be that one percent. If the one percent is composed of regulatory genes—probable since the chimp's maximum life span potential is much shorter than ours—you see the benefit Evan would reap from the DNA of a primate *closer* to us? A primate on the hominid branch, not the pongid fork?"

A copy of *Bagpipes, Blood, and Glory* lay on the table. Joe opened it to Chapter Nine. "I drew some additions on your diagram.

"By comparing our DNA with that of another hominid, Evan could isolate our mutant supergene. The closer the relationship, the narrower his search. If *Gigantopithecus* lived on Windigo Mountain, what better environment to preserve its DNA? The peak is ice-locked year-round."

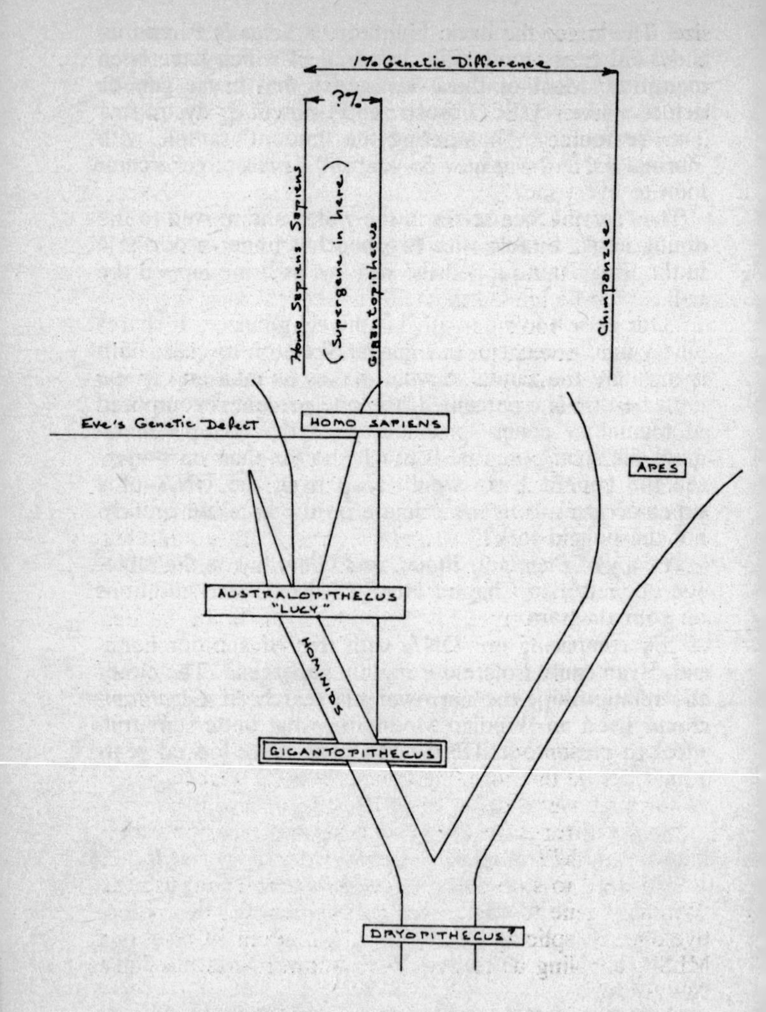

"Why *Gigantopithecus*?" Robert asked. "Any hominid predating Eve would do."

"Daniells said Evan was interested in Sacher and Cutler's work. They found as longevity increases across species, there's a corresponding increase in brain-to-body size. The larger the brain, the more efficiently it runs its body. Efficient brains burn fewer calories. Fewer calories require less cooling. Less cooling needs a lower DECO level. A lower DECO level means slower aging. If not for Eve's defect, that would be us."

Joe turned the pages in Robert's book to *Parker's Journal*.

"Look at the size of the Yellow Skull. Its cranial vault would hold a brain larger than that of every known primate. Even at nine or ten feet tall, the brain-to-body ratio would be immense. That's why the Kwans are fired up over your book."

The tide beneath them changed from ebb to flow. The stereo played a gospel version of "Jacob's Ladder."

"Evan finds the supergene. Then what?" Robert asked.

"Genetic engineering is out of control. It's a revolution equal to unlocking the atom, escaping gravity, and building the computer. Certain bacteria secrete enzymes that cut single genes from a DNA strand. Ligase, another enzyme, glues the orphan gene into a foreign strand. The hybrid created is 'recombinant DNA.' By splicing the gene into a bacterium, it's reproduced in hours instead of generations. If the gene manufactured a hormone in its original strand, as the bacteria multiply into a colony of billions, the 'clone' secretes a steady flow of the hormone too."

"*Gigantopithecus* DECO?" Robert said.

"Or maybe the hormone that screens it, retarding age. A hormone we're deficient in because of Eve."

"So Evan turns on the good gene and taps the Fountain of Youth?"

"No need to stop there," Joe said. "He could use the 'Windigo' gene to engineer a replacement for our defective one. By splicing it into our DNA, he might reset our MLSP, enabling us to live—who knows?—Methuselah's 969 years?"

"Use a monster to make a monster," Robert said.

RELIC HOMINIDS

Kowloon, Hong Kong
Monday, March 23, 10:22 A.M.

Scuffling echoed down the subterranean corridor as the Alma was dragged past the Pit and up the stone stairs.

Beyond the trapdoor to the Sacrificial Altar, Cutthroat whetted a beheading sword.

The Warlord was hungry.

Time to harvest the yang.

Vancouver
Sunday, March 22, 6:55 P.M.

"Bizarre," DeClercq said, "if Murdoch, Maxwell, and Daniells died so the Kwans can hunt extinct monsters."

"Extinct?" Joe said. "Maybe not. Yesterday's myths are today's realities."

The Mountie frowned as if to say, "How many beers did you have before I arrived?"

In his Blake biography DeClercq had written:

> Long before Spaniard Juan Perez "discovered" the West Coast in 1774, men the Indians called "the eaters of maggots" arrived. At Chinlac village near Vanderhoof, B.C., a twelfth-century Chinese coin was dug from strata levels predating 1730. Did ancient Asian explorers bring the Yellow Skull, which through trade or war fell into Kwakiutl hands? The Kwakiutls had a myth centered on the Rockies, where they believed a cannibal god lived in his spirit house. Did they transport the skull east in a ritual? Was that how it passed to the Plains tribes and ultimately to Parker?
>
> Near Purgatory Hill in present-day Montana, the molar of a primate was recently sifted from rubble

forty million years old. Likewise, was the Yellow Skull from an extinct species . . .

What he had not suggested was the species was alive. Why damage his credibility when there was no need?

"Myths are the archetypes of the collective unconscious," Joe said. "Jung believed the sum of our psychic history is distilled in them. The power of myth lies in the fact legends don't develop in one person's mind, but are inherited with our primal memory. Myths are limbic thoughts that pass with our genes. That's why the same myths turn up in different cultures."

The boat rocked as Elvis sang "I Believe."

"*Current Anthropology* surveyed scientists. Thirteen percent thought Bigfoot a non-extinct species, while twenty-three percent said the Loch Ness monster lives. We *still* classify twenty new mammals every year."

"Were you polled?"

Joe nodded.

"How did you respond?"

"With a big question mark. By nature I'm a skeptic. I scarcely believe *I* exist. But in 1958 the Soviet Academy accepted that two unknown manlike creatures live in Central Asia. Both inhabit the Pamir, Himalaya, Tien Shan mountains. My friend Dmitri sent me the Snowman Commission Report in Moscow's Darwin Museum. It makes you wonder."

DeClercq thumbed the books from the expedition's room. "It's a long jump from *Gigantopithecus* bones to saying Bigfoot exists. Similar fossils in Asia didn't prove the Yeti."

"No, but the Yellow Skull is an amazing coincidence. *Gigantopithecus* fossils are found in 'Yeti-land,' then a similar bone turns up in Bigfoot's haunt."

"Anything's possible, I suppose. Look at the coelacanth."

In 1938 scientists thought the coelacanth—a primitive fish that evolved into amphibians—had been extinct for sixty million years. Then Captain Hendrik Goosen, a South African fisherman, caught one off the Comoro Islands near Madagascar.

"Same with the giant panda, pygmy hippopotamus, and Komodo dragon. All were myths," Joe said, "until we 'discovered' them. Then they crossed from cryptozoology to legitimate science. The mountain gorilla is the best example."

Whites exploring Rwanda were told a huge manlike beast swung through the treetops emitting frightful cries. Europeans dismissed this as black superstition until Captain Oscar von Beringe returned with a mountain gorilla skin in 1901.

Joe said, "The 'African Sasquatch' was proved real. How many planes go missing a year in the local mountains? The ones we never find?"

"Two or three."

"Ideal country for a relic hominid."

"Are you playing devil's advocate? Or do you now believe?"

Joe indicated the books left by the expedition.

"It's what the Kwans believe that interests me."

In *Systema Naturae* (1775), Swedish zoologist Carl Linnaeus introduced modern biological names. He listed *two* subspecies of man: *Homo sapiens* (us) and *Homo ferus* (wild man). Seventy-five years before Neanderthal Man was discovered, he wrote at a time when no hominid fossils were known.

For centuries natives and whites alike have said a hairy monster lives in the wilds of North America. In 1784 *The Times* reported such a beast was killed by Indians at Lake of the Woods. As European settlers colonized the prairies, "Bigfoot" sightings moved west to the Rocky Mountains. Retreat is common to threatened wildlife.

On October 20, 1967, Roger Patterson was riding horseback in the Bluff Creek Valley of northern California. There he shot twenty feet of film. The film shows what appears to be a female Sasquatch seven feet tall. About four hundred pounds, she's covered with black hair. When the film was shown to the F/X men who built King Kong, they thought it impossible for an actor to walk like her. "Patty" had different musculature.

On October 21, 1972, Alan Berry recorded whistles and calls in the High Sierras. Signal processing later confirmed they were from a primate with a vocal tract larger than ours. The tape wasn't tampered with or studio-produced.

Near Walla Walla, Washington, in 1982, a Forest Service ranger found a set of footprints fifteen inches long. Pressed in soil ideal for casts, they revealed dermal ridges like we have on the soles of our feet.

Thirty-six to twenty thousand years ago, a land bridge joined Alaska and Asia. During this period, an ice-free corridor ran south into America's heartland. Prehistoric man crossed from the Orient, so Indians are of the Mongoloid race. Did the Yeti migrate then? Or when an early Ice Age froze the Bering Sea?

Long before Westerners reached Central Asia, the Abominable Snowman was there. Tibet's B'on religion sacrificed its blood, while Buddhist monks sought Yeti flesh as a general cure-all and aphrodisiac.

From 1820 to 1843, B. H. Hodgson was British resident at the Nepalese court. First to bring the Yeti to Western attention, he wrote his porters were frightened by a hairy mountain man.

In 1889, climbing in Sikkim, British Major L. A. Waddell spotted giant footprints at seventeen thousand feet. When Edmund Hillary conquered Everest in 1953, he reported sighting similar tracks. Lord Hunt, who led the expedition, heard high-pitched yelps in the Himalayas.

For three thousand years peasants have claimed a hairy beast lives in the Shennongjia Mountains of South China. Recent expeditions to the area returned with hair samples from an unknown primate. Like its Soviet counterpart, China's Academy of Sciences accepts the Yeti.

On April 22, 1979, London's *Sunday Telegraph* ran the headline "SOLDIERS ATE A YETI." The Chinese journal *Huashi*—translation "Fossils"—said back in 1962 Himalayan troops had killed a Snowman for its meat. . . .

DEATH HORMONE

Kowloon/Rosetown, Saskatchewan
Monday, March 23, 12:05 P.M./Sunday, March 22, 10:05 P.M.

> "If I were hanged on the highest hill,
> Mother o' mine, O mother o' mine!
> I know whose love would follow me still,
> Mother o' mine, O mother o' mine!"

"Zinc?"
"Rudyard Kipling, Mom. Happy Birthday."
"Sometimes you're just like your father. You sound far away."
"Hong Kong. It's tomorrow afternoon."
"Your voice is different."
"Cracked a tooth. Just came from the dentist, so my mouth is frozen solid. Still picking that gunk they use to make impressions from my teeth."
"I hope you saw a *good* dentist. Not some quack."
"Teeth of the man who referred me are like pearls."
"Are you boiling the water, son?"
"Everything's under control. By the way, when I return I'm bringing someone to meet you."
"It's about time," his mother sighed.
"Her name's Carol Tate. You'll like her."
"Where'd you meet?"
"Through the job."
"Not a criminal?"
"She's a cop. American, Mom."
"Sometimes I worry, the people you encounter at work."
"Tom back from gallivanting?"
"Not yet. He sent me a lovely card from Greece. I expect him any day."
"Tell him to get a haircut if he wants to be best man."

"Son . . ."

"Yes, Mom?"

"Be careful over there. We hear such terrible things about those Asian gangs."

"Piece of cake," Chandler said. "Small-time thugs. Gotta run. Important meeting. Just called to say you're the best mom a kid ever had."

"And you're the *second*-best son," she teased.

Laughing, they hung up.

Before calling up to Chandler's room on the hotel phone, Ong entered a small office off the Blackfriars lobby. There, a sallow-faced man with headphones and a tape recorder sat eating dim sum.

"Well?" Ong asked, picking his teeth.

"The *gweilo* just phoned his mother in Saskatchewan. Now he's talking to someone named Carol."

"Track down the mother's address. It may be of use."

Hong Kong, Hong Kong
1:16 P.M.

Ong dropped Zinc in the Central District, where Fankuang Tzu's office tower hugged the foot of the Peak. Central was a humming powerhouse of commercial banks, stock exchanges, and plush boardrooms behind glittering glass and steel. The building faced the stream of traffic along Connaught Road, close to Exchange Square. Zinc rode the elevator up to the forty-fourth floor.

As the doors whispered open, yes-men sprang into action, offering instant service with mandarin charm. Security guards lurked behind every potted palm as a bimbo in a tight *cheongsam* ushered him away to wait in luxury. The sway of her hips made him think, *Money, power, and sex.*

The Observatory was spacious and reeked of arrogance. The north wall a panorama of glass, the room commanded the harbor, Kowloon, the New Territories, and Red China beyond. A brass telescope, fixed in its mount, offered him a look at the Kwans' factory. Hunkered beneath a dishwater sky streaked with mustard yellow, the mountains in the distance a dismal gray, the drug complex resembled a concentration camp. The way it was fortified, Chandler wondered what went on inside.

His back to the vista, Zinc surveyed the room. Opposite, red-carpeted steps climbed to a higher level, the staircase flanked by two stone dragons. Right of the stairs, a well-stocked bar served a cluster of leather sofas and lacquered cabinets. The east wall was hung with Chinese theater masks. The west displayed Monet, Degas, and Renoir. A yellowing seventeenth-century globe sat on a marble pedestal in the center of the room, ringed by blowups of Asians exploring far-off lands. Beside the globe was an architect's model of the Kwans' factory planned for Vancouver. Gracing the Fraser River like some neo-Garden of Eden, it didn't look anything like a concentration camp.

Evolution, he thought.

Chandler wandered over to the lacquered cabinets. He noticed each was wired to an alarm. The nearest contained a Chinese manuscript. From its ragged condition he knew it was old.

As Zinc's attention shifted to the next display, soft footfalls sounded on the stairs. Turning, he saw a high-heeled pump and shapely calf, then an hourglass figure decked out in red silk. *Hubba hubba,* he thought.

"Inspector Chandler? I'm Lotus Kwan."

Offering him a fine-boned hand.

"The book you're admiring is five thousand years old. *Shennong's Materia Medica* lists 365 drugs. The manuscript in that case"—pointing to Zinc's left—"is *The Yellow Emperor's Canon of Internal Medicine*. It predates the Great Wall, three hundred years before Christ. Mao proclaimed it China's traditional pharmacology."

"The *Canon*'s still in use?"

"By a billion people. Chinese medicine goes back seven thousand years. Longer, except then we're into prehistory."

A garter appeared in the slit of the dress as Lotus sat down. A ruby red suspender against a dark stocking top. Zinc moved to the next case as the garter winked.

"Precious Supplementary Prescriptions," Lotus said. "A classic Taoist treatise from the Tang Dynasty. One prescription offers the world's first hormone treatment.

Eating human umbilical cord with the liver of a pig. It suggests consuming a mad dog's brain to ward off rabies. The same principle underlies modern immunology."

As Lotus stood up, red panties flashed in the slit.

"This one is Li Shih-chen's *General Catalogue of Herbs*. Only one of the fifty-two volumes is displayed. For twenty-seven years, he collected the family remedies of Ming Dynasty medicine men. Eighteen hundred drugs and eleven thousand prescriptions are described. Darwin quoted Li with respect."

"And these?" Chandler asked. "They look like carved bones."

"Chia-ku-wen," Lotus replied. "Prescriptions that predate recorded history. They're called Oracle Bones."

"Quite a collection," he said. "Must be worth a fortune."

"Legend is my family goes back twelve thousand years. We Kwans have always practiced medicine. My ancestors acquired these works over centuries, bequeathing them to future generations. My grandfather reveres our history."

"Actually, it's Kwan Kok-su I came to see."

"He has pneumonia, so I'll have to do. What is it you wish to see him about?"

"Evan Kwan," Zinc said, playing the faceless card.

"Who's he?" Not a flinch. Quizzical eyebrow raised.

"A student who came to Canada in 1978. When he ran into trouble, his lawyer flew here to confer with your grandfather."

"And the lawyer's name?"

"Hutton Murdoch."

"I was at the hotel the night he was shot."

"Small world," Zinc said. "Full of coincidence."

"Not really," Lotus said, flashing the garter again. "My brother attended the convention, so I went along. My first trip to San Francisco. Beautiful city."

"Your brother knew Murdoch?"

"We all met him. He was the one who suggested Martin attend U of T. That's why Grandfather flew him to Hong Kong."

"To ask which law school Martin should attend?"

"Fankuang Tzu is moving to Canada. The move has been on the drawing board for ten years. Grandfather had questions concerning Canadian company law, so hosting Murdoch killed two birds with one stone."

"Instead of going to Canada for a firsthand look?"

"My father was assassinated in 1963. Grandfather fears a similar fate. In twenty-four years he hasn't set foot outside our factory."

"What's your company's interest in Windigo Mountain?"

Not a flicker.

Not a flinch.

Just a beguiling smile.

Lady, you are one cool customer, he thought.

"What do you know about the Curse of King Tut's Tomb, Inspector?"

"It starred Boris Karloff. Or was it Lon Chaney?"

Lotus laughed the throaty laugh of Lauren Bacall. Zinc thought, *She's studied femme fatales.*

"Tutankhamen's tomb was breached in 1922. Soon its discoverers were all dead. Egyptologist Hugh Evelyn-White hanged himself. *I have succumbed to a curse,* he wrote in his own blood. Can you guess what caused their deaths?"

"Vengeful spirits?" Zinc said. "Undead mummies?"

"Pharaohs were buried with fruits and vegetables for the afterlife. During the 3,350 years the tomb was sealed, this organic matter decayed to mold. The fungi turned antigenic over the centuries, inducing allergic reactions in those who opened the tomb. Pink and gray patches on the walls drove them mad.

"Fifteen years back, a hiker in Norway collected two spoons of mud from a swamp. He was employed by the Sandoz company of Switzerland. When the mud was analyzed in Basel, druggists discovered a fungus they'd never seen before. Cyclosporin counteracts tissue rejection in organ transplants. Since it went on the market in 1983, the success rate of such operations has jumped to eighty percent. That hidden power of plants is what we seek around the world."

"On Windigo Mountain? In winter? There's nothing there but snow."

"Nature's untapped chemistry is everywhere. That's like saying there's nothing but water in the sea. The willow gave us aspirin. The foxglove digitalis. The strongest drugs come from the harshest climates. Who knows what we'll find where?"

Lotus crossed to the antique globe. Red fingernails gave it a spin.

"Every year Brazil destroys more of the Amazon jungle. Will the cure for cancer be lost in that slash-and-burn? Fankuang Tzu saves and clones threatened plants."

Zinc followed the Asian around the revolving globe. Lotus tapped the blowups one by one.

"Here an expedition harvests the ocean depths. Miracle drugs hide in aquatic weeds. Here an expedition nears the South Pole. Sub-thermal organisms aid cryonics research. Surely you see why Windigo Mountain attracts Fankuang Tzu? Its scientific secrets have never been explored."

"How does Bigfoot's supergene fit into your work?"

Bingo.

There it was.

Caught her off guard.

Nice recovery, Lotus. But not quick enough.

"You have heard of DECO?"

Pressing the advantage.

"Some call it the death hormone because it makes us age."

"DECO?" Lotus said, a nonchalant shrug. "There are many theories why we grow old. MHC. DHEA. Free radicals. Take your pick."

"True, but the supergene is Fankuang's theory."

"Who told you that?"

"Your company has a leak."

"Which is precisely why I decline to answer your question. Scientific espionage is rampant."

"Come on. A little hint? What's your theory? We age because we inherited a defective supergene from Eve?"

Bull's-eye.

Got you, lady.

Try deflecting that with your underwear.

"The U.S. Supreme Court has ruled genetically modified DNA can be patented. Biotechnical research is a multibillion-dollar industry. Recently I attended a meeting of pharmaceutical executives in Japan. The speaker was a U.S. patent attorney. He advised we have all research notes certified by a lawyer before discussing them with our peers. That's why our Kowloon labs are protected like they are. I can't answer your questions."

"Why do *Gigantopithecus* bones interest you? Because 'dragon teeth' are sought as Taoist medicine?"

"You do go on," Lotus said.

"It's my job."

"Did you read too much *Terry and the Pirates* as a boy? What do you think we're doing? Chinese alchemy? Cloning monsters back alive to conquer the world? Grandfather isn't Fu Manchu and I'm not the Dragon Lady. Sinister Orientals passed with the 1930s."

"The world isn't round or flat. It's crooked," Zinc said.

"How old are you, Inspector?"

"Almost forty."

"Which means your decay is well-advanced. For ten years your immune system has been in decline. Your bone mass is dropping one percent a year. Already you've lost an eighth of an inch from your height. Hair is sprouting where it's never grown before because your genetic code is breaking down. Testosterone is thinning the hair on your head. And your sexual prowess, I'm sorry to say, peaked at twenty."

"You do know how to make a fellow's day, Ms. Kwan."

"As your skull thickens, your head will enlarge. But inside, your brain will lose twenty percent of its weight, slowing your reflexes and the speed at which you think. Your midsection will bag no matter how hard you exercise, and your shoulders will narrow as your muscles waste. Your lungs will lose forty percent of their capacity, while your blood vessels will harden like uncooked spaghetti. The more your skin stretches, the more your face will sag. Soon you won't be able to hear high frequencies. Rigid eye lenses will blur your vision, as tightening vocal cords strain your voice. Whoever coined the phrase 'improved with age' was full of shit. And that's why you, like the rest of the world, *need* Fankuang Tzu."

Lotus led him to the panorama window high above Hong Kong. The "fragrant harbor" at their feet was polluted and gray. Junks and sampans bobbed on the waves, while freighters and navy frigates bumped the wharves. Green double-decker Star Ferries weaved from shore to shore, as the streets on both sides of the harbor seethed with a human tide.

"What you see is capitalism in its purest form. The colony is a British experiment in Darwin's theory—a laboratory where the market system rules without control. Hong Kong exists for profit, pure and simple. And that is a concept Americans understand.

"Do you watch American television, Inspector? Has there ever been a culture so obsessed with youth? Have you any idea how much they spend on face-lifts, tummy tucks, hair implants, and liposuction a year? How many jars of replenishing cream do American women purchase annually? Did you know Elizabeth Taylor, Gloria Swanson, George Hamilton, and Larry Hagman were injected with ground-up sheep fetus in the hope it retards age? Why? Because America idolizes youth. An American over forty is fit for society's slag heap. Thin, unwrinkled bodies, that's what Americans want. Imagine the market open to someone with the Fountain of Youth? The streets of America truly would be paved with gold.

"In America, medicine belongs to those who pay. Unlike Canada, they don't let social parasites drag the fittest down. A sixth of the population—thirty-seven million people—have no medicine. Those who succeed in America succeed well, and those who don't can wither and die. Why else would they maintain the highest infant-mortality rate among the developed nations? Obviously to weed out the weak and genetically unfit. In America health is bought and sold in the marketplace. Americans understand natural selection.

"Let me paint you a picture of America's future. The baby boomers are aging fast, shifting the center of gravity upwards every year. Soon coast-to-coast the States will look like Florida today, with forty-five million Americans over sixty-five. Even with sixty percent of the federal budget serving the old, the fund for Medicare will be bankrupt by then. Unless a two hundred-bed hospital is built every day from now until the next century, there won't be the facilities to offer medical care. The health of each American will depend on his or her bank account, and Fankuang Tzu will rejuvenate those who can pay.

"You wonder what we're doing here? Does that answer your question?"

"Why emigrate to Canada? Why not the States?"

"A slight hitch in how we raised venture capital. But once free trade goes through, the American market is ours.

"You should be grateful," Lotus said. "Not distressed. Until the twentieth century, the Chinese language couldn't translate the word *individual*. Anything less than the family was insignificant.

"The British lent you money like a pampered child.

"The Americans bought up your industries and siphoned off the profits.

"Hong Kong is sending an asset. Its business families."

"Depends on *which* families," Chandler said.

No sooner was Zinc out the door than footsteps descended the stairs.

"He got to Daniells."

"Obviously."

"The Horsemen know too much."

"Did you check the report?"

"It's confirmed. They arrested our man in the Force an hour ago."

"If Chandler has seen the DECO map, Qi is involved. If they're not working together, they will be soon."

"We must find the DNA. The blocker is useless without it. Everything is for nothing if we fail in the Search. With it we'll be welcome anywhere in the world. We must buy time until we search Windigo Mountain."

CANNIBAL

Kowloon
5:31 P.M.

The Californian stood beside the butchered refugee. The camera moved in for a close-up of the missing heart and kidney, then panned left to the bloody smears on Jackson's hands. Sitting in the viewing room watching the videotape, Cutthroat studied the look of concern on the American's face. Concern for his son currently undergoing the transplant. Concern for himself because of the videotape.

"We must insure," Martin had said the day the deal was closed, "both sides keep the organ source a secret. Your involvement will be taped and stored in a burn box to which I have sole access. Breach our confidence and the tape will be revealed. Keep our secret and it will stay hidden. If someone tampers with the box, the tape incinerates. Both sides are threatened. Both protected. The term, I believe, is a 'Mexican stand-off'?"

Cutthroat rewound the tape and watched it from the beginning:

. . . shot of the refugee in the Donor Farm, Jackson unlocking the bars of his cage . . .

. . . shot of the refugee lashed to a table, body bucking as Jackson shoots the abattoir bolt into his brain . . .

. . . shot of anonymous surgeons harvesting the spares, Jackson visible to one side . . .

. . . shot of the organs going to his son, Jackson at the window of the operating room.

Satisfied, Cutthroat removed the tape and stored it in the burn box. He left the viewing room for the underground Labs, clearing Security to enter beside the Cryonics Freezer. Through the Labs and out the door, he walked the tunnel past the Pit and climbed the stone stairs. As he entered the Sacrificial Altar above the trapdoor, hollow laughter echoed from the Ancestral Shrine.

He pushed the button under the table to close the sliding floor.

Displayed on the table were the beacons guiding the Search. The Oracle Bone which first prescribed Immortality Yang. Zhamtsarano's map indicating where Almas could be found. The *Field Notes* seized from General Pratt the previous century. And *Parker's Journal* stolen from DeClercq. The key to the Shrine lay in front of them.

As he unlocked the door, Cutthroat looked around. The Alma was still on the altar, its hair matted with blood. The beheading sword lay across the stump of its neck. Greasy tapers burned behind the corpse, casting dirty light about the room. Smudging the spirit jars, smoke touched the yang knives and longevity symbols on the walls.

Cutthroat entered the Shrine.

Inside, the air stank of incense, insanity, and decay. Paper lanterns threw blood red light. The Dragon Throne of burnished gold wrapped around the Warlord, its filigree back and arms a reptile breathing flames. Behind the throne was a jade and ivory screen. Its inlay depicted the Kwans' *zong pu*. The wall around the screen was squared with cubicles, each nook housing a lacquered skull. Some of the ancient bones were gilded with gold. As Cutthroat approached the wretch slumped on the throne, piped-in gongs and flutes accompanied the giggles.

"Yang!" the Warlord tittered, grinning like the skulls. A few of his teeth were sharpened to points.

"Yang!" he cackled, drooling down his clothes, eyeballs rolling back in his head.

"Yang!" he shouted, banging the tray. "Alma Yang is no cure! Immortality Yang!"

"I too want the Yang of the Great Hairy Beast," Cutthroat said.

The old man grunted, and picked at his food.

In front of the Dragon Throne was a mahogany table. A silver tray sat on it. The head of the Alma was on the tray. Peeled of skin, the crown of its skull was cracked like an egg. Cupped in the cranial vault was a half-eaten brain. The Alma's eyes were wide with fear.

Gore-stained and sweet with blood, the Warlord's imperial robes were torn. His one-inch fingernails curled like talons. Listlessly he diced the brain with his yang knife, moving a morsel toward his mouth with silver chopsticks. Tears ran down the old man's cheeks as he giggled.

If Cutthroat had his way, he'd cut the Warlord's throat. He itched to store Grandfather's skull in the rack with the skulls of the Ancestral Warlords. Unfortunately, the Code of Succession was strict, enforced by an Inner Council of octogenarians who predated Chingho. "His death must be natural," Chung Chong had warned. The council still had power. It held the Warlord's shares.

Ironically, Cutthroat was thankful for the Code, knowing how the Inner Council felt about him. The incident in Daniells' lab had tried their tolerance, but nothing like what he had demanded on his return. Still, he was eldest son and they were conservative, so with *joss* the council would adhere to the rules. *First son born is Warlord. Followed by his first son.* For twelve thousand years that had been the Way of the Fankuang Tzu. If you believed the myth.

"Yang!" the Warlord screeched, knocking over the tray. The open skull and mangled brain rolled across the floor. Laughing hysterically, he clawed the side of his face.

Cutthroat smiled.

A few days—a week perhaps—and Grandfather would be dead.

As new Warlord, he would own the shares.

The company would be his to do with as he pleased.

Sleek and modern, it would face the twenty-first century.

Assuming they still had a future in a week.

"Grandfather, your fear for the succession brought us to this brink. Had you not tried to impregnate that woman, Minister Qi would not have the map. Without the map, the Mounted Police wouldn't know our plans. This afternoon, without telling Ong, Chandler left for Beijing.

"Because of you, our move to Canada is threatened.

Had you not interfered, Qi would soon be dead. Now he will try to win the RCMP to his cause. We must stop that until we search Windigo Mountain. Without the DNA there is no future anywhere.

"If I kill Chandler, the Mounted will come in force. There will be no second expedition to the mountain.

"If I do nothing, Qi will link with them. Again there will be no expedition.

"The only way to buy time is distract the police. And the only way to do that is crack Chandler's mind.

" 'Our most severe punishment,' you taught me, 'is killing nine generations of a family. Great-great-grandfather to great-great-grandchild we cut every throat, eradicating the family from the face of this Earth.'

"Tomorrow I adapt that Way of the Fankuang Tzu.

"Tonight I leave for Rosetown, Saskatchewan."

THE TIEN SHAN MASSACRE

Beijing
Tuesday, March 24, 8:10 A.M.

China.

Communist China.

Hard to believe the deaths of Murdoch, Maxwell, and Daniells had led him here.

Here to this city of Mongols, Mings, Manchus, and Mao.

Here to the Northern Capital of Genghis Khan.

Chandler stood on the balcony of his Beijing hotel, eating an orange for breakfast and thinking about Carol. Last night a "yellow wind" had blown through the *hutongs,* graying gray Beijing with Gobi Desert dust. Beyond the drab housing blocks that ringed the capital, blue mountains marked the edge of the North China Plain. High above the russet roofs of the Forbidden City, colorful kites flew in Tiananmen Square.

China.

Red China.

Would he unmask Evan Kwan here?

South of Tiananmen Square, Qianmen Gate had once separated the Inner and Outer cities, protecting the emperor from those he supposedly served. Today, the wall that flanked the gate is gone, replaced by red slogans and portraits of Mao. But in the *hutongs* of the Outer City, Old China lives on.

Each *hutong* has its own history. There are three thousand back streets in Beijing, most so narrow nothing but a handcart will pass. All are single-story so no one could look down on the emperor in his palanquin. In Wet Nurse Lane, surrogate mothers suckled imperial young. In Flower Lane, the Empress Dowager bought silk petals. In Clothes Washing Lane, gossip ran rife about royal underwear. In Grass Mist Lane, torture became an art.

Beijing is a city where ten million people ride five million bikes. This morning its broad avenues and tree-lined boulevards were a blue-gray tide of whirling wheels. In the *hutongs,* however, time stood still. There the smoke of breakfast fires curled over crooked gates behind which houses with paper windows huddled.

Zinc watched an old man practice tai chi.

Two lanes over, a child with a monkey played a flute.

Three men passed with loads on their backs, hands in sleeves as they spit in unison.

A woman in the next *hutong* caught his eye.

At first he thought she was sick, the way she wobbled.

Then he saw her bound feet were just three inches long.

10:00 A.M.

Beijing headquarters of the Gong An Ju faced the east wall of the Forbidden City. Chan had driven Chandler to the airport in Vancouver, briefing him on China's Public Security Bureau. Now as he sat in the Foreigners' Section waiting for Minister Qi, watched by tandem portraits of Deng Xiaoping and Mao, Zinc mulled over Eric's sketch of the Red Chinese police.

Before the Communist Revolution of 1949, the People's Public Security Forces had assassinated supporters of the Kuomintang. Once Chiang Kai-shek's army was on the run, they turned on those who had transgressed before the Liberation ("persons with a counterrevolutionary past") and subsequent criminals ("active counterrevolutionaries").

The Gong An Ju was formed in 1955. Qi Yuxiang, a friend of Mao's from the Long March, became minister in charge of China's police. That year he broadcast a warning on Radio Peking. "The eyes of the masses are bright as snow. They report anything suspicious to me. Don't think I don't know what you're doing. I know, comrades."

During the Bamboo Curtain years, Qi was a mystery. His character was discerned from the prison he ran.

At Number 13, Tsao Lan Tse Hutong, Grass Mist Lane Prison enforced the party line. "Men commit crimes," Qi told the populace, "because they have bad thoughts in their heads. My function is to rid them of these thoughts, and in so doing make them new men."

Step one in making a new man was the Study Group. Daily, a meeting was held in each cell to hammer home the guiding words of Chairman Mao. "Facing the government, we must study together and watch each other." Failures moved on to step two, known as the Struggle.

This began with the offender standing in a courtyard surrounded by screaming mouths. "Confess!" the crowd demanded, jeering his answers with raucous hoots. Later he was led to the Interrogation Hall. It was an endless corridor of dark green doors, their frosted panes labeled "52ND ROOM," "63RD ROOM," etc. Shouts, threats, and sobs escaped from the rooms.

Each interrogation room was an austere box with whitewashed walls and a tile floor. Two desks separated by a wooden locker with a red star on top faced the prisoner's stool. Harsh fluorescent lights backlit the officers behind the desks, faceless party functionaries in dark blue uniforms. Above them stretched a red banner with white calligraphy: "Leniency to those who confess. Severity to those who resist. Rewards to those who earn big merits." A portrait of Mao stared at the prisoner's back.

For hours, days, and sometimes weeks, the brainwashing continued. The interrogators were trained by Qi. "Prisoners divide into toothpaste and water-tap men. The toothpaste prisoner must be squeezed occasionally to keep him talking. The water-tap prisoner needs one hard twist and everything comes out. How hard you squeeze or twist depends on the man."

Recalcitrant offenders were dragged to the Underground Cell. There imperial torturers, then Kuomintang torturers, and now Communist torturers perfected their art.

The Cell's main attraction was the "tiger bench," a hinged platform that bent in excruciating ways. The hip bones of a prisoner tied to it cracked first, followed by the weak parts of his skeleton. A towel and bucket were nearby for Chinese water torture: not the drip on the forehead used psychologically, but slow suffocation by draping the face with a wet cloth. Bamboo splinters and red-hot forks were available.

When Mao turned the Red Guards loose in the sixties, Qi spent time in his own jail.

"For what?" Zinc asked.

"His 'bourgeois past.' "

"Meaning what?"

Eric shrugged. "Party-speak."

"Who redeemed him?"

"Deng Xiaoping. Another friend from the early days who fell victim to the Cultural Revolution. When Mao died in '76, Deng took over. Once more Qi's star was on the rise. All the way up to the Leading Group for Political and Legal Affairs under the Central Committee. Not only does he control prisons and the police, but Qi's now the Politburo's number three man. He's a tough son of a bitch."

The man who hobbled into the Foreigners' Section didn't look tough. He looked like someone with weeks to live. His shriveled-up body was hunched over a cane. His mouth was lopsided from a stroke. His liver-spotted face was pinched with pain. Today he'd shed his Mao-jacket for an ill-fitting suit, a sure sign a Red Chinese wants something from the West. *He's a paper tiger,* Chandler thought.

Like its occupant, Qi's office was a shell. Where pictures of Nixon, Thatcher, and Mao had hung yesterday, there were yellow squares on a sun-bleached wall. The trappings of his party life were packed in boxes, a clean desk and two chairs all that remained.

"Liver cancer," Qi said, closing the door. "Tomorrow my successor arrives and I go home."

Chandler said nothing.

What was there to say?

The gulf between their realities was too wide.

He wondered where Qi had learned English with a strong British accent.

"Inspector Chan and I spoke this morning. My health delayed our discussion until today. We talked about your murders and Windigo Mountain. I'm pleased you share my interest in Kwan Kok-su."

Qi withdrew some photographs from the desk drawer. As he and Chandler sat down, light reflecting off the roofs of the Forbidden City fell across their laps.

"The story I have to tell, you may not believe. Had I

not lived it, I might not either. Only by telling you the truth will I accomplish my goal. Eradicating the warlords of the Fankuang Tzu."

Qi passed Chandler a photo from the pile. It showed a young Asian punting on the Backs, Queen's College and Mathematical Bridge behind.

"Recognize the setting?"

"Oxford?" Zinc said.

"Cambridge. 1933. The year I graduated."

Chandler had seen the next photograph before, in *Time, Life,* or *Newsweek,* one of those magazines. Barefoot peasants marched behind the hammer and sickle, led by Mao Tse-tung and two cohorts.

"Me," Qi said. "The one with the shoes."

"Year?"

"1935. On the Long March."

The third was of a mansion in classic Chinese style, with curved-up eaves and ornate balconies. A cruel-eyed man stood in front.

"My father," said Qi. "Our home in Shanghai. He was a wealthy landlord with plans for me. He knew a Western education would ensure a quick rise in the Kuomintang. Are you acquainted with Chinese history?"

"Just the basics," Zinc said. "With a lot of gaps."

"The emperor was dethroned in 1911. China became a republic under Sun Yat-sen. His Kuomintang government controlled the south, while imperial warlords held the rest. Until Sun's death from cancer in 1925, the Communist Party backed the Kuomintang. After Sun's death, a split developed. The Communists wanted social change on Marxist-Leninist lines, while Chiang Kai-shek demanded a capitalist state. He wanted it run by a privileged elite backed by his army, so he hated the Communists as much as the warlords."

"Was Kwan Kok-su a warlord?"

"No, his father was."

"Where'd the family live?"

"Near the Shennongjia Mountains south of Xian."

"Practicing medicine?"

"Yes, and hunting drugs. Chiang and my father were close friends. Both opposed any reform threatening their position. In 1926, Chiang led his army north to subdue the warlords. The Kwans were trapped near Xian. You know of the family's position at the imperial court?"

"They were alchemists who served the emperor. The one who built the Great Wall . . ."

"Qin Shihuang."

". . . wanted them to find an elixir of immortality. For two thousand years they were druggists in the Forbidden City."

"Kwan's father struck a deal with Chiang Kai-shek. In exchange for the drug of long life, the Kwans were granted safe passage to Xinjiang. Xinjiang is China's western province between the Himalayas and Tien Shans. Chiang pressed on to Shanghai."

A uniformed man knocked on the door and entered with Chinese tea. Serving the jasmine in handleless cups, he retreated.

"Is the Shanghai Coup of 1927 a gap?"

Chandler rocked his hand. "Refresh my memory."

"Chou En-lai's men fomented labor unrest to undermine the warlord of Shanghai. Industrialists like my father feared the effect unions would have on their profits, so when Chiang arrived to overthrow the warlord, his army turned its guns on the Communists instead. Five thousand men died by slow strangulation as civil war broke out."

"You saw the massacre?"

"The month I left for Britain."

"How old were you?"

"Twenty-one."

Qi passed Zinc a pair of photographs. In one his father and Chiang Kai-shek posed in front of a factory billowing black smoke. "That was to be mine on graduation."

The second was taken against the Backs. "Philby, Burgess, Blunt, Maclean, and me. Marx and Engels flowered at Cambridge that year."

Qi paused for a moment to gasp for breath. Zinc prayed he didn't die while they were alone.

"Children worked as slaves in that factory, sleeping under their machines at night. Female employees prostituted themselves for food, and strikes were suppressed by beheading the strikers. On my father's rural estates, taxes were collected sixty years in advance, with interest calculated at seven hundred percent. Debtors avoided prison by sending their wives and children to work in the factory. That was to be my legacy.

"Chiang was obsessed with killing Communists. Mao was hiding in the mountains of the south. He converted the peasants to his cause, enlisting guerrillas for the Red Army. 'The enemy advances, we retreat. The enemy camps, we harass. The enemy tires, we attack. The enemy retreats, we pursue.'

"I returned to China as Chiang's extermination sweep reached its height. The Communists offered fraternity and hope. The Kuomintang offered a factory of slaves. Did I embrace capitalism and my ancestral line? Or change my name, forget my past, and join the Revolution?

"If you were me, Inspector, what would you have done?"

It seemed as if we had been fighting forever, Qi told Zinc. First against sickness and fatigue on the Long March, for only one in five survived the six thousand-mile-trek to Shaanxi. Then against the Kuomintang in that endless Civil War. Then against the Japanese in 1937. Then against the Kuomintang at the Battle for Chingho . . .

"When was that?" Zinc asked.

"Nineteen forty-five. Fought in the Tien Shan Mountains of Xinjiang."

"Where the Kwans went after their deal with Chiang?"

The minister nodded.

Xinjiang is an area, Qi explained, as vast as Britain, Germany, France, and Italy combined. A pair of basins—once great lakes—flatten this rugged wasteland; the Dzungarian north, the Tarim south, with the Tien Shans in between. Below eternally snow-capped peaks of 23,000 feet, the road from Ili to Urumqi passes through Chingho. There the Kuomintang had 15,000 troops.

"Our strategy was to catch them in a vise," said Qi. "My battalion would circle north in a 280-mile arc to block retreat, then our main force would attack from Ili. Once through the Tien Shans, we were to cross the Dzungarian Desert by the Mongols' route, turning south behind Chingho.

"We found the massacre by accident. To scale the mountains we had broken into groups of ten, hoping to avoid detection from the air. Our goal that day was an abandoned lama temple, the route to which was across a rocky plateau. Rounding a jagged outcrop, we stumbled on the corpses. Thirty bodies rotting in a pile. Each skull was cracked open and missing its brain."

The old man paused to catch his breath. Zinc had to concentrate because of the stroke's effect. Only one side of Qi's mouth moved as he spoke.

"Head to toe, the bodies were covered with red hair. All except the faces, palms, and soles. The features, though like ours, were more pronounced. Flat foreheads, brow ridges, jutting jaws. The knees were semi-flexed like an ape's. The feet turned inward, with big toes spread. Nine were males. The rest females and children. The females all had long, drooping breasts."

"Yetis?" Zinc said, eyebrows raised.

"Too small and manlike," Qi replied.

"Did you get a picture?"

"Unfortunately, no. Stripped for the climb, we had no camera."

"When I was a boy," Zinc said, "every circus had a sideshow of freaks. The 'hairy man' was a common geek."

"Here too we have 'hairy people.' But they're unlike the bodies I saw."

"What became of the remains?"

"Food for the birds. We were on a forced march twenty hours a day."

"Did the Kwans kill them?"

"So I was told. The Kuomintang lost the Battle for Chingho. I interrogated the prisoners of war. Each was given a choice between execution or purge and redemption. That's how I learned about the Kwans and the massacre. They butchered Almas, I was told, for the yang in their brains. That's why the skulls I saw were cracked open."

"Almas?" Zinc said.

"Hairy Ones. The Kwans believe them a cross between us and the Great Hairy Beast."

"The 'beast' is the Yeti?"

The minister nodded.

Chandler fought to suppress a cynical smile. This case got weirder every day.

"Chingho was my first brush with the family. Those I interrogated said the search for the Great Hairy Beast was their ancestral quest. The Kwans possessed a *Chia-ku-wen*—an Oracle Bone—which promised eternal life to those who ate the Beast's brain. The bone was why Emperor Qin summoned them to his court."

Chandler recalled the *Chia-ku-wen* he and Lotus discussed. "Where'd they supposedly get this bone?"

"From the Fankuang Tzu. The Sons of Reflected Light. They're a prehistoric mythical race. Like Christianity, every Taoist sect claims to have the one true Way. The Kwans adopted the myth for their own well-being."

"Shennongjia?" Zinc said, recalling what Joseph had told him when he phoned in his report. "That's a Yeti haunt?"

"Xian was the ancient capital of Emperor Qin. That's where the terracotta soldiers were found. Working from the imperial court, the Kwans searched Shennongjia to the south. For three thousand years, peasants there have claimed sighting the Beast.

"The Shennongjia Mountains are rugged and remote. Ten thousand feet high, they cover more than a thousand square miles. Even in sweltering July, a winter climate prevails. The peaks abound in legends fostered by rare species like the white bear, dove tree, and arrow bamboo. Shennong, our first herbalist, gathered drugs there. Due to the steepness of the slopes, he had to build scaffolding to reach the plants. *Jia* is our word for ladder."

Zinc flashed on one of the old texts the Kwans had on display. *Shennong's Materia Medica,* Lotus said.

"The family advanced its search in two regions," said Qi. "Shennongjia, where the first 'dragon teeth' were found. And the Tien Shan Mountains of Xinjiang. In Xinjiang their henchmen hunted Alma Yang, which was fed to the emperor as a substitute for the Beast. Without that drug they'd never have survived our turbulent past."

"And after the emperor fell?"

"They sold to an elite within the Kuomintang. Now they sell to the wealthy of Hong Kong. Hairy Ones are descended from the Beast. Alma Yang, therefore, prolongs life. The effect is weak because it's not as wild."

"Wildness is important?"

"Wildness *is* yang. The wilder the animal, the stronger its drug."

"The Tien Shan massacre was to restock?"

"The Kwans backed the wrong side in the Civil War. When the fighting reached Xinjiang, they had to flee. The brains were starting capital to invest in Hong Kong. Taoist drug practice applies there too."

"Why hunt Almas? Why not lie and pass off a domestic substitute?"

"Because Kwan believes in the yang himself and astute gourmets would know. Wildness weakens in captivity. Off Qianmen Street, here in Beijing, is the Tongrentang. Since the seventeenth century, its druggists have sold 'summer horn' for fertility. Summer horn occurs in June when the antlers of immature caribou are velvet-covered and rich in blood. One lick tells a druggist whether a sample is genuine or from domestic reindeer, the caribou's cousin. Same with any yang."

"Is Alma brain available at the Kwans' restaurant?"

"Probably. For the right price. The snakeheads bring it in."

"Snakeheads?"

"Smugglers. Traffickers in flesh. The Kwans have henchmen in Xinjiang. Drug and gun peddlers still in their employ."

"They send the brains?"

"Send the Almas. The fresher the yang, the stronger the drug."

Zinc shook his head. "Hard to believe. If you were told the truth, their clients are cannibals."

"I know it's true," Qi said, "because of kuru disease."

"What's that?"

"Laughing sickness. A virus that rots the brain. It's only passed by eating human flesh. The incubation period is thirty years. The doctor who discovered it won the Nobel prize. *Kuru* is a Papua New Guinea word meaning tremors or shakes. Once it attacks, the victim loses nervous control. The Nationalists who ate the yang giggled to death."

"The Almas got the last laugh, huh?" Chandler said.

THE THOUSAND CUTS

Rosetown, Saskatchewan
Tuesday, March 24, 7:45 P.M.

"If you should die," the Warlord said, "who will carry on? First son born is Warlord. Followed by his first son. *To protect the succession, we must store your seed."*

Each Monday of his thirteenth year, a naked woman came to milk him of sperm. "Ayeeyah," *she would tease, tugging on his penis. "How much will you spill for Grandfather today?"*

The shame of it incensed him. Such revolting hands. Smiling at him as he dribbled in the cup.

Cutthroat endured by finding the cold place in his mind . . .

"The shallower you cut him, the longer it will last." The Warlord put the yang knife in his hand.

Stripped and screaming, the man hung by meat hooks through his wrists. Feet suspended inches from the floor of the Pit, he jerked to escape the relentless blade. Every square inch of skin bore at least one slash.

Cutthroat was nine when he learned the Thousand Cuts.

He endured by finding the cold place in his mind. . . .

Earlier, he had parked beside a snowy woods.

Hidden by the trees he'd performed tai chi, imagining water on smooth rocks as he "presented the gift."

During the ritual he found the cold place in his mind. . . .

Snow, as far as the eye could see, nothing but snow.

He crouched behind the snowdrift at the foot of the drive, casing the farmhouse through night-vision glasses. Phosphorescent green in the binoculars, the gabled roof had a lightning rod and a rooster weather vane. Shuttered windows fringed with lace crowned the porch, while icicles hung from the eaves like Old Man Winter's beard. The panes flanking the front door glowed from the hearth.

Cutthroat was sheathed in white instead of his usual black. White parka with white gloves and white eye-slit hood. A crescent moon and starry sky shone above.

Cold land.

Cold mind.

Frigid heart.

He unzipped the bag and took out the gun.

Her arthritis was bad tonight, so she sat rocking by the Home Comfort stove. Gnarled fingers leafed through the album in her lap. The tea in her cup had gone cold, she was that absorbed. The memories in the book warmed her.

There was Zinc, five years old, crying for his mom, tongue stuck to the iron railing beside the icy barn. *Twice* he'd learned that winter lesson. Such a headstrong boy.

Her sons poured syrup on the snow in the next photo, maple sugar *habitants* while their father hosed the garden to freeze a skating rink. Maple and ginger: Zinc's favorites. Vanilla and licorice: Tom's.

She grinned at the snapshot of a snowman in the yard, turning to gaze at the one Zinc had built when he was here. Through cloudy eyes she could just make out the stovepipe hat and moth-eaten scarf, its eyes and nose coal and a carrot from the cellar. Bark and Bite romped by the light of a silver moon.

A few minutes more and she'd bring in the dogs.

Cutthroat shot Bark and Bite as they ran around the house, picking the German shepherds off with the silenced rifle.

Storing the gun, he drew the yang knife.

White on white, he circled around to the backyard.

The grandfather clock chimed eight as she struggled from the chair. Every joint ached when she moved. How she dreaded opening the door to let the dogs in, giving the hoary demon of winter a chance to chew on her bones. Spring was late this year. So was Tom.

At first she thought she saw a ghost outside the open door, a trick cataracts played on her eyes. Then the knife cut her cheek and she knew the specter was real. Drops of blood spattered the snow-white mask.

The next two cuts slashed her palms, raised in terror to protect her face. The honed blade sliced to the bone.

The old woman staggered back against the butter urn. Her wedding ring clanged the copper boiler as she stumbled. Cutthroat sliced the back of her neck while she struggled to stand.

From stove to china hutch, to pioneer water pump, beneath her copper pots and coronation mugs, past Irish crochet and Nottingham lace and rustic sepia prints, the killer stalked her ruthlessly.

"Out with the old."

He cut her.

"In with the new."

He cut her.

"You pay the price for spawning a nosy son."

He cut her again.

And again . . .

And again . . .

And again . . .

THE FINAL CUT

Vancouver
9:15 P.M.

DeClercq reread Chan's interrogation of the Kwans' spy within the Force. The man was an Asian recruited two years before. While on a gang course in San Francisco, he'd made computer inquiries at Yale University concerning Francis Parker and his Black Hills research. Another request went to the U.S. Army for information about a Civil War general named Gideon Pratt. Who Pratt was, DeClercq had no inkling, but both requests predated his own inquiries within the Force. Were the Kwans tracking Parker *before* they knew about Blake? The spy wasn't talking.

"Got a minute?"

Joe poked his head in the door.

"I just got off the phone with Dmitri in Moscow."

"Read him Zinc's report?"

"He was fascinated. Remember I told you the Snowman Commission thought *two* unclassified hominids live in the heights around Xinjiang? One's the Yeti. The other is the Alma."

Joe consulted notes he'd jotted during the call.

" 'Alma' is Mongolian for 'strange species between ape and man.' Tien Shan sightings date back to the fifteenth century. Tibetans say its meat cures mental disease. In Gandan Monastery in what's now Ulan Bator, there's a woodcut of a 'wild man' like Qi described."

"How would the Kwans find them if others can't?"

"Like any hunt, you must know where to look. At the turn of the century, the czarist government exiled a professor named Zhamtsarano to the Tien Shans. He did field work there until 1928. Hoping to verify Alma sightings, he plotted them on a map, along with the names of his nomad sources. An artist drew a picture from each description."

"The Darwin Museum has the map?"

"No, it was stolen. But Zhamtsarano's papers are in Leningrad and Ulan Ude."

"Perhaps the Kwans stole the map like my notes on Blake?"

"And have hunted the Almas to near extinction."

"Do the Russians think the species a cross between the Yeti and us?"

Joe shook his head. "Porshnev is the greatest name in Soviet 'wild man' studies. He spent thirty years assessing Zhamtsarano's work. In 1974 he published his conclusions. His book is titled *Neanderthal Man Is Still Alive.*"

Robert let out a deep sigh and sat back in his chair. He felt like the first time he saw an atom bomb explode, like the day he watched Neil Armstrong walk on the moon. His mind had to expand to match reality. "Is that possible?" he asked.

"The overlap of Alma sightings with known Neanderthal sites is remarkable.

"What happened to the Neanderthals is the most disputed question in paleontology. From 125,000 to 30,000 years ago they flourished in Eurasia, then suddenly disappeared when we arrived.

"Did they go extinct? Probably. Or did we drive them out of the best hunting grounds into remote areas where small groups survive?

"Did they evolve into us? Unlikely. There's too great a difference between our physiques. More likely, we both descended from Archaic *Homo sapiens.*"

"From Eve?" Robert said.

"Who knows?" Joe replied. "But if the Almas are descended from her, their supergene postdates any defect."

"*Australopithecus* and *Homo habilis* overlapped," Robert said. "So did *Homo habilis* and *Homo erectus*. I guess there's precedent for the Neanderthals and us."

"People think Darwin said evolution is a slow process affecting everyone. What he actually said is that natural selection acts on a few inhabitants in any particular region. Evolution is jerky, with bursts of activity separated by static plateaus. That's why different hominids coexist, and why some make dramatic leaps forward, backward, and even sideways."

Joe searched his jacket for a cigar. "The Tien Shan

Mountains are unexplored. We still find Stone Age tribes in the jungle."

"No more devil's advocate. What's your honest opinion?"

Joe lit the cigar and fanned the match. He blew a smoke ring, tapping his cheek.

"Almas are throwbacks. Devolved human beings. There's nothing to stop evolution taking a backward turn. Because they're human, they pass kuru disease. And that's why their DNA is no use to Evan."

The telephone rang.

"DeClercq," Robert said.

"Chief, there's a distraught woman on the line. Insists on speaking to Chandler. Says it's about his son."

"His son?" Robert said.

"Surprised me too."

"What's her name?"

"Won't say."

"Put her through."

No sooner did he hang up from talking with Deborah Lane than the telephone jangled again.

"Chief, another call for Zinc."

"Take a message."

"This one's urgent. Rosetown Detachment."

Saskatoon, Saskatchewan/Kowloon
Tuesday, March 24, 11:12 P.M./Wednesday, March 25, 1:12 P.M.

"It's done."

"Good. Want a *coup de grâce*?"

"Who?" Cutthroat asked.

"Chandler's son."

Canton, People's Republic of China
Wednesday, March 25, 2:17 P.M.

Canton is a noisy, humid city of old temples, dusty trees, wide boulevards, narrow alleys, and sprawling factories. The muddy Pearl bisects the city east to west, with Shamian Island hugging its north bank. Wrested from China as a concession won in the Opium Wars, the island was an enclave of stately mansions, colonial churches, embassies, banks, football grounds, and tennis courts. The buildings that survive today are shabby with decay, dwarfed by the new White Swan Hotel.

North of Shamian Island, across the Canal, Qingping Market feeds Canton. Whether today was market day or just the regular fair, Chandler was shoved, jostled, and bruised by a madding throng. Hemmed in by a crowd with no concept of personal space, many spitting to rid themselves of "unhealthy" phlegm, he struggled past the herb stalls at the market's gate, heading for what Qi described as "a take-out zoo."

A take-out zoo it was.

The first sign of the public abattoir was rhinoceros horn for sale. On a cart with a moon and serpent painted on its side, snakes wriggled and slithered in glass terrariums. As each customer made a choice, the vendor grabbed the reptile and bit off its head, slitting the snake's belly to skin its meat. All sorts of domestic, wild, and endangered species were for sale. Sad-eyed monkeys rattled the bars of their wooden cages, while terrified deer were jammed in pens so small they couldn't move. Owls were chained to kennels paced by civet cats, and turtles crawled on one another in shallow tin trays. A rare snow leopard lay hobbled by handcuffed paws, as eagles, badgers, pythons, dogs, pangolins, and salamanders went to the chopping block. Surrounded by carcasses still twitching from recent death, the gutted ones spiked on hooks hanging overhead, chatting butchers with cleavers and knives skinned some alive, stunning others with blows to the skull before plunging them into boiling water to ease their flaying. Calm amid the screams of wildlife being slaughtered, a woman wearing designer jeans sniffed a bloody paw.

Chandler was revolted.

He made his way back to the car under a curdled sky. Everyone around him was in someone else's face. "Now do you find my story hard to accept?" Qi asked.

Zinc climbed in back with the minister and the car drove away. "For a prairie boy raised in the wide open spaces, that was a living hell."

"We are born in a crowd, live in a crowd, and die in

a crowd," said Qi. "That is the reality of most Chinese. I was there when Deng Xiaoping met Jimmy Carter. The president began to lecture him on human rights, decrying the fact our citizens cannot leave. Deng smiled and replied, 'How many hundred millions do you want?' That ended the lecture."

They sat in the stuffy government car breathing diesel fumes, slowed by a tide of bicycles, carts, and rusted automobiles. Four-story buildings with street arcades lined the main roads, drab ribbons that stretched north toward the White Cloud Hills. Moon gates led to back streets wafting odors of greasy pork, rotting fish, stale urine, and unwashed bodies. Too many wretched faces stared from packed flats.

The car turned north on Jiefang Zhonglu, heading for Baiyun Airport. In a weak attempt at capitalism, billboards advertised Moon Rabbit batteries and Long March tires.

"In the White Cloud Hills," Qi said, "is Cheng Precipice. Emperor Qin, legend tells, dispatched Minister Cheng On Kee to find him the herb of immortality. Years later Cheng found the drug in the Baiyun Shan, but when he tasted it, the other plants disappeared. Ashamed of returning empty-handed, he threw himself off the cliff, where a stork caught him in midair and flew him to Heaven. If only the Kwans had been as noble when they failed in their quest."

The road became Jiefang Beilu, the Orchid Garden and Yuexiu Park appearing ahead.

"The Tien Shan massacre was forty years ago," Zinc said. "Why the sudden interest of the Gong An Ju?"

"The interest is mine, Inspector. Not the Gong An Ju's. Kwan's younger son was killed escaping in 1945. After the Revolution, I tried the family in absentia for the massacre and other crimes. Kwan Kok-su was sentenced to death. Since then I've become the focus of his hate. He blames me for the loss of both his sons."

"Did you bomb Stephen in 1963?"

"No, but he thinks I did."

Qi withdrew a photograph from his jacket, a morgue shot of two bodies in autopsy trays. Both skulls were cracked open and missing their brains.

"The woman is my wife. The boy my younger son. The mutilation informs me who killed them.

"It took my elder son years to breach Kwan's factory. There he met a woman and fell in love. Recently Kwan summoned her to his Ancestral Hall, a feudal inner sanctum at the heart of his company. Kwan behaved strangely, laughing out of control. Obviously he too has kuru disease. He asked her to bear a child by artificial insemination, for which she would be handsomely paid. During the visit she stole the map my son sent to me, the one I later sent to you. Kwan was delirious from the disease, and let slip the fact he had *two* grandsons. The elder was causing trouble and wouldn't provide an heir."

"Was a name mentioned?"

"Evan," said Qi.

The car was nearing Yuexiu Park when its radio squawked. The driver reported in while the men in back talked.

"Kwan Kok-su is a devious fiend. Who knows what went on in the Inner Sanctum after Stephen's death? Perhaps there was a *third* grandchild hidden out of fear. An heir kept secret so assassins couldn't wipe out his line."

"There'd be a record of the birth in the colony."

"The Hong Kong police are paid to protect the Kwans. Documents go missing if the price is right."

"Kwan summoned the woman to bear *him* a son?"

"So it appears."

"Artificial insemination? Is he impotent?"

"Probably a side effect of the disease. The family passes power generation to generation through the eldest son. That son—the Cutthroat—does the Warlord's bidding, undergoing an apprenticeship that trains him to lead. Kwan Kok-su was Cutthroat at the Alma massacre. He assumed command during the flight to Hong Kong when his father was killed. With Stephen's death, the new Cutthroat was *his* eldest son. Kwan must want to replace Evan."

Qi handed Zinc another photograph. It showed a suspended body skewered on a rod. Again the brain was missing—the Kwans' calling card.

"My son and his lover were caught last week. Kwan's Cutthroat did that to him. The body was then sent home to me."

"The words on the wall? What do they mean?"

"There was a man who had two sons . . ." said Qi.

Past Panfu Lu the car veered left. The minister spoke to the driver in Mandarin. They stopped at the public security building facing the park. "You have an urgent call from Canada," Qi said.

Chandler's knuckles turned white as he listened to DeClercq. Enlarged, the veins in both temples pulsed blue. Shaking with anger he passed the telephone to Qi and without a word left the building ashen-faced.

Outside, a somber sky threatened rain. Seething with an irrational urge to lash out blindly, Zinc dashed across the road to the park's south gate. Heart pounding and shedding sweat in his wake, he ran around Sun Yat-sen Monument with its granite obelisk, once the site of a temple to goddess Kuan Yin. He sprinted northeast by the People's Stadium, closing on Zhenhai Tower, seized by the British in the Opium Wars, passing the twelve cannons in front of the Five Story Pagoda. From the Old City Wall of the Ming Dynasty, he circled Nanxui Lake as startled parents yanked their children out of his way. Only when he was exhausted and his limbic rage spent did he slump at the foot of the Five Rams Sculpture. Eyeing him warily, people shied away.

When Zinc was seventeen, he had bought his first car. Within a week it slipped on ice and smashed into their fence.

His mother came out of the farmhouse to console him. "Never cry over anything that won't cry over you."

She'd have cried over him.

He buried his face in his palms.

He heard the cane tapping far away.

It took a long time for the taps to reach him.

A bottle in a paper bag appeared in front of his face. Johnnie Walker, judging from the cap.

"I too had a mother," Qi said. "Tell me about yours."

ROGUE COP

Kowloon
5:20 P.M.

Chandler was half-drunk when his CAAC flight touched down in the colony. From Kai Tak Airport he cabbed to Blackfriars Hotel intent on checking out to return to Canada. He was settling his account with the cashier when the desk clerk handed him several messages. Glancing at the top one, his past reached out and grabbed him by the throat. "Fuck me," he muttered. "No," the clerk replied.

So many times had Zinc relived that night at the Red Serge Ball that he no longer envisioned it as a cohesive whole. Instead a single image repeated endlessly like a snippet of film looped on a projector.

Fade in at the Red Serge Ball.

The scene is set on the glassed-in balcony of the Hyatt Hotel. Stars wink overhead as music drifts through French doors from the ballroom beyond. Zinc is dressed in the mess kit of an RCMP inspector: waist jacket of red serge over a blue vest, white ruffled shirt with a black bow tie, blue yellow-striped trousers with black half-Wellington boots and box spurs. Gold crowns gleam on his epaulets. Gold regimental crests sparkle on his lapels. Worry lines his face.

Deborah Lane is also dressed in formal wear. A long black gown crossed over her breasts is tied behind her neck to leave her back bare. As she sobs, wayward strands of honey blond hair adhere to her tears.

"Deborah, please. I had to know. We couldn't just—"

"Well, there's something else *you ought to know," she says, blue eyes trailing mascara streaks. "I'm two months pregnant . . ."*

. . . pregnant . . .

. . . pregnant . . .

The loop goes around and around.

"Us?" he says, caught off guard.

"That night in the lair of the Ghoul."

"Deborah, I—"

"Good-bye, Zinc."

. . . good-bye . . .

. . . good-bye . . .

. . . good-bye . . .

As her bare back departs through the French doors to rising strains of Floyd Cramer's "Last Date."

Fade out and wrap it.

A year had passed since then without a word from her, convincing him she'd lied about her pregnancy, throwing a spur-of-the-moment barb in the heat of their argument. Also, schizophrenia ran in Deborah's family.

Several times he'd tried to reach her in Rhode Island, only to find she'd quit her job and moved elsewhere.

He'd lost Carol.

He'd lost Deborah.

Served him right.

Now Carol was back.

And so was Deborah.

With his son.

Kowloon/Maui, Hawaii
Wednesday, March 25, 5:35 P.M./Tuesday, March 24, 11:35 P.M.

"Hello."

Voice strained.

Baby crying behind.

"It's Zinc. I have a plane to catch. What's wrong, Deborah?"

Now she was crying.

Like their son.

"Deborah—"

"Help me, Zinc. I'm so scared."

"You're in Hawaii? Doing what?"

"Hiding from her."

"Who?"

"She wants to hurt our son."

"*Who,* Deborah?"

"Mother. She's going to cleanse my sin."

Jesus Christ, he thought, sobering up.

Deborah's mom had died insane years ago.

Honolulu
Wednesday, March 25, 7:05 P.M.

Cutthroat examined his mouth in the mirror.

Chandler's teeth smiled back at him.

In order to repair Zinc's broken molar with a crown, on Monday the Kwans' dentist had made models of his teeth. Mixing alginate powder and water into a pink goo, he filled a full-arch impression tray with the gunk and placed it over Chandler's upper bite. After the mixture hardened into a rubber-like mold, he removed the tray to do the same with the lower teeth. Then he filled both impressions with dental plaster.

The result: perfect duplicates of Zinc's bite.

Today the dentist had used those models to make another mold, pressing Chandler's plaster teeth into silicone for a new impression. Partly filling the silicone mold with quick-setting acrylic, he pushed a model of Cutthroat's teeth into the drying resin.

The result: appliances that fit over the killer's teeth and left Zinc's bite.

Now to try them out on Deborah Lane.

Thursday, March 26, 7:02 A.M.

Chandler was exhausted.

The only flight from Hong Kong to Hawaii had been through Japan, where an airport curfew and bomb threat had delayed him.

All night across the Pacific, drunken Japanese sang *karaoke* songs, so he arrived wasted to face Deborah Lane.

Emotionally he was spent.

Zinc was standing in line to purchase a ticket to Maui

when he caught sight of Ong's dentist boarding an Asian flight.

Short vacation, he thought.

Maui, Hawaii
8:11. A.M.

Combing the beach, Cutthroat watched her answer the phone. He knew the caller was Chandler from the way she played with her hair. Seconds later, his cellular phone confirmed the fact.

Deborah hung up and checked the baby in his pen, cracking the lanai door for fresh air. Moving toward the bathroom, she loosened her robe.

The bathroom door was closing as Cutthroat left the beach.

8:29 A.M.

To visit his mom in Rosetown, Zinc had rented a car. Just his luck the heater was on the fritz.

To visit his son on Maui, he rented another one. This time the air conditioner didn't work.

From Kahului Airport he drove south to Kihei along the valley separating Puu Kukui and Haleakala Crater. The car passed the twin stacks of the Puunene Sugar Mill as gusts of wind ruffled the cane in undulating waves. No sooner had Maalaea Bay appeared to the right than a humpback whale blew misty vapors in the harbor. Except for ticky-tacky tourists unwilling to leave McDonald's and Burger King behind, it was a perfect day in sunny paradise. Coconut palms sixty feet high caught the offshore breeze, clicking their fronds like typewriter keys. The car hugged the shore along South Kihei Road as women wearing muumuus shuffled by. Inland to his left, aloha-shirted Japanese thwacked golf balls. Across the road, waves broke on fine white sand and the ocean changed from azure to aquamarine to cerulean blue. Zinc was in no mood for a holiday.

South of Kamaole Beach he found the condo lot. Parking the car behind the units, he sighed with relief. While on the phone with Deborah in Hong Kong, Zinc had made a judgment call. He knew she'd freak out if he suggested medical help, for since the day her mother had died in a Providence asylum she'd been paranoid about psychiatrists. Reporting her to the Maui police was another option, but what if she saw them coming and winged out? Finally he'd decided to take a chance with her, knowing how much she loved the boy. Now he was on the spot to protect their son.

No one answered his knock on the door.

A garden path along one side of the condo led to the beach. Colorful koi swam lazily in a reflecting pond as fragrant eucalyptus and jacaranda trees with purple lilac-shaped blossoms overhung the water. Beyond a well-kept lawn edged by dazzling sand, Shipwreck Beach on far Lanai beckoned him. Windsurfers rode the waves as boats of divers headed for Molokini Island.

"Deborah?"

No answer.

His eyes searched the beach.

"Deborah? You here?"

He stepped onto the lanai.

A teddy bear lay on the threshold of the open glass door.

The feet of a child were visible in a playpen to the right.

"God, no!" he gasped, stepping inside.

A praying mantis skittered along the playpen's rail.

Of all the murders he had witnessed, this was the worst. Inside the pen, a Pamper and two chubby legs extended from beneath a large throw pillow. Tiny toes, curled in death, had wrinkled the baby blanket as Travis fought for breath. Steeling himself, Chandler lifted the pillow with his pen. Features a miniature of his own, a small blue face stared up at him.

She killed him, he thought.

Zinc was about to call the police when he spied a woman's foot through the bathroom door. *Killed him and topped herself,* he thought—but that gave way to disbelief when he saw Deborah's body. Someone had murdered the two of them within the past hour.

Mom.

Son.
Deborah.
Zinc knew who.
Stark naked, feet on the floor, head submerged, she lay face-up with her back arched over the side of the tub. The belt of a bathrobe was cinched around her throat, one end floating on the suds with strands of blond hair. He brushed the water with his hand to clear it of soap. Bulging eyes red with Tardieu spots met his. As with most strangling victims, her tongue stuck out, her teeth ivory white against a cyanotic face. At death she'd voided both her bladder and her bowels, but what caught his attention were the marks on her breasts. Zinc had eaten too many apples not to know that bite.

How? he wondered.

The dentist, he thought.

When he heard the siren, he knew the killer had called the cops, another anonymous tip like the one about his mom.

How long would the Maui police hold him while they investigated—if not in a jail cell, at least confined to the islands?

Was that what this was all about?

Buying time?

Jerking him like a puppet to suit the Kwans' needs?

Zinc hadn't slept since he and Minister Qi were in Beijing.

In his overwrought brain, reasoning shut down.

Thoughts from deep in the limbic system took control.

"I'll find you, you bastard. And when I do, I'll tear you apart with my bare hands."

Honolulu
11:12 A.M.

The Mounted Police do not play by the Marquis of Queensberry Rules.

Not when those they're up against play by the Law of the Jungle.

At Honolulu Airport, Zinc rented a day room at the Mini Hotel, purchasing a few supplies before double-locking the door. With a Gillette Blue Blade he slit the seams of his passport folder, revealing another passport inside. Propping it open against a mirror, he set to work.

The man who slipped out of the Mini Hotel to board a flight to Asia had brown hair, bald on top, and thick-rimmed glasses. The mustache on his upper lip rivaled Tom Selleck's, his passport identifying him as Barry Horne.

Winging over the Pacific heading east, Chandler jotted his suspicions on a scrap of paper.

How did the Kwans know about his mother and his son?

Because his room at Blackfriars Hotel was bugged?

Who got him that room?

David Ong.

How had the Kwans gone undetected for so long?

Because they were protected by a dirty cop?

Who gave him a whitewash of their crimes?

Superintendent David Ong.

Assuming Evan hid behind false documents, who was in position to make the switch?

If the marks on Deborah's breasts matched his bite, who recommended the dentist in Hong Kong?

David Fucking Ong, he thought, pocketing the notes.

Vancouver
6:05 P.M.

DeClercq was in his office when the Maui sergeant phoned.

Hearing the names of the victims, he remembered Deborah's call.

"We need his dental records," the Maui cop said.

While hanging up, DeClercq recalled Zinc's battle with the Ghoul.

Chandler was unpredictable when the knife was at his throat.

There's going to be trouble, Robert thought. *Major trouble.*

He called Chan and Tate.

THE TEAHOUSE

Hong Kong
Saturday, March 28, 8:02 P.M.

David Ong was worried.

The Kwans had gone too far.

The manhunt for Chandler threatened to enmesh him in its net.

Time to cash out.

Time to be gone.

The superintendent had spent the day on the phone with other cops: Hawaiian police, the FBI, the RCMP. Each had a different perspective on Chandler's involvement in this mess, from perpetrating a double murder to him being framed. Bite marks were mentioned. So was the cracked tooth. The Mounties wanted him to track the dentist in Hong Kong. The Kwans' dentist. Ong's dentist. What if they made the link?

Worse, no one knew where Chandler was.

Nothing was deadlier than a rogue cop on the run.

A rogue cop with an ax to grind with Ong.

From RHKP headquarters on Arsenal Street he hurried south to Queensway to catch a tram. If Chandler had the building staked out, he'd be watching the parking lot. HQ brass didn't use public transport.

Boarding the tram at back, he chose a seat with a view of the door and the traffic. As a youth he had liked to sit top-front in the tall green double-deckers and watch Wanchai jerk by. He would dream of being the most feared man in Hong Kong, nemesis of the Triads and the British police. His stranglehold on Kwan Kok-su had sated his desire, filling his offshore account with millions while the Triads cursed his name. Like most Hongkongers he planned to be gone by 1997—his escape was to Taiwan, then on to the States—but this debacle with Chandler convinced him the time to retire was now.

One more trip to the money well.

The Kwans owed him that.

As the streetcar trundled west toward the Central District, Ong kept track of the cars behind and round-eyes who boarded the tram. He scrutinized each white face for giveaway signs. The Maui police suspected Chandler was in disguise.

Dropping the fare in a box by the driver before he swung down, Ong left the tram at the Hilton Hotel. From there he hiked up Garden Road toward the Mid-Levels, past the governor's residence and the U.S. consulate, watching for Chandler every step of the way.

The Peak Tram terminal was a glass-faced building hiding the funicular railway beyond. Ong arrived as the tram was ready to depart, so he leaped into the last car as the doors slid shut. Anyone following was left behind.

Victoria Peak is the highest point on Hong Kong Island. So steep is its gradient, the towers of the Central District seem to lean backward into its slope. The tourist seated next to Ong rose at a forty-five-degree angle to snap a photograph. Steps gouged in the floor braced his heels. Cables five thousand feet long hauled the tram smoothly up the sheer incline as the superintendent fingered the gun in his pocket. The city below was a purple carpet spread with jewels. Neon reflected off the black waters of the harbor while shadows lurked among the spires lining both shores. Across the Pearl River estuary to the west, a dying sun smoldered behind Portuguese Macau. Tail swishing above the smoggy hills of Kowloon and the New Territories north, the Dragon of Red China prepared to eat the British Lion.

The tram made five stops up the Peak.

Kennedy Road and Macdonnell Road: the Botanical Gardens.

Bowen Road: sweaty joggers and wild monkeys.

May Road: the steepest part.

Barker Road: the finest views.

While searching for Chandler at one stop, Ong spotted a rat. Rats have always been a problem in the colony. A bounty of twenty cents a tail was offered to stamp out the scourge. The bounty was withdrawn when so many fishermen took up rat farming they had no time to fish.

Eight minutes bottom to top and the tram reached the Peak Tower.

That was insufficient time to scale the slope by road, so if Chandler was stalking Ong he was ditched.

Two-thirds below ground, one-third above, the Peak Tower can withstand winds of a hundred miles an hour. Some of the passengers oohed and aahed at the panorama below. Others ambled toward the overpriced restaurants. Ong branched left down Harlech Road.

The Peak has always been *the* place to live in Hong Kong. Back when transport up and down was by coolie-powered sedan chair, Sir Hercules Robinson had recommended British *taipans* build their manors here to avoid the humidity. Until World War II, the price of Peak real estate included a white skin. Status depended on how high you lived on the slope, a game the Chinese adopted with relish when they were allowed to move in.

Harlech Road and Lugard Road circle the Peak like a collar. Thickets of bamboo and stunted pines mix with fragrant hibiscus and creeping vines. The governor's lodge at the summit had been burned by the Japanese, but white colonial mansions with big bay windows and blackwood furniture still dominate the jade green folds. Sparrow hawks and blue magpies soar above. Homes with southern exposures overlook Deep Water Bay and the junks of Aberdeen. Swimming pools have replaced the verandahs of yesteryear, and modern bungalows now dot the greenswards like a pox, but wilderness and garden estates do survive. The Teahouse was tucked away in one of these.

Glancing over his shoulder, Ong abandoned the road. He followed a bowered driveway to a spiked iron gate, punching a code into its lock to pass through the old brick wall. Parked inside was a silver Jag. The Kwans were coming separately. Only one had arrived.

Wisps of mist veiled the path and a chill was in the air. Between the ginkgo trees ahead the garden unfolded like a painted Chinese scroll. The moon did a fan dance behind scudding clouds, sheening the lake when its face appeared. The Teahouse crowned an island in the center of the pond, a water pavilion with upswept eaves and a moon gate door. A pebbled bridge connected the island to the shore while fish surfaced in the water to sip the lunar glow. The only tree on the island was a blossoming plum arched over the lake to admire its reflection. Water lilies graced the silver mirror.

Ong desired a cigarette.

Ghostly shrubs lined the edge of the spectral pond. Magnolias, azaleas, rhododendrons, and winter jasmines. He found a bench among them and sat down. Fragrances mingled to please his sense of smell. The sounds he heard were those of wind, water, and flitting birds. Through branches etched black against the shining lake he saw a silhouette move behind the Teahouse windows. He wondered who it was.

Selecting a Benson and Hedges from the mother-of-pearl case, he tapped the smoke, lit it, and savored the nicotine.

In all his dealings with the Kwans they'd kept him clean, knowing he'd destroy them if placed in jeopardy. Now inexplicably they had thrown caution to the wind, exposing him to suspicion to frame the Canadian. Was Chandler that loose a cannon? That great a threat?

The calls from the foreign cops had stoked his unease. The Kwans had neglected to tell about the shootout in Stanley Park and the double murder in Hawaii. What sort of fool faced an Uzi with a .38? Ong remembered Chandler eating more ants. For some reason that bothered him most of all.

As he was butting the smoke, a twig behind him snapped.

Before he could turn, a muscular arm locked around his neck, lifting his chin to expose his throat. Razor-sharp steel caressed his jugular vein.

"You're fucking with the wrong guy," Chandler whispered in his ear.

Cursing himself, Ong recognized his mistake. While he was ditching no one, the Mountie was tailing Kwan. Chandler had followed the silver Jag up the Peak.

Rage trembled in the arm under his chin.

The knife at his throat drew surface blood.

"Reach for the gun and I'll slit you ear to ear."

Ong swallowed dryly.

He raised his hands.

"Is Evan coming? Lie and you'll bleed."

"Yes," Ong croaked as the knife pressured his neck.

The swiftness of Chandler's next move took him by surprise.

Ong was spun around so fast he sprained his ankle.

By the light of a grinning moon he saw death in the *gweilo*'s eyes.

His death.

Here and now.

Ong pissed his pants.

"Take it!" Chandler snarled, ramming the knife under his rib cage and through his heart.

When a cloud masked the face of the moon, Zinc crossed the bridge.

The windows of the Teahouse were lattice screens, intricately patterned with chrysanthemums.

Back to the door, the figure inside watched ripples play across the lake.

Ong's gun in one hand, knife in the other, Chandler was a shadow in the moon gate.

Lotus Kwan turned.

"Where's Evan?" Zinc asked, scanning the pavilion.

"Behind you," Lotus said, East confronting West.

The look that passed between them spoke a thousand words.

To imperial China, the Middle Kingdom was the center of the world.

Everyone not Chinese was a barbarian.

The "Red Beards"—Englishmen—were hated most of all.

Lotus Kwan was heir to that reality.

To imperial Britain, everyman's land was theirs to seize.

Colonists had a right to go where they had no right to be.

God, Queen, Country, and the White Man's Burden sent armies and corporations forth to "civilize" the world.

Chandler was heir to that reality.

"White monkey," Lotus said, pulling a gun.

Zinc heard running behind him, coming across the bridge.

Shots rang out.

Part Four

MIND

Whoever fights monsters should see to it that in the process he does not become a monster. And when you look long into an abyss, the abyss also looks into you.

—Nietzsche

STILL LIVING?

Moaning . . .
Hissing . . .
Bubbling . . .
Breathing . . .
. . . *blip* . . . *blip* . . . *blip* . . .
Followed by a final gasp strangled at its source.
Hissing . . .
Bubbling . . .
Breathing . . .
. . . *blip* . . . *blip* . . . *blip* . . .

Time and place meant nothing to him.

Then bit by bit reality bled into his dreams.

The hissing and breathing—that was him, behind an oxygen mask.

The bubbling came from a suction tube hooked in his mouth.

The . . . *blip* . . . *blip* . . . *blip* . . . was a cardiac monitor tracking his heart.

The moan and gasp, thank God, issued from someone else.

". . . what a shame . . ."

Fade in, fade out.

". . . such a good-looking man . . ."

Fade in, fade out.

". . . what happened to him . . ."

the hum of an air conditioner over the throb of a city beyond

snoring, coughing, retching, and the whir of a vacuum cleaner

rubber soles and a rolling tray rumbling down a hall,

lost in the *kraang-awaang-awangawangawang*! of a bed-pan striking the floor

the insistent call of an emergency alarm.

The first thing he saw when he opened his eyes was a vase of daffodils

glorious yellow trumpets wearing Elizabethan ruffs

which transmogrified to purple tulips when he blinked.

Beyond the glass wall of his cubicle was the hub of Intensive Care

where Asian nurses in starched whites monitored gauges, gadgets, and gizmos on high-tech machines

while medics in Nikes and wrinkled greens ran, stethoscopes flapping, into the cubicle opposite his.

A curtain was pulled around the bed as a doctor jabbed a hypodermic into someone's heart

then others zapped the patient with defibrillator paddles from a crash cart.

He thought of the gardens he'd passed in his life and had never stopped to admire.

IV bags overhead, ringed by a curtain rod and traction bar

a different room—private—where squiggly green lines revealed his brain waves

soft, subdued light, distorting human features into Halloween masks

". . . concussion . . ."

". . . grazed his skull . . ."

". . . where'd they find him . . ."

". . . wounded in a teahouse here on the Peak . . ."

". . . an inch to the left . . ."

". . . enter his brain . . ."

Good night, ladies.

"Good morning, Rip Van Winkle. How do you feel?"

"Like Humpty Dumpty. After the fall."

"Headache?"

"A screamer."

"That's to be expected. The scar on your forehead will match the one on your jaw."

"Where am I?"

"Pokfulam Road. Queen Mary Hospital."

"What day is it?"

"Monday. March thirtieth."

"I've been out a day and a half?"

"In and out's more like it. Combined effect of drugs and exhaustion, plus a mild concussion. A better shot and you'd have been out permanently."

The Asian nurse who shaved him smelled of Pears soap.

Mom, he thought, closing his eyes.

The ghost of David Ong floated through his mind.

Take it
Take it
In your spectral ribs.

"There," said the nurse, holding up a mirror.

He opened his eyes to face the killer inside.

Out, damned spot!

An hour?
A day?
A week later?
Robert DeClercq called.
Time and place had slipped again
as
if
he
now
viewed
life
from
five
miles
up.

"How's the head?"

"Scrambled. Hurts like a son of a bitch."

"Stupid what you did. You were almost killed."

Mexico
Slaughterhouse
Park
Lair
Aquarium
and Teahouse

Who remembers Elfego Baca?

I have three lives left.

"Zinc?"

"Yeah."

"With me? You're in the clear. The RHKP found the notes in your pocket. They tracked down the dentist and he confirmed the frame. DNA fingerprinting proved saliva around the bite marks didn't come from you. Carol convinced the Maui cops the killer's Evan Kwan."

"Who'd I get at the Teahouse?"

"Lotus and Ong. She was in the pavilion with two slugs in her heart. He was found stabbed to death by the lake. The bridge was smeared with blood as if someone had crawled or was dragged away."

"Police know Ong was dirty?"

"They do now. Evidence turned up when they searched his home."

"How have they tagged the deaths?"

"Self-defense. Guns against a knife and three on one."

"What about Evan?"

"Was he there?"

"I didn't get a look at who was on the bridge."

"There's no sign of Evan or Martin. But Kwan Koksu's dead from kuru disease. Police are presently searching his factory."

"Where now?"

"Windigo Mountain. We're going to stake it out. Evan wants that DNA. My gut says he'll show."

"It's too risky. Cutthroat's no fool."

"Evan's only future is that DNA. With it he'll be welcome around the world. Without it he's just another fugitive. Besides, he thrives on risk."

The Wheel of Fortune spun around and around, hurling dark visions through his mind . . .

urban sprawls
and toxic dumps awash with PCBs . . .
oil spills
and drift nets
and radioactive seas . . .
spreading deserts
shrinking forests
falling water levels . . .
nuclear bungles

droughts
plagues
and tainted food . . .
gas leaks
ozone holes
greenhouse effect . . .
this species threatened
that species gone
gutless politicians . . .
population growth
at an alarming rate
rising to 14 billion in 50 years . . .
too many people thinking
plenty is not enough
while others go hungry
on less land
with less room to move . . .
mass insanity
wasting the future
for selfish greed today . . .
as time runs out
on a bankrupt dream
countdown to calamity . . .
witness the ladder
of devolution
stepping
down
to

h
e
l
l

He awoke to find himself on a plane with no idea how he got there. Concussion, drugs, and exhaustion: a wonky combination.

Outside the cabin, alien stars shone down on a helpless world.

The pain in his forehead
(take it)
was a persistent throb.
He closed his eyes to block it out.

* * *

"Hey, Mad Dog."

"Chandler."

"What you doing here?"

"Catching a flight to Quesnel. We're going up the mountain."

"Who?"

"Chief, Jack, Joe, and the American broad."

"When?"

"Dawn tomorrow. Weather's s'pose to clear."

"Hang on. I'll get my bags and buy a ticket."

"Meet me at the gate. I need permission for this."

Rabidowski hefted a heavy rifle bag.

They locked themselves in the men's room off the boarding gate. Unzipping the bag, Rabidowski pulled out a weapon.

"Your Iver Johnson .338/416," he said. "Bolt-action. Fluted barrel. Parallel stock. Delivers a 250 boat-tail slug at 3,000 feet per second. Brought down a grizzly at Kakwa River with it last fall. Put every shot in a pie plate at a distance of a mile."

He pulled a second rifle from the bag.

"Your AM-180 laser supergun. Most advanced hand-held piece around. Only shoots .22s, but spits 'em out at the rate of 2,150 Stingers a minute. Cluster 'em and it chews up concrete or metal. Two seconds, I finished a pack of wolves near Tweedsmuir Park."

Mad Dog activated the mounted sights. A thin beam of red light struck the urinal.

"Transmits two hundred yards," he said. "Fire from the hip or hanging upside down, whatever the laser pin-points, the slugs'll hit."

He pulled a copy of *Soldier of Fortune* from the bag.

"Remember in *Dirty Harry* when Clint does the punk? 'This is a .44 Magnum, the most powerful handgun in the world'?"

Wrapped in the magazine was the meanest-looking six-shooter Zinc had ever seen.

"Meet your Dan Wesson .445. Kick'll snap your nuts up to your chin. Makes Clint's .44 a cereal toy. Not on the market yet. Mine's a prototype. Straight from the factory in Monson, Massachusetts. Dropped an elk on Pink Mountain with one blast."

The last gun was all black with a military grip.

"Your Franchi 12-gauge SPAS automatic shotgun. Eight wads in the magazine, ninth in the chamber. AAI 32s packed with flechettes. Darts went right through a moose I cornered at Vanderhoof."

Ed pumped the slide and tickled the trigger.

"Whatever's up that mountain, one *boommph*! and this cunt'll nail it to the rocks."

"Mad Dog" Rabidowski was a backwoods recruit. Son of a Yukon trapper, he lived to kill. Ed was a brawny loner with a heavy-browed scowl. ERT assaults were his favorite sport. One thing about DeClercq: he knew how to pick a team.

"True you got the hots for the Yank broad?"

"Something like that," Zinc said.

"Me, I never been on a date in my life. Rather pay a pro than mess with amateurs. Them, you get your rocks off, they leave you alone."

"You look like shit," MacDougall said, answering their knock on the motel door.

Joe glanced up from the book he was reading.

"I thought you were out of it in Hong Kong."

"Couldn't take any more hospital food."

"The chief won't like it. You're too involved."

"That didn't stop him with Kate and Jane."

"No," Jack said. "And look at the price he paid."

Joe spread a map of western Canada across the desk. MacDougall circled Windigo Mountain with his pen.

"DeClercq's in Jasper, east of the peak. Tate's bussing in to join him tonight. Tomorrow, if the weather clears, they'll drive to the mountain. We'll pick them up at its foot."

Jack tapped Quesnel in central B.C.

"The Cowboy's down at Williams Lake searching for a body. He'll bring the LongRanger up tonight. At dawn we fly east to Tête Jaune Cache, refuel, and press on to the peak. After we meet DeClercq and Tate, we scale the mountain."

They retired to get some sleep.

Dawn in the Rockies.

A glory to behold!

The Bell LongRanger II came out of the west, rotors nipping the tail of retreating night. From the front it looked like Huey, Louie, or Dewey Duck: big-eyed cockpit windows with a small blue bill. Zinc sat in the passenger seat beside the Cowboy as rose, to pink, to salmon, to gold, the mountains colored ahead. Rank-and-file the lower peaks were black silhouettes until dawn washed down to give them life. The northern lights danced beneath an anemic moon as summits marched left and right for three thousand miles. Three thousand miles of ice, snow, and deadly drops, one tusk of which was the grave of Wilfred Blake.

"Now what?" the Cowboy yelled, craning his neck.

"Circle the mountain," Jack shouted from the rear.

"What about the others?"

"Change of plans. We're to take advantage of this break between storms. They'll radio when they arrive."

"Roger," the pilot said, checking his map.

Of all the peaks in the Rockies, ahead was the most forbidding. The Earthquake of '97 had split it in two, sundering the hunchbacked lower mass from its pinnacle. Jutting straight up like a butcher knife gutting the sky, the rib/fang/spire/needle was slick with ice. The fissure between the halves was four thousand feet deep, a yawning crevasse hungry for human meat. Wind whined through the chasm like a coward on the rack.

The Bell was halfway around the pinnacle when Jack tapped the pilot on the shoulder.

"See those cabins? Across the valley? That's where we meet DeClercq and Tate. They'll come in off the Yellowhead in a Jeep. Hover near the summit and let's take a look."

A glacier tongue covered the valley beneath the chopper, overstaying its welcome since the last ice age. Along the tongue's far edge, three cabins hugged the foot of Viking Peak. They were linked to the highway north by a rugged access road. Opposite, across the cracked surface of the tongue, loomed the pinnacle of Windigo Mountain. The only ledge on the ruin was an ice field near its top, tucked in the concave of its slightly bent tip. The field was overhung by corniced snow that freezing winds had caked above the niche. Should this armor ever shake loose from the rock, it would plummet toward the valley in an avalanche. If the cornice gave way, the ledge would be buried.

"See anything?" the Cowboy asked.

Zinc swept the ice field with binoculars.

"A helicopter rotor. Sticking from the snow."

Ice rimed the windows of Jasper Park Lodge, distorting her view of the Whistlers and Pyramid Mountain.

Shivering with goose bumps, Carol pulled on her clothes, then went down to meet DeClercq.

The night before, her bus from Edmonton had passed Miette Hot Springs north of Medicine Lake.

That's where she and Zinc would go after Windigo Mountain.

DeClercq ate a lumberjack breakfast in the restaurant of the lodge, fueling his metabolism against the cold.

Tate came down as he was packing the Jeep.

"Hold on," the pilot shouted over the *whup-whup* of the blades. "The skids might break through when we land."

Aviator shades reflecting the glare of the sun, headphones clamped over his ears, he lowered the collective pitch lever to bring them down. As the helicopter entered ground effect, a white whirlwind engulfed the windows.

The LongRanger rocked when its skids hit ice. "Touchdown," the pilot said, the *whup* dying to a whistle. Rabidowski opened the port side doors. Single file, the Mounties climbed down.

The five were bundled up in the Force's arctic dress: navy fur-lined parkas with yellow bottom stripes, whipcord trousers tucked into sealskin mukluk boots, beaver caps with ear flaps tied under their chins.

They waited for their lungs to adjust to the thinner air. The snow blown up by the rotors settled. Gradually the mountaintop reappeared, icicle swords of Damocles hanging overhead.

The wreck was buried thirty feet from the Bell. A single rotor foil marked its grave. The blade protruded from the snow like a zombie arm.

"Let's start digging," MacDougall said.

"Who was Jasper?" Carol asked, consulting the *Canadian Book of the Road* in her lap.

"How much for this one?"

"Make it a dime."

They were in the Jeep, heading out of town.

"Jasper Hawes ran Jasper House near Punchbowl Falls. It was a North West Company base for fur traders crossing the Great Divide. You passed it on your way in from Edmonton."

"For a penny more, built what year?"

"Eighteen thirteen, I believe."

Carol whistled. "You sure know your stuff."

"Don't forget I spent a month researching here."

"Ten cents on the next one?"

"Make it a quarter."

"Blue phenomena" plagued Zinc worse than the others. He assumed this was because of his wound. Hallucinations brought on by rarefied atmosphere are dangerous. Altitude depression has sent too many climbers over a cliff without a rope. In relays they returned to the Bell for oxygen.

On one trek Zinc saw David Ong. He was pinned to the fuselage by a knife, his body slumped near the RCMP crest. "Maintiens le Droit," the Force motto, was replaced by "Take it" scrawled in blood. A hit of oxygen made the vision disappear.

At twelve thousand feet the atmosphere is so thin it never warms up, yet flesh exposed to the sun bakes in minutes. Snow and ice have a magnifying effect, tripling the power of reflected rays. The Mounties had smeared their faces with cream and wore dark glasses.

"See anything?" MacDougall asked, standing at the edge of the excavation.

On hands and knees. Rabidowski hacked at the ice. "The cockpit windows are white with frost."

"Looks like a Sikorsky," the Cowboy said. "S-76, probably."

"Hand me the blow torch. We're almost through."

Successive arctic storms had hardened the snow to concrete, locking the wreck in a deep deep-freeze. For an hour they had chipped the ice with picks and shovels, ribbing the pilot's concern about the skids breaking through. Now, fanning the ground with the torch, Rabidowski melted the pack around the cockpit.

"Everybody back while I break the glass."

One blow from a pick smashed the window. Shards tinkled inside.

MacDougall shone his flashlight into the hole. "The chopper's empty. Where'd they go?"

West of Jasper the highway passed the Whistlers and Indian Ridge, then climbed the Miette Valley toward the Yellowhead Pass.

"Who was Yellowhead?" Carol asked.

"How much have I won so far?"

"$3.56."

"You're sure you can afford this?"

"I'll rob a bank."

"Yellowhead—Tête Jaune—was a fair-haired Indian trapper. His white name was Pierre Hatsinaton. Tête Jaune Cache, through the pass, is where he stored his furs."

"Why's the B.C.–Alberta border uneven to the south?"

"Because it follows the Great Divide."

"Piss west from the Divide and you pollute the Pacific. Pee east and your contribution joins what sea?"

"Five cents?"

"Seems fair."

"The Arctic Ocean. Down the Miette, Athabasca, and Mackenzie rivers."

"Time to play dirty," Carol said.

They found the cave where the ice field met the vertical wall of the peak, its mouth hidden behind a drift of snow. The fissure was a four-foot gap in the rock. Mad Dog primed the shotgun. "I'll go first."

MacDougall crawled in after him, followed by the others.

The cavern, pitch black, resembled the mouth of a

whale, with stalagmites and stalactites the size of giant's teeth. Daylight from the opening died a few yards in, forsaking all who entered to what lurked within. The beams of their flashlights crisscrossed like dueling swords.

"Watch your step . . ."

"step . . .

"step . . .

"step . . ."

the cave echoed.

"The Rockies were formed by crust upheaval," Joe added. "Imagine the cracking and faulting it took to move the site of Calgary twenty-five miles west. The mountains are wormed with tunnels . . ."

"tunnels . . .

"tunnels . . .

"tunnels . . ."

"Holy shit!"

The Mounties stopped dead in their tracks when Mad Dog cursed.

"There," he said, pointing with the gun.

The other four torch beams joined his.

In their pool was a pile of bloody bones.

A mile before the Yellowhead Highway crossed the Great Divide, they turned south on a rugged access road. Behind them, "mares' tails" harbingered another storm.

"All or nothing," Tate said. "You a gambling man?"

The Jeep bumped along the washboard ribbon.

"This one has two parts, but they're related. Answer both and dinner's on me. Miss one and I get to keep your winnings."

The Jeep swerved to avoid a startled rabbit, fishtailing as it hopped away.

"Along the Great Divide is Mount Robson Park. What two attractions make it unique?"

"The park has the Canadian Rockies' highest peak *and* Canada's deepest cavern."

"To the foot, how deep is Arctomys Cave?"

"No fair," DeClercq said. "We use meters."

"Sorry," Tate said. "The question stays. Years ago I lost money up here and swore never again."

It began to snow.

* * *

Human bones, cracked open to get at the marrow.

Human skulls, cracked open to get at the brains.

They squatted in a circle around the skeletons, like primitive hunters reading a spoor.

"Gnaw marks," Zinc said. "Eaten alive?"

"Have to be to pool this much blood," Joe replied.

MacDougall indicated a clump of hair. "You're the hunter, Mad Dog. Recognize it?"

Rabidowski fingered the fur, shaking his head.

"Labels on the tatters are Chinese," Joe said. "Definitely the Kwans' expedition."

"Wait here," MacDougall said. "I'll fetch the other weapons. And try to raise DeClercq on the radio . . ."

"radio . . .

"radio . . ."

His footsteps retreated.

Blinded by the snowfall, they couldn't see a thing. "For all I know, we're off the road," DeClercq said.

"I hope the others aren't in the air. Not in this wind."

"Worse if they're on the mountain. This could sock in for a week."

"The weather in this country really is—"

With a jolt, the Jeep hit a frost heave and began to slide. "Hold on," DeClercq warned as they sideswiped a tree. The vehicle flipped and the engine died.

"Here," said Rabidowski, pulling the Dan Wesson from his parka pocket. "Take this and give Joe your Smith."

Chandler hefted the .445 as they exchanged guns.

"What's that?" the Cowboy said, his torch knifing the dark.

"Where?"

"Over there."

"Looks like another cave."

"Easy does it," Chandler said. "Remember those bones."

The cave within a cave led to the mountain's throat, a vein of velvet blackness that disappeared below. Around them layers of verglas coated the antechamber's walls, through the silver-blue of which winked knobs of quartz. The floor of the mini-cavern was a rink of ice, its smoothness broken by a semicircle of giant skulls. The skulls faced a crude throne chipped in the rock.

"I've seen weird," the Mad Dog said. "But nothing weird as this."

"Let's get outa here," the Cowboy suggested.

Cautious of their footing, Zinc and Joe approached the throne.

Around it were pictographs drawn on the rock, images akin to those in France's Lascaux Cave. In one a red-chested man fought a hairy beast, lightning from his fist striking the giant's head. Next to it, the same man confronted similar monsters, while one offered him the heart cut from the vanquished primate. In a third, he mounted a hairy female from behind.

The mummy seated on the throne was hoary with ice. Rime stiffened its white hair and grizzled mustache, aging the parchment-like skin and glazing the milky eyeballs that stared vacantly. Desiccated flesh had pulled back from the teeth, curling blue lips in an ivory grin. The tunic fused to the chest like a second skin humped where the rib cage gave it shape. Over the years the corpse had sat in the hall of the mountain king, scarlet red had faded to pink. In one mummified hand it held the Yellow Skull.

"Blake," said Zinc.

"Now what?" Tate said, shivering by the Jeep. The whiteout was so thick she couldn't see three feet. "Engine's dead. Heater's gone. Radio's kaput. If we don't find shelter, we'll freeze to death."

"They must have left the chopper," DeClercq said, giving the portable transmitter a shake. All that came through was static and hiss.

"If we try to walk it, which way do we go? Snow's so deep there's no road."

"Keep to the swath through the trees and we'll reach the cabins."

"Trees?" Tate said. "You see trees?"

The skulls that faced the throne were like the one in *Parker's Journal*. The bone ring on the floor paid homage to the mummy.

"You're the anthropologist. Explain this, Joe."

"*Gigantopithecus* bones were found in Chinese caves.

Blake was on the mountain when the earthquake hit. He shot the Bigfoot patriarch and assumed his role. Same ritual as apes in Africa."

"Wouldn't the quake's survivors be extinct by now? Trapped inside the mountain, what would they eat?"

"Caverns have an ecosystem too. Maybe they ate each other when game was scarce. If the species has inbred for a century, turning Windigo is a likely devolution."

Zinc studied the pictographs, then the skulls. "So Blake's revolver was found at the foot of this cliff."

Joe touched the sagittal crest on one of the bones. "You're witnessing the zoological find of all time. A missing link in our evolution that's still alive."

A howl of raw hunger echoed up the mountain's throat.

"What was that?" Rabidowski glanced at the mouth of the cave.

"Just the wind."

"Not that. I heard a rifle shot."

LAST STAND

Rabidowski in the lead with Chandler on his heels, they crawled through the hole behind the drift. Outside, snow was falling in big white flakes, driven by a gusting wind. How had the weather changed so fast?

"There!" Zinc said, pointing up.

Twenty feet from the Bell and sixty feet from them, MacDougall struggled across the field toward the Long-Ranger. A trail of blood stained the snow behind him, while buffeted by the wind above their heads, a chopper like the Kwans' wreck hovered over the valley. The Sikorsky was turned sideways with its main door open, a black-masked sniper kneeling in the loading bay. As the rifle muzzle flashed, a plume of powder burst from the ground near Jack.

"Come on!" the Mad Dog shouted, tugging Zinc's arm. "You get him and I'll get the guns."

Ten feet apart to split the target, both cops started across the field.

Converting the shotgun to semiauto, the Mad Dog opened fire. *Boommph! boommph! boommph!* The SPAS hurled darts. Missiles plinked on metal around the sniper.

The chopper was kept away by the threat of downdrafts. Wind spilled over Viking Peak and roared into the valley, then shot back up Windigo Mountain to strike the main flow. Vertical wind shear threatened to slam the Sikorsky against the cliff, so until the storm lulled the chopper couldn't land.

As Chandler neared MacDougall, a slug whined by his ear. Chips from the ice crust stung his face. Shoving the .445 in his pocket, he reached for Jack and pulled him to his feet. The wounded man let out a cry of pain.

"Where'd he get you?"

"In the leg."

"Lean on me. We can't stay here."

Chandler hooked an arm around MacDougall's waist as eddies of snow swirled toward them.

Rotors deafening in a sharp descent, the Sikorsky passed overhead. A dip in the storm gave it access to the ledge.

"Zinc!" MacDougall shouted.

Chandler looked up.

The sniper's rifle was aimed at his heart.

Releasing MacDougall to clear him from the shot, he fumbled in his parka for the .445.

Too late, he heard a whipcrack on the air, and braced himself for a slug in the chest.

One of the Sikorsky's cockpit windows disappeared, suddenly blasted to smithereens. Blood and gore splattered the window opposite. Hitting the cyclic control stick, the pilot spun around. As he crumpled on the collective pitch lever, the rotors jerked up, plunging the chopper toward the ledge. It hit the ice field with a jolt that sent the sniper flying, shaking several icicles loose from the overhanging cornice. In a rain of javelins, they hit the whirling blades, spewing ice through the crystals blown up by the crash. The chopper disappeared.

"Get down!" the Mad Dog shouted, ejecting a spent cartridge from the Iver Johnson. He was in the loading bay of the Bell. "They won't be comin' out with their dicks in their hands."

As Zinc and Jack hit the ground, he swapped the Iver Johnson for the AM-180. A red laser beam streaked through the tumbling flakes. It dotted the forehead of an Asian emerging from the haze.

Pfffdrdrdrt! Pfffdrdrdrt! Pfffdrdrdrt! Snow puffed from the man's clothes. Spine arched back, his finger jerked, discharging an Uzi erratically in the air.

Zinc searched the settling snow for Cutthroat's mask.

The Mad Dog sent three more spinning back.

There it was.

To the left.

Buried in a parka hood, like the Grim Reaper.

Zinc aimed the Wesson as the laser hit his target.

"No!"

Pfffdrdrdrt!

A line of holes ripped across the parka.

"He's mine!"

Again too late.
The Mad Dog wanted them all.

"Cool Clear Water" by Marty Robbins played in her mind, for that was how Tate felt in this godforsaken land. Like a doomed wretch crawling across Death Valley sands—except here the temperature was forty below.

High up, the shifting wind howled through the saddles of the mountains.

Down here it sucked drifts from the ground that mixed with the snowfall to confuse her completely.

For all she knew, they were trudging in circles.

Freezing her clothes and freezing her hair as it tried to put out her eyes, the storm was a fury of flying ice.

Her face was so swollen she could hardly breathe.

Her underwear was so stiff it chafed her skin.

Keep moving, Tate, she thought.

Like a freighter in the fog, the Sikorsky reappeared.

The Mad Dog ran toward it, shotgun in hand.

Zinc stood over Cutthroat's body sprawled in the snow, feeling hollow from unrequited revenge.

Reaching down, he tore the mask from the face, revealing the features of Evan Kwan.

Traces of Martin and Lotus were evident in the jaw, the cupid's-bow mouth a genetic link.

Otherwise, Evan was a face in the crowd.

From Zinc's point of view, the mask and face were one.

How anticlimactic.

No Jekyll and Hyde.

Chandler tensed when the eyes popped open.

Cutthroat lay on his back with four holes in his chest, bleeding a crimson pool absorbed by the snow. His tongue flicked between his lips as if in thirst. His mouth curled slightly when he recognized Zinc. Chandler had the .445 in his fist.

MacDougall and Avacomovitch were in the Bell, their backs to him as Joe bandaged Jack's leg.

The Mad Dog and the Cowboy were by the Sikorsky, their attention on what was inside.

Unobserved, Chandler crouched beside Kwan.

"This is for my mother."

He cocked the gun.

"This is for Deborah."

He aimed between the eyes.

"This is for my son, you son of a bitch."

Teeth bared . . .

Nostrils flared . . .

Finger on the trigger . . .

He itched to blow Cutthroat's head apart.

(take it)

Take it.

"Take it," he snarled.

The wound in his head pounded with hate.

Oh cease! must hate and death return?
Cease! must men kill and die?
Cease! drain not to its dregs the urn
Of bitter prophecy.

Name the bard, son.

Shelley, Pop.

His finger faltered on the trigger as reason made a stand.

With Ong he let the monster win.

With Evan he let the man.

Zinc was uncocking the pistol when Rabidowski approached. Placing its barrel to Evan's head, the Mad Dog fired the shotgun. The force of the contact wound disintegrated his skull, spewing a circumjacence of blood for yards around. The stump of Evan's limbic brain twitched at the top of his spine.

That's where mankind came from.

That's where it was going.

"Feel better now?" the Mad Dog asked.

Luckily, no one was in the chopper when the lightning hit.

Unfortunately, they were on the ledge when the earthquake followed.

The shotgun blast had brought the five together, knotted in a circle around Evan's corpse. The Mad Dog was recounting how Cutthroat went for his Uzi when a dark thunderhead spiked itself on the peak.

"What—"

"Can't—"

"Hold—"

"We're—"

Feeble voices faded, swallowed up in a booming barrage.

Smiting the mountain with sheets of livid flame, the epicenter of the storm detonated above. Ghostly flashes sparked off their wet uniforms as fans of fire encased the Sikorsky and the Bell. Spooky three-inch auras danced along their guns.

No sooner had the storm moved on, thundering southwest, than the ledge beneath their feet quivered and grumbled.

With an earsplitting *CRAAACCCKKKK*! that threw them to the ground, the spire of Windigo Mountain jerked like a tree in a hurricane. The chasm between the halves yawned wider.

CRACK! CRack! Crack! crack! The cliff beneath them fractured, as aftershocks shimmied up the pinnacle.

Dumbstruck, they were slid toward the precipice.

Then, like a whip the ledge yanked back, skidding them toward the cave.

Shhhhwoooooghhhh! Whhhoughh . . . A twenty-foot icicle snapped off the cornice, screaming past them into the valley.

Shhhhhwouuughhhh! Fffwwackkkk! The next lance speared the Sikorsky, pinning it to the field like a butterfly.

Shhougghh!
Ffooonk!
Ffooonk!
Ffooonk!

they were under attack, as icicle after icicle broke from the overhang.

"Into the cave," MacDougall shouted, "or we'll be impaled!"

Feet slipping on the ice, they scrambled for the hole, crawling in like Neanderthal men.

Gaining access far below, the storm bellowed up the cavern's throat.

"The tremor must have cracked an opening," Joe said.

An eerie shriek of triumph echoed up the tunnel.

"That's not wind," the Cowboy said.

"Something got in?" MacDougall wondered.

"Something got *out*," Joe replied.

"Look," DeClercq said, pointing through ice-plumed gargoyles that had once been trees.

"Glory be. A cabin," Tate sighed.

The quake had added a new dimension to their ordeal: slabs of ice breaking off the Windigo spire. They heard the whistle of unseen chunks plummeting from the sky, hysterical whines of unchecked descent exploding like artillery shells in the valley. Debris skittered toward them across the glacier.

But now they had sanctuary.

The chalet was made of fir logs stacked one upon another, rough-hewn, dove-tailed, and chinked with oakum. The A-frame's gabled roof was angled into the wind, a precaution necessary to equalize the snow load. The door opened off a second-floor deck, designed to keep it free from drifts. The windows were shuttered against the blizzard. Smoke belched from the chimney, then vanished on the wind.

"Fire's going," DeClercq said, shivering with relief.

"A sauna if we're lucky," Tate replied.

"This one's the owners'. Let's get our key."

"Where's our cabin?"

"Down that path."

Stomping snow from their boots, they started up the stairs.

Right arm in a sling, Tate gripped the rail.

Near the deck DeClercq motioned her to halt.

Torn from one of its hinges, the door hung ajar.

An antler rack over the threshold lay smashed on the deck.

Carol drew her Colt as Robert stepped inside.

"Let's get off this mountain before the main jolt hits."

"Main jolt?" Zinc and Ed said in unison.

Joe led the way out of the cave.

"During the last ice age this area was compressed. Isostatic rebound's been happening ever since. A delayed release of stress caused the tremor. Once a quake starts, cracks and faults give way. The spire of Windigo Mountain is the Rockies' weakest point."

The cabin door opened on a "decompression chamber" with a pine bench for removing boots. Peg racks held pairs of cross-country skis flanked by hooks hung with outdoor clothing. Left, a set of stairs ascended to the sleeping loft.

Beyond the entrance foyer was an unlit hall, with bathroom, sauna, and kitchen off it. The parlor at the far end glowed with firelight, a welcoming hearth drawing them on. Tate followed a step behind DeClercq.

Nearing the end of the hall they saw a sawbuck table with four barrel chairs, two overturned and another smashed.

Then the fireplace came into view, nail keg to one side and milk can to the other.

The macramé rug in front was littered with dominoes.

The church pew facing it was knocked askew.

The overmantel was spattered with blood.

Intestine cords dangled from the lamp.

"Back!" DeClercq yelled as something blocked the hall.

Then a mammoth hairy hand grabbed him by the throat.

"Frozen solid," the Cowboy said, kneeling between the LongRanger's struts. "Have to use the blow torch to thaw them out."

Lightning striking the chopper had melted the ice underneath, which had then refrozen around the skids. The Bell was now cemented to the ledge.

"Rotor's okay," the Cowboy said, opening the cowling to inspect the engine. The 500 shp Allison 250-C28B turboshaft was rimed with ice.

MacDougall was in the cockpit trying the radio.

The monster was the stuff of which nightmares are made. Whatever the species originally—for the head had the basic shape of the Yellow Skull—genetic inbreeding had riddled it with mutation. Its King Kong body was hunched and deformed. Its leathery black face was knobbed like the Elephant Man. Hair sloughed off its pustular skin in ugly pink patches, oozing slime into its matted fur. Drool that smelled like goat cheese dribbled from its fangs, two inches long and caked with raw meat. Bloodshot, its piggy eyes were rabidly insane, a condition echoed in its ravenous growl. Nine feet tall, the rotting Sasquatch filled the end of the hall.

Her arm over DeClercq's shoulder, Tate shot it in the eye.

With an enraged shriek, the beast released its hold.

Robert fell to his hands and knees, gasping for air.

The radio he carried struck the floor.

Carol fired four more shots.

Each slug hit the eye, now a ragged hole where the eyeball had been.

The Bigfoot levered back and toppled with a crash, shaking the chalet to its foundation.

Another monster appeared in the doorway.

Tate put the Colt's last round in its mouth.

"Run!" she cried.

The blow torch ran out of fuel halfway through the job.

Wind chill increased in the wake of the gale, threatening frostbite to exposed skin.

Zinc closed the parka hood about his face, then wrapped a scarf around his head.

Sinews straining as cramps set in, he tried to free the frozen skids with a shovel.

Blisters burst inside his gloves.

Scabs peeled off the piranha bites.

Flashes of light popped behind his eyes.

Then, heart palpitating, reality slipped.

A path opened through the blizzard across to Viking Peak. There three giants sat on rock-hewn thrones: Odin, Thor, and Tyr, surrounded by Valkyries. One god blew the wind; another clapped the thunder; while the third threw lightning bolts. The Valkyries beckoned him to Valhalla.

"Easy," Joe said, gripping his arm. "Falling nitrogen pressure is affecting your brain. If automatic breathing goes, Cheyne-Stokes will set in. You rolling around in your death rattle won't help anyone."

"My head aches."

"Uh-huh."

"And I'm hallucinating."

"What do you see now?"

"DeClercq. Calling us."

They came down the stairs like the Flying Wallendas, a broken neck preferable to the alternative.

"That way," DeClercq said, pointing down the path. He still gripped the radio in his hand.

A snow-covered bower led to the other cabins, barely visible through the swirling flakes. Wherever these ogres came from it wasn't a chalet, so indoors was safer than thrashing about in the woods. Hemmed in by underbrush and overhanging branches, they had a sixty-foot dash to the next cabin. Tate was in the lead with DeClercq close behind.

"Jack? Joe? Ed? Can you hear me?"

Robert tried the radio as he ran.

"We're at the cabins. Under attack."

A hairy arm shot from the trees to his right, clamping strong fingers over his skull.

DeClercq jerked away to leave the beast with just his hat, then the creature lumbered out to cut him off.

When he turned to retreat back the way he had come, the Bigfoot Carol had shot in the mouth took a swipe at him. It used a human arm as a club.

Caught in a hot box with basemen closing in, he hurled the radio at the monster clutching his hat.

The hominid grunted as the missile mashed its nose, giving the Mountie a chance to slip by.

Tate was halfway up the stairs to the next cabin when she remembered they didn't have the key.

It was back at the owners' place.

"Hear that?" Jack said from the cockpit. "Let's quit farting around and get in the air."

The Mad Dog searched the Bell for a siphon. He emerged with a length of hose. Opening the fuel tank, he sucked the tube until it was full of gas, then sprayed the petrol along the skids.

"No," warned the Cowboy. "That's suicide."

"Get the rotors going or—"

The mountain began to shake.

"Told you," Joe said. "Here it comes."

The door was unlocked in anticipation of their arrival. The key was on the bench in the "decompression" room.

This cabin had the same layout as the other: entrance foyer fronting a hall; bathroom, sauna, and kitchen off that; parlor protected from the wind at back. The door was fashioned from pine planks set diagonally, with wrought iron latchings and a dinky Yale lock. Here in the middle of nowhere crime was nonexistent, so one well-placed kick would knock it open.

"Find an ax," DeClercq said, thumbing the Yale as one of the monsters topped the stairs.

Tate ran down the hall to the kitchen, eyes scanning the room for any and all weapons. Split-log ceiling laid round side down. Empty coal oil lamp hanging from a log. Antique cooking utensils hooked on the walls. Shelving with basic food stuffs and a bottle of rum. Large, enameled wood-burning stove. Brass wood basket and hickory-handled ax.

Grabbing the ax, she ran back.

DeClercq had upended the boot bench flat against the door. He used the ax to gouge a deep groove in the floor. Wedging one end of the bench under the handle, he dropped the other end into the groove. Now the door was braced against assault.

"The windows," Tate said.

All eight windows were shuttered outside. They weren't large because of the cold. Those north and east faced the woods. Those south and west opened onto the deck. So did another door off the parlor. Outside, they heard the deck boards creak.

"Forget the windows," Tate said. "Barricade the door."

They pushed the parlor furniture across the floor. They stood the pew on end against the deck door, then fortified it with the sawbuck table and chairs. Above the stone fireplace was a rusted bear trap a century old. With nothing left to block the door to the hall, they took the trap down and set it on the threshold. Using their combined strength they levered the jaws apart.

Sweating from exertion, Tate flicked open her Colt. She emptied the spent shells into the milk can, then reached in her pocket for the reloader. It wasn't there.

"Damn," she said, remembering her coat. She had borrowed a parka from Jasper Detachment. Her own lightweight was still in the Jeep.

"I'm outa rounds. We're down to your piece."

"I don't carry one," DeClercq said.

Tate was in the kitchen when the beast broke in. The parlor shutters were torn off and the deck windows smashed. Holding the ax, two knives, and the bottle of rum in her good arm, she returned to the parlor as the monster stuck its head into the room. DeClercq sprayed it in the face with a fire extinguisher.

The tremor hit as the Bigfoot struggled to retreat.

At first Carol thought it was the beast Robert blinded, flailing about on the deck outside before crashing through the rail. Then the entire cabin shook and a tree cleaved the roof. Losing her footing, she dropped one knife and the bottle of rum. The bench bracing the main door jumped free from its groove. A moment after it banged to the floor, the door was shouldered in.

White-haired, with pink eyes and ivory fangs, an albino Bigfoot shambled down the hall. As Tate scrambled to meet it at the parlor door, an arm came through the window and grabbed her by the hair.

Twisting, she saw a female ogre outside on the deck, tits devoid of fur and leaking yellow pus.

Carol jammed the ax handle into her sling. She used the kitchen knife to stab the monster in the arm.

Screeching, the female shoved its head in through the window, breathing foul breath in Carol's face.

Above, the ceiling buckled as feet landed in the loft. One or more of the creatures had climbed the tree that breached the roof.

Avoiding the bear trap, the albino went for DeClercq. He was spraying another Sasquatch at the window when the giant fist knocked him halfway across the room. The fire extinguisher flew from his hands. He landed on the bear rug in front of the hearth. He tried to gain his feet, but the quake threw him back. On hands and knees, the albino attacked.

Throughout the chalet the tremor was hurling knick-knacks from the walls, producing a symphony of clanging metal.

Tate brought the ax down hard on the female's skull, the blow deflecting off its sagittal crest. Sheared from the bone, a clump of hair slapped the floor. Howling, the half-scalped beast let her go.

In retreat, the female clutched the windowsill. It caught its head on the window frame. Tate chopped the ax across its hand. Hairy fingers fell to the floor.

Grabbing Carol's parka with the bleeding stumps, the enraged monster opened its jaws.

Backhand, Tate swung the ax through its mouth, snapping off teeth with the rear of the blade.

Wrenching back, she brought the wedge down full force, burying the ax head in its skull.

Across the room, fangs wide, the albino went for Robert's throat.

He did the only thing he could.

He stuck his arm in its mouth.

One foot in the chopper, the Mad Dog torched the skids. Flames shot up with a *whooooosh*! as he climbed into the Bell. They licked the royal blue RCMP markings on the side.

In the cockpit, the Cowboy's eyes were glued to the console. He watched the manifold pressure gauge and rotor rpm. As he cranked the throttle and raised the collective pitch lever, the tach's needle crept past the danger line.

Outside, the peak was shedding its skin like a snake. The quake had fractured and splintered the ice in all directions, laying the foundation for a slab avalanche. Tired of holding out, the frozen shell gave in, hurling great blocks of ice down the mountainside. The bare rock exposed beneath was veined with faults.

Inside the Bell, a whole lotta shakin' was goin' on. The peak to which they were frozen had St. Vitus's dance, jerking to and fro with terminal jitters. The chopper shimmied as its engine revved to overspeed, losing the dampening effect of the Noda-Matic. How long until one of the cam lobes or rod bolts went, assuming the falling chunks didn't get them first?

One rock was all it would take to snap the rotor blades.

With a tortured groan, the cliff above gave way.

With a sickening crack, the bones in DeClercq's forearm snapped. The albino's fangs bit through his flesh.

The Bigfoot with its head cleaved went into convulsions, falling to the deck with the ax in its skull.

Carol turned when the Mountie cried out in pain. Sharp white bones stuck from his wrist.

The size of the albino made her forsake the knives. Gritting her teeth against the price of tearing her stitches, Tate used both arms to heft the bear trap from the floor. She turned it upside down on the albino's head.

Like a shark bite, the jaws snapped shut. Crimson geysers spurted from the metal teeth. The beast turned two-tone, red on top. With a thunderous crash it toppled dead beside DeClercq.

Too big for the windows, the monsters on the deck keened a horrid dirge.

Above, the ones in the loft moved toward the stairs, which descended to the foyer, blocking any escape.

Now the monsters on the deck were heading for the door ripped from its hinges by the albino's blow.

Tate retrieved the bottle of rum from the floor. One hundred fifty-one proof for après-ski toddies, the Appleton J. Wray was 75.5 percent alcohol by volume.

Reaching for a matchbook above the hearth, she spied another ax in the nail keg. Matches between her teeth and bottle in the sling, she looped her good arm, ax in hand, around DeClercq. His wrist hung at an ugly angle as she led him along the hall.

The Bigfoot she had shot in the mouth appeared outside the door.

Two more descended the steps from the loft.

Releasing DeClercq, Tate chopped the feet on the stairs, hacking two off at the ankle.

Swapping the ax for the bottle of rum, she hurled it full force out the door.

The Appletons shattered in the Bigfoot's face, spraying it and the other beasts on the deck.

Tate lit the matchbook and tossed it out the door.

Shrieking like witches burned at the stake, the monsters outside burst into flames. The hall filled with the stench of singed hair.

One of the crippled Sasquatch grabbed her leg. It had tumbled to the foot of the stairs. Swinging the ax in a roundhouse, she caved in its face.

Outside, the flaming monsters flapped about the deck or broke through the rail to roll in the snow.

Guided by Tate, DeClercq stumbled out the door, bleeding profusely from his lacerated arm. Gripping the hood of his parka, Carol maneuvered him down the stairs.

The noise of other monsters issued from the woods.

Tate knew DeClercq would falter in the underbrush.

That left one route.

Across the glacier.

* * *

Damn the torpedoes and his fear the engine would stall, the Cowboy wrenched the throttle and yanked up on the lever.

Screaming with protest, the rotor jerked up, tearing the LongRanger from the icy ledge.

The pilot shoved the cyclic control stick toward the valley, sucking the chopper sideways clear of the avalanche.

Chunks of the cliff missed them by inches.

"We did it!" the Cowboy exulted as the Bell gained altitude.

"Good work," MacDougall said. "Now take us down."

The pilot turned to face him. "Are you crazy? We just escaped by the skin of our teeth. You want to risk icing, avalanche, wind shear, downdrafts, and zero visibility? The whole fucking mountain could crumble any minute."

"A member's down, son. We have no choice."

"The hell we don't. We're members *alive* up here. I'm captain of this aircraft, and I say no."

Jack MacDougall stared him down. Fear sparked in one man. Tradition in the other.

"You're a special constable. I'm an inspector. You're in the Mounted and it doesn't work that way. Now take us down. That's an order!"

Carol cinched her sling around DeClercq's arm, hoping the makeshift tourniquet would stem his loss of blood.

The peaks above raked the last flakes from the clouds, increasing visibility as the snowfall waned.

Trailing a hundred feet behind, a gang of four monsters trudged after them.

Across the valley, wind hummed inside the hollow mountain, the crack at its base converting it into a reverberating drum.

Now another sound hitched a death ride on the wind, a creaking, squeaking, growling rumble high above. With a sibilant roar, the tip of Windigo Mountain broke away, tumbling end over end down the precipice. Spewing ice and crushed rock in a mushroom billow, it pulverized the glacier's edge like an atomic bomb.

The force of the impact tossed them into the air.

* * *

The chopper rode the updraft down the mountainside, their ears popping as turbulence tested their dental work.

Watching Rabidowski rearm his arsenal, Zinc wondered if Carol was still alive.

Depend upon it, sir. When a man knows he is to be hanged in a fortnight, it concentrates his mind wonderfully.

The Teahouse bullet grazing his head had done that for him.

He found himself dreaming of life as it used to be, before urban thinking turned his world surreal.

How he'd loved winter mornings with fresh snow on the fields, his horse's warm breath enveloping them.

How he'd loved the swimming hole and fishing in the stream, whiling away a summer day with nowhere else to be.

How he'd loved the wheat stalks at harvesttime, walking through them palms down so they tickled his hands.

Forty years along the way he'd come full circle, pining for what he'd left behind.

He yearned for the farmhouse.

He longed to work the land.

He envied his brother in Saskatchewan.

He wanted kids in the yard, in touch with the soil. Not pacing concrete malls in overpriced sneakers.

If he suggested that to Carol, would she think him crazy?

The Mad Dog passed him the laser gun.

Landing on his broken arm, DeClercq passed out.

Tate staggered to her feet to find the glacier a web of fissures. In front of her yawned a deep crevasse six feet wide. Behind her, closing rapidly, were the four monsters.

With a running leap she could jump across the chasm, stranding the lumbering heavyweights on this side.

No way could they follow.

She'd be safe.

All she had to do was abandon DeClercq.

Howling for blood, the hungry beasts were thirty feet away . . .

Twenty-five . . .

Twenty . . .

Gnashing their fangs.

What's it gonna be, Tate?

Time to decide.

The Lady or the Tiger?

Which is coming out?

If she turned and ran, no one would ever know.

Except her.

Facing the coward each day in the mirror.

The coward who proved her father right about women and true grit.

Fifteen feet . . .

Fourteen feet . . .

They would eat her alive.

Tears streaming down her cheeks, she gripped the ax in both hands.

Breath pluming in ragged gasps, she steeled her nerves.

What did the Indians used to say?

Today's a good day to die.

Rebel yell as a battle cry, Carol charged.

The Bell was coming across the white eye of the glacier, Rabidowski kneeling in the open door.

"Let's spill some blood," the Mad Dog said, aiming the Iver Johnson.

"Don't shoot!" Zinc yelled. "Carol's in the way!"

The whipcrack from the shot filled the LongRanger. The bullet passed six inches over Tate's head, blowing a hole clean through the Bigfoot's throat.

"Think I'd miss?" the Mad Dog said, ejecting the shell.

"Let's get it together," MacDougall said, "with no mistakes. We'll lose the chopper if we land on those cracks. Joe, take the winch. Zinc, you're going down. Mad Dog—"

"Got it. Cover the broad."

Chandler wriggled into a body harness as Joe hooked three lifelines to the winch. Pair of harnesses in hand, Zinc swung out of the chopper. Avacomovitch lowered him to the ice.

"Carol!" Zinc shouted, straddling DeClercq.

The ground effect from the Bell swirled about them.

Ten feet away, Tate turned to run.

Her foot caught in one of the cracks, bringing her down.

The nearest monster grabbed her ankle.

There were so many shots at once Zinc couldn't distinguish the weapons. The Iver Johnson blew the face off Carol's attacker, releasing her to crawl toward him. Joe fired two wads from the Franchi SPAS, blinding the far beast with darts. Jack opened up with the laser to cut down the third.

As Zinc tightened one of the harnesses about DeClercq, a groan of resignation grumbled above.

Like solid lava, hundreds of thousands of tons of rock tumbled down Windigo Mountain.

Five feet away, Carol reached for Zinc.

He advanced as far as the leash would allow.

In the hovering chopper, the Cowboy panicked. Anyone not linked to the Bell had to be left behind or they'd all be bloody rags crushed by the rock. He raised the collective pitch lever and pushed the cyclic control stick toward Viking Peak.

Zinc and Carol's fingers touched as the rotor whined.

A second more and she'd slip away.

He strained against the lifeline like a two-year-old fighting its mother's will.

His hand closed around her wrist and held on for dear life.

Up they went like puppets as
the
ruin
came
down

Hong Kong
Saturday, March 28, 10:22 P.M.

down
down
down.

Zinc Chandler lay on an operating table with a bullet in his brain. His head was now completely shaved in preparation for surgery. Electrodes taped to his scalp fed a bank of neurological machines, the monitors of which dis-

played his alpha, beta, and delta rhythms. Several interns watched his brain waves spike across the screens.

"Dreams? Stories? Myths? What's going on in there?"

"To seek to know what determines the knowing is an impossible task."

The Welshman eyed the Londoner over his glasses. "Feeling philosophical, are we, Taylor?"

"These rhythms are deep-sourced. Limbic perhaps. Maybe his collective unconscious is taking flight."

"Good Lord," the Welshman sighed. "A Jungian in our midst."

"What a shame," the Kenyan said. "Such a good-looking man. What happened to him? Why all the police?"

"Chap's wanted for murder in Hawaii, I hear. Sex killing of a woman and her child. Rumor is he stabbed Superintendent Ong."

"The Terror of the Triads?"

"Knifed him here on the Peak. Sung says Ong is in our morgue."

"Who's operating?"

"Huang's scrubbing up."

"Thought he was in Australia."

"Conference finished."

"They say you see your whole life just before you die. Could be that's what's going on inside this fellow's head."

"They say the body's six ounces lighter after death. Could be that loss is taking place."

The Welshman cast the Londoner a wry glance. "Don't tell me you're touting the soul, Taylor? And you a medical man?"

Part Five

SOUL

The greatest single achievement of nature to date was surely the invention of DNA. We have had it from the beginning, built into the first cell to emerge, membrane and all, somewhere in the soupy waters of the cooling planet.

—Lewis Thomas

BRAIN WAVES

10:43 P.M.

Carol stood vigil in the hospital corridor. The Mounties were off trying to find out what had happened at the Teahouse. DeClercq had been right in his guess Zinc would return to Hong Kong, bent on revenge against a killer still without a face. With those odds, getting shot was almost preordained. In the East, the *I Ching* divined your fate. Now she was left alone to grasp what would never be.

While flying here she'd thought about their talk in Stanley Park, just before the killer fed Daniells to the bears.

One thing we haven't discussed, she'd said, *is where we're going to live.*

The answer that came to her in the air was *Why not the farm*?

Zinc had told her how his father had left it to his sons, and how he had abandoned it out of rebellion.

The farm was paid for. Half was his. And Zinc's brother, Tom, lived a pretty good life.

Why not us? she'd thought. *At least give it a try. Unless people slow down, the world will soon be gone. Rooster crowing in the morning. Sunset from the porch at night. If I suggest the farm to Zinc, will he think me crazy?*

She wondered if she'd ever know.

DeClercq stepped from the elevator, dressed in uniform. Blue serge tunic and forage cap with braid. Blue trousers to match with a yellow stripe. Black congress boots with box spurs. In his hand he carried a pair of white gloves.

"How is he, Carol?"

"They're operating. His brain waves are active. That's

a good sign. Thoughts of some sort are sparking in his mind."

"When will we know?"

"Not for hours."

"I spoke to MacDougall. He and Joe landed on the peak. They found the Kwans' first expedition crashed at the bottom. Calgary Detachment stopped their second at the airport."

"What about the Yellow Skull? What about Blake?"

"They found both up the mountain but didn't solve the mystery. Blake's body was interred in six feet of ice. His head was gone and in its place was the Yellow Skull."

"Someone—or something—*buried* him?" Tate exclaimed.

DeClercq shrugged. "Both, it seems, will remain the stuff of myth."

"My God," she said. "Haunted by ghosts. A nineteenth-century revenant took Zinc from me?"

"Attitudes, not ghosts, are what survive. The past is prologue to the now. It haunts us all."

Carol eyed him askance, searching his face. "What's wrong?"

"The Hong Kong police are closing ranks."

She exhaled deeply and leaned against the wall. She ran the fingers of her good arm through her hair. "A cover-up?"

"Something's going on. We're to meet a high-up in an hour."

"What'd you find out?"

"Very little. Police responded to a report of shots on the Peak. They found Zinc wounded in an empty teahouse. The teahouse crowns an island in a lake. Blood was smeared on the bridge connecting it to shore. Someone, apparently, was dragged or crawled away. David Ong, our contact here, lay dead by the lake. Zinc held the knife which stabbed him and Ong's gun."

"Shells fired?"

"Three."

"The blood on the bridge?"

DeClercq nodded. "Looks that way."

"Was Ong dirty?"

"There's the rub. He's the current golden boy of the

RHKP. Press calls him the Terror of the Triads. He's the Untouchable of the Anti-Triad Unit."

"What about Zinc's effects?"

"Police won't let us see them. Nor can we watch Ong's house being searched."

"Why?" Tate asked.

"Why, indeed?"

"Being American, I don't quite trust the British."

"Being French-Canadian, I don't either. We're in the last outpost of an empire that doesn't exist. Farewell the trumpet. Furl the flag. They'll want to go out clean."

Carol glanced at the door to the operating room. "It's all for nothing, isn't it?"

"Not for nothing," Robert said. "Someone's going to pay."

"Excuse please. You police?"

The Asian stepped out of the elevator as they were stepping in. The man was dressed in hospital whites.

"Yes," DeClercq said. Carol tensed.

"This left in ambulance. We just find. Fall from man's pocket when we pump heart."

The medic handed them a scrap of paper.

On it were the notes Zinc had jotted in the plane.

11:30 P.M.

Senior Superintendent Humphrey Thorpe-Baker was a little pissed and royally pissed off. The Humper was a relic of a dying breed: colonial troubleshooter to Her Majesty the Queen. He'd whipped the Mau Mau in Kenya when the map was mostly red, and other insurgent wogs in Rhodesia, Malaya, and Aden. After the corruption trials of the 1960s, he was sent to "Honkers" to clean up the RHKP. This evening the Humper was being feted for a job well done, before retiring to London to receive a gong. Now these two interrupted the party to piss on his carpet.

"Rubbish," Thorpe-Baker scoffed. "Where's the proof? That allegation is tommyrot. Did you throw out the law of evidence along with the wig?"

"I'm not finished," said DeClercq.

"My club is waiting. And I've heard enough. I have no time to waste with some befuddled Holmes."

Folderol and medals displayed on his puffed blue chest, Thorpe-Baker reminded Carol of Captain Bligh. He stood, swagger stick in hand, by a gilded portrait of the Queen, cheeks ruddy from too many G-and-Ts on verandahs around the realm. Kikuyu spears and a zebra-skin shield adorned one wall. Opposite was Elizabeth Butler's *The Defence of Rorke's Drift*. Under a bell jar on his desk was a shrunken head.

"Shall I pigstick, old boy, to show how silly you sound?" The Humper's breath reeked of single malt.

"You say my best man was bribed by the Kwans. Ignore the fact Fankuang is a leading industry with no need to dabble in crime. Ignore the fact David Ong has filled the brig with villains despite countless attempts to corrupt him. You say he kept the Kwans from legal scrutiny, and when your man got too close framed him with false teeth. Really, old chap. How penny dreadful."

"We have Chandler's notes."

"Self-serving drivel. Your man was"—he looked at Tate—"on the lam?"

"What turned up at Ong's house?"

"Not a thing."

"Is the search complete?"

"All but the report."

"When do you expect it?"

"Imminently."

"Good. We'll wait."

The Humper lit a pipe as if born to the bowl. Smoke hazed the Indonesian shadow puppets above both doors. When a knock sounded at one of them, he harrumphed, "Enter."

An Asian cop in uniform stepped into the room.

"Either of you speak Cantonese?" Thorpe-Baker asked.

The North Americans shook their heads as the colonists spoke that tongue.

"Confirmation," the Humper said. "Ong's house is clean."

Carol caught the look that passed between the Hong Kong cops. Thorpe-Baker motioned the Asian toward the door. *They found something they're covering up,* she thought.

Thorpe-Baker saw her shoulders slump as suspicion narrowed her eyes. He cast her that special smirk the British Army saves for Yanks. "The cavalry only arrives in your Western myths," he said.

The Asian cop neared one door as the other door swung wide. Framed in it was a Chinese Thorpe-Baker had never met.

DeClercq revealed the microphone tucked up his sleeve.

The intruder held a receiver-recorder in his hand.

"They may not speak Cantonese. But I do," said Inspector Eric Chan.

A Commonwealth outsider, Tate couldn't fully fathom the psychology here—but she knew two royal stalwarts were going man to man. Between them DeClercq and Thorpe-Baker had so many badges, aiguillettes, crowns and pips, service ribbons, and shiny brass buttons she felt she ought to salute. If only they were dressed in red, not blue.

"Inspector Chan, what did they say?"

"The search uncovered proof Ong worked for the Kwans. It was hidden in a safe. The senior superintendent told his subordinate to suppress it. He'd decide what to do once you were gone."

DeClercq took a step toward Thorpe-Baker.

The senior superintendent stood his ground.

"Are you dirty? Or influenced by drink?"

Two more steps brought them face to face.

"My man's in hospital with a bullet in his brain. Your man helped put him there."

Thorpe-Baker, chin out, didn't cede an inch.

"I demand to see the evidence in your hands. Give me what I want or fight this out in the press. Don't forget I have your words on tape, *old chap*. Either you do the right thing, or I'm taking you down."

One of them blinked.

"Good work, Eric. Fine idea."

"Dammit," Carol said. "Why was I left in the dark?"

They were waiting to see Ong's cache. It was in transport from his home. Boxes of it.

"With you to look at, who'd watch me? I wanted Thorpe-Baker to think he had us. Your frustration was the bait."

* * *

When Stephen Kwan was bombed in 1963, Ong had capitalized on the Warlord's resulting fear. Kwan Kok-su had paid him millions for protection, suspecting the Triads, the RHKP, and the Gong An Ju. His all-consuming obsession was to save the family line, which no doubt motivated fashioning the mask. Evan had to survive at all cost, including Kwan family pride.

Ong was too street-smart not to protect himself. Over the years he had built an insurance file, stocking it with everything threatening to the Kwans. If anything happened to him, they were finished too.

In that file were the psych reports from the deportation hearing.

In that file were photographs of Evan Kwan.

In that file was a map of the Kowloon complex security system.

In that file were *two* colony birth certificates.

Jekyll and Hyde.

JEKYLL AND HYDE

Kowloon
Sunday, March 29, 3:41 A.M.

There are no finer soldiers than the Gurkhas of Nepal. Since 1815 they have served in the British Army, winning the Victoria Cross thirteen times. In recent years the Gurkhas have guarded the borders of Hong Kong, stationed at a base in the New Territories. Tonight a Gurkha vanguard led the assault.

According to the map found in Ong's safe, there was an escape route from the Ancestral Hall. It opened off a tunnel beneath the Sacrificial Altar, then ran underground to a safe house streets away.

While DeClercq, Chan, Tate, and Thorpe-Baker waited outside, the assault team broke into the house, located the subterranean passage, and disappeared.

First came the news Ong was dead. No wonder he failed to show at the Teahouse tonight. Then the dentist called in a panic. The RHKP were at his door. Now the surgeons told him his brother was dead. For hours they'd labored to save him in the Fankuang hospital. Cutthroat was with them when the alarm sounded. Someone in the safe house had found the secret passage. The game was over.

The killer ran underground to the Labs. He entered by the door beside the Cryonics Freezer. The security screen above the exit opposite was flashing. A camera in the passage showed Nepalese soldiers approaching fast.

Unknown to all but the Kwans, the research center was a giant burn box. Only the family knew the computer sequence that sealed the Labs and minutes later converted the underground chamber into a crematorium.

Exiting, Cutthroat used the door release to punch in the destruction code, then ran past the Pit and up the stone stairs. He slid back the trapdoor to the Sacrificial Altar as a Gurkha stun grenade exploded below. Pushing the button that closed the trap, he grabbed the key from the table bearing *Parker's Journal* and *Field Notes*. He unlocked the door to the Ancestral Shrine.

The Warlord, soul gone, was a skeleton of a man. He sat gripping the arms of the Dragon Throne with broken talons. One side of his face was clawed to tatters in a vain attempt to gouge the virus from his brain. The eyeball in the raw meat hung from its stalk. Bathed in the glow of red paper lanterns, he shook like a man with cerebral palsy. His teeth, bared by grinning lips, clacked like castanets.

Cutthroat yanked him from the throne. He drew a .380 SIG/Sauer from his belt. Muzzle to the Warlord's head, he pulled the trigger. Grume and rotted gray matter spattered the skulls in the bone rack beyond. It sprayed the jade and ivory screen inlaid with their imperial *zong pu*. The chattering stopped.

Straddling the raw-head who crumpled to the floor, Cutthroat tore the signet ring from his bony finger.

As he raised the seat of the Dragon Throne, exposing the puzzle box within, a Gurkha mine blew the trapdoor open. Military boots scrambled up the stairs.

The ring fit a hole in the top of the box. Inserting it popped the lid, revealing a set of keys inside. The keys opened bank vaults around the world where a hundred million dollars in cash was stored. More than enough for him to start anew.

A Gurkha stun grenade was lobbed into the shrine.

Keys in one hand, gun in the other, Cutthroat hurled himself at the screen behind the throne.

The jade and ivory *zong pu* opened into a chute, down which Cutthroat was swallowed as the grenade exploded.

Rows of spikes locked in place to block any pursuit.

The sheer audacity of the escape took Carol by surprise.

Once the assault was underway, as evidenced by the blasts—though no one could explain the hellish heat that suddenly blew from the mouth of the safe house passage—she'd left the three men to find a phone.

Wandering the streets around the drug complex, she spotted one across from the compound wall.

As she phoned the hospital to check on Zinc, entranced

by moonbeams glinting off the razor wire atop the fortress, a figure burst through the wall high above the street.

She thought she was hallucinating from stress and lack of sleep.

The acrobat hit an awning positioned strategically, then somersaulted to the sidewalk and dashed for the nearest lane.

Tate was at the corner of the next lane down the street.

It's him, she thought.

Through shadows from the tenements, Cutthroat made his escape.

The unexpected fooled the unimaginative every time. Chutes like that were common at amusement parks. Medieval castles employed the same trick. False bricks above the encircling moat.

The killer glanced over his shoulder for one last look. The wall beyond which he was born and raised retreated with every step. In doing so he missed the foot that kicked from the side passage.

Arms outflung, Cutthroat tripped and fell to the cobblestones.

The .380 SIG/Sauer clattered from his hand.

"FBI," Tate yelled. "Freeze or I'll blow your head off."

Cutthroat looked up to face a new adversary.

The SIG/Sauer lay two feet from his hand.

"I mean it, Evan. Or should I call you Lotus?"

POINT OF VIEW

4:09 A.M.

"I don't see why the old boy accepted the switch," Thorpe-Baker said. "Flies in the teeth of Chinese tradition. Boys preferred, and all that."

"Go back to 1963, when Stephen Kwan was killed. The Warlord lost his Cutthroat in that blast," said DeClercq, "seriously threatening the family line. He was left with two infant grandsons to protect: Evan, the elder, his new heir, and one-year-old Martin, born in Canada."

"Ong killed Stephen?"

"Possibly. He certainly used the death to approach Kwan. Whoever was responsible—Ong or someone else—the Warlord blamed Minister Qi. Qi had tried him in absentia for the Tien Shan massacre and other crimes, hounding his Xinjiang henchmen ever since. Retaliating for Stephen's death, Kwan killed the minister's wife and son."

Thorpe-Baker nodded. "Still fighting the Civil War. Two old pigtails pigsticking each other."

"Kwan was afraid Qi's agents might breach the Kowloon compound, so that's when he decided to dress Evan as a girl. If Martin was the only boy, he must be the Cutthroat, protecting the real heir from assassination."

"Rum ploy," Thorpe-Baker said. "Making him killer's bait."

"Evan was registered as a boy on his birth certificate. When he was born in 1961 there was no threat, but after the bombing two years later he was in jeopardy. Ong switched certificates in the colony registry, converting the boy to Lotus Kwan. Evan ceased to exist, except on the certificate stored in Ong's safe."

"What about those who knew him before?"

"Near as we can tell, Evan didn't leave the Kowloon complex until his teens. Not until he went to study in Canada."

Thorpe-Baker snorted. "Dressing him queer made him queer, uh?"

"No, the boy's effeminacy gave Kwan the idea. Ironically, Minister Qi wasn't after the heir. All he wanted was Kwan Kok-su."

"So when did Evan have the nip and tuck?"

"After he ran afoul of Daniells in 1978. Gender confusion was part of what she witnessed in the lab. From puberty on, Evan's sperm had been stocked in a freezer, ending the need for him to cross-dress. Once the family line was safe from assassination, 'Lotus' could continue life as a man."

"Except he didn't want to? A true-blue faggot?"

"Martin's birth in Canada secured the Kwans a haven. Should Hong Kong ever sour, they could emigrate. To build a base, both grandkids were sent to college there, Evan in science and Martin in law. What better opportunity for Evan to reappear? Until then he'd never been outside the compound. 'Lotus' was shed in Hong Kong and he arrived a man. Ong secured papers in the new identity."

"So what went wrong?" Thorpe-Baker asked.

"Culture shock. Here's a mixed-up kid who's never been outside the cocoon, living in an alien country on his own. For the first time he's expected to relate as a man, while mentally gender-confused and a psychopath. One night he ends up in the lab swacked on drugs, cross-dressing while experimenting with cryonics. Daniells catches him and complains to Immigration. It's all in the psych reports from Ong's safe.

"Kwan hired Murdoch to save their future plans, since a deportation order would bar Evan from Canada. Evan returned to the colony demanding an operation so he could *physically* become Lotus Kwan."

"I don't understand why the old bugger relented," Thorpe-Baker said.

"If he refused, Evan threatened to go elsewhere."

"Why not conceive another heir himself?"

"Age and latent kuru disease had made him impotent."

"The woman he tried to impregnate? Qi's son's lover? Why wait so long to beget Evan's heir?"

"The longer they waited, the further genetics would advance. They hoped to tinker with the heir's aging gene."

"If Evan were killed, would Martin not take his place?"

"He wasn't the one with the intellect to find the Fountain of Youth. And he too was sterile.

"Everything fell apart when the Warlord got sick. Suddenly their timetable ran out of time. Lotus was cleared for immigration and the company half-moved, but there was still the outstanding deportation matter. Kwan demanded the grandkids follow up on my book, hoping for a cure to his new affliction. A family as prominent as the Kwans attracts the media, and those who knew about Evan were still alive. If Evan was linked to Lotus, their haven would be gone, so all the hearing participants had to be killed. It might have worked had the person in control not gone insane."

"So your man paid the price of a bullet in his brain."

"Like all of us," DeClercq said, "he was fooled by the mask. Years ago I was in remand court when the most stunning hooker I've ever seen approached the judge. The sheriffs around me were muttering how they'd like a piece of her, until the clerk read the charge against William Hall.

"Sex is determined by a single gene—the Testes Determining Factor on the Y chromosome.

"Objectively, we remain the gender programmed in our cells, no matter what we do to our outer shell.

"Subjectively, however, the eyes deceive, so we ignored Lotus while looking for Evan Kwan.

"He or she," DeClercq said. "It all depends on point of view."

"Very clever," Tate said. "Seducing Arnie Smolensky in his top-floor suite. Gave you both an alibi and access to the roof up the fire escape. What'd you do, Evan? Shower between fucks? Shoot Murdoch while the water ran, then slip back into bed? Easy if the gun was already on the roof."

Raising his chest from the cobblestones to look at her, Cutthroat recognized Tate from the shootout in the zoo. She stood two yards away, gun aimed at his head. Her eyes were on the SIG/Sauer near his outstretched hand. The way her gun hand wavered, he knew her good arm was in the sling. His other hand was beneath his breasts, allowing the spring sheath around his wrist to slip a German throwing knife into his palm. *Have to get her in the heart,* he thought.

"I want to kill you," Tate said, "for what you did to Chandler."

Eyes on the SIG/Sauer, she watched his outstretched hand.

"Go on. Give me reason. Try it."

So he tried.

AUTHOR'S NOTE

This is a work of fiction. The plot and characters are a product of the author's imagination. Where real persons, places, or institutions are incorporated to create the illusion of authenticity, they are used fictitiously.

Inspiration was drawn from the following nonfiction sources, though facts were freely altered for the purpose of the story. That, after all, is what fantasy is about.

AC/DC, for a jolt when juice was low.

Arens, W. *The Man-Eating Myth: Anthropology and Anthropophagy.* Oxford University Press, 1979.

Bao Ruo-Wang and Rudolph Chelminski. *Prisoner of Mao.* Coward, McCann, 1973.

Berton, Pierre. *The Wild Frontier: More Tales From the Remarkable Past.* McClelland and Stewart, 1978.

Brininstool, E. A. *Troopers With Custer: Historic Incidents of the Battle of the Little Bighorn.* University of Nebraska Press, 1989.

Butler, William F. *The Great Lone Land.* Hurtig, 1968.

Campbell, Joseph. *The Power of Myth.* Doubleday, 1988.

Chiarelli, A. B. *Evolution of the Primates: An Introduction to the Biology of Man.* Academic Press, 1973.

Ching, Frank. *Ancestors: 900 Years in the Life of a Chinese Family.* Morrow, 1988.

Colombo, John Robert, ed. *Windigo: An Anthology of Fact and Fantastic Fiction.* Western Producer, 1982.

Cowan, Don. "Medicine That Kills." *The Globe and Mail.*

Gaute J. H. H. and Robin Odell. *Murder "Whatdunit": An Illustrated Account of the Methods of Murder.* Pan, 1984.

Gillespie, Neal C. *Charles Darwin and the Problem of Creation.* University of Chicago Press, 1979.

Graham, W. A. *The Custer Myth: A Source Book of Custeriana.* Bonanza, 1953.

Graysmith, Robert. *Zodiac*. St. Martin's, 1986.
Hogg, Garry. *Cannibalism and Human Sacrifice.* Pan, 1958.
Horrall, S. W. *The Pictorial History of the Royal Canadian Mounted Police.* McGraw-Hill, 1973.
Hunter, Don and Rene Dahinden. *Sasquatch.* McClelland and Stewart, 1973.
Hsu, Hong-yen and William G. Peacher. *Chinese Herb Medicine and Therapy.* Oriental Healing Arts Institute, 1982.
"Interview: Richard Cutler." *Omni,* 1986.
Johanson, Donald C. and Maitland A. Edey. *Lucy: The Beginnings of Humankind.* Simon and Schuster, 1981.
Lasker, Gabriel Ward. *Physical Anthropology*. Holt, Rinehart, 1976.
Le Gros Clark, Sir Wilfred E. *History of the Primates: An Introduction to the Study of Fossil Man.* British Museum, 1970.
Lotz, Jim. *The Mounties: The History of the Royal Canadian Mounted Police.* Bison, 1984.
Lueras, Leonard and R. Ian Lloyd. *Hong Kong.* APA, 1987.
Maitland, Derek. *The Insider's Guide to Hong Kong.* Hunter, 1988.
Malloy, Ruth Lor. *Fielding's People's Republic of China 1988.* Fielding Travel, 1988.
Mandelbaum, David G. *The Plains Cree: An Ethnographic, Historical, and Comparative Study*. University of Regina Press, 1979.
Morris, James. *Heaven's Command: An Imperial Progress.* Penguin, 1979.
Napier, John Russell. *Bigfoot: The Yeti and Sasquatch in Myth and Reality*. Cape, 1972.
Poirier, Frank E. *Fossil Evidence: The Human Evolutionary Journey*. Mosby, 1977.
Posner, Gerald L. *Warlords of Crime: Chinese Secret Societies: The New Mafia.* Penguin, 1988.
Restak, Richard M. *The Brain: The Last Frontier.* Warner, 1980.
Royal Canadian Mounted Police Fact Sheets. RCMP, 1990.
Rosenberg, Bruce A. *Custer and the Epic of Defeat.* Pennsylvania State University Press, 1974.

Samagalski, Alan, Robert Strauss, and Michael Buckley. *China: A Travel Survival Kit.* Lonely Planet, 1988.
Simpson, Keith. *Police: The Investigation of Violence.* Macdonald and Evans, 1978.
Shackley, Myra. *Still Living? Yeti, Sasquatch and the Neanderthal Enigma.* Thames and Hudson, 1983.
Sheehy, Gail. *Passages: Predictable Crises of Adult Life.* Dutton, 1976.
Sherman, Patrick. *Cloud Walkers: Six Climbs on Major Canadian Peaks.* St. Martin's, 1965.
Shipman, Pat. "Baffling Limb on the Family Tree." *Discover,* 1986.
Simons, Elwyn L. *Primate Evolution: An Introduction to Man's Place in Nature.* Macmillan, 1972.
Smith, Frank. *Cause of Death: A History of Forensic Science.* Pan, 1982.
Soo, Chee. *The Taoist Ways of Healing.* Aquarian Press, 1986.
Stewart, Edgar I. *Custer's Luck.* University of Oklahoma Press, 1955.
Teresi, Dick and Patrice G. Adcroft, eds. *Omni's Future Medical Almanac.* McGraw-Hill, 1987.
Tierney, John, Lynda Wright, and Karen Springen. "The Search for Adam and Eve." *Newsweek,* 1988.
The Vancouver Sun (for a wealth of news clippings).
Turner, C. Frank. *Across the Medicine Line.* McClelland and Stewart, 1973.
Turner, J. P. *The North-West Mounted Police 1873–1893.* Queen's Printer, 1950.
Williams, B. J. *Evolution and Human Origins: An Introduction to Physical Anthropology.* Harper and Row, 1973.
Young, J. Z. *An Introduction to the Study of Man.* Clarendon Press, 1971.

Contrary to myth, Custer wasn't a general at the time of the Little Bighorn. He held the rank of lieutenant colonel.

Since 1979 the pinyin system of romanizing Chinese script has replaced the Wade-Giles method. Mao Tse-tung is now Mao Zedong, and Peking is Beijing. To avoid confusing the reader, the spelling most recognizable in the West was used at the expense of consistency.

For visual effect I moved the Headquarters of the Gong An Ju to the local office beside the Forbidden City. The real HQ is off Tiananmen Square.

To thank all those who answered my research questions would take another volume. You know who you are, so here's a toast and a tip of the hat.

An extra sip to the Anvil Chorus—Bill, Ted, Bev, Jim, Susan, Glen, Lee, Erin, and Les—for hammering out the bumps.

And to Renée for a tour through the mysteries of China.

And to John and Barney, for casting the runes.

The story survivors will return in *Skull and Crossbones*.

SLADE
Vancouver, B.C.

MICHAEL SLADE

HEADHUNTER

By the time the second mutilated body was found, the Press were talking about the Headhunter and the city of Vancouver was ready to explode with fear.

And then the photographs arrived. Carefully posed shots of the women's heads stuck on poles. Enough to convince Superintendent Robert DeClercq that they were dealing with a very special kind of killer. A killer who inhabited a bizarre world of cannibalism, torture and sexual perversion.

A killer who was only just beginning . . .

'Bizarre . . . full of tension and mystery with unforgettable scenes and weird happenings' *The Scotsman*

'Well written, very well researched . . . a gripper' *Daily Mail*

'Macabre . . . a very polished tale' *Sunday Telegraph*

'A thinking man's Texas Chainsaw Massacre' *The Vancouver Sun*

MICHAEL SLADE

GHOUL

A violent spectre is haunting London.

Dressed in a grey cape and a top hat, with a bone-white face and a madman's eyes, the Ghoul crawls from the London sewers to kill – bloodily, perversely and inexplicably.

For Detective Chief Superintendent Hilary Rand, an ambitious woman in a man's world, the carnage must stop or her career will be finished. But hunting the Ghoul means stepping into her worst nightmare . . .

'As alarming a piece of Gothic as I've read in many a black moon . . . treads a perverted fantastic with droll skill' *The Times*

'Slade runs a three-ring circus of suspense, salting the plot with red herrings and keeping the reader guessing until the truth is revealed in a grisly, sensational climax to which is appended yet another gut-wrenching revelation' *Booklist*

'*Ghoul* almost finished me . . . Here's a book that gives you real shock value for the money'
Robert Bloch, author of PSYCHO

HODDER AND STOUGHTON PAPERBACKS